A LAIR OF BONES

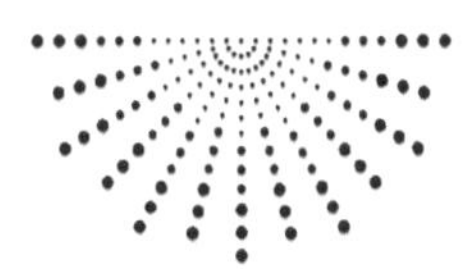

A LAIR OF BONES

HELEN SCHEUERER

This book could only ever be for Gary.

Because of you, my world, and the world within these pages, is all the richer.

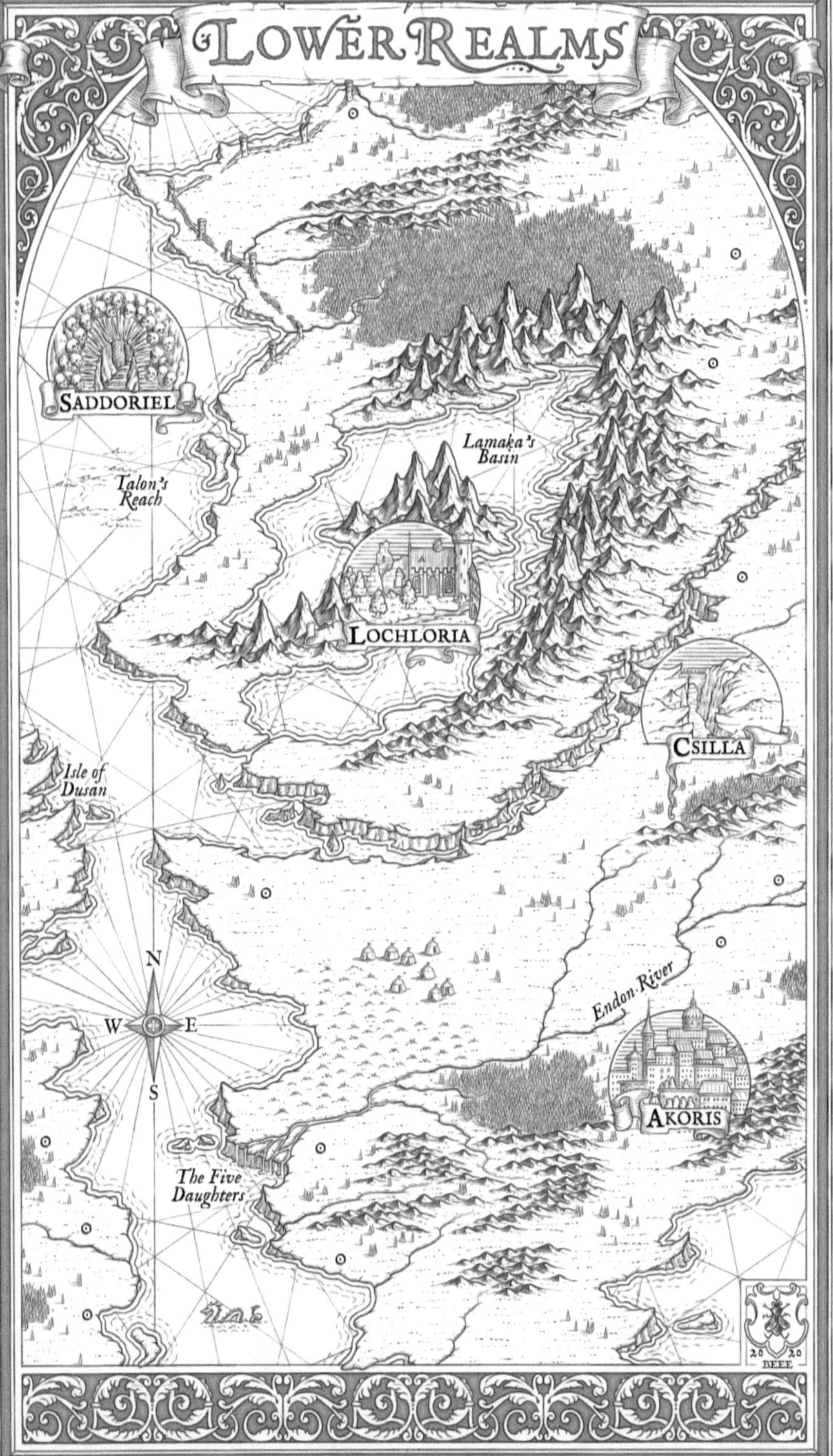

LOWER REALMS
SADDORIEL
Talon's Reach
Lamaka's Basin
LOCHLORIA
CSILLA
Isle of Dusan
Endon River
AKORIS
N
W E
S
The Five Daughters
2020
BEEE

PROLOGUE

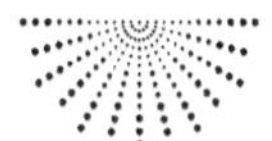

F ar below the darkest waters, in a cell made of bones, a creature was born. She was the only one of her kind to have entered the realm in such a way: on the cold, bloody stones of Saddoriel's prison. In the waning torchlight, her mother, the prisoner, closed her lilac eyes. Bracing herself against the raw beat of lingering pain, she already sensed the deathsong that hummed within her daughter, as strong as the ancestors before her. It was the quiet promise of poignant keys and mesmerising notes: magic, ready to be honed into one of the most powerful weapons known to the realms above, belonging to a cyren of the vast and ancient deep.

The prisoner gazed down at the small being in the crook of her elbow. In all her centuries of existence, she had never seen a newborn up close before, and this one was *hers*. She peered at the tiny, pink face in wonder. Without the glimmer of scales at her temples, or the dark fingernails that turned to talons, the infant could have been human. The prisoner unsheathed her own talons, studying the jagged and torn points – a consequence of the manic etchings on the rocky walls around her: drawings, rhymes and snippets of songs long lost. Once, there had been scores that marked the passing days, too, but as decades turned to centuries, time became but one endless darkness.

The gleam of blood on the stone beneath her caught her attention. Ribbons of crimson flowed freely from her still, forming narrow rivers in the cracks of the prison floor, slipping beneath the bars of bone that held her captive. She followed their course, until they reached a pair of familiar boots. Opposite her cell were bodies, standing preserved in all their former glory but for a blue tinge to their skin: the water warlocks. Their vacant stares had kept her company for quite some time now. Her gaze fell to the man in the middle, positioned for her best viewing. His name tasted hauntingly familiar on her lips, but she did not speak it; she had promised herself long ago that she had said it aloud for the last time. More often than not, as the years blurred and the torches became faint embers, she saw his ice-green eyes blink at her through the darkness, or his grip on the quartz dagger shift just a little. But it was only a trick of the light, or of the mind.

She adjusted herself on the stone, trying to ease her pain. Now, more than ever, she yearned for music. To feel song coursing through her very being like her life's blood through her veins. But the vibrant melodies of the lair above did not reach the confines of the cells. As though sensing her mother's turmoil, the infant stirred, her little face scrunching into a would-be cry. A long-forgotten tune fluttered at the back of the prisoner's mind, the words forming on her cracked lips.

'*Hush, little cyren ...*' Her song voice was raw from decades of silence and she clutched desperately at any semblance of melody. The child drew a trembling breath and the prisoner hesitated no longer:

'*Little nestling, little nestling,*
We cry not in the ancient deep.
Little nestling, little nestling,
Follow my voice, to the land of sleep.
Hush, hush, little cyren, so strong yet so small,
For down in deep Saddoriel, we let no tears fall.
Oh hush now, little nestling,
One day you will find your song.
But quiet now, little nestling,
For in dream is where you belong.
Hush, hush, little cyren, listen to my call,
For under these starless nights, we let no tears fall ...'

The soft scrape of shoes upon the gravelled path sounded, and a long shadow was cast across the prisoner and her child.

'What did you think would happen, Cerys?' the onlooker asked quietly, scales glimmering at her temples. 'Did you really think we would allow you to raise your nestling within this cell?'

Cerys ... It had been an age since someone had spoken her name aloud, let alone with such familiarity. *Cerys.* If she closed her eyes, she could pretend they were in another place, another time ... But she kept her eyes open.

The cyren outside her cell hadn't changed. Her lilac eyes were as bright as ever, her dark hair brushing her hips. She stood before the bars of bone, wearing a coloured silk robe, belted with jewels at the waist, and flowing pants, the hem dark with the filth of the prison. Cerys squinted. Sometimes she saw great wings behind the onlooker, sometimes she didn't, but always, she saw shadows.

Her guest gripped the bars of the cell gently, eyeing the child in her arms with concern. 'Don't you want her to know *music?*'

Cerys peered down. The heat from the bundle she carried pressed against her cold, clammy skin as she imagined what a gift a *real* melody would be. For her daughter to hear the music she herself could not ...

'What will you call her?' The onlooker's voice was a whisper, as though she feared disturbing the sleeping child.

'You ... you would allow me to ...?'

The other cyren's eyes swept across the cell, to the blood that neared her slippered feet. 'A courtesy, Cerys. A final tribute to a friendship that once was.'

For a moment, as the words lingered between them, the onlooker and prisoner locked eyes. A fleeting acknowledgement of a past so tangled and distant, it was but a dream.

'You requested my presence?' said a quiet voice. A male cyren appeared from the passageway, clad in plain grey robes. From beneath his sharp collar, a small patch of discoloured skin peeked. He glanced from the guest to the prisoner, his own lilac eyes intense.

'I did. Take the child,' the onlooker ordered.

It was only then that the male cyren's gaze fell upon the blood and the newborn clutched in the prisoner's talons. If he was shocked, he didn't show it. He produced a crowded ring of keys from his robes and went to work on the multiple locks and chains.

At last, the cell gate swung inwards with a screech and he stepped inside, eyeing Cerys warily. But she didn't move. Her face was blank as he reached down and took the infant from her. She did not fight, despite the sudden cold in her arms.

It wasn't until cyren and infant were on the other side of the cell, and each lock had clicked back into place, that Cerys spoke. 'Rohesia,' she said.

Her guest took half a step forward. 'What?'

'Rohesia. That is the name I choose for her.'

Sadness crossed the onlooker's face as the male cyren left without a moment's pause, taking the child with him.

The onlooker gave Cerys one final, lingering look. 'No harm will come to her,' she vowed.

. . .

Hours after her visitors had departed, the old lullaby still swam in Cerys' mind. She swayed with the pain, watching more blood seep through the cracks in the stone, wondering if she was going to die. Part of her very much wished she would. She had spent so long cloaked in darkness.

But she knew the onlooker would never allow it. Cerys was to live. Soon, fresh torchlight flooded the passageway and a heavily guarded healer began attending to her. As a pain-relief serum clouded her senses, Cerys' unfocused gaze swept from one blue-tinged warlock to another and the words of the old nursery tune found her once again …

'Hush, hush, little cyren, so strong yet so small,

For down in deep Saddoriel, we let no tears fall …'

As gentle hands washed her, Cerys thought hazily of how cold and alone she felt without her infant nestled against her. But something else warmed her from within, an ember of hope, slowly flaring to life in her chest. It didn't matter that she lay here bleeding, empty and abandoned. Her nestling, Rohesia, was exactly where she needed to be.

CHAPTER ONE

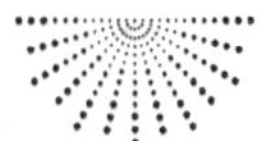

The quiet, square workshop smelled of bone shavings and sawdust, and specks of ivory gleamed on the floor in the flickering torchlight. In the early, eerie hours, if Roh stilled her aching fingers and strained her ears, she could hear the faint notes of music trickling down from the Upper Sector of Saddoriel. Delicate sea-blue scales glimmered at her temples, and dark, wavy hair fell across her face as she rested on her elbows against the workbench and closed her eyes, savouring the delicate sound of harp strings being plucked far above. The melody stirred ancient magic in her chest; a beast awakening after a long winter. Roh imagined the feeling was akin to the sun warming her skin. As quickly as it had come, though, the music was snatched away, leaving only the stifling quiet once more.

Roh stretched and turned back to her work. On the bench before her was the project that had her out of her bed hours before any of the other fledglings. The measurements and sketches alone had taken her at least eight moons to finalise, but there was no point in creating a working model if it wasn't to scale. Ames, her mentor, had taught her that. His stern respect for the finer details of architecture had rubbed off on her and she was begrudgingly grateful. She studied her project carefully. Made with bone splinters she'd saved from around the workshop, her creation mirrored everything she yearned for: a place where melodies could be captured and driven upwards to starving ears, a colosseum with a semi-circular stage, a space where cyrens like her could at last hear the same rich notes and cresting choruses as those above.

Sighing, she consulted her drawings and sought the particular piece of bone she needed. With her dark talons retracted, this sort of work was much easier. She double- and triple-checked before fixing the piece into place and stepping back to survey her progress. As she tucked a loose strand of hair behind her ear, her fingers brushed the thin line of gold that circled her head. The pulse of a longstanding grievance thrummed through her. *Gold ...* The weakest, most meagre metal the cyrens possessed; a circlet of it, to mark those lesser than the rest. It was a humiliation she'd worn since she could remember, a permanent reminder of her place in Talon's Reach. Only a handful of cyrens bore this particular shame: the offspring of criminals – not that she'd ever seen another like her. They were probably hidden away in the darkest pockets of the territory, just as she was.

Determined not to dwell on her shortcomings, Roh returned her focus to the project at hand. The model was far from finished. She could only work on it in the brief moments of time she stole for herself while the rest of her cohort slept. But she was glad for the months of distraction it had gifted her. Months … Barely a blink in the long life of a cyren, but she was thankful all the same. The soft notes of music drifted down again, a hint at the breathtaking sounds the Upper Sector enjoyed —

An ear-piercing scraping noise cut the melody short and Roh jumped in surprise. Her head snapped up to see her friend, Harlyn, dragging her talons down the grimy workshop window. Harlyn grinned, her razor-sharp cheekbones all the more prominent. Behind her was a huge trolley, stacked with half a dozen barrels.

'Draw the short straw again?' Roh asked as she held the door open.

Harlyn scowled as she pushed the trolley through the wide doorway. 'I always draw the damn short straw. Been carting these barrels around all night, haven't I?' Harlyn had a permanent crease between her brows, a pointed chin and unusual white-blonde hair that was currently swept off the back of her neck with a leather strap. 'Why in the names of Dresmis and Thera are you here so early?' she asked.

Roh waved a hand at the structure sitting atop their workbench. Only three people knew of its existence: Harlyn, their friend, Orson, and Ames.

Harlyn nodded knowingly. 'You can't keep away from that thing, can you? Rohesia the bone cleaner's secret passion …' She brought the trolley to a stop in the far corner of the workshop and twisted her body, cracking her back with a satisfied groan.

'Like you can talk.' Roh gave a pointed look to the handcrafted lute strapped across Harlyn's shoulders. Her friend had made it herself by carving wood from an old bench, spending days meticulously setting the strings. Harlyn was as obsessed with her lute as Roh was with her design work. But it was against the Law of the Lair for cyrens to play music; that was what humans were for. Cyrens were *supposed* to focus all their energies on honing their deathsong, cultivating their power from within. To spend talent and time giving their musical gift to human instruments was considered an insult to their kind. But a bone cleaner was low on the Council of Seven Elders' list of priorities, and so Harlyn had taught herself how to play the one-of-a-kind instrument. It was one of the rare sources of music for the cyrens of the Lower Sector.

Harlyn elbowed her. 'No need to *stare.*'

'Sorry,' Roh muttered. She hadn't realised she had been gawking at the lute. Still a fledgling, her wide, moss-green eyes hadn't yet taken on the striking lilac hue of the fully matured cyrens. Even for a youngster they were considered an unusual colour, and Harlyn insisted that they made Roh unnerving. The dark shadows below her bottom lashes were permanent features thanks to exhaustion, while her dark brows and the speckle of blue scales at her temples intensified her discerning gaze.

Harlyn was now wrangling a barrel from the trolley

dramatically and Roh clicked her tongue impatiently. 'Can you hurry this up? I want to finish this section of the model before the others get here.'

But Harlyn leaned back against the trolley leisurely and picked her teeth with an extended black talon. 'I'd love to. I'm just *dying* to count these bones all on my lonesome.'

Roh couldn't help the smile that tugged at her face. Harlyn's humour was one of the reasons Roh loved her. With a resigned sigh, she threw the dirty cloth over her project and moved it to the far end of the workshop, where she kept it hidden from sight. 'Can't have you counting bones solo,' she told Harlyn. 'We both know you'd make a mess of it.'

'Too true, Rohesia. Too true.' Harlyn carefully swung the lute strap from her shoulders and hid the instrument alongside Roh's model.

Using an iron rod, the two fledglings prised the lid off the first barrel. The foul stench of rotting flesh within assaulted their senses and had them dry-retching.

Eyes watering, with a hand over her mouth and nose, Harlyn looked at Roh with a deadpan face. 'I do love how rewarding this job is.'

Roh snorted.

Elbow-deep in pungent vinegar water, Roh and Harlyn had just finished their count as the other fifteen fledglings and cyrens filed in. All had completed the sixteen years of education required of their kind, like Roh and Harlyn, and some were fresh from their lessons, while others had cleaned bones in the workshop for decades. Then there was the occasional younger face, like Jesmond, who apparently had no affinity for learning and so had been allowed to split her time between the workshop and the lesson rooms.

'You've been here a while?' a familiar soft voice sounded. Orson slid into her seat at the bench between Roh and Harlyn. Her face was the other side of Harlyn's harsh coin: round, with gentle, wide-set, almost-lilac eyes. When she smiled shyly, her chin dimpled. It made her seem more youthful, though she was a whole decade older than both Roh and Harlyn.

'About three hours,' Roh told her, spotting Ames entering the room. Roh had known him her whole life. A quiet but steely creature, he was the poor male cyren who'd been charged with her care from infancy, though why she had become the ward of the workshop master, she did not know. Ames was older than any cyren Roh knew. He'd been around for centuries, if lair gossip was to be believed, and was one of the few cyrens who actually aged. His weathered skin was lined and he wore a permanent expression of exasperation.

Harlyn elbowed Roh and her attention snapped back to the new crate of bones that had just been emptied onto their bench with a loud rattle.

'Perfect,' she sighed.

Someone sidled up in between them. 'Need a hand?'

Harlyn let out an impatient *tsk*. 'What are you doing here, Jesmond?'

At fourteen years of age, Jesmond was the youngest fledgling in their ranks, who made it her mission to interrupt the trio any chance she got.

She flashed Harlyn a grin. 'Helping you three.'

'You're not a bone cleaner yet, Jes,' Orson said gently.

'Ahhh, yes,' Roh retorted. 'Something to aim high for.'

'Shouldn't you be learning about long-forgotten cyren wars and deathsongs?' Harlyn added less kindly, flicking a bone splinter at the youngster.

Jesmond didn't so much as flinch, but merely batted the fragment away and waited expectantly to be included. Roh loved watching the verbal sparring matches Jesmond started; she had a way of getting under all of their skins. When she wasn't driving them mad, they couldn't help laughing at her antics. She was akin to the younger sister none of them had, persistent and always having heard things she shouldn't have.

'Jesmond, get back to the lesson rooms.' Ames' voice cleaved through the chatter. Jes slipped away without another word and Ames' gaze fell to Roh, Harlyn and Orson. 'You three,' he said sharply. 'Less talk, more work.'

Roh had lost count of how many times Ames had scolded them over the years. The rest of the workshop knew that if their mentor was in a foul mood, it was more than likely that the 'trio of terrors' was behind it. That was what Ames had called them as youngsters. Despite the fact that he had always said it with a sharp voice and stern expression, Roh, Harlyn and Orson knew there was some semblance of fondness buried beneath, and thus they always dared to push Ames that little bit further than the rest of their cohort.

'Rohesia.' Ames had moved closer to Roh. 'Have you looked at the design for the new nobles' quarters yet?'

She shook her head, still studying the skeletal piece in her hand. 'I haven't had time —'

'Do it now.'

'But Ames —' She couldn't help the longing glance in the direction of her secret project.

He made a point of ignoring this. 'Now. They want it built yesterday.' His cutting expression told her there would be no negotiating. He dropped a rolled piece of parchment on top of the bones in front of her. 'Stop hunching,' he added, tugging his collar; a tic he had to cover the strange mark on his neck.

Roh stretched her arms behind her with a groan.

Harlyn rejoined them at the workbench. 'Why in the realm should you be looking at designs? You're just a bone cleaner like the rest of us.'

Orson looked worriedly between Harlyn and Roh. 'What she *means* is: they shouldn't be taking advantage of you.'

Harlyn rolled her eyes in frustration. '*Obviously* that's what I was saying.' Harlyn had a harsh way with words, but she meant well, usually.

Roh knew her friends were right. Looking at designs was not part of her job. But she didn't care. Reviewing plans for the lair, analysing the architectural integrity of Saddoriel and the outer borders of Talon's Reach, was far more stimulating than picking rotten skin off bones could ever be. And she was *good at it*. She had an instinct for assessing the landscape, Ames always said. When she wasn't working on her own design, she practised drawing exercises in her sketchbook, perfecting the basic principles of architecture. Amidst the monotony of the workshop, pre-empting a fault in a floor plan or poking holes in the scale of someone's carefully built model gave her a thrill. So when Ames sought her help, Roh jumped at the chance, despite the fact that she never received credit for her input. The main problem was how little time she had. She was never excused from her duties in the workshop, so she often found herself trying to catch up well into the early hours of the morning.

Roh now turned to the curling piece of parchment Ames had given her. The design for the nobles' quarters. She scowled, studying the crisp lines and measurements. It wasn't architecture for a new wing at all. Far from it. She stared, disbelief clenching her insides. It was a *cage*. Roh didn't want to guess at what, or *whom* it was for. She took a breath and examined it critically. She could already see the flaw in the design – the levers where the cage would open and close weren't positioned correctly. The system of pulleys would snap at the incorrect weight distribution. She took out a stick of charcoal and began to make her adjustments.

She had just found her rhythm, blocking out the endless distractions of the workshop, when Ames cleared his throat pointedly. He stood at the front of the room, long fingers pressed together, waiting coolly for all movement and chatter to cease.

'You will need to have all bones cleaned and sorted by the eighteenth hour today,' he said. His high collar seemed sharper, making him look even more severe than usual.

He was answered with an outburst of loud protests.

'Master Ames, there's no way we can possibly —'

'That's not fair. There's just not enough time —'

'Why? We can't be expected to work like that —'

The scrape of something sharp on a workbench set Roh's teeth on edge. Harlyn had dragged her long, black talons across the surface, her face dark with fury. 'He can't be serious,' she hissed.

'Calm down, Har,' Orson whispered, placing a soft hand on Harlyn's arm. 'I'm sure there's a reason.'

Roh took in the sight of her friends, both tense in their own different ways. Harlyn, on the verge of a violent explosion, Orson poised to intervene at a second's notice.

Roh straightened on her stool and sought her mentor's attention. 'Ames,' she called, her voice louder than the unified cry of objections. 'It's not possible. We can't complete —'

But Ames' icy lilac glare silenced her. 'Her Majesty has called a territory-wide assembly in the Upper Sector this evening,' he said, his words cold.

Roh blinked, not daring to glance at Harlyn and Orson. '*What?*'

Ames' voice cleaved through the workshop and seemed to forge it anew. 'It appears the Queen's Tournament is upon us once more.'

Suddenly, Roh couldn't swallow. It was as though the back of her throat was swelling with every burning question that sprang to her mind. At last, she turned to her friends, their expressions just as shocked and then eager as her own …

The Queen's Tournament. It's finally here.

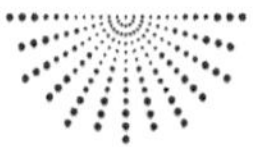

CHAPTER TWO

The bone Roh was holding clattered to the ground and the entire workshop burst into excited chatter while the trio of friends stared at each other in disbelief. They had been waiting for the Queen's Tournament their entire lives. The mere mention of its name flipped Roh's stomach. Held only every five decades, this would be the first in her brief lifetime of seventeen years. On more than one occasion, she had wished herself older to have witnessed the tournaments before, so she knew what to expect and how many years, months, days until the next. But no amount of wishing would change things; being a bone cleaner of Saddoriel had taught her that much at least.

The tournament was *everything*. It gave cyrens from all over the realms the opportunity to compete for the coral crown. It offered a chance for glory, a chance to see Saddoriel and escape the confines of monotony. Since they were youngsters, the trio had lived off the stories of past tournaments. Over the years, they had taken every chance to interrogate Ames about the ones he had seen. They'd questioned him about the previous competitors, the dirty tactics, the cunning trials and the bloodlust of the crowd. The three friends had inhaled every morsel of detail, noting down everything that might help them one day … If Ames was in a good mood, he would humour them, describing the set-up of the arena: a series of deadly circuits one tournament, a race through the human realms above the next, and one of the most recent … A cage battle. The tournament encapsulated the nature and history of their kind: brutal, bloody and cunning. Roh had always been fascinated with the idea of the tournaments, but as she and the others grew from nestlings to fledglings, they became obsessed. Soon they began to whisper plans of their own. *Imagine … If one of us were to be crowned queen …*

But Ames finished his tales the same way every time: with a sigh and the words, 'It's called *the Queen's Tournament* for a reason.'

This always made Roh, Orson and Harlyn roll their eyes. They *knew* Queen Delja was the most powerful cyren to have ruled Talon's Reach in thousands of years. She wasn't called Delja the Triumphant for nothing. For *six centuries* she had reigned over Talon's Reach and the cyren territories beyond. Their winged queen was a descendant of the great water goddesses, and because of her heritage had been blessed with an unusually long life, even for a cyren. But that didn't mean she would reign forever. The trio was determined to prove that to the rest of Saddoriel. For nearly a decade, they had repeated that promise to one another. Together, they would show their kind that lowborns could do more than clean bones. Together, they would make their mark on Saddoriel, because at long last, the tournament was here. And Roh, Orson and Harlyn were all old enough to enter.

As per the tournament rules, there was only one place open to their subsector. Long ago, they had agreed to play each other for it, vowing that the two who lost would be happy for the victor. It was as simple and as hard as that.

Roh looked down at the bloody mess in front of them. A collection of bones, human and other, with strips of flesh and whatever else still attached. Centuries ago, the cyrens of the world had done whatever they pleased; luring their prey into dark passages, tempting victims from ships into the churning currents … Wherever they roamed, they took what they wanted: music, magic, power. Now, it was different. Now, cyrens stayed within the cyren territories, depending on melodies to preserve their might. And Roh and her friends had no idea where the bones came from. Any queries fell on deaf ears. Lowborns weren't to concern themselves with questions.

Roh returned her focus to the blueprint before her. The sooner she completed her work, the sooner the trio could discuss the Queen's Tournament and what, exactly, they intended to do about it.

. . .

Somehow, their cohort managed to complete the day's work in time, and that evening the dining hall was buzzing. Everyone was to go to the Upper Sector after supper, and that alone was cause enough for excitement. Like many of their peers, Roh and her friends had never seen past the lower levels of their sector. Only the more senior cyrens were allowed into the Mid and Upper Sectors for trade, and of course, to maintain the bone architecture above. The trio sat huddled at the end of the table, away from the rest, taking in the energy of the room.

'It's happening … It's *finally* happening,' Orson said, voice hushed. 'Part of me can't believe it.'

Harlyn slung her arm around their friend's shoulder. 'Well, believe it. Not long now until one of us is an official competitor.'

Roh could hardly stomach her dinner, so bad were the nerves writhing inside her. Their lives were about to change forever. There would be no going back; once a competitor entered, that was it. Many died during the trials, which was often preferable to the shame of failing. Roh only knew of four living cyrens who had survived a Queen's Tournament and remained in Saddoriel; they did so only by the grace of the Council of Elders, apparently having shown enough valiance to sate the pride of their queen. The tournament was perilous at best, deadly at worst, and Roh had never wanted anything more in her life.

'It's called the Queen's Tournament *for a reason.'* Ames' words echoed in her mind.

Yes, she thought. *And there will be a new queen soon enough.* Only on occasion had Roh dared to dream of what might be should they succeed, should *she* succeed. She imagined her friends and peers cheering her on as she faced challenge after challenge. Banners with her name scrawled across them in big letters, cyrens who had painted lines of gold across their foreheads so they could be just like her. She pictured a great feast, proud faces and words of congratulations as the coral crown was at last bestowed upon her. Her life as a bone cleaner would be no more. What then? Would she and the others live as highborns in the Upper Sector? Experiencing music every single day?

Roh shook the daydreams from her head. 'When are we going to decide?' she asked Harlyn and Orson, pushing away her bowl.

'First thing tomorrow? Gives us the night to think about whether we want to back out …' Harlyn grinned as she said the last words.

Roh forced herself to return the grin, knowing full well that *none of them* would pass up the chance to compete.

'What game are we going to play?' Orson said.

Harlyn shrugged. 'We always said we'd choose at the last minute.'

'We did?'

'Yes,' Roh replied, knowing full well the terms of what they had discussed over the years, knowing that the others did too. 'So none of us have time to prepare or plan anything prior.'

A bell rang and Ames appeared in the doorway of the dining hall alongside the other mentors of the Lower Sector.

Roh was already standing. 'It's time …'

The trio stayed close as the hall burst into activity. Benches scraped back, bowls and cutlery were deposited at the kitchen window and the crowd of lowborns bottlenecked at the exit. Roh linked arms with her friends and joined the rest of the jostling group, spotting Ames in the lead as they made their way towards the elaborate pulley system that would transport them to the entrance of Saddoriel. Roh's throat went dry. She had no idea what to expect from the Upper Sector or its inhabitants. They were going in blind.

Packed into a metal box, they lurched upwards and Roh clutched the railing, her stomach squirming. With their entire workshop group squeezed into the tiny space, it was instantly stuffy and made Roh nauseous. She hated the sensation. Ignoring the animated chatter around her, she focused her attention outwards, peering through the bodies as the various levels began to pass. Talon's Reach was an immense, cavernous territory, with its city, Saddoriel, at its heart. A cylindrical fortress, holding three sectors, twelve subsectors and countless levels, tunnelling deep, dark leagues under the seabed.

The pulley system jolted violently as they continued upwards and Roh gasped. Orson squeezed her arm; she too was suffering. When they passed the Mid Sector, Roh's ears felt strange, as though something had popped within them. As the pulley system took them higher still, the light changed. Roh knew from what Ames had told them that the Upper Sector of Saddoriel was enchanted to reflect the natural light of the sun and moon in the sky above the seas, while the Lower Sector made do with torches and jars of glowing valo beetles. Roh craned her neck to see the levels as they passed.

There was a collective intake of breath as suddenly, it sounded. *Music.* The mournful notes of a fiddle carved through the lair. Clear and brilliant, the sound skittered across Roh's skin and sank into her chest, where it belonged. She felt the contentment only music could bring, a kind of peace within herself that was so often just a mirage.

The screech of chains cut through the melody as they came to a halt.

'This way,' Ames called. They stepped out into a cavernous passage, with sparse light flickering, catching the glint of salt crystals in the walls.

Following her peers, Roh was mesmerised as a different sort of light beamed down, revealing the official entrance to Saddoriel ... An archway of bones. Its ivory tones gleamed bright. Immaculately sculpted and preserved, the sheer volume of them ... The way they were expertly placed ... It was both horrifying and beautiful. As they passed under the towering structure, the music that filled the air around them became even clearer.

Imagine hearing this all the time, Roh marvelled, pressing her hand to her chest in wonder. Around her, her fellow fledglings wore the same awed expressions.

This ... this is what the Upper Sector is like ...

Beyond the archway of bones was the inside of a great cylinder, with numerous stone galleries peering down at them, stretching over a hundred feet above. Rocky bridges joined the upper levels, and in the centre of it all was a thick, jagged column, a throne looming high. Roh admired the structure, wishing she'd brought her sketchbook and stick of charcoal to capture the architecture, to break down the form and function of the design. There was nothing like this down in the Lower Sector. It was like an everted tower, brimming with magic and complexities she longed to study and understand. Ames had taught her the tenets of architecture, and his words echoed in her mind now:

'Space, concept, function and structure. Once you understand these principles of design, Rohesia, you can build anything, and take anything apart ...'

Roh didn't know where to look. Thousands of cyrens from all over Talon's Reach were crammed into the entrance of the lair. The populations of the Upper, Mid and Lower Sectors were, for once, all in the one place.

Was that a ...? Roh stared after a lowborn she'd never seen before, ducking into the crowd. Sometimes it was hard to believe she wasn't the only circlet-wearer in Saddoriel. But she was sure she'd seen a flash of gold, and for that she was grateful, knowing the existence of others granted her a sliver of anonymity. She might be the offspring of a criminal, but no one knew *which* criminal – except for Harlyn and Orson, of course. However, there was no denying what she was.

Roh's skin crawled as the nearby highborns noticed her, their eyes catching on the gold circlet around her head, noses wrinkling in disgust. Heat flooded her face and she wanted to shrink back from the slippered feet, flowing robes and jewelled belts. Some sported silver jewellery along their exposed arms, others displayed their nobility with small serpents coiling around their necks. These snakes were the distant relation to the legendary sea serpents and drakes who accompanied the goddesses Dresmis and Thera everywhere. To have one was to be in the inner circle of the Council of Seven Elders – or to be the queen herself.

Beside Roh, Orson was fidgeting in her discomfort, whereas Harlyn had plastered an aggressive, narrow-eyed stare upon her face. They too were being gawked at, though not with quite as much loathing. Roh had to clamp her hands to her sides to stop herself from trying to cover the ring of gold that marked her as different. Instead, she took in the extraordinary surroundings. She gaped at the vertical gardens of rare flowers that inched up the walls of the galleries above. Inside, bone framed almost everything. The work of so many cyrens who had come before her and her friends.

She froze mid-step. For standing in a gallery high above was the Council of Seven Elders. She nudged Harlyn and Orson, nodding to the balcony.

Harlyn followed her line of sight and let out a low whistle. 'Do you know who's who?'

Roh gazed up at the straight-backed figures. Like all cyrens, she knew the names of the seven members: the two Haertels (a couple), Mercer, Ward, Colter, Rasaat, Sigra. But this was the first time she had seen them in person.

Orson pointed. 'The light brown-haired duo, there, that's Taro and Bloodwyn Haertel.'

Harlyn scoffed. 'How do *you* know?'

'When I was a nestling, they visited the Lower Sector. They oversee the population of Talon's Reach. I think they're seen as the unofficial leaders of the council.'

'And the rest?' Roh asked.

'That's Arcus Mercer,' Jesmond piped up. Roh had to stop herself from cursing the youngster. She really did manage to sneak up on them. Roh followed Jesmond's pointed finger to the tallest of the elders, whose hair was shaved close to the skull. 'He came to our lessons a few moons back. He's the education master. And that elder there ...' Jesmond added, shifting her focus to another male cyren whose arms were crossed over his chest. He looked severe, with sharp features, a zigzag line shaved through his hair and his talons unsheathed.

'That's Erdites Colter. He oversees the Law of the Lair, and the Jaktaren.'

Roh's stomach dropped. 'The Jaktaren? Are they here?' She pivoted, searching the crowds for any sign of the legendary guild.

Harlyn nudged her in the ribs with her elbow and thrust her chin upwards. In the gallery beside the Council of Seven Elders was a small group standing stoically side by side. All five of them had the same thin zigzagged line shaved – or was it scarred? – into the right side of their head, just like their elder. Roh let out a breath. She could only really make out the two at the front – a male and a female cyren, who watched the crowd below, still as death. The Jaktaren was a guild of highborn cyrens who had mastered their deathsongs early in life, who had been trained to scour the vast realms above, hunting human musicians to bring back to Saddoriel.

Roh realised she was still staring at the handsome pair. The female was short for a cyren and wore a sling at her jewel-belted hip, while the male's mouth was set in a straight line, his jaw square and aggressive, with chestnut brown hair to his collarbone. Roh started. There was something familiar about him …

'That's Finn Haertel,' Jesmond said with a wink. 'According to my sources, he's one of the best Jaktaren in the last century. He's brought fifteen musicians back to Saddoriel in this past moonspan alone.'

Roh frowned at the youngster. 'Your sources?' she laughed. 'Who do you think you are, Jes? Some sort of secret informer?'

Harlyn snorted beside her. 'Jesmond thinks she's got a future in gambling, haven't you heard, Roh? She constantly combs the lair for the best tips.'

'And what in the name of Dresmis and Thera do the Jaktaren have to do with lowborns gambling away their hard-earned bronze keys?' Roh said.

Jesmond sighed dramatically, not yet having taken her eyes off the highborn male. 'Thought you three were savvier than that. Everything's got to do with everything,' she said with a shrug.

Orson leaned in with a finger pressed to her lips. 'Shhh … You're drawing too much attention. It's going to start soon.'

Roh and Harlyn conceded, throwing their hands up in mock surrender and exchanging quietly amused glances. Orson was always overly cautious, so much so that she hadn't realised the whole of Saddoriel was too caught up in their own chatter to pay any attention to the trivial conversations of a couple of lowborns. All the same, Roh returned her gaze to the galleries above, scanning the faces of the elders in awe. They and their ancestors had been in the council for as long as Delja had reigned, perhaps even longer. She couldn't imagine having that sense of history, or power.

Nervous energy rushed through Roh's veins as she craned her neck towards the throne and spotted Queen Delja the Triumphant upon it. The rocky column on which the throne was carved gave an unexpected groan, and to Roh's amazement, the structure began to lower. As the queen drew closer, Roh gasped at the horned viper that was curled around Delja's arm, the *direct descendant* of a sea drake.

'I heard she has three,' Jesmond said matter-of-factly.

'Rubbish,' Harlyn scorned.

Roh couldn't take her eyes off it. She had had no idea there was *one* in Talon's Reach, let alone *three*.

The column came to a stop, not completely at ground level, but somewhere in between the lower and middle galleries. Roh had never been this close to the queen before. Her gaze snagged on the crown of coral atop the beautiful cyren's head of dark, waist-length hair. Embedded at the front three apexes were glinting jewels: the birthstones of Saddoriel. Even from a distance, Roh could appreciate their breathtaking beauty; so unique, so rich in colour and magic. The Gauntlet Ruby, the Mercy's Topaz and the Willow's Sapphire.

The music around them ceased and a powerful surge of air swept through the space, strong enough to flutter the long tresses and robes around Roh. Above her, the queen had unfolded a giant pair of wings at her back. Dark membrane blocked out the light and she hovered, with an effortless beat of those wings, above them all. The very wings that marked her as *chosen* by the goddesses.

'Welcome to Saddoriel.' Somehow, a subtle melody laced between the queen's first three words and Roh couldn't tear her attention from her; she was hooked.

'The Council of Seven Elders and I welcome one and all here today.' Queen Delja's opening address projected to the far reaches of the stone galleries and the ground below. There was no other sound but for the crisp notes of her voice ringing outwards. The crowd was full of simmering anticipation; Roh could feel it, palpable between the cyrens around her.

'You all know why we are here,' the queen continued. 'Every five decades, we hold the tournament. For the longest time, it was known as The Dawning, but for the past six centuries, it has been mine, and so it remains in this moment: the Queen's Tournament. Today, you are given the opportunity to challenge my reign.'

The queen smiled.

'For those of you too young to know, the tournament consists of three trials, which will be completed within three moonspan or less. The cyren standing at the end, *if there is one*, will be crowned victor. And thus, the new king or queen of our kind. Should there be no such victor, I shall continue to rule, as I have done these past six hundred years.'

With her mouth slightly open, Roh studied the queen. She was too young to fathom that length of time, if one ever could. Cyrens had always been blessed by the goddesses with long life – usually around two hundred years – but six? It dawned on her then that to enter the Queen's Tournament was to face cunning honed by six centuries' worth of experience ... Cunning that had seen twelve tournaments and their competitors come and go, to no avail ... A wave of goosebumps rushed across Roh's arms.

'Orientation for chosen competitors will be held at the twelfth hour tomorrow and the opening gala will be hosted tomorrow evening. The tournament officially begins in three days' time, at the commencement of the first trial.' Delja's melodic voice was like silk, soft but unyieldingly strong. Roh had only heard historic tales of the queen's deathsong. Of how she was only eight when she sang its first note. Of how it had been wielded against human warships in the seas above. It was rumoured to be the deadliest and most powerful in all of history.

'Sectors will decide their competitors by the ninth hour tomorrow.'

Roh closed her eyes against the rush of wind that

pushed through the cavern. When she opened them again, the queen was gone.

In the crowded entrance, Harlyn and Orson stood before her now, their eyes bright and eager. Roh forced herself to smile back at her friends, her *family*. They had been through everything together for as long as she could remember. They were the two cyrens Roh admired most, the two she depended on for everything, and now, they were the two cyrens she would do anything to beat for her place in the tournament.

CHAPTER THREE

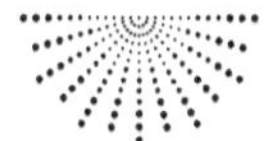

Roh hardly noticed as the bone cleaners were ushered back towards the pulley system. This time, she barely felt her stomach churn as they started their descent with a jolting drop. Thoughts of the tournament consumed her. She had always known that only one of their trio would compete; *only one*. The friends had spoken about it for years, content to let fate decide between them when the day came. But now that day was upon them, it wasn't until the queen had actually said the words that Roh realised just how desperately she needed that *one* to be *her*.

As the crate descended through the lair and the Lower Sector swallowed them once more, the music that had been so vibrant and *filling*, faded. It grew further and further away, becoming just the faintest of notes until they hit the ground. Suddenly, Roh could hardly breathe, as though she had left a part of herself under the archway of bones above. Thankfully, the crate gates opened and the crowd dispersed in a wave. Saying nothing, Roh pushed on after the others, following them back to their sleeping quarters. While the queen's address had left her silent, it had spawned a hushed, incessant chatter between Harlyn and Orson.

'We could play slates for it?' Orson said as they crossed the common area, making for their chamber.

'*Slates?* Not a chance,' Harlyn replied. 'You only suggest that because you leave us in debt every round.'

'Well, what's your brilliant suggestion, then?'

'We could get the rest of the bone cleaners to vote.'

It was Orson's turn to laugh, though she did so with a lot more respect than Harlyn had. 'A vote? A vote of popularity, you mean. Which *you* would win, no doubt.'

'You don't know that —'

Roh followed the banter back and forth between her two friends – it was light-hearted for the moment – but her mouth stayed clamped shut. How *would* they determine their champion? In all these years, they had never decided a method. It gave too much time for preparation, for scheming, as was in their blood. Now, however, Roh desperately wished she knew what was coming, and how to make it work in her favour. Could she wait another five decades before she had the chance to enter again? Panic blurred her vision momentarily and she raised a hand to her eyes, brushing the gold circlet. *It has to be me*, she told herself. She pictured colourful blooms being thrown at her feet and the birthstones of

Saddoriel glinting at her as she studied the coral crown in her hands —

A flare of flame brought her out of her thoughts with a jump. Like most cyrens, she was wary of open fire, but the small, circular room needed a source of light and warmth, which came from the fire pit at its centre. Orson was standing by the charred bricks, stoking the flames to life with a poker. She had volunteered for the job when they had first been allocated these quarters and took great pride in keeping the fire going in the cold depths of Saddoriel. Six beds fanned out around the fire pit like hands to a clock face, a trunk at the end of each for the lodgers' possessions. It was a cosy space; the only room in Talon's Reach Roh knew to describe as such. Their quarters shared a connected bathing chamber with the water runners – the cyrens who transported fresh water around the lair. Right now, though, their room was empty but for the trio. Their fellow bone cleaners, Jesmond, Krea and Manelda, had not yet returned from the announcement, or were likely giving their little group the space to digest the news. It was no secret that Ames' favourite workers wanted to enter.

Roh sat on the end of her bed, tracing shapes in her sketchbook while she watched her friends. Orson busied herself feeding the fire with kindling, while Harlyn, her white-blonde hair loose at her collarbone, sat cross-legged on her own bed, her lute in her lap, her fingers still on its frets as she gazed, transfixed, at the flames licking at the kindling. Roh longed for her to play, then, knowing it would fill them all with some semblance of comfort, perhaps even hope, that this would somehow work out.

'What are we going to do?' Harlyn said finally, looking up from her instrument.

'We could draw straws,' Orson offered. 'Or get Ames to decide.'

'Straws and Ames? Those are our only options?' Harlyn jeered. 'I can hardly wait.'

Roh shook her head. 'That's not helping.' What she didn't say was that *nothing* would help them. She was going to be ruthless, no matter what.

'Well, first of all, we need it to be fair,' Harlyn said, chewing her bottom lip.

Orson waved her hands at the pair of them, forever the peacekeeper. 'This must have happened before.'

'What?' Harlyn asked, her expression softening as she saw the anguish on poor Orson's face.

'Friends having to decide between themselves. If it has, what happened? How did they choose?'

Harlyn sighed. 'You're forgetting that it's not just us, Orson. The other bone cleaners might want to enter.'

But Orson pushed on. 'We need to choose between ourselves, and then worry about the rest. Surely we can look to the past for guidance? What are some of the scenarios from before?'

'How would we know?' Roh asked. 'We've been around even less time than you.'

'Well,' Harlyn said slowly, her gaze falling to the jagged white scar that ran from Roh's left nostril through her lips and down her chin. 'There is one person who might know.'

'I'm going to assume you're talking about Ames,' Roh warned, knowing exactly what Harlyn was getting at.

'No, that's not who I meant.'

Uncontained fury surged through Roh and she stood abruptly, rounding on Harlyn. 'Why do you do it? Why do you insist on bringing her up?'

'She's your mother.'

Roh's talons flashed. 'Leave it alone, Har.' The words were vicious.

Harlyn's eyes didn't leave her scar. 'She could tell you. She's one of the oldest living cyrens in the lair —'

'But she's not *in* the lair, *is she*? You don't know anything about her, Harlyn.'

'Neither do you —'

'I know enough —'

Harlyn snorted. 'No one *really knows* what happened in that chamber.'

'She *annihilated the entire Council of Elders*. She used her *deathsong* against our own kind,' Roh seethed. 'What more do you need to know? She's not like your mother, who used to carry your bag to lessons for you. Or like Orson's, who still visits with meals from the markets every few days. Think about it, Harlyn. She is Cerys *the Elder Slayer*, not Cerys, Holy Mother of Talon's Reach.'

Orson threw her hands up. 'Roh, Harlyn,' she implored. '*Please*. This won't help *anything*. If Roh doesn't want to see Cerys, she shouldn't. And Roh, Har didn't mean any harm. We're in this together, always have been … Let's not turn on each other, alright?'

The heat was already leaving Roh's blood at the sight of her distressed friend. She turned to Harlyn in surrender. 'You know I can't just demand to see her,' she said quietly. 'It's once a month. That's the Law of the Lair.'

Roh tried to keep the lie from her eyes. While it *was* the Law of the Lair, she didn't always *abide* by it. Roh nursed a certain fascination with her mother, a curiosity which couldn't be dampened, not even by cold disappointment or fear. But it was not something she shared openly, not even with Harlyn and Orson. The line of gold across her forehead and the legend of her mother's crimes coerced her into silence.

'She doesn't speak to me,' Roh pleaded with her friend. 'She's … she's not right, I've told you.' Although they didn't know everything, they knew seeing Cerys was never easy.

Harlyn placed her lute carefully on her bed before crossing to Roh. With a glance at Orson, she reached out, squeezing Roh's shoulder. 'I know,' she said. 'I shouldn't have pushed.'

Roh nodded, running her talon down the scar on her face; its ragged ridge was as familiar as any part of her. She had been visiting her mother in the prison as a small nestling when, unprovoked, Cerys had lashed out with her talons, slicing into Roh's face in a manic rage. Roh remembered the white-hot pain and the warm blood gushing down her cheek, but the memory ceased there. She must have passed out.

The trio ran out of time alone. Krea and Manelda entered the sleeping quarters flushed and in a flurry of chatter.

Manelda shrugged. 'All I'm saying is that he's —'

'He wouldn't look at you if you ran face-first into him.' Krea laughed.

'Who are you talking about?' Roh asked, relieved that there was some distraction from the intensity of the trio's conversation and enjoying the brilliant red blush spreading across Manelda's cheeks.

'The Jaktaren,' Krea replied gleefully. 'Manelda here thinks he's —'

'Finn Haertel?' Harlyn smirked.

'Oh, shush,' Manelda snapped, rummaging for her nightclothes. 'I said he cut a decent figure, and now Krea thinks I'm in love with him.'

Roh exchanged an amused glance with Harlyn, who was already bright-eyed, perked up and ready to stir the pot further, always finding joy in the subtle torment of others.

'Where's Jesmond?' Orson interrupted, forever checking up on the younger fledgling.

Krea shrugged. 'Making a menace of herself in the hall. Some of the older cyrens are placing bets on who will enter. She's taken on the role of master of coin.'

Harlyn huffed a laugh. 'She hasn't.'

'Has. We tried to bring her back here, but … Well, you know what she's like.'

Orson was already making for the door.

'Good luck,' Manelda called after her.

. . .

Roh couldn't sleep that night, not with thoughts of her mother swirling around in her head like a whirlpool threatening to suck her in. *Mother* ... The word almost didn't apply. It certainly seemed foreign in reference to Cerys.

Over the years, Roh had come to experience the notion of motherhood from afar, from witnessing her friends with their parents and the love they so obviously shared. Roh didn't know if she loved her mother. Could someone love the Elder Slayer of Talon's Reach? If they could, did such a bond form over the course of prison visits, in stolen snatches of time, while staring at one another through bars of bone? For the most part, Roh didn't feel anything when she saw Cerys, didn't feel for her mother the way she knew Orson felt for hers, or Harlyn had felt for her parents at one point or another. Perhaps Roh had been born without that particular ability. All she knew was that she and Cerys were different. The word 'mother' was not so much a title as it was a question. What they shared more than anything was a peculiar curiosity about one another. A lingering sense of wonderment at the fact that amidst the complexities and long history of Saddoriel, they were somehow connected.

Roh turned onto her other side, adjusting the blankets around her and watching the embers of the fire glowing. She had never fully explained her prison visits to her friends, never told them about how her mother stared at her with unfocused eyes, or how she manically carved strange patterns into the stone walls, a mural of madness from her broken talons. Roh had never told Orson and Harlyn that each month when she visited Cerys, she spent more time playing cards with the guard, Bryah, than speaking with her mother. It was far easier to win at cards than it was to face that part of herself.

The others were all sleeping soundly. Harlyn's scowl was softened by slumber and the glowing embers of the fire, while Orson was buried beneath her quilt like a child. Over the course of her life, they had been the only ones to ignore the gold circlet around her head. They had welcomed her into their lives, into their families where they could. Without them, her life would have been very different. Perhaps she would have gone mad like Cerys. But now, everything was at stake: everything she had ever wanted … Could she leave that up to chance? No, she couldn't. Roh knew what she had to do, had known for a long time now. And if she looked deep down, the plans she'd kept hidden, even from herself, began to slide into place.

Yes, she knew what to do. Come morning, she would stir with the rest of the bone cleaners, for what she hoped was the last time.

'She's gone again.' Roh woke up to the sound of Orson's worried tone. 'Has anyone seen Jesmond?'

Roh blinked blearily at the unmade, empty bed.

'Somewhere she's not supposed to be, no doubt,' she muttered.

'That's what concerns me.' Orson opened the door to the bathing chamber and peered inside to no avail, sighing in frustration.

Swinging her legs out of bed, Roh pulled on her pants and stood up to stretch, slowly sifting through the plan she'd been piecing together. 'I'll find her,' she offered.

''Bout time,' Harlyn grumbled from beneath her quilt. 'You never deal with her.'

'She's more trouble than she's worth.'

Orson had her hands on her hips. 'That's what I used to say about you two.'

Roh huffed a laugh as she tugged on her boots. 'Well, she's usually far more interested in having Harlyn deal with her.'

Harlyn pulled her pillow over her head with a groan. 'She's too damn young for me. And I've got too many other options.'

'Will you two stop?' Orson cried, talons out. 'Roh, please find her. The whole lair is up early this morning for tournament deciders, but Ames trusts us to keep her in line.'

'I'm going, I'm going,' Roh told her.

She found Jesmond exactly where she thought she would: in the private chambers of some older cyrens, attempting to hustle them out of their already scarce bronze keys and silver marks.

'Orson's looking for you,' Roh said, folding her arms over her chest in the doorway.

Neither Jes nor the other cyrens looked up from where they were crowded around a cup of dice.

'She's always looking for me,' Jes retorted, scooping the dice up in her palms.

'We're meant to keep an eye on you.'

'An eye, not full-time surveillance.'

The other cyrens laughed at that. 'Looks like you're out of luck anyway, Jes,' one of them said. 'Be on your way now.'

'*Tchah.*' Jes clicked her tongue. 'Fine. You lot are no use to me, anyway.'

'Watch yourself,' another cyren chided.

'Come on,' Roh muttered as the youngster joined her at the door.

'Surprised you're not wrapped up in deciding who's taking the tournament place.' Jesmond pocketed her pouch of bronze keys and dice as they walked through the common areas.

'Orson wanted to make sure you were alright first.'

'And Harlyn?' Jes asked, eyes bright.

'Harlyn wasn't bothered,' Roh said. The sooner she stamped out Jes' crush on her friend, the better. Harlyn tended to leave a trail of broken hearts wherever she went. Besides, she wasn't here to talk about Harlyn's love interests.

Jesmond didn't so much as flinch. 'So, have you decided?'

'Decided what?' Roh said coolly.

'I'm not an idiot, Rohesia.'

Roh shrugged. 'No, we haven't decided.'

'I'll wager there's a reason you volunteered to retrieve me.'

'You'll wager on anything.'

Jesmond halted with a grin. 'That's a yes.'

Roh faced Jesmond. 'I had an idea … about how the bone cleaners could decide their representative.'

'Oh?'

'But it can't come from me.'

Jesmond's expression was sly. 'Makes sense. And the idea?'

Voice lowered, Roh made quick work of telling her.

'What's in it for you?' Jesmond asked when Roh was finished. They continued to walk, this time towards the dining hall.

'The real question, Jes, is what's in it for *you*?' Roh smiled. 'Double the wagers. On the manoeuvres of the game itself as well as the final cyren standing. It's not about me, it's about how much you stand to make in commission. Which is why you're still here having this conversation.'

They had reached the entrance of the dining hall, where within, their cohort was in the midst of a very early first meal.

'I'll think about it,' Jesmond said.

Roh nodded as she walked off. 'You do that.'

'Where'd you find her?' a voice said from behind her.

'Exactly where she shouldn't have been,' Roh replied to Orson without turning around.

'Figures. She's a nightmare,' Orson allowed, tugging Roh into the dining hall.

'You're telling me …'

The trio ate breakfast together, quietly discussing their options for selecting their representative. With their heads huddled close, they ignored the flurry of movement and lively chatter around them, Roh savouring the sense of camaraderie for as long as they would share it.

'Orson,' a panicked voice sounded, interrupting their whispers. Orson's mother was there, forcing her way onto the bench and pushing Harlyn aside. 'Orson, *meesha*, tell me you're not still planning on involving yourself in this madness?'

Meesha, the New Saddorien word for 'my love', always sparked an ember of envy within Roh.

But a pained expression tightened Orson's gentle face, the younger mirror image of her mother's. 'Ma … I have always been honest about this.'

'No, *meesha*. I will not allow it.'

Roh and Harlyn tried to fade into the background, but Orson's mother was having none of it. 'This is your fault,' she spat at them. 'You two blood-hungry orphans, no? You put these ideas in *meesha*'s head.'

Both fledglings kept their mouths clamped shut. They had learned long ago that nothing good came from talking back to the whirlwind that was their friend's ma.

'Ma!' Orson snapped. 'They did no such thing. In case you have forgotten, I'm ten years *their senior*. If anything, I'm the one who's influencing them.'

From the corner of her eye, Roh saw Harlyn bite down on a bark of laughter.

'Ma,' Orson implored, more gently this time. 'I am a fully fledged cyren. It is my choice to put my name in the ring with the other willing bone cleaners. It will be alright, I promise.'

Tears lined the older cyren's eyes. 'These things are never alright, Orson. You can make no such promise.' She kissed the top of her daughter's head, muttering, '*Meesha*,' one more time before taking her leave with a final glare of disdain in Harlyn and Roh's direction.

Roh raised a brow. 'Blood-hungry orphans, eh?'

A dark laugh bubbled from Harlyn. 'We've been called worse.'

Orson flushed. 'I'm *so sorry* —'

Roh waved the apology away. 'Har's right. We've been called worse.'

'That doesn't make it alright,' Orson said crossly.

'I think we've got bigger matters to worry about.'

Someone cleared their throat pointedly. *Jesmond.* 'I hope I'm not interrupting,' she said.

'You're always interrupting,' Harlyn quipped.

'Well, forgive me for thinking you were interested in how the bone cleaners intend on choosing their competitor,' Jesmond shot back.

'Sorry, Jes,' Orson said. 'We're all a bit on edge this morning. What's going on?'

Jesmond paused, giving each of them an even stare. 'The bone cleaners want to play Thieves for the place in the tournament.'

'Thieves?' Orson frowned. 'Really?'

'Really,' Jes replied, her voice deadpan. 'You three in?'

The trio exchanged worried looks.

'*Tchah.*' Jesmond rolled her eyes. 'Let me know within the next twenty minutes.'

'Wait,' Harlyn said. 'So it's been decided? That's how we're electing a competitor.'

'I didn't realise what I said was so confusing.' Jesmond sidled up to Harlyn. 'I can talk you through it in detail if you like?'

'Oh, for Thera's sake,' Harlyn exclaimed, shoving Jes away. 'Go find some fledglings your own damn age.'

Jesmond shrugged. 'Let me know if you want to play.' With that, she left them.

'Looks like things have been decided for us,' Harlyn said slowly, the crease in her brow deepening.

'Looks like it,' Roh ventured, a finger tracing her circlet absentmindedly.

'But ...' Orson started.

'What?'

Orson gave Roh an apologetic grimace. 'Are you certain you want to play? I'm sure we could find a fairer way.'

'What do you mean?' Roh frowned.

'It's just that ...' Orson struggled to finish her sentence.

'*What?*'

Orson shifted in her seat. 'It's just that —'

'You're terrible at Thieves,' Harlyn finished for her cheerfully.

'I am not,' Roh objected.

'We're just more practised than you,' Orson reasoned,

shooting Harlyn a warning glare. 'You're always working on your … project when we play.'

'I'm not *that* bad.'

Harlyn scoffed. 'Roh, last time you were called *Thief* within the first three minutes.'

'Was not.'

'Were too. I caught you mid-sleight of hand – over a damn nucrite card no less.'

Roh fell silent. Every word was true. Those few times she had played with them, she had never played well.

She took a breath. 'Regardless of that, what do *we* want to do? It has to be *our* choice.'

Harlyn ran a hand through her hair. 'It looks like it's Thieves or no tournament chance at all.'

Orson still wasn't done trying to make it fair for everyone. 'We could —'

'I think we're out of time for other options,' Roh interrupted, spotting Jesmond loitering at the hall's edge.

'Roh's right,' Harlyn agreed, ever the opportunist. 'Jesmond,' she called across the room. 'We're in.'

'Good,' Jes replied. 'Meet at the workshop in thirty minutes. Oh,' she added. 'If you have a spare deck, bring it along, will you? It's looking to be a big game.'

Thieves was a cyren's game through and through; a display of strategy, cunning and risk. Which was why Roh wasn't surprised to find the workshop full, with Jesmond and her ledger in the midst of the fray. The youngster was directing a few older cyrens to push two tables together to form a large one, and move the benches against the walls to make room for the crowd. There were three bone cleaner workshops in Saddoriel, the workers of which had all managed to cram themselves into Ames'. Thankfully, it was too early for Roh's mentor to be here, for none would dare attempt this under his watch.

Roh, Harlyn and Orson forced their way into the room, the air thick with excitement. Jesmond waved them over and Roh had to admire the sheer force of her. No matter how many times she was told *no*, she persisted.

'For Thera's sake,' Orson muttered as numerous cyrens clapped Harlyn on the back as they made their way to the table. Harlyn grinned until they reached Jesmond.

'This is it?' she asked, looking around.

She'd said aloud what Roh had been thinking … There were only ten players in total.

'Perhaps I wasn't the only one Ma went around lecturing,' Orson offered quietly.

Roh couldn't quite manage a laugh. Instead, she wiped her clammy hands on the sides of her pants. 'You might be right there.'

She recognised Andwana, an older cyren who usually pushed a trolley of books from the Mid Sector archives around the dining hall. There was Mikael, a fledgling from their workshop who had made the unfortunate mistake of trying to mimic the way the Jaktaren wore their hair. Renee, a cyren with a sinewy frame who'd caused much drama when choosing her trade between water runners and bone cleaners. Freya, Ames' counterpart in another workshop group; Thomes, Freya's partner; and two other older cyrens Roh didn't know by name. Between them, they shared a wealth of knowledge and potentially hundreds of years of experience that could work against her. Roh surveyed the group, including her friends, her chest constricting. She would face the cunning of nine different cyrens, each one with their own unique set of rules and morals to test. How prepared were they? How long had each of them planned for this moment? How much did they want to win?

Roh and the others were jostled by the crowd as final bets were placed with what little coin the lowborns had. It was rare that Roh saw bronze keys slide across a table so freely, but for some, it was the first and only time in their lives that they would wager on a Queen's Tournament. From the corner of her eye, Roh saw Jesmond documenting the wagers and counting the small pile of bronze before her. A quick tally told Roh that Harlyn was the favourite. That fact didn't surprise her – people knew Harlyn because she played the lute at the evening meal sometimes. Starved for melodies down in the dark reaches of the lair, it was no wonder that people recognised Roh's friend and wanted to back her.

Orson tapped Jesmond and handed her Roh's deck. Jesmond smoothly slid the cards into the pile she was already holding and began to shuffle.

'Players at the table,' Jesmond said, her voice authoritative.

Gods ... Roh steadied her breathing as she sat down

beside Orson, with Harlyn opposite. Mikael took up the place to her right and the rest spaced themselves out. These were the cyrens standing between Roh and her place in the tournament … She silently cursed her sweating palms and her irregular heartbeat. She needed to stay calm and focused, to keep herself in check so she could see when others were losing their cool.

Jesmond started to deal.

Roh kept her hands under the table as the cards were laid out before them. A seven-card draw, as expected, with another ten placed in rows facedown in the centre of the table: the thief's temptation. Roh had seen it become the downfall of many a player, including herself on occasion. The thief's temptation offered the opportunity for a 'legal' sleight of hand, but if the player was called 'thief' mid-action, they were eliminated. If they were found to be bluffing the sleight of hand, the caller was eliminated. It was a tactic usually left until later in the game.

Roh's seventh card was placed in front of her.

'Alright,' Jesmond said, signalling for quiet. 'Let's —'

'What in *Dresmis and Thera's names* is going on here?' Ames' voice didn't boom. It brushed against them softly like a silk scarf before it squeezed around one's neck.

The room fell silent and Ames' face tightened with fury. 'Well?'

It was Orson, quiet, sweet Orson, who spoke. 'Our apologies, Master Ames. We sought a way to elect a representative for our subsector in the Queen's

Tournament.' Only Orson could make a game of Thieves sound so official and reasonable.

'So, you decided to turn my workshop into a gaming hall?'

'It seemed the fairest way, Master Ames,' Harlyn piped up.

The ancient cyren scanned the desperate faces before him, his own expression unreadable. The tension in the air was palpable, and Roh found herself clenching her fists so hard that her talons unsheathed and dug into her flesh. She *needed* this game to go ahead. With the competitor orientation only a few hours away, *all* the bone cleaners did.

'I hope anyone considering this,' Ames began darkly, 'knows *exactly* what they're getting into. There are no fair fights in Saddoriel, only the cunning of your fellow cyrens. The trials will get harder and deadlier as the tournament goes on. Few survive. And of those who do, most wish they hadn't.'

No one said a word.

Ames sighed. 'Get on with it, then.'

A collective murmur of relief washed over the workshop and Roh unclenched her fists. At Jesmond's signal, she turned her cards and assessed her hand. She bit her lip and then silently cursed herself for doing so. No doubt the others would be watching her for any tells. She schooled her features into neutrality as she scanned the cards again. *Not terrible, but not terribly good, either.* A backahast – a type of water horse hailing from Lochloria, the third-highest card; two nucrites – moth-like creatures that were only powerful in swarms; two humans, as well as a land card and a sea card.

Slowly, she turned her gaze to the other players. First, the two she knew best: Harlyn was chewing the inside of her cheek and Orson's posture was straight, too straight, which meant both had strong hands. She didn't know the others nearly as well, but she had a knack for reading people, or so Bryah had told her during one of their many games. She could tell by the way Mikael held his cards that he was no threat.

Unless he's bluffing, a voice in her head said. But no, she knew Mikael from around the workshop. He'd likely just entered the game for the notoriety of having put his name forward for the tournament. *He doesn't expect to win,* Roh thought. *Nor does he wish to – he has too much self-preservation for that.*

Roh looked to the cyren she didn't know on Mikael's right. The hand that held his cards was shaking ever so slightly. Beside him, Roh saw Harlyn's sharp eyes note the small detail as well. On the other side of the table, Freya smirked into her cards, and Thomes —

Roh's assessments were cut short as Jesmond spun a small wheel to determine who turned the first card. The needle landed on Andwana, who, with a steady hand, reached towards the thief's temptation and turned a card over, the card that would set the tone of the entire game. It was a klyree – a horned hare that usually found a way into the Lower Sector crops; a low-value card. Roh noted the water-element symbol in the top corner with a surge of relief; if the element stayed the same, she wouldn't have to pick up cards this round.

She watched intently as the game began to unfold. It was Harlyn's turn next. She coolly placed two water-elemented cyren cards down and sat back. The cyren whose name Roh didn't know followed them with a single water warlock. A gasp from the crowd sounded. It was the first high-value card to be played.

Suddenly uncomfortable in her seat, Roh shifted awkwardly and glanced at her cards. Depending on what Mikael put down, she'd be alright for this round … She hoped.

Mikael matched the water warlock with one of the fire element. Someone in the crowd whistled. An element change. Fine. That suited her just fine. She played a water warlock with the air element. There was a murmur of approval from around her, but Roh kept her eyes on the game and her cards covered. She knew she wouldn't be the only cyren channelling her cunning today. While Orson mulled over her hand, Roh recounted what had been played so far. It was early in the game, too early to mark the threats – the round was not yet half complete. A flicker of movement caught her eye —

'Thief,' a stony voice sounded.

Roh recognised that voice. She went cold as she looked across the table to see Harlyn staring down at Renee. The entire room fell silent again. It was a bold move to call 'thief' so soon, but that was Harlyn. Roh had seen Renee's sleight of hand, but had kept quiet, not wanting to draw attention to herself. However, it wasn't in Harlyn's nature to be cautious.

'Thief,' Harlyn said again, waiting for Renee to challenge her.

The quiet pulsed as the workshop tensed for the explosion that so often occurred around these calls. But Renee tossed her hands up and threw eight, not seven cards onto the table. She hadn't yet completed the sleight of hand – placing the card that she didn't want back into the thief's temptation. Her stool scraped against the floor as she exited the game, muttering curses under her breath.

'Play on,' Jesmond prompted.

Soft gasps sounded from the crowd as Orson played a sea drake: the highest card, the one cyrens usually left until last. Roh felt her palms grow clammy again; she needed to keep track of the sea drakes more than anything.

One player down, eight more to go ...

The game continued, finally making it the whole way around the table, and again. Players began to use combinations, changing their strategies as the game progressed. Roh kept her cards close, watching every tell, every play, alert and ready. She knew Orson had lost some of her better cards and was now playing conservatively, while Harlyn, being Harlyn, was quite arrogant in her approach, which made Roh think that she too was playing with a weak hand.

'Thief.' It was Mikael who called it this time, looking

across the table at Thomes. But Thomes grinned and shook his head. A bluff manoeuvre. Mikael was out.

'Good luck,' he said as he placed his cards facedown and left the table.

Four cards out of play, unknown to the players. Roh knew she wasn't the only one assessing these details, but she watched Mikael leave, satisfied that she'd been right about his motivations.

Another round, an offering of much lower cards, though the stakes only seemed to get higher and higher. Roh fanned her cards out close to her chest and considered the pair of humans the cyren beside Harlyn had just played. Roh played three of a kind, her best hand yet: klyrees, two land and one fire element. She finished with the fire element, knowing they had played more fire than anything else so far. As she did, she saw Thomes slide a card from the thief's temptation into his hand and replace it with one of his own. It wasn't a seamless act and Roh knew she couldn't have been the only one to notice it, but no one called it this time, not even Harlyn. To call 'thief' was to draw attention to your own level of skill and observation, which meant Harlyn in particular wanted the heat off her for the time being.

Interesting.

A tightness grew in Roh's chest the longer the game went on. She was aware of every movement around her, including Ames' constant pacing around the table. He was eager to have his workshop returned to him, of course, yet Roh suspected it was more than that on his mind. She chanced a glance in his direction, but he wouldn't meet her gaze, and she couldn't split her focus between the cards before her and whatever turmoil her mentor was experiencing.

A moment later, Andwana was eliminated.

Six more to beat ...

As cards were played and picked up, Jesmond refilled the thief's temptation from the remaining deck. At last, Roh spotted what she had been looking for. A barely noticeable dot of shine on the back of two cards ... But it wasn't time yet. *A little longer —*

'Thief,' Roh heard herself say, looking directly at Harlyn.

Harlyn blinked as the rest of the workshop stilled.

'What?' she said.

Roh didn't break eye contact. '*Thief,*' she repeated clearly.

One of the cards in Harlyn's hands bent.

'Harlyn?' Jesmond prompted. 'Your response?'

It had been a good manoeuvre, subtle and weightless, but Roh knew Harlyn, knew when she would try the steal, and she'd done exactly as Roh had anticipated. A slew of curses escaped Harlyn as she flung her cards down on the table, the stolen card in question still bent in her grasp.

Roh bit back the apology on the tip of her tongue. Harlyn shoved her chair back so aggressively that it knocked to the floor and the crowd behind her dispersed. Had Harlyn been in Roh's shoes, Roh knew she would have done the same. There was no room for the courtesies of friendship when a place for the Queen's Tournament was at stake.

Roh eyed the two cards glinting at her from the thief's temptation. *Soon.* Soon it would be time.

Jesmond cleared her throat. 'Play on.'

'I fold,' said the cyren who'd sat next to Harlyn, placing her cards facedown on the table and sliding them away from her as she left.

Another four cards out of play, unknown to the players ... *Good ...* The more cards unknown to them all, the better. Roh felt stiff in her seat as the tension around her grew more and more palpable with every card played.

Freya put a combination hand in play – two teerah panthers and a land card. Roh froze as the realisation dawned on her. She'd made a mistake, she'd miscounted ...

Ames was still pacing, his movements distracting Roh to frustration. She shook her head, trying to maintain her composure and attention on Freya's recent hand. *There should only be ... Unless ...* There was one more panther in play than she'd counted, which was strange. She'd kept a sharp eye and even sharper count. Frowning, she stared at her own hand. She hadn't made a mistake, she *couldn't* have. She had played this game, tried and perfected this technique dozens of times before, which meant ... She wasn't the only one testing the limits of a cyren's cunning nature today. Freya was cheating.

Now, only Roh, Orson, Thomes, Freya and the cyren Roh didn't know remained. The pace of the game quickened. Roh beat Freya's backahast with a pair of airelemented cyrens, her confidence growing. No one had yet touched the cards in the thief's temptation she had her eye on. To the rest of the players, the thief's temptation offered a chance for a better card and a risk for a worse one. But Roh had taken the chance from the game.

Tensions rose as Orson applied pressure with a pair of water warlocks. Roh checked her friend's posture. As it had been at the start of the game, Orson's back was slightly too straight.

She has a strong hand, then ... Roh's gaze flicked to the cards in the thief's temptation and weighed up the probabilities ... With the two combined decks and the cards that had already been played ... It was possible Orson had what Roh needed, or that what she needed was amidst the pile of discarded, forfeited cards. Without meaning to, the talons of Roh's spare hand unsheathed sharply, and eyes were upon her immediately. Her cheeks grew hot under the scrutiny.

'Thief,' the nameless cyren stated bluntly, looking at Roh.

Roh's heart almost lodged itself in her throat, but she shook her head. No, she was no thief, not this time. The cyren left without a word, her cards discarded at her place.

And then there were three ... Roh looked around at the other cyrens, who were inevitably thinking the same thing. They were all so close; they were within arm's reach of the Queen's Tournament – the glory, the notoriety, and of course, the chance that they might just become the next ruler of Saddoriel. She could hear the throngs of cyrens chanting her name —

Roh reined in her thoughts. She had a tendency to get swept away with the 'what-ifs' and the far-off dreams of her imagination, but she would not let that happen in this moment. She would not let her overactive mind become her downfall today.

Thomes looked anything but sure of himself as he considered his hand. Roh took the opportunity to do the same, looking down at her four cards. Her whole body was taut with anticipation. There was work to be done with her hand, which was risky so close to the end. From where she was sitting, Roh could see the sheen of sweat lining Thomes' upper lip.

She wondered if she looked as worried. She couldn't win with the cards she had. A sleight of hand was in order, but ... she needed to know what three Orson held.

Unable to best Orson's water-warlock pair, Thomes folded in an aggressive display of disappointment.

Now. Roh made her move. In one fluid motion, she relieved herself of one of her unwanted cards, without dipping into the thief's temptation. She found her salvation elsewhere.

She nearly jumped when Freya swore. It wasn't to do with Roh, though. The older cyren threw down her hand and stormed off after her partner.

The end is so close. But I still need to know ... Roh twisted in her stool to properly face Orson, and her friend gazed at her with a knowing smile.

It's just us two, she seemed to say.

Roh tried to smile back and failed. This was the moment she'd been waiting for, for the better part of the last decade. She had to act, she had to snatch up the chance, *her* chance, *now*.

She nearly screamed in frustration as Ames started up his incessant pacing again. Couldn't he just leave them be, *for once*? Couldn't he understand why she had to do this? Why was he making it so hard to concentrate?

Ames' pace didn't falter, but this time, when he reached the spot behind Orson, his gaze lingered on Roh for just a fraction too long … as if … as if to convey …

She knew what she needed to know about Orson's hand.

Swallowing the hard lump in her throat, Roh played a single cyren card. Nothing special. Nothing that would make history. Around her, she heard movement and murmuring from the crowd; her peers were inching towards the table, all too keenly aware that the final result was mere moments away. Roh looked to Orson, who was doing her utmost to keep a victorious grin in check.

Orson played her hand to a collective gasp around the workshop: three water warlocks. An incredible feat.

Roh stared at the three of a kind and then looked up, her eyes meeting Orson's. There was no going back now. She would do whatever it took … including breaking the rules.

Roh placed her final cards, three sea drakes, upon the bench.

And the workshop erupted.

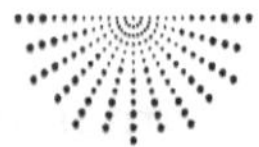

Roh had *won*. She had actually *won*. The slight crease in Orson's forehead and Harlyn's arched brows told her it was true. Roh withdrew a trembling hand from her winning cards on the bench, her gaze shifting from one friend to the other, hardly drawing breath. Body tense, she waited – for the outbursts, the accusations, the renouncing of friendship. An image came to her then: amidst the rubble of scattered bone shavings on the floor, she was on her knees, completely alone. Had she *really* thought she was more deserving? More worthy than them?

But then ... What makes someone worthy, if not that they'll do whatever it takes?

Her vision blurred. Roh caught herself teetering on the edge of that dark, familiar spiral and forced herself to look up, finding Orson and Harlyn's faces again amongst the crowd. They were smiling, as per the vow they had made to each other.

All eyes were on Roh and her sea-drake cards. She fought the desire to shrink back, all too aware that her victory might also be her undoing. The smattering of applause and shouts of disbelief swelled around her, swallowing her whole and slowing time. The claps of congratulations upon her back felt so forceful that they might knock her forward, and her name on her fellow fledglings' lips sounded foreign. She swayed, now unable to see Orson and Harlyn because she was hemmed in by other cyren bodies around her: glimmering scales, dark talons and tangles of long, wavy hair.

'That's enough.' Ames' voice cut through the chaos and silence fell immediately. He paused, long enough for faces to flush and bodies to disperse. 'Now this stupid business is done with, everyone get back to their stations, or you'll find yourselves working triple shifts.'

The cyrens scattered, the excitement forgotten in the wake of reality: only one would leave the Lower Sector. The rest of them, as always, had bones to clean.

Roh's heart rate spiked as she saw Jesmond scoop up the cards from the bench.

'I'll take those,' Ames said, his hand outstretched.

Jesmond started, clutching the cards to her chest. 'But, Master Am—'

'You think I'm going to allow this to become a regular occurrence? The cards, Jesmond. Now.'

The nestling handed over the deck of cards reluctantly.

'You should be in lessons,' the workshop master told her sternly, 'not gambling with the older cyrens.'

'But —'

Ames narrowed his eyes in a challenge. Jesmond knew when to fold, and the youngster scurried off before punishments were doled out. The deck of cards vanished into the folds of Ames' grey robes, along with any proof of Roh's deception. She knew they would never surface again, and that Ames would deny what they had done until his last breath. Which was why she couldn't meet his gaze. No matter what happened next, Ames was now entangled in her misdeed. From now on, he would feel a sense of responsibility … When she finally worked up the nerve to look at him, he was at the front of the workshop, calling out instructions to the rest of the bone cleaners as though nothing had ever happened.

Roh then found herself at her workbench, her stomach writhing under Orson and Harlyn's scrutiny.

'Roh … that was …' Orson started, her voice quavering. She offered her hand. 'That was some game.'

Not trusting herself to speak, Roh took her friend's hand, which was warm against her clammy palm.

Harlyn stepped in and offered her hand as well, her grip firm but genuine. 'Well done, Roh.' Then, with a glance at Ames, who was now waiting impatiently by the workshop door, she added, 'Looks like you're not long for this place now.'

But all at once, Roh's feet became rooted to the spot and she couldn't release Harlyn's hand. She looked down at her dirty old boots, standing atop the litter of bone fragments, the laces fraying and the soles peeling away from the leather. This was where she belonged, wasn't it?

'Roh?' Harlyn's voice brought her back.

Roh dropped her hand and smiled tightly. Forcing one foot in front of the other, she made her way to Ames.

'The tournament position is yours, it seems,' he said quietly. 'You have the morning to pack up your belongings. You will be staying in the competitors' quarters in the Upper Sector. All entrants are due at the Great Hall at the twelfth hour. I will collect you and escort you there. Then … then you're on your own, Rohesia.'

In the doorway, Roh nodded. She had done it. She was competing in the tournament. It was the start of everything she had dreamed of since she was a nestling. She had spent every day working towards this, readying herself for this very moment. From the door, her gaze shifted back to her friends. Their heads were down, their taloned fingers sifting through a new assortment of messy bones. Roh slipped away from the workshop, making for their quarters. Yes, she was in the tournament … but at what cost?

Roh couldn't remember the last time she'd been in the sleeping quarters alone. There was always at least one other cyren there. Usually it was her, Orson and Harlyn all together. Privacy was unheard of in the Lower Sector and she'd yearned for a space of her own for as long as she could recall. But as she found a spare rucksack, she marvelled at the eerie emptiness of their quarters: so quiet, the once-glowing embers of the fire now mere ash in the pit. The rucksack made a mockery of her as she attempted to pack it. She owned very little: a few sets of plain clothes and the heavy worker's boots she was already wearing. She didn't have one item of sentimental value, and why would she? Who would it be from? Her mother? The only things her mother had ever given her were the scar across her face and a fragment of a broken talon.

Roh pictured Cerys in her cell, frail and manic, her long, unruly hair matted and damp with sweat. Would Cerys even be informed that her daughter was now a competitor in the Queen's Tournament? Would she understand what that meant? And if she did, would she care?

My sketchbook and charcoal, Roh realised, snatching the items from her trunk. Perhaps not sentimental in the strictest sense, but they mattered to her. And she had exercises to practise. Tournament or no tournament, she was still in the midst of training her architectural eye, and she wasn't about to fall behind on the principles of design. She tucked her sketchbook under her arm and pocketed the stick of charcoal.

As Roh turned to leave, she caught a glimpse of herself in the looking glass on the wall. Did they look alike? She and her mother? The thought was fleeting, and as it always did, her gaze went to the circlet of gold at her forehead. Without thinking, her fingers brushed against its smooth surface, remembering the stares she'd experienced at the queen's announcement. The way they'd made her skin crawl and her cheeks flush. She knew there was little chance another circlet-wearer would compete in the tournament. There was no denying that she would stand out in the Upper Sector. But this time, she would refuse the brand of shame their glares demanded. She lifted her chin and dropped her hand. She was a competitor in the Queen's Tournament now.

With her rucksack packed, Roh sat on the end of her bed, unsure of what to do. It was the first time in her life that she'd been excused from her duties in the workshop. She spotted Harlyn's lute, left atop her trunk. Notes of a melody Harlyn had played a few mornings ago sprang into Roh's mind and she clung to them like a lifeline; the recollection of the rise and fall of the song soothed her as she waited. Studying the lute, Roh thought of her own secret project. She recalled the tweaks she'd made to the design only a few nights before and wondered if she'd ever get to work on it again.

She shook her head. *That doesn't matter now,* she told herself. *If you win, you can have the damn thing built.*

'I've been waiting,' Ames said from the door, jolting her from her reverie. Her mentor stood straight-backed, adjusting his high collar. He looked even older than usual today, his weathered face somehow more lined than the day before. His expression was unreadable, and Roh was desperate to read it. Had her actions, or his actions, for that matter, changed things between them? Or was he being his usual, stern self? He had disapproved of her entry in the tournament from the start, but now … What did he think of her now? After what she had done? What he had *helped* her do?

Roh shouldered her rucksack and went after him. His robes billowed as he strode through the residences, down to the lower level, towards the same pulley system they had used only the day before. Roh's stomach flipped. Orson wasn't here to hold her hand this time.

'What happens now?' Roh managed as they stepped into the crate and it lurched upwards.

'Orientation. You will meet the other competitors and learn the rules.' The tournament rules. The new laws by which she would live.

'What about my work?' she asked, gripping the rail hard.

'You are excused from your duties, but your work must still be completed. Orson and Harlyn will take on your workload while you compete.'

Roh's eyes flew open. It felt like she'd been punched in the gut. 'I … didn't know …'

Ames' brows rose. 'Would that knowledge have changed anything?' he asked.

'I …' Roh stammered.

'What's done is done.'

He was right. She'd made her choice; every action had a consequence. Playing that sea-drake hand, it seemed, would have many.

'Am I the first?' she heard herself ask.

'First what?'

'The first … circlet-wearer to enter the tournament?'

Ames fiddled with his collar. 'Yes. Others like you tend to keep to the shadows.'

'But … they won't know who I am, will they?' Roh braced herself. *They won't know whose daughter I am,* was what she meant. She needed to know what she was about to walk into.

'It's a bit late to be having second thoughts,' Ames retorted. Upon seeing her horrified expression, he sighed. 'No, the competitors and the public won't know,' he told her. 'Here, you are merely a representative of the bone cleaner subsector.'

As they ascended the levels of Saddoriel, music took hold of Roh entirely and she forgot where she was. Ancient magic flickered in her veins, in her chest, and she closed her eyes against the force of it. It skittered across her skin and —

There was a loud screech as the pulley system came to a stop. Ames pushed the gates open and gestured for her to follow. 'This way,' he snapped, stepping into a brisk walk. 'You're not here to sight-see.'

They had passed under the formidable archway of bones and crossed the entrance when Roh stopped short, her attention wrenched away from Ames and his reprimands. Before them stood the entrance to the Great Hall of Saddoriel. It was a magnificent feat of architecture, even just from the outside. The entrance was shaped like a giant keyhole, with great, thick iron doors, panelled with an array of gleaming white bones. On either side of the doors were marble statues that towered above at least three storeys of the stone galleries.

Roh had to crane her neck to see them. The daughters of the water goddess, Lamaka: Dresmis and Thera, the ancestors of the queen; their wings flared outwards, framing the entrance to the hall. Roh felt dazed as she took in the astonishing structure for the very first time. *This* was the true Saddoriel. *This* was the definition of cyren magic.

She was so transfixed that she almost didn't hear Ames as he said, 'This is where I leave you.' But his words pierced her sense of wonderment and the bubble of music that had followed her since she'd stepped foot in the Upper Sector. She didn't want to acknowledge them. She didn't know whether it was because of the secret they now shared, or because he was her last tether to normality, and *home* ... When she finally got up the courage to turn away from the face of the Great Hall to bid her mentor farewell, he was already gone.

Her skin prickled in his absence. Roh tried to rub the goosebumps from her arms as she turned back to the hall and stared at the great statues once more. She shoved her hands in her pockets, unable to shake the chill. She didn't feel how she'd expected to feel, Roh realised. She had imagined this moment so many times, had yearned for the momentous change that was bound to accompany such a milestone. And yet, nothing came to her. Nothing changed. She was as she had always been, felt as she had always felt. Ordinary. Average. And there was not a single hint of her deathsong within.

Roh adjusted the strap of her rucksack, willing herself to move —

Someone collided with her shoulder. The drastic light change within the hall had her blinking rapidly before she could focus on the stocky figure beside her. The first thing Roh saw was the sharp zigzag line shaved into the side of the cyren's head. She stifled a gasp.

'I'd watch where you're going in here,' the Jaktaren said, her lilac gaze cool, framed by unusually pale lashes.

Roh swallowed. It was the cyren she'd spotted in the galleries at the queen's announcement, a sling and a pouch of stones still belted at her waist. 'I …' Roh fumbled for words, not quite able to believe she was standing face to face with a member of Saddoriel's most revered guild.

'What are you waiting for?' the Jaktaren ground out, her brow knitted in a scowl worthy of Harlyn.

'Sorry,' Roh muttered, moving aside.

Without another word, the Jaktaren swept past her.

Roh stared after her in awe. When she had first learned of the guild as a nestling, she'd envisioned joining one day, shaving a zigzag through her own hair and searching the vast realms above for music worthy of Saddoriel. That was before she'd found out that the Jaktaren were all highborn.

The others aren't going to believe this, she thought, as she too stepped inside.

Like much of Saddoriel, the Great Hall was cylindrical, but that was where the similarities ended. It was not a hall in a traditional sense, not in the way Roh had imagined it to be: with big square rooms and a stage. Below the unguarded stone bridge she was standing on was a bottomless drop. Her gaze followed the path that led from the entrance doors to a vast platform in the centre. As she looked, Roh suddenly felt a wave of dizziness wash over her. One wrong step and she would plummet to her death, down into a deadly gorge in the dark depths of the lair. Below and above her were rail-less arching bridges that crossed to the galleries. Further above, great domes released beams of enchanted sunlight into the hall, and Roh's gaze followed the shafts of golden light upwards. It was so realistic; she could just about feel the warmth of the sun kissing her skin. She relished it, promising herself that one day, she would see the real sun and bask in its rays in the realms above.

Roh turned slowly on the balls of her feet, wary of the edge of the bridge. There was so much to see here. Upon the curved ceilings of the domes were great murals: paintings created with enchanted seagrass to make the art glimmer and its subjects' eyes seem to follow its viewer. The murals told stories of cyren history, of their beginnings as winged gods with powerful songs. They showed the creation of the *Tome of Kyeos* – the all-knowing book enchanted by the first water warlock, and the rule of their first king, Taaldin the Great. As a nestling, Roh had heard tales about the famous book: the all-seeing tome that wrote itself and documented every detail of cyren history. She had dreamed of taking it in her hands and finding her mother's name within its pages, finally learning what she had always longed to know.

The scenes of epic, bloody history brought Roh back

to her humble reality, as did the immensity of the hall itself. Here, in this great cavern, she was small, insignificant against all that had already come to pass. And yet, she hoped to somehow matter.

The quiet shuffle of slippered feet reminded Roh she was not alone. Dark shadows swept across the bridges as patterned silk robes fluttered along with hushed whispers. There were eleven other cyrens. Most of them were of full maturity, their lilac eyes bright with cunning as they scrutinised her. Their gazes sought her eyes – moss-green – before landing on her circlet. In her daze of admiration, Roh had wandered out to the centre of the bridge, while the other competitors had kept to the edges of the entrance. It left her exposed, vulnerable. For a moment, she saw herself through their eyes: a fledgling cyren from the Lower Sector with no allies or obvious strengths – *definitely a target.*

She forced herself to join the company at the doors. The female Jaktaren and competitors, marked as nobles by their jewelled belts, shifted away from her. Roh steeled herself against the slight. There would be more of that before the day was done. And at the end of the tournament, they would be sorry.

'Rohesia?' said a timid voice.

Roh turned to find Neith, a scrawny water-runner fledgling, peering hopefully at her. Roh recognised her as one of the cyrens who shared their common bathing chamber in the Lower Sector.

Roh's chest became tight. 'Neith? I didn't know you were competing?'

The delicate water runner came to stand beside her. 'It wasn't my idea,' she replied, nervously surveying the competitors around them.

'What?' Roh took a step closer to Neith, who had hugged her arms tightly around herself. Roh stopped short of putting her own arm around the fledgling's shoulder, conflicted by the realisation that Neith's visible fear comforted her in some dark, selfish way.

'None of the water runners wanted to enter. Understandably,' Neith sniffed. 'You know what happens at these things, don't you?'

Roh nodded stiffly. 'As much as I can know ... So, you were *forced* to enter?' The notion that a subsector had failed to find a willing competitor while the bone cleaners had fought over their place was ludicrous. It could have been Orson or Harlyn standing beside Roh now ...

Before Neith could answer, a high-pitched squeaking echoed through the hall.

'What's that?' the water runner asked, her talon trembling as she pointed.

Roh followed her gaze to see several porters wheeling a large structure covered in a dark sheet from the far side of the hall across the narrow bridge. They were panicked, shouting to each other in Old Saddorien as they dragged their cargo across, watching it sway precariously near the edges. When they reached the platform in the middle and placed blocks of wood behind the wheels, there was an audible sigh of relief. Whatever it was, it was half the size of the workshop in the Lower Sector.

'Is it some sort of weapon?' Roh muttered, mainly to herself. But as the words left her mouth, she found herself confronted with a hard lilac stare from afar. There was no mistaking the chestnut hair and glimmering scales at the temples of Finn Haertel, the arms of his crossbow peeking from behind his back. Another arms-bearing Jaktaren.

Roh looked away, pretending she'd accidentally met his gaze while casually scanning the faces of the other competitors. They were all here now, she realised with a start. Saddoriel's most cunning, most ambitious cyrens … Well, except for Neith.

Anticipation was clear on each and every face in small tells: pursed lips, protracted talons, shifting slippered feet and furrowed brows … Roh found small comfort in those details; none of them, it seemed, knew what was to come, or what awaited them beneath the folds of that thick, dark fabric.

The music changed. What had been a quiet melody delicately toying with the ancient magic of the hall became sharper. A tighter, louder verse began, drawing everyone's attention to the far side of the hall once more. There, an elaborate pair of double doors swung open soundlessly, and from the shadows, the great Council of Seven Elders appeared. They stepped into the hall, each of their postures perfect, their robes of the deepest, darkest blue, cinched at the waist with silver cording. What little exposed skin showed was adorned with silver cuffs and rings, while a small serpent coiled around one of the shorter elder's arms. The music that filled the hall narrowed in on them, as though it were drawn to the magic, the knowledge and power the elders possessed. Roh recognised Taro and Bloodwyn Haertel at the apex of the group. Taro shared the same square jaw as his son, while Bloodwyn's hard gaze was even more terrifying. The fair-haired duo led their fellow elders across the narrow bridge, robes billowing, to the platform at the heart of the hall.

There was no sign of the queen. Roh craned her neck, searching the galleries above for their legendary ruler, hoping to catch another glimpse of those great wings and the coral crown. *Where is she? Surely she wouldn't miss the official start to her own tournament?*

One of the elders stepped forward, palms upturned towards the competitors. Roh couldn't recall his name.

'Come, competitors,' he said, his voice cutting through the building melody around them.

The nobles were the first to move, clearly familiar with the cyrens standing before them. Roh and Neith followed them across the bridge in silence and came to the platform warily.

'I am Erdites Colter.' The elder's voice was gravelly, and as he looked down to his pockets, retrieving a scroll, Roh saw that a zigzag pattern had been shaved into his hair on the right side of his head. 'I oversee the Law of the Lair,' he continued, surveying them with violet eyes and unravelling the parchment. *And the Jaktaren*, Roh recalled Jesmond telling them. His eyes were ... strange. Roh had never seen a mature cyren with eyes any colour other than lilac.

Elder Colter cleared his throat. 'You are the competitors the subsectors of Saddoriel have selected as their representation. I welcome you to the official orientation of the Queen's Tournament. The rules are brief but exact: first, the tournament consists of three individual trials. However, it is not solely confined to these trials. It will take place within three moonspan – ninety days or less, for those inept with numbers.'

Roh swore Elder Colter's gaze paused on her and Neith as he spoke. She cursed him silently. She may have been a bone cleaner, but she knew damn well how to count.

'Each competitor will be given rooms in the Upper Sector. These will be the only space where the common Laws of the Lair protect you. You will learn of the trials as they occur. The first trial is the day after tomorrow and will be held in the outer forests of Talon's Reach.'

Roh had heard of these enchanted water forests that acted as the lungs of the lair; they pushed air throughout Saddoriel and greater Talon's Reach. And she was going to see them.

Elder Colter was still speaking. 'You are required to sign an entry contract. When I call you, please come forward and sign next to your name.'

Roh's mouth went dry. In the past, she had never minded speaking before a group, or standing at the front of the workshop, but this ... She gazed upon the Council of Seven Elders, their severe expressions unreadable, their sheer presence utterly intimidating. This was different.

Elder Colter cleared his throat again. 'Finn Haertel.'

Finn strode forward, impeccably clean and straight-backed. He bowed swiftly to the council and then went to the small table Roh had failed to notice behind Elder Colter. Though the supposed contract was thick with pages, Finn made no move to even scan its contents. He swiped an extended talon across his wrist without so much as a flinch and signed the parchment in his own blood.

Roh stared. *What an* ... Her thoughts trailed off as she watched him rejoin the group and readjust his sleeve to cover the small cut.

'Yrsa Ward,' Elder Colter called.

Another offspring of the council elders. Roh's skin prickled as the Jaktaren she'd run into earlier stepped forward with a bow. She was one of the few cyrens who wore her hair short. Her dark locks, cropped straight at her shoulders, swayed as she followed Finn's example, signing her name in blood.

'Savalise Vinnet.' A tall, pretty fledgling glided forward, dipped her talon in what must have been an inkpot and signed.

Roh recognised the next name – *Arcelia Bellfast* – and craned her neck to see her old lessons master move to the front to sign her name. Though Tutor Bellfast had always been hard on her, Roh had admired her, and despite failing miserably at producing a single note of her deathsong, she had always strived to impress her.

Cyrens by the names of Zokez Rasaat, Darden Crezat and Miriald Montalle followed. They all did as they were told without flourish or fanfare. Roh decided she respected that approach far more.

'Estin Ruhne.' Not even Elder Colter's gravelly drawl could dull the importance of *that* name. Roh held her breath as the renowned bone architect broke away from the other competitors and approached the Council of Elders with a low bow. Roh stared after her. It had been Estin Ruhne's designs that had first ignited her passion for architecture. Roh had even reviewed some of Estin's earlier work with Ames, not that the famous architect would know it. *Holy gods*, Roh gushed to herself, only tearing her eyes away from the cyren as she found her place once more in the group.

'Neith.' There was an immediate change in the atmosphere as Elder Colter started on the lowborns, the competitors whose birth status warranted only one name, not two. They lacked the honour of a family name, showing the lair that they belonged to no one.

Her shaking limbs clearly evident, Neith went to the table to sign, forgetting to bow to the council and only remembering after her signature was scrawled across the parchment. She gave a messy curtsy and Roh cringed inwardly; she'd never known cyrens to curtsy on any occasion. Neith practically ran back to the group, like a terrified mouse fleeing the pursuit of a viper, only to realise it had been herded into a nest.

Finn Haertel and Zokez Rasaat mimicked Neith's failed curtsy. The sound of their stifled laughter flooded Roh's cheeks with heat.

A kitchen hand by the name of Ferron and a cleaner named Lillas were called, and before Roh knew it ...

'Rohesia.'

Forgetting Neith and the others, she tried to hold her chin high as she approached the council, but every pair of eyes went straight to the gold glinting around her head. She was not just a lowborn here; she was the offspring of a criminal. She only prayed they didn't know *which* criminal. She felt their stares like a brand on the back of her neck as she bowed to the elders. Inwardly, she warred with herself, pitting the part of her that wanted to remain invisible to these cyrens, hidden away in the Lower Sector, against the part of her that wanted to rule over them, to be the most powerful cyren in all of Talon's Reach. When she reached the table, the sheer number of pages in the contract made her stomach squirm. But ... no one else had read through them, no one else had so much as *glanced* at the terms outlined beneath the list of names. She wouldn't be the outlier of the group. Not this soon. Making a quick decision, she dipped her talon into the inkpot and signed her name, trying not to wince at her messy scrawl compared to the numerous lines of florid penmanship above. As she withdrew from the parchment, she managed to smudge her name, and she silently berated herself as she returned to the competitors.

'Thank you,' Elder Colter said blandly. 'Now ...' He turned, drawing their attention back to the covered structure in the centre of the platform. 'There is one more element to Her Majesty's Tournament.'

'Gods,' Neith murmured beside Roh, loud enough that a few heads turned.

Roh fought the urge to reprimand the water runner; the last thing they wanted was to publicly disrespect the council. Instead, she kept her eyes ahead, hands clasped together tightly. From the tales Ames had told her and the others, she knew that whatever lay beneath the fabric would not be good news for her. *Is it some sort of torture device? A beast we have to battle? A weapon we must wield —*

With a flash of his long talons, Elder Colter reached for the cloth and pulled.

Roh was hemmed in by the silence; trapped by the force, the heaviness of it as she stared at the monstrosity that had just been revealed: a cage. Not just any cage, but the cage of bones she herself had helped design.

And inside it were *humans*. Live humans.

She could practically smell their terror. No doubt they had been told stories of Saddorien cyrens' cruelty, just as she had been told tales of humankind's weakness. From her lessons on the Age of Chaos wars, she knew humans bore a resemblance to cyrens, but had swapped delicate scales and fierce talons for blandness and fragility. She started to count, if only to get her mind working again. Silently, she worked through the huddle of bodies, ignoring the eyes staring back, wide with horror. There were twelve of them. Each clutching a piece of timber with a number carved into it. Each bearing the marks of struggle: torn clothes, bruises blooming across sallow skin, bloodied lips and missing shoes. Roh forced herself to exhale steadily through her nose as she took in their varying ages and sizes. *Humans, alive in Saddoriel. What is the council playing at?* The only humans allowed in Saddoriel were the musicians the Jaktaren captured, those whose music filled the lair.

Roh trained her gaze on the levers of the cage, wanting to extract herself from the reality before her. She noted that her changes had been implemented, more bones added. *I probably cleaned some of those myself,* she thought, dazed as she took in the gleaming ivory.

'You will each be assigned a human,' Elder Colter announced, his drawl tearing through the quiet. 'Throughout the tournament, you must keep them alive. Your human will be your constant companion. If they die on your watch, you will be disqualified. If they are injured, you will be disqualified. If they are misplaced, you will be disqualified. This is the Queen's Tournament; it is no place for excuses.'

Lamaka's heart ... Roh wasn't the only one looking around in disbelief. As if these trials weren't going to be hard enough, now she had to keep herself *and* a fragile human in one piece? Roh couldn't help but steal a glance at the Jaktaren, well aware that their experience in handling humans gave them an unfair advantage. She traced her scar with a short, black talon and waited.

'Each human has been given an enchanted token,' Elder Colter continued, holding up what looked like a shell necklace. 'This makes them immune to our deathsongs and the lure of the lair. They are also able to see Saddoriel for what it truly is, not the enchanted glamour they usually see if they happen to wander down a passage. Each human is given one and only one. Lose it, and they will be at the lair's mercy. This ongoing task is designed to test your responsibility and your patience throughout the trials. Traits you will need in the *unlikely* event that you should succeed in this tournament. Should you be eliminated or killed, your human's token will be taken and they will be turned out into the passages of the lair. Should they find their way out of Talon's Reach, they will have earned their freedom. If not …'

Elder Colter's words cast a dark shadow over Roh. *Certain death for the humans, then …* And yet, against all reason, she willingly took the number six that was pushed into her hand by one of the elders.

'Whatever number you are dealt correlates to one of these humans.'

The humans looked pitiful, like stray animals caught for the slaughter, trapped inside the cage she'd helped make stronger. A cage made out of their own kind's bones. The cruelty of it was inherently Saddorien. Roh's eyes went to the levers she had advised be reinforced … They mocked her now.

'What are you waiting for?' a cold voice sounded. Bloodwyn Haertel approached the cage and crushed the lock in her hand, sending the door swinging inwards. The humans shrank back, or rather, tried to push each other forward. Roh knew from her lessons as a nestling that those actions were to be expected from the weaker species. That in sea battles long past, men had thrown their fellow crew members overboard in hopes of placating the cyrens. They had no cunning, only fear and selfishness.

'For Lamaka's sake,' Finn Haertel muttered impatiently, breaking away from the group and entering the cage.

One of the humans screamed. The high-pitched shriek echoed up into the stone galleries of the hall, drowning out the notes of music that still danced between them. Finn ignored the cry for mercy as he approached the humans, yanking at their wooden boards and scanning their numbers until he found the man belonging to him. Finn took him by the upper arm without a word and dragged him from the cage.

All at once, the cyrens around Roh shoved forward, now suddenly eager. Roh pushed her way into the cage with the rest of them and started to scan the terrified faces and the numbers around their necks for her human.

Number six. A male. He was tall and lean, not much older than Roh herself, by the look of him. Toffee-coloured hair fell over his amber eyes as she approached, and as he pushed it back from his forehead, Roh noted the fingerless gloves covering his large hands. A mottled bruise of blue and green bloomed around his left eye. When she reached him, she didn't know what to do. She didn't want to touch him, and she certainly didn't want to drag him out as Finn had done. The human didn't meet her gaze, but seeing the matching number in her hand, seemed to understand it was in his best interests to follow her out.

The competitors and their humans stood outside the

cage now. Roh kept stealing glances at hers; his pulse was jumping in his neck. Her heart sank. Looking around, the other competitors had older, stronger-looking humans. Her eyes snagged on Finn Haertel's and Yrsa Ward's – two healthy-looking charges. *Typical.*

Roh sought Neith in the crowd then, and was filled with instant gratitude for her own fortune as she spotted the tanned, withered old man at the young water runner's side. His back was hunched over, as though he needed the support of a staff to walk, and the skin around his eyes and jaw sagged. Was this what it looked like to age? She had never seen the full effects of the process before. It looked *awful*. In comparison, Ames seemed positively sprightly. Roh's body sagged with relief; she hadn't drawn the shortest straw, after all …

She turned back to her human. 'I'm Roh,' she said.

He shook his head and realisation dawned on her. She was speaking Saddorien. 'My name is Roh,' she said in the common tongue of the realms above. His eyes flicked to her in understanding, but he remained silent.

Roh ground her teeth. *Of course, a mute …*

Elder Colter motioned for the competitors to follow him, leaving the rest of the council behind. He led them across another narrow bridge, out through a different exit of the Great Hall and into a vibrant foyer beyond. The Upper Sector residences. Dozens of levels towered above, where cyrens lounged on their balconies, looking down. It was brighter than Roh had ever imagined, and the music … The delicate notes of a fiddle – no, two –

danced along her skin, singing to her soul. She took a moment, savouring the sound.

But Elder Colter did not pause. The open foyer and colourful gardens were a blur to Roh as she followed the group, unable to take in details fast enough: the odd human at her side, the smooth silver-and-bone pulley system, the marble floors, the elaborate torches lining the walls …

'You have one hour to prepare for tonight's gala,' the elder was saying, his eyes roaming across Roh and Neith's dirty tunics and pants. 'Your presence is mandatory in the Queen's Conservatory at the twentieth hour.'

With that he left them, and within moments porters swept in and Roh, with her human in tow, was directed to her quarters. Double doors were opened for her and inside was the most opulent space Roh had ever seen. Her knees buckled as she stepped inside and her rucksack dropped to the floor with a loud thud. The walls were a deep teal colour, and all the furnishings were accented with gold. There were two giant beds with gold lattice headboards and bedside tables with gold clawed feet. A door trimmed with gold foiling led to a bathing chamber beyond. There were gold candle holders and sconces, not to mention the gold-lined plant holders housing rare water ferns. It was … *unbelievable.*

The low whistle of breath escaping between her human's teeth told her he felt the same. But Roh's hand went to her circlet. Gold … the weakest substance the cyrens possessed. Was it all just an extension of the insult? She flitted between that paranoia and the pangs of guilt in her gut. She had cheated Orson and Harlyn out of experiencing this. If she lost, they might never see such things in all their lives. She wandered around the room, running her talons across the luscious fabrics and valuable furnishings. What she'd done had not been fair. But what did fair matter in a place like this?

She paused by one of the bedside tables. A place card of sorts had been made. She read the name it displayed in scrawling cursive.

Odi Arrowood. She looked from the parchment to the human now standing at the window, looking out. 'What sort of a name is that?' she muttered, placing the card back on the bedside table.

She eyed him warily as he reached with his half-gloved hands for the window latch. As he pushed the window outwards, music flooded the room and the chorus of the two fiddles built to a powerful crescendo.

At last, from across the room, he met her gaze. 'I know this song,' he said.

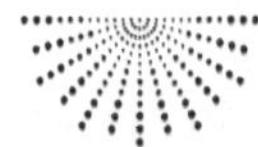

CHAPTER FIVE

Roh stared at the strange human, all long-limbed and wide-eyed. He stood at the window, leaning out into the melody that drifted from somewhere below, his fingers twitching in time with the music, those ridiculous half-gloves frayed around his hands.

'What do you mean, you know this song?' Roh demanded in the common tongue.

Odi's amber gaze went to her talons and he took a step back from the window, flattening himself against the wall.

A thrill rushed through Roh. So he *should* be scared – he was in the heart of Saddoriel, with a cyren as his keeper.

'I mean …' he stammered. 'I mean I've heard it before.'

Roh paused, frowning as she listened to the long, mournful notes of the fiddles. The music was a seductive call to her cyren instincts, beckoning the ancient magic within her to escape its confines, to play. She shut it down. 'Where?' she asked.

Odi's dark brows furrowed. 'It's a well-known song, it's played all over.'

Just as Roh was about to interrogate him further, there was a knock at the door. Two porters entered, carrying boxes and hangers of clothing. Without a word, they laid out the items on the beds. Roh watched them, unnerved by their silence. She knew they were *called* porters, but there was no hiding what they really were: servants. Not for the first time, Roh considered the inner workings of Saddoriel, baffled. Here in the Upper Sector residences, they had 'porters', but these porters were not lowborn. She had never seen their likes in the Lower Sector. So how did it work? Were there hierarchies within hierarchies? And if so, how did they feel, tending to the likes of *her*? She shook her head as she closed the door behind them.

'Everything looks different to when I first got here,' Odi told her.

'How?'

Odi considered her question and their opulent surroundings. 'It … it looked like a nightmare. More than just the bones. Everything was so dark and wet.'

'Saddoriel is enchanted to look barren and haunted to outsiders. Cyren rulers have always insisted that the strength and prosperity of our territory remain unknown to the realms above.'

Odi remained on the far side of the room with his back pressed to the wall. Roh ignored him as she went to the beds to examine what the porters had left. Her fingers found silk – the skirt of a long, flowing dress made in the fashion of the Upper Sector. The fabric slid over her palms as she picked it up; she had never touched something so fine before. There was a jewelled belt to match and a pair of tan leather sandals, just like the nobility wore. She touched the supple leather of the shoes, smelling the high quality, and noting the workmanship that had gone into detailing the straps. Someone had made them with pride. Again, she found herself puzzling over the hierarchy of the lair, wondering where a cordwainer might fit … In the Mid Sector? Or perhaps even the Upper Sector if they supplied the nobles with high-quality products such as these.

'What's that?'

Roh nearly jumped, having forgotten the human was there. Suppressing the desire to throttle him, she looked to where he was pointing. A necklace lay on the bed. It was a large piece, created with dozens and dozens of fragments. She lifted it from the quilt, immediately recognising the smooth surface and delicately balanced weight. It was a necklace of bones. It rattled softly in her hands.

'Are they human?' Odi murmured, crossing the room to examine the jewellery. His face had gone deathly pale. He didn't take his eyes from the necklace draped between her talons.

'I don't know,' Roh told him truthfully. 'It's possible.'

'This whole place is made of bones.'

'Some of it,' Roh corrected, still studying the elaborate piece.

Odi met her gaze, his amber eyes wary. 'The bones at the entrance, in the giant archway. Those are human.'

Roh undid the clasp of the necklace and brought the ends around to the nape of her neck, latching it together, letting the white pieces rest against her own collarbone. How could something so beautiful be so horrifying? 'Yes,' she told him. 'We have a history with your kind.'

'A *history*?' Odi scoffed. 'That's putting it lightly. Your kind *went to war* against us. You tried to take every coastline —'

'*That*,' Roh spat, scooping up the clothes and turning towards the bathing chamber, 'was a *long* time ago.'

It had been over eight hundred years ago, to be more accurate, during Asros the Conqueror's reign. Roh and the other fledglings had learned about it in their lessons. Asros had wanted dominion over all seas and coastlines of the realms and had waged war against the humans for decades. After some time, the humans devised talismans to repel the cyrens' lure, not unlike the token that hung around Odi's neck now. But more than that, the humans developed contraptions capable of capturing a hundred cyrens at a time. The losses were unfathomable, but even so Asros had pushed on, consumed by greed. Asros had used the bones of the victims of war to build upon Saddoriel and Talon's Reach. It had become known as the Age of Chaos.

'You brought it up,' Odi muttered.

'Mentioned it.' Roh didn't know why she had. To

educate a human on the history of the lair? To defend the Saddorien cyrens' predisposition towards bone architecture? Who was she to do so, anyway? She was a cleaner of bones, and when told, a designer of those very structures. No, he had earned no such explanations, not from her. Frustrated, she made for the bathing chamber, eager for a few moments of peace without the human eyeing her every move.

'Roh?' His voice was tentative, as though sensing her growing impatience.

'What?'

'When are you going to tell me why I'm here?'

With the clawfoot bathtub in sight, Roh paused in the doorway and blinked at him. 'What?' she repeated.

'They didn't tell us anything … Those others … Well, nothing we understood, anyway.'

'Dresmis and Thera, help me,' Roh muttered. She should have realised. The elders had been speaking Saddorien the entire time, and the humans would know nothing of their language. For a moment, she imagined what it would have felt like, trapped in a cage of bones cloaked in darkness, hearing whispers of words she didn't understand, the deep instinct within screaming of danger, of death … She slammed the lid down on those thoughts. Her role was not to imagine the experiences of strange humans. Her role was to compete, to *win* this damn tournament. Perhaps it was wiser to keep the truth from Odi, just for a while? He was already frightened of her. What would he be like in the trials? It was possible his fear would send him into a panic, and that wouldn't be good for her strategy, once she had one. Making up her mind, Roh hung her clothes in the bathing chamber.

'We need to get ready,' she said. 'Don't go anywhere,' she added, shutting the door hard behind her. With a heavy sigh, she sagged against it, fighting the urge to sink to the gold-plated tiles spanning the floor. She looked harder, realising that the tiles had been designed to resemble scales. Crouching, she ran her fingertips across the cool, smooth surface. She remembered seeing the mosaic tiles depicting legendary creatures during her lesson in the Passage of Kings as a nestling. For a moment, she felt nostalgic for those simpler times, learning and scheming beside Orson and Harlyn, plotting their futures while Arcelia Bellfast spoke of centuries past. But the future was here, and she was living it, right now.

Getting to her feet, she made quick work of removing her boots, tunic and pants. She used the tepid water in the basin to wash herself, vowing that she would make good use of the luxurious tub later. The bathing facilities in the Lower Sector didn't offer large tubs like this. Lowborns bathed in barrels when they could, but more often than not, merely had to tip water over themselves after they'd scrubbed the dirt away with coarse sponges.

When she was clean, she tugged the dress over her head and adjusted what seemed like yards of fabric. The softness of the silk was foreign against her skin, and she turned once, twice, just to feel the folds of it flutter delicately into place. Feeling self-conscious, she clipped the belt into place, mimicking the style she'd seen on the highborns at the tournament announcement. She went to the full-length looking glass on the far wall of the chamber and studied herself. Her reflection resembled something akin to the fashion of the Upper Sector: comfortable, flowing and luxurious. The gown trailed across the tiled floor – was it meant to do that? There was something not right about the picture, though … Roh corrected her slouching posture and looked again. *Better, but still not quite there.* As if in answer, the gold across her forehead glinted.

'Well, there's no escaping that,' she muttered. She assessed the rest of her face, thankful that cosmetics were not widely used, even in the Upper Sector of Saddoriel. They had been taught from a young age that cyrens possessed natural beauty, and that their best features – their lilac eyes and the subtle glimmer of scales at their temples – ought not to be trifled with. Roh stared at her moss-green eyes, wondering when their colour would start to change. Orson's had changed in her twenty-third year, and more recently, Harlyn's would gleam lilac in the light, before changing back to her usual sea-blue. Roh willed hers to change too, but the green remained.

She turned to the sandals resting on the vanity before looking down at the length of her skirts. She thought of the human on the other side of the door, waiting to pepper her with questions, and considered the dozens of nobles who would no doubt be staring down at her all evening. Nodding to herself, she tugged her own boots back on. Small comforts … No one would see them, anyway.

. . .

A porter led Roh and her human through the residences of the Upper Sector and down a number of brightly lit, twisting paths, where music followed them. Roh breathed in the series of unhurried notes that spoke to one another, a thriving conversation in melody, a subtle arrangement of elegant chords that sent a rush of goosebumps across her arms. Determined not to lose herself in the music, she rushed after the porter, whose name she still didn't know. Her skirts swished about her ankles and she bunched the fabric up in her fists, worried that she might trip. To her annoyance, the human, Odi, kept glancing in her direction.

She clenched her jaw and looked away. *Gods, must I really put up with him for the whole tournament?* His presence was already testing her patience and the trials hadn't even begun yet. She eyed the protective shell token bouncing against his chest as they moved.

'Tuck that in,' she hissed, throwing a pointed look at the talisman.

Odi glanced down and fumbled with the necklace, finally shoving it down the front of his shirt so only the leather thong peeked out behind his collar.

'If that's the only thing defending you against the lure of the lair, *keep it safe.*' Her words came out harshly, her tone reminding her of Ames whenever he reprimanded her. She shook off the thought; she had to be harsh if the human was to survive here.

They came to a halt outside the Queen's

Conservatory. The porter knocked twice and the doors swung inwards.

Roh didn't know what a conservatory was, but she hadn't expected *this*. An enormous rectangular room greeted them, all of its walls made entirely of floor-to-ceiling windows that looked out into the surrounding private gardens. Even at a glance, Roh could see there were hundreds, if not thousands of species of trees and flowers. There was so much colour. She gazed longingly at the deep-blue blooms of the towering Aching Fiirs, a single flower atop a shoulder-height stem. She recognised miniature willow trees, their branches bowing beneath the weight of their blue-green leaves, and a species of water roses, fresh droplets forming across their petals. She had only ever seen such things in books before, and that had been a long time ago.

The conservatory was brightly lit with chandeliers made of crystal and bone. Either side of the room were long, decorated tables displaying decadent food and drink. The rich scents were enough to make Roh's mouth water, and she realised she hadn't eaten since that half-bowl of slop early that morning. Here, there was no slop in sight. Trays of exotically spiced pies, tiers of petite sweet cakes and goblets filled with the queen's own smoked wines circulated the room in the steady hands of the Upper Sector servants.

Wandering slowly into the conservatory, Roh was so lost in the opulence and wealth that she nearly forgot about the human at her side. He was fidgeting, his fingers twitching erratically at his sides. To her dismay, she realised he'd kept his fingerless gloves on.

'Why do you wear those things?' she whispered in the common tongue.

Odi glanced down at his hands. 'I need them.'

She scowled. 'What sort of a reason is *that*?' Between his gloves and her circlet, there was no chance of blending in here. She had been thrown into a raging whirlpool, and she wasn't sure she remembered how to breathe under water. If they stopped walking, it would draw more attention to them, so Roh forced one booted foot in front of the other and began a slow turn around the room. She saw that the other competitors had begun to arrive. Tutor Bellfast was by the refreshments table, assessing the room with the same critical gaze Roh knew she used to survey her students. Her human, a middle-aged woman, was standing shoulder to shoulder with her.

At least Odi doesn't stand that *close*, Roh mused, eyeing her human, who trailed behind like a shadow.

She continued her study of the room, spotting Finn Haertel, who looked right at home standing in the centre of a group of nobles. His human, a muscular, bearded man, stood a few paces back, beady eyes alert as he watched the nobles. They all wore elaborate, wide-sleeved robes over their loose-fitting clothes. They were speaking animatedly, in Old Saddorien, Roh realised as she drew closer. The words that rolled off their tongues were long and drawn out, their sentences rich with rhythm. Although Roh could guess a phrase or two, the dialect as a whole was unfamiliar to her. The ancient language was reserved for the highborns of the Upper Sector, while the Mid and Lower Sectors were all educated in New Saddorien, as well as a number of foreign tongues from the realms above. The other Jaktaren, Yrsa Ward, approached Finn, placing a gentle hand on his arm and leaning in close to whisper something. Roh watched curiously.

I suppose they do make a handsome couple, she mused.

Odi's shoulder brushed hers as he followed her gaze. 'I didn't know there were males of your kind.'

'What?'

'In … in all the stories, the lisloiks singing at sea are women.'

'Lisloiks? We do not call ourselves *lisloiks*,' Roh said, cringing at the human term for her kind. 'We are Saddorien cyrens. You would do well to leave that ugly common-tongue word behind.'

'Saddorien cyrens …' Odi seemed to mull the word over. 'And what about the tales?'

'Of us being a women-only race?' she sneered, gesturing around the room. 'Does it look that way to you?'

'No, but …'

'Our armies are female only,' she told him, gathering her skirts and making for the closest table. 'Only female cyrens can partake in the death chorus. That's why your fishermen tell such stories.'

As soon as Roh moved, she felt eyes on her. Her stomach churned as she realised the subject of the attention – the black boots peeking from beneath her gown. She dropped her skirts, but the damage was done. With a deep breath, she straightened her posture and lifted her chin. So be it. She was out of place here no matter what.

'I've seen drawings of ... cyrens,' Odi ventured, following her to the table. 'You don't look like what I expected.'

Roh resisted the overpowering urge to shoo him away. She was going to have to get used to him, to endure the additional shadow, and no doubt, the endless questions, for the duration of the tournament.

'Humans see what we want them to see,' she said. She pointed to where she knew the shell token rested against his chest beneath his shirt. 'Right now, that is what allows you to see us for what we are, and what the lair is.'

Roh reached for a pie, before realising that everyone else was using small plates. Spotting a stack of these, she got one for herself, and on second thought, got one for Odi, too. She handed it to him wordlessly. He needed more meat on his bones if he was going to be of any use to her. She couldn't have him starving to death before the first trial.

All thoughts emptied from Roh's head as she bit into the most delicious thing she'd ever tasted. A savoury pie, spiced with peppers she'd never dreamed of.

Thera's heart, I could eat twenty of these ... The complexity of flavour was a far cry from the soggy gruel of the Lower Sector, that was for sure. Still chewing, she began to make another lap around the conservatory. It was near capacity now, Roh's fellow competitors lost amidst the crowd of highborns. Queen Delja was nowhere in sight, but there was a handful of council elders present, and a lot of nobility. A glimmer of silver was gone as fast as it appeared: silver marks exchanged between soft, clean hands. She'd only ever seen a silver mark once before, in a lesson on sums and currency. Now, seeing a handful of such wealth exchanged so casually made her jaw clench. She had all but thirteen bronze keys to her name, tucked away in a sock, hidden in a spare pair of boots back in her quarters.

She caught a noble pointing subtly to Finn Haertel. *Of course, a wager.* It seemed that placing bets was not above the highborns. Jesmond would be pleased to hear it.

A server offered Roh a selection of wine. She took a glass, marvelling at what looked like liquid rose gold within, tiny bubbles rising to the surface. They danced across her tongue with sweet bursts of flavour as she took her first sip. This was nothing like the stuff Harlyn made from potato skins.

Across the room, Neith, the water runner, was indulging in the petite sweet cakes. She caught Roh's gaze and waved. Flushing, Roh gave a small wave back, torn between finding comfort in the familiar and knowing that the tournament would only have one winner, if at all. Neith had no such concerns, it seemed. She crossed the room, her withered human in tow.

'Roh!' she said brightly upon approach. 'Isn't this amazing?' She gestured around at the food and drink. 'Imagine if the others could see us now. Wouldn't Harlyn and Orson be jealous?'

Roh's face burned hot as she felt the unwanted attention of the nobles. The water runner was making a spectacle of them, but to tell her so would only exacerbate the situation. Roh gave a tight smile. 'The wine is excellent,' she said, her voice low.

'I haven't tried it yet,' Neith gushed, though thankfully she matched Roh's volume. 'Can you believe the residences?'

'They're beautiful,' Roh allowed, as she tried to subtly extract herself from the situation. However, as she took a step away, she collided with a sharp shoulder.

'Watch where you're going, *isruhe*,' Finn spat under his breath, hot in her ear.

Roh heard the vile word clearly. The one reserved exclusively for the likes of her: the lowborn offspring of criminals, wearers of circlets. Fury surged through her as it seared like a brand. *Isruhe*. It had only been directed at her once before, but she knew its meaning well enough: *vermin of the deep*.

Roh only just managed to suck in an outburst of rage and hold back her talons. She couldn't react, not here in the Queen's Conservatory, not amongst the highborn nobles of Saddoriel. She backed away, and to her frustration, smacked right into Odi.

'Stay out of my way,' she hissed. The last thing she wanted was to look like a bumbling fool. Reining in her temper, she clutched her wineglass and wandered to the outskirts of the conservatory, the vibrant colours beyond the glass soothing her as she walked. Around her, there were dozens of conversations in Old Saddorien she didn't understand, but perhaps that was for the best, especially if Finn Haertel was the example to heed.

A familiar, subtle scent suddenly filled Roh's nostrils, somehow sweet and bitter all at once. She whirled around as Odi put a goblet of wine to his lips.

'Don't!' Her sharp command had frozen Odi's hand midway to his mouth. 'Don't drink that,' she said more calmly. 'It's poisoned.'

The blood drained from Odi's face as he peered into the crimson liquid. 'What? How … how do you know?'

Roh sniffed casually in the goblet's direction. 'It smells of coral larkspur.'

'Of what?'

'A poisonous coral flower we harvest from the seabed. At the very least it causes all sorts of irritation, rashes and internal complaints. At its worst, it can cause paralysis, even death. Don't drink it,' she instructed. The harvest had only occurred twice in Roh's lifetime, but the smell of the coral was something she would never forget. 'But keep ahold of it,' she added. 'We might be able to use it later.'

Looking shocked, Odi sniffed the edge of the goblet. 'Use it how?'

'I'll think of something. Now, can you try to not get yourself killed before this tournament begins?'

Odi didn't look particularly pleased at that remark, despite the fact that Roh had just saved his life. She led him to an unoccupied space by one of the tables at the back of the conservatory, trying to force her heartbeat to a normal pace. Her time in the tournament had almost been brought to an abrupt end, before the trials had even got underway. She hadn't been paying attention and Odi had nearly died because of it. She scanned the room, spotting Finn Haertel smirking by the refreshment table.

That bastard. He'd laced Odi's wine, or had his human do it for him as he'd insulted her. She met his lilac gaze. *You're going to pay for that*, she promised silently.

Roh looked back to Odi just in time to see the human turn a sickly shade of green. 'What is it?' Her eyes went to his goblet instantly – had he forgotten? But the poisoned wine within was untouched. 'What is it?' she demanded, scanning the room, trying to locate the source of his transfixed attention.

There. Taro and Bloodwyn Haertel had entered the conservatory. They may as well have been royalty themselves, the way the room quietened to whispers and the music softened. The nobility bowed their heads as the Elder Council couple swept into the room.

'Do you know them?' Roh asked Odi.

His eyes slid to hers. 'They are the ones who found me.'

'Found you?'

'Wandering the tunnels.'

'Oh.' Roh had assumed he'd been captured in his own realm. She wanted to ask if they had hurt him, how they had brought him here, but the questions seemed too personal somehow.

Odi brushed a strand of dark hair from his eyes and seemed to sense her curiosity. 'I was in the woods near my village foraging for truffles and came across the entrance to some sort of cave. That's when I heard my stepbrothers – I heard them so clearly. I just walked in.'

'The lure of the lair …' Roh nodded distantly. 'The lair can enchant a cyren song to sound familiar to prey.'

'I'm not anyone's prey,' Odi snapped, his amber eyes filled with determination.

Roh toyed with the bones of the necklace she wore. 'Not for the next few moons you're not.'

Odi's nostrils flared, but he continued. 'Those two …' He nodded to the Haertel couple. 'I was lost when they found me. They brought me to the cage where the others were already trapped —'

Odi fell silent as a hand reached between them and touched Roh's shoulder. Tutor Bellfast gazed into her face, seeking recognition.

'Fledgling, do I know you?' the teacher asked. 'You look familiar to me.'

Roh took a much-needed sip of her sparkling wine. 'You taught me as a nestling, Tutor Bellfast. I was in your lessons for melody and history. I'm Rohesia.'

Her teacher nodded. 'That's right, Rohesia. I remember you now. You were more of a keen soloist than one for harmonies, if I recall correctly?'

Roh was grateful her tutor hadn't mentioned their deathsong practice and how Roh, after hundreds of lessons, still hadn't managed a single note.

'That sounds like me,' Roh said quietly, not wanting to encourage that particular direction of conversation.

However, Tutor Bellfast had already moved on and was running a critical gaze over Odi. 'He's not in bad shape, considering. I cannot believe this addition to the tournament. In all my years of studying and teaching, this is by far the most outlandish and complex stipulation.'

'Where's yours?' Roh asked, brow furrowed as she scanned the crowd.

Her former teacher waved vaguely across the room. 'Oh, somewhere over there, by the pastries.'

'I'd keep a closer eye,' Roh said, not taking her eyes from the human in question. The middle-aged woman sported some deep cuts on her forearms.

'What?' Tutor Bellfast appeared taken aback.

'We had our first sabotage attempt a few moments ago,' Roh explained, unsure why she was warning her competition. One human down would also mean one less cyren for her to beat in whatever trials awaited them. 'Coral larkspur, in the wine,' Roh offered.

The tutor's lilac eyes filled with alarm. 'Is that so?' She beckoned frantically to her human, calling her over. The woman eyed Roh fearfully as she approached.

But Roh's attention snagged on something else: a flicker of movement to her left. She glanced in time to see Odi slide a knife from the nearby table up his sleeve.

'We're well past your lessons, Rohesia,' Tutor Bellfast was saying. 'You may call me Arcelia. I'm sure —'

Arcelia's words were drowned out by the loud strike of a cymbal. The sound cut through the chatter and the music, and only once it had finished echoing did the double doors open. Roh saw the wings first, dark and membranous, tucked tightly behind Queen Delja's back as she stepped into the now-silent conservatory. She wore a flowing gown, the same shade of rose gold as the wine in Roh's cup. Her midnight curls hung to her waist, and atop her head, the coral crown sat proudly, gems gleaming.

All around, cyrens dropped into low bows. Roh did the same, tugging Odi down with her. Bent at the waist, all she could see were the queen's slippered feet and hem as she strode across the marble floor. She walked the length of the conservatory slowly, until she reached the end of the room, where she stepped up onto a small dais.

'Rise, cyrens of Saddoriel.' Roh swayed at the melodic sound of Queen Delja's voice. She stood along with the rest of the crowd, her eager eyes seeking the queen, who was accepting a goblet of wine offered by a server, her dark talons out as she surveyed the party. She was magnificent. Power seemed to drip from her very being, and it wasn't long before Taro and Bloodwyn Haertel were at her sides, the rest of the Council of Seven Elders loitering nearby, ready to have her ear. Roh watched the queen in awe. *This* was the cyren who was known as the youngest deathsong singer in their history, the cyren who had overthrown the fanatical king, Uniir the Blessed, the cyren who had single-handedly saved Saddoriel from insanity centuries before.

'That's your ruler?' Odi whispered at Roh's side.

Roh nodded. 'Queen Delja. The first queen to ever reign over Talon's Reach.'

'Why does she have wings and you don't?'

Roh sighed. 'She was chosen by the goddesses.' At her words, the queen's lilac gaze snapped up and met Roh's from across the room. Roh nearly grabbed Odi's arm in shock. The intensity of her stare was tinged with a glimmer of recognition.

Roh tugged Odi's sleeve. 'Come, we're staring.' She led him to the other side of the room, carefully avoiding the highborn competitors and Neith, not wanting to create any sort of scene, especially now. With concentrated effort, Roh slowed her breathing, exhaling steadily through her nose as the music began to play once more and the conservatory came back to life.

As she drained the last of her wine, her stomach gurgled loudly. Odi threw her a sideways glance. A moment later, her insides shifted again, this time twisting painfully.

Gods, she thought, sniffing her wineglass. *Have I failed to catch my own poison?* She couldn't smell anything around the rim of her glass, but that meant nothing now that she'd downed the whole drink. Sweat began to form at her brow and her stomach clenched in another agonising cramp.

'We have to leave,' she hissed in Odi's direction. Her stomach whined again, rumbling inside her. '*Now.*'

'Are you —'

Roh had to stop herself sprinting across the conservatory as cold sweats set in, sending shivers down her spine. Propriety be damned, she hiked up the fabric of her dress and rushed towards the doors. Odi was right behind her, and thank the gods for that, because she would have left him amongst the vipers in the state she was in. She raced through the tunnels, hand clapped over her mouth as she followed her inner compass desperately back to the Upper Sector residences.

How could I have been so stupid? At last, she burst into their rooms and threw herself towards the bathing chamber. She slammed the door shut behind her. If she was going to die, she wasn't going to do it in front of the human.

You absolute fool, Rohesia, she cursed herself, collapsing on the cool tiles. *You got so arrogant with Odi's wine that you missed the poison in your own.*

Nausea rolled through her, a massive wave hitting her right in the gut. Roh threw up on the floor. This was it. She was going to die, before she'd even heard what the first trial was. Before the queen had seen her compete, before she'd even made a dent in the competition. Some Saddorien cyren she had turned out to be.

Her stomach emptied onto the tiles again and she moaned, before letting the poison claim her.

Hours later, Roh peeled herself off the cold floor. She wasn't dead. Although, she didn't feel far from it. As she sat up, cringing at the mess on the tiles, it dawned on her: there had been no poison. It had been the rich, decadent food and sparkling wine. She should have known better. She wasn't used to such gluttonous consumption. She did her best to clean the floor before rinsing out her mouth and splashing her face with water.

Roh emerged from the bathing chambers sheepishly.

From his bed, Odi watched her collapse onto hers. 'Are you … alright?'

Roh inhaled shakily.

Odi didn't take his eyes off her. 'You … you detected the poison in my drink, but not your own?'

Roh found herself nodding weakly, her pride more injured now than her stomach. She wasn't about to correct him, not for a thousand silver marks. She closed her eyes briefly. She needed to pull herself together, and fast. She had been foolish, oh so foolish. But she was allowed one mistake. This had been it. No more.

'Roh?' Odi asked. 'How is it that you know my language?'

Roh didn't bother opening her eyes. 'We are taught many tongues when we are nestlings. It's so we can sing our deathsong in whatever language our prey understands.'

The rustling of fabric sounded and Roh opened one eye. She saw a glint of silver.

'You need not worry. I need you alive to win the tournament. That's why you're here,' she said, as Odi hurriedly stuffed the stolen knife under his pillow. 'So I won't be killing you,' she added. 'Yet.'

CHAPTER SIX

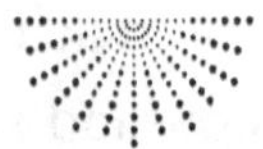

Roh dreamed of music, of elegant, refined notes dancing along her bones and filling her soul. Two fiddles in perfect harmony started out with soft, sweet chords only to build and build to an explosive crescendo. She thought she would burst, and never again feel so complete, so truly whole and herself. When she awoke, she could still hear the fiddles playing, and she realised with a start where she was: the Upper Sector, in the competitors' quarters for the Queen's Tournament.

From her lavish bed, she spotted an opened letter discarded on one of the gold-trimmed end tables. Frowning, she swung her legs from beneath the covers and padded across the room, snatching it up in her talons. It was the instructions from the council regarding the first trial. Her eyes snagged on several words that made her heart sink, but suddenly, she stopped reading. Skin prickling, she scanned the room.

Empty.

The door to the bathing chamber was ajar. She pushed it open.

Empty.

A ragged gasp of realisation escaped her. *The damn fool.* Her hands shook as she struggled into her clothes and yanked on her boots, not stopping to tie her laces. Her chest was tight as she shoved the torn envelope in her pocket. *Doesn't he know how much danger he's in out there?* She had to find him. With the council's letter burning a hole in her jacket, she darted for the door and raced from the residences, not caring whom she woke in the process.

Odi, where are you? She wanted to scream it across the foyer, but the last thing she needed was her fellow competitors knowing her human was out on the loose – that was, unless they already had him.

The fiddles continued to play somewhere in the near distance, but for once, music offered Roh no comfort. She couldn't have reached this point only to fail before the tournament began. She had not dreamed of this opportunity her whole life and cheated her friends to get here for nothing. She refused to accept that possibility. Roh ran the perimeter of the foyer, ignoring the startled cries of several highborn cyrens milling beneath the archways. All the while, the tantalising notes of the fiddles mocked her.

'I know this song.'

With panic clenching an unforgiving fist around her heart, Roh raced towards the music, towards the song

Odi supposedly knew, through the foyer and to the entrance and surrounding galleries of the Upper Sector.

The Great Hall. Her inner compass dragged her towards it and she at last found an opening. In the shadows, she nearly fell to her knees.

There he was, at the centre of the hall, standing before a cage of bones, peering inside. Behind the bars were two human men, fiddles tucked beneath their chins. With their knees bent, they swayed in time with the melody, their muscular arms guiding their bows across the strings. It was the music from her dreams. It was even more beautiful here, the sound bouncing from the hall's cylindrical walls and echoing in the light-filled domes. The notes wrapped around Roh, like the currents of the sea did when she dived deep into its waters. She stood transfixed. She had never seen music in the flesh before, never watched as a master, or *masters*, created a soul-changing sound from practically nothing. The fiddles played complementary melodies, rising and falling with each other, shifting from a slow, joyful pace to double-time, peaking at a sorrowful climax.

Movement from Odi broke her reverie. He pressed himself close against the bars of the cage, but Roh was too far away to see what he was doing, or hear what he was saying. It looked like he was talking to the musicians, as though *sharing information.* She approached on light feet now, determined to catch a snippet of conversation, but the human musicians saw her, both taking a step back within the cage, alerting Odi to her presence. He whirled around, eyes wide.

'Do you have any idea what could have happened to you without me?' she hissed as she reached him, a taloned hand clamping around his forearm.

'I … I just …'

'You just *nothing*. You *aren't safe* out here. Do you understand that?' As she spoke, Roh's gaze fell to the lock of the cage. A jewelled hairpin from her chambers was sticking out, its gems glinting in the enchanted light. As realisation dawned, she inhaled hotly, her grip tightening on Odi's arm as she turned to him, only to then notice a rucksack – *her* rucksack – at his feet.

'How far did you think you would get?' she asked quietly, allowing the fury to surge through her veins. Her talons threatened to pierce his soft skin.

Colour bloomed on Odi's cheeks. 'I —'

'The only way you'll ever leave Saddoriel alive is if we win this tournament. Do you hear me?'

Odi looked at the ground, shifting from foot to foot while the musicians continued to play – Roh guessed they knew better than to stop. They watched her closely, their bodies rigid, as though expecting her to pounce on Odi.

'You know them,' she said to him, matter-of-factly.

'Everyone knows them,' he allowed. 'They're the Eery Brothers. They're famous throughout our realm, the best fiddlers in our lands.'

'And you thought by springing them free and miraculously returning them to their own territory that you'd earn some quick coin?'

'No, I —'

Roh cut him off with a shake of her head. *Famous ...* She supposed the men were attractive, by human standards, at least, and the way they stood, despite their obvious fear, with their chests puffed out and their backs straight, gave them the confidence of performers. Their bows continued to draw expertly across the strings of the fiddles, birthing a melody that was melancholy, resigned to its own finality. The notes were long and rich, full of a yearning that Roh recognised in herself. The musicians' elegant fingers danced across the strings, creating wordless poetry, a whorl of invention that settled deep in Roh's chest. Music poured from the fiddles' hollows. The notes held, arresting, spiralling upwards. Both players hunched over their instruments, eyes now closed as they rocked back and forth with the intensity of their song —

'What are you doing?' a male voice cut through the music like a honed blade. 'You have no business interfering with property of the Jaktaren.'

Roh whirled around to see Finn Haertel charging towards them, his crossbow gleaming at his back. For a split second, the music behind her faltered and Roh swept the rucksack from the ground and shouldered it, pulling Odi closer to her side as Finn stormed up to them. Though Roh was tall, Finn was taller and seemed to tower over her as he glared down.

'I said, what are you doing?' he demanded.

Roh fought the instinct to shrink away, and she met his hard gaze. 'That's none of your concern.'

'It's my concern when you're loitering around two of Saddoriel's most prized possessions.'

'We're not *loitering*.' Roh spat the words. 'We're passing through.'

But Finn's eyes roamed over her, the bag at her shoulder, her forced expression of neutrality. They lingered on her loose bootlaces, before scanning the bars of the cage.

The hairpin, she realised with a jolt. *This is bad. Very, very bad. He's going to think ...* Roh forced herself to remain still. Finn's view of the lock was obstructed by Odi, but it was only a matter of moments before the Jaktaren moved closer and discovered the escape attempt, in which she was now entangled. To make matters worse, Odi was fidgeting incessantly, drawing more attention to himself. Finn took a step forward.

'Is it true?' she asked, nudging Odi aside and taking his place in front of the lock. She turned to face the musicians, as though she were studying them.

'Is *what* true?'

She placed her hands on the bars, pretending to rest against them, praying to Dresmis and Thera that Finn couldn't see the talon of her smallest finger unsheathe and inch towards the hairpin. She could sense him getting closer, and hear the breath escaping his lips. 'That you've single-handedly brought fifteen musicians back to Saddoriel this month alone?'

She heard him pause. Just as her talon dislodged the pin.

'No,' he said slowly.

In one swift motion, Roh swiped the pin from the lock and spun around to face Finn expectantly.

He eyed her warily. 'That was Yrsa.'

His partner. 'Oh.'

The Jaktaren gave the cage, Roh and Odi one final scan and turned on his heel. 'Keep away from here.'

Roh waited until he was out of sight before she rounded on Odi. 'Do you know what you could have cost me just now? Do you know what could have happened to *you*?' She wanted to shove him, to slash him with her talons. She wanted to instil in him the shard of fear that throbbed in her own heart.

But Odi had returned his gaze to the empty lock and the musicians within the cage of bones. 'What will happen to them?'

'They will play their music until they have no more to give.'

'But —'

Rage still coursed through her as she clutched the hairpin. She considered driving it into his stupid neck. 'Enough,' she snapped. 'They belong to Saddoriel now.'

Something dangerous must have flashed in her eyes, because the human fell silent.

Roh pulled the council's letter from her pocket and shoved it into his chest. 'We have bigger problems,' she said. 'Did you read this?'

Odi pushed her hands and the parchment back gently. 'I couldn't understand a word of it.'

'It's the instructions regarding the first trial,' she murmured, re-reading the few lines.

'Are you going to tell me what these trials are about at last? Why I'm your gods-damned prisoner?' The words came out thick and fast as the human eyed her exposed talons warily, but he stood his ground.

Roh stared at him, finding herself strangely pleased. At last, the boy had shown some *backbone*. *This* was the sort of human she would need by her side throughout the games ahead. She crossed her arms over her chest. 'Very well,' she said.

Roh explained the Queen's Tournament and its new rule, sparing Odi no detail. She outlined all she knew of the previous trials, the savagery behind them and the ruthlessness of the competitors.

'And I am forced to partake?' Odi said bluntly when she was done.

'Yes.'

'In not one, but three separate trials?'

'That's correct.'

Odi shook his head and ran his half-gloved fingers through his hair before jerking his chin towards the parchment. 'What does it say?'

'*Join the hunt ...*' She read to him, wary of the music slowing as she did. '*Dear competitor, at the seventh hour tomorrow, join the queen's hunt. You may bring a weapon of your choice and a single pack of supplies. Each competitor's human must be in attendance. More instructions shall be given upon arrival. Sincerely, Erdites Colter, Council of the Seven Elders.*'

'A hunt ...?'

Roh nodded, only half listening to him. She had no *inkling* of what the trial would entail, or how long it would last. Weapons ... Where would she find those? And what of food? Drink? What if they were required to spend the night somewhere? She might know nothing, but she was willing to bet all the bronze keys in her hidden sock that Finn Haertel and Yrsa Ward had a wealth of knowledge that she did not.

'What sort of hunt?' Odi pressed.

'Why? Are you any good at hunting?'

Odi shook his head. 'I'm a … craftsman. A shopkeeper of sorts. I spend most of my time indoors.'

Roh gave a huff of frustration. 'Of course you do,' she muttered. 'Follow me.'

Her human hesitated a moment, as though he didn't want to leave the musicians behind.

'For Lamaka's sake,' she muttered, pulling him in the right direction, away from the chaotic notes and golden harmonies that were trapped in the cage of bones. If Odi didn't get himself killed, she might well kill him out of irritation herself. Of all the additions to the tournaments over the centuries that she knew of, this new human element was the absolute worst. Humans … Their barely existing attention span, their tendency to freeze in tight situations, their complete and utter uselessness …

Yes, Odi was likely to get himself, or both of them, killed.

It was only when the crate of the pulley system opened up to the passage of the Lower Sector that Roh noticed Odi was shaking.

'Well, I know you're not cold,' she said. 'You're wearing those ridiculous gloves.'

Odi tucked his hands in his pockets, his shoulders hunched inwards.

'Spit it out.' The screech of the crate being drawn back up sounded.

'They … they were in a cage.'

'So were you. You could have been shoved back into one after what you just attempted.'

The melody from the Great Hall had faded as they'd descended into the lower levels of Saddoriel, and Roh felt as though she were being spread out thin across two places, like part of her had been left in the Upper Sector with the Eery Brothers.

As they started down a dark passage, Odi's gaze scanned the wet walls.

'This …' he murmured. '*This* is what the place looked like to me at first.'

Roh huffed a dark laugh. 'Welcome to the Lower Sector,' she grunted, heading for the workshop. 'Where is it you're from?' she found herself asking.

'Why?' Odi retorted, considering her warily. 'Are you going to take me back?'

'No,' Roh said.

'Then it doesn't matter, does it?'

Roh's eyes narrowed. 'I suppose not.'

There was a long pause as they walked the passage, the silence curdling. 'What happens after?' Odi asked finally.

'After?'

'After your damn tournament.' Odi's cheeks flushed pink. 'What happens to us humans then?'

Roh frowned and rubbed the bridge of her nose. 'I don't know.'

'You mean you don't care,' Odi said, crossing his arms over his chest.

Roh didn't know if she cared. She certainly felt sorry for the poor creatures who had been lured into the lair only to find themselves caught up in the biggest cyren event of the past five decades. But did she *care*? Had she even considered their fate beyond the next few moons? Not quite.

When they arrived at the bone workshop, Roh was dismayed to find it full. She hadn't thought to check the hour. Peering through the dirty window, she spotted Harlyn and Orson, bleary-eyed and sorting through yet another barrel of bones.

'If all you were going to do when you got to the Upper Sector was return to us lowborns, then what was the point?' Ames' silken voice sounded.

Odi jumped and made to scurry behind Roh, but she faced her mentor. He stood leaning against the doorframe to the workshop, arms folded over his chest, waiting expectantly.

'I need weapons.' The words were out of her mouth before she could think better of it. And she had used the common tongue of the human realms instead of New Saddorien.

'Weapons?' Ames' expression was deadpan as he too spoke in the common tongue. 'Do you even know how to swing a sword? Lift a shield? Have you ever even seen a cyren with a weapon before?'

Although her mentor had made no comment on her choice of language, she did not miss his eyes sliding to Odi, forever assessing, analysing.

Roh shifted from one foot to the other. 'The Jaktaren … and the guards —'

'The *prison* guards?'

Roh's gaze went to the ground.

'You're not thinking strategically,' Ames said more quietly, checking over his shoulder.

'How can I, when I know nothing?'

Odi was fidgeting again, his fingers performing some sort of elaborate dance at his sides. Roh threw him a pointed look and he stilled.

Ames glanced from the human back to her, curiosity piquing on his lined face for a moment before his voice turned stern.

'I did not help secure you a place in this tournament only for you to return to whine before it even begins.'

Roh's face burned as she felt Odi's inquisitive gaze flick to her. It wasn't fair that she had to take him everywhere with her. He was here to *see* everything, *hear* everything. She had never had much privacy before, but this … With a human here to witness every humiliating moment … She ignored Odi, returning her focus to Ames, her mouth opening and closing under the pressure. 'I …'

'What is the use of a weapon if you don't know how to wield it? What *do* you know how to wield? What *do* you know about the tournament? About your fellow competitors? There are lessons and tactics to be taken from all around you. If only you would open your eyes.' Her mentor's questions were relentless, and as always, struck a hard chord of truth. She knew nothing of daggers and swords. A cyren's deathsong was the only weapon she needed, but Roh didn't know a single note of her own. Whatever her song, it was buried deep within her, yet to be discovered. She inhaled through her nose and nodded slowly. What *did* she know? She knew about bone cleaning. She knew the workshop like the back of her hand. She knew every corner, every tool, every design, every damn bone splinter on the ground.

'Is there something else?' Ames' arms were folded across his chest, the creases in his forehead deepening. 'Is there some other reason you're down here wasting my time and taking me away from the bone cleaners in my charge?'

Roh couldn't help it. Her eyes went straight to the workshop window and her friends who sat beyond it. Orson and Harlyn, sitting up straighter than usual, were doing their best not to look in her direction.

Ames threw his hands up in exasperation. 'Twenty minutes. And that's twenty minutes too long.' Shaking his head, his lilac eyes bright with frustration, he returned to the workshop. Moments later, Orson and Harlyn rushed out, scooping her up into their arms in a hard embrace. She breathed in their scents. It had only been one night, but … They had been together every day and night from the moment they had met. Harlyn released her, pulling back to examine the new clothes Roh wore, the fresh shirt and loose pants, simple but of fine make, a far cry from the grubby, coarse fabrics of the Lower Sector. Roh's shoulder was damp as Orson pulled away, her face wet with tears.

'It hasn't been that long,' Roh quipped despite herself, trying to break the tension.

But her comment only made Orson cry harder. 'I can't believe you're here.'

Fascinated as always, Roh watched her friend's tears spill as she had many times before. Orson cried often – when she was happy, when she was sad, when she was angry … Her tears were an emotional outlet that Roh envied. Roh couldn't remember the last time she herself had shed a single tear. It wasn't as though she hadn't wanted to cry – many a time – but somehow, the tears never broke. However, it did not leave her without empathy.

Roh squeezed Orson a little harder. '*For under these starless nights, we let no tears fall,*' she whispered to her friend. It was a lullaby for cyren infants, but whenever Orson needed comforting, which she did often, it was the only thing Roh knew to do.

Orson gave a sad smile at the familiar words and sniffed. 'You're in it, Roh. And you might not walk away from it.'

Roh squeezed Orson's hand. 'I'm not going to let that happen,' she said, suddenly filled with conviction at the sight of her weeping friend.

Harlyn cleared her throat loudly. 'Is anyone going to *mention* that there's a gods-damned *human* standing here?'

Harlyn was towering over Odi, a single talon poised at his throat.

'Har, no!' Roh exclaimed, rushing to Odi's side.

Harlyn's brows furrowed in confusion as Roh pushed her off him. If Roh hadn't been so invested in Odi's safety, she would have laughed. It was a surreal sight – the three of them down in the Lower Sector of Saddoriel, with a human boy flattened in fear against the wet passage wall.

'I have to keep him alive,' Roh explained.

'What?' Harlyn spluttered.

'I know. That's the least of it.'

Shaking her head in disbelief, Harlyn examined Odi critically. 'Well, you're doomed, aren't you?'

Odi's amber stare implored Roh. 'Is she going to eat me?' he asked, backing away from Harlyn.

At that, Roh and Harlyn *did* burst out laughing.

'*Eat you?*' Harlyn gibed, using the common tongue. 'Why *in the name of Dresmis and Thera* would I do that?'

'And *what*, exactly, would she eat? There's barely any meat on you,' Roh added, holding her aching stomach. Gods, it felt good to laugh.

'Harlyn, Roh,' Orson reprimanded them. 'Don't be cruel.' She turned to Odi. 'Do you have a name?'

Odi threw Roh a dirty look before nodding. 'Odi Arrowood.'

Roh flicked her extended talons menacingly in his direction and shook her head at Harlyn.

Orson, however, took a step towards the human.

'What is it that you do in your realm, Odi?' Her voice was gentle and her eyes warm.

It was typical of Orson, really. She cared so much; human or not, her kindness shone through. And even though she was wary of the waning time she had left with her friends, Roh waited.

'My father owns a shop,' Odi answered cautiously, still eyeing Harlyn. 'We fix instruments mostly. Sometimes we make them.'

'How?'

'With different types of tools and machines —'

'As nice as it is, playing "get-to-know-the-human", do we not have bigger matters to discuss?' Harlyn drawled.

Orson gave Odi an apologetic grimace. 'Of course.' She turned back to Roh, her bright eyes eager. 'Tell us, how can we help? What can we do?'

What do you know how to wield? ... There are lessons and tactics to be taken from all around you. If only you would open your eyes.

Ames was right. Roh knew things that no one from the Upper Sector would even dream of. *That* was her advantage. All those years of interrogating Ames about the tournaments. All those years of playing pranks as nesters. All her unofficial visits to Saddoriel's prison ...

You may bring a weapon of your choice and a single pack of supplies.

She was already running through a list in her head. Of essentials, basic items that would help her endure a hunt, whatever that might mean. But the trials weren't just about enduring, they were about outsmarting the competition, about using a cyren's cunning at whatever cost. The poison in Odi's wine was only the beginning. A savage move by Finn Haertel, aimed at the weak link in Roh's armour. Betrayal, sabotage, undercutting … There would be plenty of that before the tournament was done. Roh paced back and forth, her heavy boots grinding the grit beneath. She had to listen to her instincts, to her inner compass. Roh straightened as a slither of realisation dawned on her. She hadn't returned to the Lower Sector because she *belonged* down here. She had returned because it was what she knew: the dark depths of Saddoriel were home to all she had learned in her seventeen years, and those lessons were her edge, her weapon against the competition.

'Roh?' Orson was reaching for her arm. 'How can we help?'

Roh nodded to herself, her gaze resting upon the flimsy old shoes Odi wore and recalling the thinly slippered feet of the highborns. Finally, her eyes met Orson's. 'There *is* something you can do for me …'

Roh lowered her voice and told her friends what she needed.

The seed of an idea had begun to form. It fed the nerves and anticipation already swirling in her gut. It would either be a monumental mistake, or the move that put her leagues ahead of her competition. Roh motioned for Odi to follow.

'Where are we going?' he asked.

Roh's mind raced through the tasks she'd set herself and the moving pieces of the plan that was slowly forming. 'There's something I need you to do.'

Odi eyed her suspiciously. 'Oh? And what's that?'

The jewelled hairpin as a makeshift lock pick flashed in her mind. 'Can you steal?'

'Steal?'

Roh gave a single nod. 'That's what I said. Let's hurry – I don't know how much time we need, or how much we have.'

'No.'

Roh's blood turned to ice. 'What did you say?'

'I said, *no*. If you're tasking me with errands, ones that will no doubt put me in deadly peril, then I deserve to know the plan. The *full* plan. You have to tell me.'

An unexpected smile tugged the corner of Roh's mouth. Perhaps she had underestimated the human. As he was now obviously underestimating her. But whatever expression she wore had silenced him.

'First,' Roh said quietly, flicking her talons towards Odi's throat, 'I don't *have to* do *anything*. *You* do not say what goes on here. A mere *boy* does not command a Saddorien cyren. Secondly' – Roh motioned for him to walk on – 'I can do better than tell you. I'll *show* you.'

After the briefest of hesitations, Odi shut his mouth for once, and followed her into the darkness.

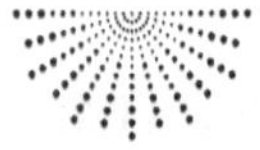

etween the bars of bone, Roh watched her mother, Cerys, slice through tendrils of her own hair with jagged, bloodstained talons. The matted midnight curls that had once hung well past her mother's waist were now severed, fanned out around her on the algae-covered stone. Painfully thin, wearing a grime-covered shift, Cerys moved with an eerie sense of tranquillity, carefully considering each lock of hair before cleaving through it and discarding it: an ancient cyren who indeed had lost her grasp on the passage of time.

Roh's skin prickled, and her own talons shot out as Cerys' gaze slowly lifted to hers. The eyes that met Roh's were bright and intense, gleaming with a sea of words that Cerys was unable to speak aloud. Roh yearned to know what went on in that manic mind and if her mother recognised her as the daughter she'd birthed in that very spot. The daughter who had been taken from her hands while she lay bloody on the cold stone. The thought made Roh's stomach churn. Ames had told her the story precisely three times as a nestling and then refused to repeat it. The story of her birth had always felt like it had happened to someone else. And yet here she was. The creature in the cell before her was her mother, a part of her, and always would be. She could close the distance between them in a single step, but there was far more than a barrier of bones separating them.

Ignoring the scraping of Odi's shoes across the gravel as he fidgeted nearby, Roh continued to watch Cerys, unnerved by the sight of her with her hair hacked away and strewn about her, the walls scratched with new stone carvings. Illustrations of strange masks … Did they mean something? Or were they merely the carvings of someone whose mind had been addled by centuries of isolation and confinement?

Ames' words returned to her. *'There are lessons and tactics to be taken from all around you. If only you would open your eyes …'* Roh had her eyes open, alright. But the cell before her offered no bolt of inspiration, no insight into the trials ahead. She glanced in Odi's direction, acutely aware of his presence in what was usually a very private space for her. The human was marvelling at the dead water warlocks behind her, pacing down the row of them. Like a child, he didn't have the ability to look and not touch. His hand reached for a brooch pinned to one of the warlock's jackets.

Roh bit back the sharp objection on her tongue. She didn't want him here at all, but at least there was something shiny to hold his attention while she talked to Cerys. If she could find the words. Most often these *conversations* were only one-way. Her mouth suddenly dry, Roh licked her lips before shoving her hands in her pockets and facing the cell once more.

'It's begun,' she said slowly, her voice sounding foreign in the echoing chambers. 'The Queen's Tournament, it has started. I'm a participant.'

For a split second, Roh could have sworn she saw the corner of her mother's mouth tug upwards. A hint of a devious smirk, as though she knew about the card game … and the fact that Roh would censor the tale for her benefit was amusing. The hairs on the back of Roh's neck prickled, but she couldn't stop now. She had risked her waning time before the trial to come here … For what? Knowledge? Support? She suppressed a scoff.

'The main ones to beat are Finn Haertel and Yrsa Ward. They're Jaktaren.' The armpits of her shirt became damp as a flicker of recognition passed over Cerys' face. If Roh had blinked she would have missed it. A bead of sweat trickled down her ribs.

'You know those names, don't you? *Haertel* and *Ward* …' Roh trailed off. Cerys' eyes widened as her gaze settled on Odi, her mouth parting as though she were remembering something.

'Marlow?' she croaked, pressing her face against the bars.

Roh stared. 'Marlow?'

'Marlow, you've come,' Cerys rasped, a thin arm reaching out.

'Who in all the realms is Marlow?' Scowling, Roh looked from Cerys to the human, who'd frozen in terror.

'*Your uncle*,' said a quiet but melodic voice from behind her.

Roh whirled around, finding herself face to face with the queen – Delja the Triumphant.

Wild panic sucked the air from Roh's lungs as she threw herself into a messy bow. Words refused to form on her lips, her tongue swollen in her mouth. What should she say? What could justify her presence here? Her visits had always seemed so insignificant, a tiny indiscretion in a sea of ordinariness. Now, in the presence of the queen, the magnitude of Roh's actions came crashing down on her like a tidal wave. Would she be disqualified from the tournament? Banished from Saddoriel?

'Your Majesty, I ...' she stammered, nearly swaying on her feet, still bent at the waist, her eyes locked on the ground.

'I have known of your secret visits for some time, Rohesia,' the queen said, her voice soft.

'I beg your forgiveness, Your Majesty.'

Silence wrapped around Roh like a heavy cloak, smothering her as her mind spiralled with every possible consequence and punishment for breaking the Law of the Lair. Imprisonment, perhaps, alongside her dear mother?

A smooth finger lifted her chin. 'Your curiosity is natural; however, I fear it will only bring you pain.'

Ames had always said as much to her, in far more colourful terms. But the queen spoke of fear and pain as though she knew all too well the weight of wearing them. The pressure of the finger under Roh's chin increased slightly, and with the queen's wordless permission, Roh straightened from her bow, finding Queen Delja's lilac eyes filled with sympathy as she turned her gaze to Cerys. Cerys had moved, as silent as death, and now was sitting in the centre of her cell, legs crossed, continuing the task of slicing through her hair. She stared through the ruler of Saddoriel like there was nothing but blank space before her, as there always was. The queen blinked several times, lines appearing at the corners of her mouth as she seemed to struggle with herself. She looked out of place down here, unnecessarily smoothing down her flowy silk pants that were dark at the hem. The coral of her crown seemed too bright in contrast to the grimy bones of the cell.

'Your Majesty,' Roh managed. 'You know my uncle?' She had no idea if questions were allowed, particularly this one, but …

'I *knew* him, yes,' the queen said. 'He perished in the Scouring of Lochloria, a long time ago.'

Once more, words failed Roh. She had never imagined family beyond her mother and the father she knew nothing of, and yet … She had an uncle. A dead one, at least.

'I come down here sometimes,' Queen Delja murmured, watching the prisoner. 'To see her.'

The quietly spoken words hit Roh in the chest with full force. A thousand questions burst into her head all at once. Cerys had had another visitor all this time? Why would *the queen* want to see *Cerys*? How long had she been visiting? How long had she known about *Roh's* visits? And how did she know about Marlow?

But a surreal wave calmed the whirlpool within, and strangely, Roh's thoughts returned to a specific moment: when she had packed her rucksack the morning before. She recalled the coarse fabric of her spare clothes as she had shoved them inside the pack. She remembered weighing up the grey sock stuffed with the coin she'd saved over the years and deciding to keep it hidden. She recalled the nagging sensation at the back of her mind as she had searched the sleeping quarters for some sentimental token that did not exist, the realisation dawning on her that she had not one personal item, *not one thing* belonging to her mother. No embellished pin or stone carving, no ribbon or old dress, not even something as small and mundane as a hairbrush. There was no evidence that Cerys had ever existed outside of the prison walls. She was a living ghost, as was Roh by extension. Until now …

'You knew her, Your Majesty? Before?' She silently cursed her trembling voice.

The queen didn't take her eyes off Cerys, as though she couldn't quite believe the prisoner was actually there. 'Yes, I knew her. Long before.'

Roh struggled with herself. Here she was, a tournament competitor, standing with the Queen of Cyrens, the most powerful ruler to have ever reigned, and all she wanted to do was ask about her mother. It seemed Queen Delja sensed it.

'You want to know what she was like ...' she murmured, her voice trailing off with the memories that dragged her back into the past.

Roh caught herself holding her breath, hands clenched at her sides. Would the queen actually tell her? Was she finally going to learn something about the cyren who'd made her?

The queen continued to peer into the cell. 'She was fearless, back then. A force unto herself. In the end, it was her undoing.' Queen Delja faced Roh and reached out, running a single finger across the circlet of gold across Roh's forehead, her voice laced with regret. 'She gave me no choice when I put her in here. The Law of the Lair was broken in ways it had never been before, shattered. Where she is now, where you ended up ... I promise, I had no choice.'

All at once, the queen's promise opened up a passageway to the past where a beam of light beckoned to Roh at the end, a perfect circle that was growing smaller and smaller as the darkness encroached. Roh wanted to run towards it, but the compass within told her she wouldn't make it in time. Instead, she swallowed. 'Of course, Your Majesty.'

Roh's self-restraint prickled in the air around them, and the queen rubbed at the goosebumps on her arms. 'And yet,' she said. 'After everything ... I still find myself wandering these lonely tunnels to see her. Perhaps one day you will understand.'

'One day?'

'Should you succeed in the tournament,' Delja said, a

note of surprise lacing her words. 'The *Tome of Kyeos* tells all.'

The *Tome of Kyeos* ... It seemed bad luck to even mention the sacred text, the self-writing book that held all of Saddoriel's secrets, if rumours were to be believed.

Roh couldn't contain the eagerness in her voice. 'So it's true? You have the tome, Your Majesty?'

'No one ever truly possesses the *Tome of Kyeos*,' the queen explained. 'But yes, I have seen it, read it. It is mine to access for the duration of my rule. One might argue I have read more of it than any king before me.'

Roh could tell by the shift in the queen's stance that she had not meant to discuss such matters with a competitor, and Roh had learned on numerous occasions with Ames that questioning subjects such as these was a delicate art, one that she herself had not yet mastered with any sort of subtlety. Roh wasn't about to take such a risk with the queen.

Clearly seeking a new topic, the queen's gaze casually flicked to Odi, who still stood in the shadows of the water warlocks. 'Your human is doing well enough.'

'Well enough, Your Majesty?' Roh had felt the boy fidgeting nearby the whole time, his nervous energy grating on her during the entire royal exchange.

A small smile tugged the corner of Queen Delja's mouth. 'His knees aren't knocking together too loudly with terror.'

Roh felt herself grin. 'That's true.'

'I should leave you to your visit, Rohesia. Just remember what I said it might bring you.'

'Yes, Your Majesty,' Roh said, bowing low.

The queen made to walk away, her hem trailing through the wet grit, but she paused. 'Rohesia?'

'Yes, Your Majesty?'

'Why did you enter my tournament?'

The question was an impossible ambush. To have entered the Queen's Tournament was to challenge the queen's rule itself, a public seeking of Delja's status and power. But was that why Roh had entered? Was that what had kept her up every night, dreaming of the event?

Roh considered her words carefully. 'Because … I want … I want *more*, Your Majesty,' she said at last.

'More?'

'Yes.'

Queen Delja nodded slowly, lifting the fabric of her trousers as she faced the path towards the exit. 'You are not the first to want. Nor will you be the last.' She started down the passage once more, and though spoken quietly, her final words echoed: 'Ambition can be a poison.'

The queen's footsteps echoed long after she had disappeared into the darkness. Roh stood listening, wringing her hands and reeling at what she had learned, what the queen had deigned to share with her. That Queen Delja and Roh's mother had *known each other* before everything. And that the 'everything' was still unknown …

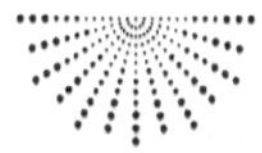

CHAPTER EIGHT

The gentle music dancing through the air did not match the sight that greeted Roh and Odi in the outskirts of Talon's Reach the next morning. The melody was unobtrusive and non-threatening with its soft notes and steady rhythm, whereas before them stood a great forest, dense with dark and twisted trees. Its edge was a precise line, as though someone had measured and drawn it before planting the saplings. Dispersed at random intervals alongside the trees within were towers of rigid, pale coral, standing like skeletal guards, watching over the forest. Roh squinted beyond the threshold, spotting head-height lengths of enchanted seaweed wavering upwards in a phantom breeze, answering the rhythm of the fiddles around them.

She knew what this place was … *One of the many lungs of Saddoriel.* A forest that had been enchanted by the water warlocks to provide the passageways and the lair with clean air to breathe. According to her lessons, there were dozens and dozens scattered all over Talon's Reach.

With the bulky pack at their feet, Roh and Odi, along with the other competitors, stood in the marshalling area: a roped-off section that acted as a buffer between the edge of the forest and the bustling stands that stretched five storeys upwards. Not knowing where to look, Roh had been trying to ignore the crowd, but their murmurs cast a loud, uniform hum across everything, their voices fighting against the music. Throughout the throngs of bodies were fashions Roh had never seen before: tightly laced sleeves and bodices, and boots that wrapped around calves to above the knee. Her ears pricked at the snippets of conversation in cyren tongues that were neither New nor Old Saddorien.

'They have come from the other territories as well,' Arcelia said, peeling away from the other competitors and approaching Roh, her human shadowing her closely. 'I can hear accents and dialects from Lochloria, Akoris, and I think, Csilla.'

'Have you been to those places?' Roh asked, whose own knowledge of other cyren territories was terribly limited. All she knew was that although they were a great distance from Talon's Reach, their clans still bowed to Queen Delja.

'Some,' Arcelia allowed. 'I have visited Lochloria and Akoris for scholarly work on Dresmis and Thera. Csilla, no, too far away for a humble educator. Only the Jaktaren roam the realms above so freely.'

Roh dared a glance across at Yrsa Ward and Finn

Haertel, and Arcelia followed her gaze across the marshalling area.

'I used to envy their travels and adventures,' the education master told her quietly. 'But I'm sure they have many dark tales to tell regarding what happens in the realms above. A Saddorien cyren belongs in Saddoriel.'

That was indeed what they were taught as nestlings, that the greatest honour was to live alongside fellow cyrens in the greatest lair of all history. But did that mean that Roh belonged in the Lower Sector cleaning bones for centuries to come? Adventures in the realms above, no matter how dark, sounded far more appealing.

Not sure how to respond, Roh turned back to the crowd and searched for familiar faces. She focused on the upper tiers, knowing that if Harlyn and Orson had managed to get away from the workshop, that was where they'd be. She took in the rows and rows, desperately scanning for Harlyn's unusual hair colour – she was always the easiest to spot in a crowd. When she couldn't see her, a weight sank in her chest. Though she knew that Har and Orson could do nothing to help her from the stands, just knowing they were there would have been an extra piece of armour Roh could have worn into the hunt. But there was no sign of them. However, a flicker of movement caught Roh's eye. It was hard to make out details from this distance, but … Yes, it was Jesmond, working her way along the aisles, her ledger pressed firmly to her chest as she navigated the spectators, taking bets.

A small smile broke across Roh's lips. *Does Ames know*

you're here? she wondered. *No doubt you've skipped your lessons to take advantage of the loose currency exchanged here.* She watched the youngster confidently barter with cyrens five times her age. *At least some things don't change.* It was a small moment of comfort in the absence of her friends.

Jesmond froze amongst her clients and a sharp intake of breath from the crowd made Roh whirl around, following pointed fingers and transfixed gazes to something hovering above the canopy ...

A floating hourglass had appeared. It was massive, poised at an angle over the top of the forest, its sand contained in the lower half, not yet in play. It glowed orange, like a beacon in the distance, its presence feeding the starved anticipation of the crowd, sucking at the air around them.

The ground quaked, enough to rattle Roh's teeth. On instinct, her hand shot out, grabbing Odi's arm. But as fast as the tremor had begun, it stopped.

'What was that?' Odi asked.

Roh released his arm, spit thick in her throat. 'I have no idea,' she told him honestly, looking to Arcelia for answers. But the education master had moved across the way to talk with Estin Ruhne. Roh reined in her admiration for the architect. Perhaps one day she would have the opportunity to speak with her, but for now, she needed to figure out what that tremor had been. Neith, the water runner, looked perturbed. She glanced around nervously, standing close to her elderly human, whose weathered face was drawn in resignation as he patted her on the shoulder. Even as the ground shook again, the others didn't look nearly as concerned, Roh noted, watching the ease with which Yrsa Ward tested the band of the sling she carried. The Jaktaren had no pack to be seen, but the young human girl at her side carried a bulging satchel of stones. Miriald Montalle was the only other carrying supplies, a sack of sorts, knotted at the top. Roh squinted. She could have sworn the material had just *moved*. But the lair rumbled once more and she awkwardly fought to keep her footing.

'Desperate to know what that was, aren't you, little bone cleaner?' a sneer sounded. Roh flinched as Zokez Rasaat sidled up next to her.

Fists clenched, she willed Odi to remain silent and still at her side. There was no way she would give this worm the satisfaction. *As if he knows what caused the tremors, anyway ...*

Zokez eyed her bulging pack and barked a laugh. 'Finn, she thinks she's going on a picnic.'

A few feet away, the Jaktaren's cool, lilac gaze slowly slid from his highborn friend to Roh's pack. He said nothing.

But Zokez wasn't done. 'Not very talkative, are you, little bone cleaner?'

'I heard a story that might make her talk,' Finn Haertel said, flicking his talons as his eyes met Roh's. He took a step towards her, crossbow held carelessly in his arms, a quiver of bolts strapped across his muscular chest.

Roh felt Odi shift uneasily beside her and she had to stop herself from delivering a sharp cuff to the back of his head. Didn't he know that to show weakness to cyrens was practically a death sentence? Roh stood her ground, but at the sight of Finn's triumphant smile, she felt trapped in a cage of her own making.

'I heard a tale,' he repeated, 'about a little cyren who doesn't know a note of her deathsong.' His words sent a rush of ice across her skin and her feet felt rooted to the spot. Bile rose in her throat. *How do they know? Who told them? How can this —*

Zokez nodded eagerly, hand on the pommel of the sword at his belt. 'Not a *single* note.'

Finn turned back to her. '*Mortifying*, isn't it? To be one of our kind but unable to do the very thing that makes us what we are.'

Roh's face burned with humiliation. She was sure the other competitors could hear every word.

'And can you imagine,' Finn pressed. 'To not only be a cyren without a song, but to be a cyren without a song *in the Queen's Tournament?*'

'Perhaps you should give her a head start, Finn? She's no match for a regular cyren, but a Jaktaren … She should just go back to her bones.'

There was no denying it; everyone's eyes were on Roh. Now, they all knew: she was just a bone cleaner without a song.

Damage inflicted, Finn and Zokez strode back to where the other highborns had gathered to make final preparations, leaving Roh breathless where she stood. Everyone knew. *Everyone.* What had she been thinking? Entering the Queen's Tournament when she hadn't even discovered a note of her song. How could she think to win against cyrens who had known theirs for decades, or even centuries? Did she truly think that *even if* she won, the cyrens of Saddoriel would accept a songless queen? Her breaths became short and shallow, and her hand flew to her chest as she struggled, still feeling the burning surveillance of the other competitors, and now, the crowd.

'Is it true?' Odi murmured.

'What?' Roh gasped.

'What he said? You have no cyren magic?'

It was only as Odi asked that Roh realised Finn had deliberately spoken in the common tongue, so that her human and the others could witness and understand her public degradation. Hand still clutching her chest, she refused to answer Odi.

'Breathe,' he told her. 'I want to live through this, remember?'

Oddly, it was those words that brought a wave of calm washing over her. He was right – this was exactly what the damn Jaktaren wanted from her; she was playing directly into his hands. With a swift nod at the human, she straightened. As she did, the atmosphere changed. A cool gust of wind swept across the stands and the marshalling area, creating a shiver through the canopy of the forest.

Queen Delja had arrived, her great wings open to their full expanse as she landed gracefully on a small platform by the Council of Seven Elders. She surveyed them all, as though time stood still until she said otherwise. Her eyes scanned the competitors and their humans, before turning back to the heaving crowd. Her crowned head was held high, her back straight, even beneath the weight of her wings, now tucked neatly behind. There was no trace of the vulnerable cyren from the prison whose words had been thick with sadness. Here stood the queen of Saddoriel and beyond.

'Welcome, all.' Somehow enchanted, Queen Delja's melodic voice projected to the far reaches of the stands, where each cyren hung onto her every word. 'Some of you have come a long way to watch our competitors today. This trial is simple. A number of beasts from all over the realms have been released into the forest before us. The competitors must capture a beast for the victor's feast tonight. The more meat a competitor contributes to the feast, the better their chance at success. Each competitor must decide how and what they wish to hunt. The last four to complete the hunt, or return, or those who fail to bring back a sizeable bounty, will be eliminated. As will those whose humans are maimed or do not survive.'

Roh couldn't swallow the thick lump in her throat. Lives were at stake here, not just reputations. There was no doubt that the hunt itself wouldn't be the only challenge within the forest.

'When the hourglass turns, the competitors may enter. When the sand stops, the trial is over. Cyrens of Saddoriel, honoured guests, let us hope it is a trial worthy of your travels.'

The crowd erupted in excited chatter, the sound near

deafening, their energy pulsing across the stands and the forest. Roh could no longer hear the music playing in the background now – the intensity of the impending trial was too great. Shouldering the bulky pack at her feet and tugging Odi's sleeve, Roh followed the other competitors, backing away from the edge of the forest so they could see the hourglass above.

Her mind was racing. *No doubt the more valuable game is at the heart of the forest, while the easier catches are on the outskirts.* If she caught something early and guaranteed her safe return to the queen, she risked being eliminated by better bounties. If she passed up a smaller creature in the hopes of capturing a larger one, she would be in the forest longer. *And who knows what lurks in the shadows in there ...* But Roh was here to *win*. She would have to use all the tricks up her sleeve, but she was here. She already knew she was willing to do whatever it took.

Around her, the other competitors were being wished well by friends and family. A petite cyren in a Mid Sector army uniform threw herself at Yrsa Ward, and to Roh's surprise, the Jaktaren's expression softened as she embraced the cyren, burying her face in the crook of her neck before pulling back to kiss her firmly on the mouth.

So, she's not with Finn Haertel, then, Roh mused, tearing her eyes away from the couple's farewell as she and the others were ushered into their positions.

As they were led to their starting points, it became abundantly clear who the favourites were. Applause erupted as Estin Ruhne was shown her position. The crowd screamed, some even throwing sea blooms onto the arena floor. Estin bowed her head in gratitude, giving her fans a small wave before turning to face the trees, resting her spear against her shoulder.

The noise died down as Neith's name was called and she was shown to her spot beside Estin. Roh had to stop herself from grimacing; she was next and would receive no such reception, either. It was oddly quiet as she and Odi followed Elder Colter to their entrance. Roh held her head high. They would be cheering for her before long, she vowed. But her vows were forgotten as the arena erupted once more. She didn't have to turn back to know whom they were cheering for.

A little further along, Finn Haertel took his position alongside his human. The cheers continued as Yrsa Ward joined Roh at her point of entry. Roh couldn't help sizing her up. Yrsa was shorter than most cyrens, stockier, and as with most of their kind, it was difficult to tell how old she was. Her raven hair was cut straight at her shoulders and her white-lashed lilac eyes met Roh's as she checked the cord of her sling and the satchel of stones her human carried.

Roh tightened the straps of her pack, envying the sheer confidence it took to only bring a sling into a trial like this.

The excited murmurs of the crowd fell silent all at once and the competitors' heads snapped upwards, all eyes alert. Roh followed their gazes. *This is it. I am about to enter the first trial of the Queen's Tournament. This is what I've been waiting for.* Her heart pounded wildly in her chest. Above the canopy, the hourglass turned.

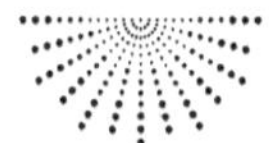

CHAPTER NINE

When the first grain of sand hit the bottom of the hourglass, the crowd erupted. Roh surged forward, rushing past the outer trees of the forest's edge, only glancing briefly behind to make sure Odi was at her heels. The trees became dense immediately, the branches tugging at her clothes and scratching at her exposed skin. Either side of her, she heard the other competitors thrashing through the undergrowth, all too aware of their proximity. How long until the sabotage began? How long until the hunters became the hunted? She needed to put as much distance between them as possible.

But Roh had to slow her pace as the forest swallowed them, and she and Odi began weaving through the thin trunks and rows of enchanted kelp that reached well above their heads. Eerily, the plants fluttered as they did when they were underwater, as though they had been bewitched to believe they still were. If there had been time, Roh would have stopped to explore the exquisite place, but the glowing hourglass hovering overhead was a stark reminder that there was not a minute to spare. Odi crept along beside her, ducking under low-hanging branches and scanning their surroundings, his jaw clenched and his amber eyes alert.

'You have your token?' Roh checked again, her own skin prickling as the magic of the forest settled around them.

The human patted his chest, where beneath the laces of his shirt, the shell token rested against his sternum.

'Good. Keep it safe,' she told him, her eyes on Yrsa, whom she could still see through the trees to their left. Roh and Odi remained within sling range, but Yrsa didn't so much as glance in their direction, and soon she turned, she and her human disappearing behind a towering column of red coral. Around them, the other competitors were doing the same – peeling away from the group to find their own paths through the strange, uneven forest. While Roh had no love for her fellow competitors, her intuition screamed that they were safer in numbers, that there was something inherently eerie about this forest. The quiet groan of the trees and the rustling of leaves made the hair on the back of her neck stand up. She fought the irrational impulse to break into a run and reached within for her inner compass. It had never failed to guide her through the winding passageways of Saddoriel, and this forest would be no different. She could trust in that at least.

She stopped short. The cyren instinct that usually

served her so well was quiet within. There was no pull or hint in any direction. She dug deeper inside herself, searching wildly.

Odi stopped, brow furrowed in concern. 'What is it?'

Roh rubbed the bridge of her nose, staring through the trees ahead. 'I … I don't know which way.'

'There is no *one way*,' he said bluntly. 'It's a forest.'

The stupid human knew nothing of cyrens.

The hum of the crowd had long ago faded, as had the music, but the forest had its own rhythm. A nearby bush rustled, leaves falling from its branches. It was enough to wrench Roh from her concerns and force her onward. It wasn't until they were well away from the bush that she realised she should have checked to see if it had been an animal.

Fool, she chastised herself; she wasn't thinking clearly. She and Odi stayed close, their shoulders brushing as they inched deeper into the forest, leaf litter sliding beneath their boots, the terrain becoming rugged and uneven. Glancing up at the hourglass, which glowed through the canopy for all to see, Roh tried to tame the sense of urgency that thrummed desperately within her. There were two parts to the strategy she had come up with, but in order to put either in place, she and Odi needed to be at the heart of the forest, where all manner of beast, cyren and human would prowl, so she pushed them on, quickening their pace.

When they stumbled upon the first glade, Roh couldn't contain her gasp. Across the damp forest floor sprouted dense hubs of glowing coral. The plants reached her hip and pulsed in an array of bright colours. She had never seen flora like it. Her skin prickled and she resisted the impulse to touch it, just. She smacked Odi's hand away as he attempted to do exactly that. 'Who knows what dangers these hold,' she said.

It was clear Odi had barely registered her words, he was so mesmerised. 'What is this place?' he breathed.

Checking that her human's token was indeed safely fastened around his neck, Roh scanned the coral warily. 'I thought it was a regular water forest, one of many used to circulate air throughout our lair, but ...' She sniffed the air, and when the cool, briny scent hit her nostrils, she couldn't believe she hadn't noticed it before. 'We're close to the sea,' she said, more to herself than to Odi. 'Which means the warlock magic used to create this forest is also drawing power from the currents. That's why there is flora from both the land and seabed.'

'I thought you said there were no more water warlocks?'

'There aren't.'

'Then how can you use their magic?'

She sidestepped the hubs of coral and beckoned to Odi to follow. 'Some of their magic remains behind ... I don't know how exactly. Cyrens can still use their healing potions, and the original enchantments of the lair still stand.' She nodded to his talisman. 'Then there's token magic, but it's nothing like it was before.'

Across the glade were shoulder-height trees, the thin branches spread out like a lace fan, intricate and beautiful, glowing a light rose-pink hue.

I wonder how long this has all been here, Roh thought, feeling dazed. She stood rooted to the spot, staring at the colours, trying to find a clue as to where the portal to the sea was hidden. Any sense of urgency within her was quelled, as though a soothing balm had been applied. The hairs on her arms stood up.

'We're falling for its trap,' she murmured, feeling the glow of the trees on her skin.

'What?' Odi asked, equally disoriented.

'This obstacle belongs to the council,' she said, wrenching herself from the trance. Purpose suddenly surging through her, Roh pulled the pack higher onto her back. 'Follow me,' she said, taking comfort in the sturdy boots at her feet and leading them on from the glowing trees. When they were once again amongst the dense boles of the trees, Roh looked up to the canopy. Through the leaves she could see the hourglass, its sand spilling slowly into its lower half.

'Can you tell how much longer?' she asked Odi, as the dream-like feeling ebbed away.

The human squinted at the hourglass. 'At the rate the sand's falling … Two hours? Maybe three?'

'That's it?'

'I can't know for sure, but no more than that, I'd say.'

'Gods,' Roh muttered.

'I'm not sure they'll be much help here,' Odi said darkly. 'We haven't seen a single animal. We're not even close to catching one. We're dead, Roh.'

Gritting her teeth, Roh grabbed his arm, letting her talons slide out slightly to press against his skin. 'Pull yourself together,' she hissed. 'You and I are in this now, like it or not.'

'*Not.* I *don't* like it at all.'

Roh felt her nostrils flare and her talons unsheathed a touch more. 'You don't have to like it. You just have to survive it.' She released his arm, and ignoring his stunned expression, started off again. They moved quickly through the forest, with Roh making fast decisions despite the ache of her missing inner compass. She followed the scent of salt in the air – turning whenever it became stronger. There was no music here, but the forest seemed to sing its own song, the limbs of the trees swaying to a rhythm inaudible to Roh and Odi.

She paused, swinging the pack around to her front. 'We start here.'

Odi turned back to her, frowning. 'Start what?'

'I'm a bone cleaner,' she said, 'not a hunter.'

'Well, that's awfully reassuring.' Odi crossed his arms over his chest, resting his half-gloved fingers in the crooks of his elbows.

'What I mean is that my hunting skills, and yours, I might add, won't be enough. So we need something else, too, a contingency plan.' She retrieved a satchel from the pack, and from within it carefully removed a bracelet. It was a dainty thing: a silver chain with charms dangling from its links. 'Remember this?' she asked, holding it up for Odi.

He took it from her. 'Yes,' he said through clenched teeth. It was one of several items she'd instructed him, against his wishes, to steal from the other humans the day before. Roh had shown him several sleight-of-hand manoeuvres she'd learned over the years and had been pleased to find Odi a natural. In the dining hall, in the pulley system, she'd encouraged him to relieve his fellow humans of their stupidly shiny sentimental trinkets. Odi's objections had mattered little to Roh.

Now, she tugged on a pair of thick leather gloves, before carefully searching another pocket in the pack. Very delicately, she took out a rag and a small vial containing a diluted extract of the coral larkspur from Odi's gala wine. Wetting the rag with several drops of the liquid, Roh took the bracelet from Odi and rubbed the rag all over it, careful not to let the soiled material anywhere near her skin. One wrong move would be all it took. She placed the jewellery deliberately on the ground in plain sight; it glinted in the thin beams of light shining down.

'That's not for an animal,' Odi murmured.

'No, it's not.' She'd known for some time that she'd have to do things like this, that she *would* do things like this, if called for. For as long as she could remember, this tournament – this victory – had been everything.

A rustle sounded. Tiny feet scurried across the leaf litter and the companions froze, listening. It sounded again, and Roh shook her head at Odi's excited expression. 'Whatever it is, it's too small,' she said, tugging his arm.

'Better small than nothing,' Odi said, his eyes betraying that he doubted her decisions and sense of direction.

With a scowl to rival Harlyn's, Roh didn't reply. He was wrong. If they caught a creature that was too small, it would be the same as catching nothing, and she had no intention of leaving the tournament early. She pushed on, following the briny air and the cold and damp. The Lower Sector of Saddoriel had been a lifelong lesson in what the deep and dark felt like. She would get them to the heart of the forest.

As they walked, something ahead caught her eye and she squinted. Something was lying on the ground. Roh approached with trepidation, her boots sinking into what had become mud beneath her. It was a quiver of arrows – the very same that had been strapped to Finn's back earlier. Half the arrows were scattered in the dirt, dry leaves caught in the fletching. A smile broke across Roh's face. *So, the arrogant bastard isn't faring as well as he thought he would.* This filled her with glee. She reached down to pick up the quiver —

A strange whistling noise sounded. A jagged dagger-sized piece of coral came shooting through the air towards her like an arrow. Her cheek stung as she was wrenched roughly from its path. She staggered into Odi's arms, heart pounding as she touched her fingers to her cheek. They came away bloody.

'What in the …?' she panted, straightening and looking from the blood on her fingertips to Odi. 'How did you know?'

He pointed to the ground, where a trip wire was revealed. 'I saw it a second too late.'

Roh's armpits were damp with sweat as she examined

the almost-deadly piece of coral that now swung uselessly on a cord before them and the discarded quiver of arrows.

'That Haertel bastard,' she spat as the blood trickled down her face. She tore a strip of fabric from her shirt and dabbed at it, amazed at the violent red against the white linen. For a moment, she pictured how her face might have looked had Odi not pulled her out of the way … In the place of a thin cut, there would have been a bloody pulp. She cursed Finn, but it was really herself she was furious at. She'd let her guard slip, and amidst her own desire to win, she'd forgotten whom she was dealing with. And now she owed her life, or at least her face, to the human beside her. That stopped *now*. She couldn't bring herself to thank Odi. Instead, she swung the pack from her shoulder once more and crouched, digging deep to find what she'd requested from Orson and Harlyn.

'He won't be far from here,' she said, weighing the bulky pouch in her palm. Her friends had done an excellent job. It was exactly what she had asked of them; the pieces within were sharp enough to poke through the fabric, jabbing at her skin. They had swept the workshop floor at her request, but had also sifted through their findings, selecting only the sharpest, strongest splinters of bone. Roh had then painted them with a sticky substance that hardened when dry, ensuring that the pieces could pierce the sturdiest of boots, even those of the Jaktaren.

'What are you doing? You don't mean to go after him?'

Roh got to her feet and tore another strip from her

shirt, smeared it with more blood from her cheek and dropped it on the ground. 'Of course. You saw what he did.'

'Roh, we've got a beast to catch, remember?'

She smiled at that. 'We do indeed. Follow me.' She dug her boots into the muddy ground, dragging them to create deep, noticeable tracks, and pushed her way through a nearby veil of kelp, ensuring that it remained slightly parted. There was no way Finn Haertel could resist returning to see the damage he'd inflicted. She was determined to use that against him.

Resigned, Odi followed her, asking no questions as she dropped another piece of blood-spotted fabric, the white and red of it a stark contrast against the leaf litter. Finn wouldn't miss it. A few steps on, she paused, tipping some of the bone splinters from the pouch into her hand. She was careful to keep her palm as flat as possible, so the jagged pieces didn't pierce her skin. Crouching, she pushed aside some of the leaf litter, scattering the bone fragments across the dirt, ensuring that their sharpest edges faced upwards. Then, she scooped up the loose leaves and sprinkled them on top, covering the gleam of ivory.

Odi bent down beside her, frowning at what she had done.

'What is it?' she snapped, preparing for the onslaught of objections. Odi, she was learning, was a generally quiet human, but when he had something to say, he said it loudly and it was usually to do with morals. He seemed to have a lot of those.

'You missed a spot,' he said, grabbing a handful of leaves and covering up a patch.

'Oh.' Roh brushed the dirt from her hands and got to her feet. She peered at the hourglass; she could only guess at the time they had left, and it wasn't much.

'What now?' Odi asked, standing beside her, wiping his hands on his pants.

'Now, we hunt,' Roh said.

She followed the salt in the air. The trees were denser here, and Roh and Odi were forced to weave through them sideways. Roh's legs burned as the terrain steepened and she led them up a rise. The ground was damp enough that it sank upon weight and scattered leaf litter was a telltale sign that something had been there before.

'Look for tracks,' she softly told Odi. They were careful not to disturb too much of the foliage around them and they treaded carefully, keeping quiet. As they went, Roh continued to place human belongings in plain sight, after she had dropped tiny doses of diluted larkspur all over them. Odi said nothing of these traps, despite the fact that they all targeted his kind, not hers. Perhaps he understood it was where the weak link lay.

Roh's shoulders were tight with tension as they pressed on through the undergrowth, her eyes scanning the forest floor for any sign of cyren or beast. She was staring so hard she almost missed them – markings in the earth: a pair of three scratches, claw marks, if she wasn't mistaken. *So, there* are *beasts in here, after all.*

'Looks like a bird,' Odi whispered, crouching by the tracks. 'It's bigger than a sparrow, that's for sure.'

'Good.' Roh moved to the next set of claw marks, and the next —

Odi grabbed Roh's arm as a klyree darted across the undergrowth before them in a flash of brown-and-white fur. It sprang from its hind legs, scattering leaves everywhere as it made another dash —

A sickening crunch sounded as a stone shot from behind the trees, cracking the creature's skull. Its limp body skidded to a halt in the dirt and Yrsa Ward emerged from the trees, sling in hand. She didn't give Roh and Odi a second glance as she stalked across the forest, picking up the dead klyree by its horns and slinging it over her shoulder. Her human, who had been waiting for her in the shadows, ducked out of sight, as did Yrsa. One moment they'd been there, the next Roh and Odi were alone again. The only evidence that it had happened at all was the smear of blood in the leaves.

'She's content with a small beast,' Odi pointed out.

'Well, we're not,' Roh said as she tried to shake the experience and relocate the bird tracks. 'A bigger beast guarantees our place in the tournament.' The sound of running water distracted her. 'Can you hear that?' she whispered.

Odi stilled and listened, nodding. 'There must be a stream nearby.'

'That could work. There might be fish,' Roh muttered, trying to follow the noise. But the babble of water drew closer and closer, faster than Roh was moving. She signalled to Odi to stop and he did as she bid, eyes wide. Something strange was afoot here. Roh surveyed the forest, the sound so close now it was nearly upon them.

'Roh,' Odi murmured, a single finger pointing to something emerging from the trees.

Roh spotted a slender silvery-blue leg extending, a hoof pawing the ground, droplets of water spraying outwards. Roh's hand went to her mouth as she stared at the backahast – a water horse hailing from the cyren territory of Lochloria. The creature was majestic, its muscular form made up of water that seemed to flow with its movements. Roh had only ever seen a backahast once before, when she was just a nestling. The backahast were no threat to cyrens. Both creatures shared a deep respect for water and ancient magic, but … When the backahast neighed, it was not looking at Roh. Its hoof stomped the ground again, body tense as it tossed its head, once more sending water flying.

'Roh?'

At the sound of the quaver in Odi's voice, the backahast charged.

'Odi!' Roh yelled, but he was no match for the powerful creature.

At a gallop, the backahast reached him in seconds, wrapping its form around him, encasing him, filling his lungs with water. Odi's shouts were drowned out, his limbs a blurry flurry of struggle within the whirlpool the backahast had created.

Roh rushed to him, diving into the cold chaos of water. Her hands found Odi and shoved him from the backahast's snare, taking his place. Odi's coughing and spluttering was distant as the roar of water consumed Roh. The water glided along her skin and down her throat, but the creature could do her no harm. She could breathe in the deepest part of the sea, and the hold of a backahast was no different, so it released her.

With a final flick of its tail and a frustrated whinny, the water horse retreated into the forest.

Odi was on all fours, coughing up water into the dirt. His hair was plastered to his head and his clothes, like Roh's, were completely soaked through.

Roh thumped him on the back as he spluttered. 'Are you alright?'

'*I nearly drowned,*' he croaked.

'True,' Roh allowed, wringing out her hair. 'But you didn't.'

Mid-scoff, Odi choked some more. 'What was that?' he managed.

'A backahast. Another challenge placed in here by the council.' She hauled Odi to his feet. 'We have to keep moving,' she said. 'This way.' She led them through the trees once more, ignoring the wet squelch of her boots and the slap of her drenched clothing. Silently, she tried to calculate how much time they might have left. They needed to get to the heart of the forest, and fast.

Eventually, they arrived at a clearing and Roh breathed a sigh of relief. Here, there was not just one set of tracks, but many – it seemed to be a crossroads, an animal thoroughfare.

'This is perfect.' She dropped the pack.

'Perfect for what?'

'You'll see. Here,' she said, using a talon to draw a circle in the dirt before passing the pack back to him. 'Dig a hole here.'

She had designed the contraption last night, sketched it in charcoal on the back of the trial instructions. It was just like designing anything, really, though regrettably, she hadn't had the time to make a working model. She left a shivering Odi to his task and set about starting on hers. She gathered a bundle of sticks from the forest floor and laid a number of them flat on the ground, assessing their lengths and fanning them out in a circular shape. Using the ball of twine she'd packed, she bound them together, creating a sturdy wheel.

'What is that?' Odi looked up, his hands muddy.

'You're not going fast enough,' was Roh's reply. She placed her wheel carefully on the ground and rushed over to him, unsheathing her talons and digging them deep into the damp earth. She lost herself in the rhythm, pummelling the dirt, her head down, perspiration stinging her eyes and the cut on her cheek.

'This is deep enough,' she told Odi, when the lip of the trench met her armpit. 'Now …' She set about fitting the wheel she'd made over the hole perfectly. Feeling grounded by the practicality of her task, Roh removed her boot and used it to hammer a stick into the ground before the trench and wheel. She used another to rest the wheel open on an angle before the hole, the new stick bridging the gap between the wheel and the pole she'd hammered in place.

Roh's fingers shook as she tied a piece of twine to

another stick. She crafted the rest of the trap as swiftly as she could, all too aware of Odi's stare bearing down on the back of her head. She used smaller sticks to create a false floor across the trench and placed half an apple she'd brought carefully on top.

'Roh?' Odi was fidgeting yet again.

'What now?'

He grimaced. 'I need to …'

'Need to what? For Thera's sake, spit it out.'

'I need to see to my needs,' he said awkwardly.

Roh huffed in irritation. 'Do you *see* a bathing chamber anywhere? Make do by the foliage over there. Be quick about it. You're lucky you're a man.'

His cheeks tipped with pink, Odi stumbled into the forest, fumbling with the ties of his pants and disappearing from her view. Shaking her head, Roh turned away, trying to ignore the quiet splashing she could now hear.

A scream pierced the air, wild and blood-curdling. The hairs on Roh's arm stood up.

'Odi!' Roh ran to him, heart hammering, but her human was safe. He was peering through a split in the kelp.

'Gods,' he gasped.

'What is it?' Roh pushed him aside so she could see herself. And wished she hadn't. Deep in the ground, someone had laid a trap, not entirely unlike Roh's, and a human man had fallen victim to it. The man, writhing in agony, was impaled on several stakes, which had been positioned upright in the trench. Blood flowed from his wounds, and pieces of flesh dangled from the tops of the stakes where they'd gone through him. He was the human belonging to the kitchen hand, Ferron.

'We have to help him,' Odi said.

Roh turned to him, incredulous. 'Are you mad?'

'No! Look at him, he needs —'

'A swift death is what he needs, and even that I'm not willing to give. Do you know what other traps could be lying around him? I will not risk us —'

The sudden caw of a bird cut Roh off and she froze, the dying human forgotten.

'Roh, we can't —'

A rush of wind swept past them, practically knocking Roh and Odi to the ground. A giant bird on long legs raced past. Roh gaped. She had never seen anything like it. From the blurred glimpse, she'd seen a long neck and muscular body on tall legs. A sizeable beast.

The ground vibrated beneath her boots and seconds later, she saw why. An enormous boar came charging down the path after the bird. Heart in her throat, Roh shoved Odi and herself back against the trees, moving just in time as the beast smashed through the foliage.

'Come on.' Roh yanked at Odi's arm. 'We're finally in luck.'

But Odi's face was pale. 'We can't just leave the man there! He's still moving.'

'He won't be much longer,' Roh said coldly, without releasing him. 'I *will not* give up my place in this tournament trying to save a dying human.'

'Roh —'

'This is not a debate.' She gripped his arm tighter, dragging him after her. Roh could tell from his weak struggles that his attempts were half-hearted. He knew it was no use, he just didn't want to be the one to say it. She'd take that burden without question, if it meant she had a chance in this trial. Silently, she followed the broken foliage. If they could capture the boar, things would look very different for them. The boar's tracks were easy enough to follow – they went deep into the mud, and anything in its path was demolished.

Odi pointed out a line drawn in the dirt. 'Someone hoping to find their way out?' he asked.

Roh shrugged and took a stick from the ground, but Odi offered his hand and slowly she gave him the stick. He went to the line and drew another forking off from it, leading elsewhere. And another, disappearing into the kelp.

Roh gave him a grim smile. 'You're starting to understand, are you?'

'I wish I wasn't,' he muttered, handing back the stick as they continued after the boar's tracks, which led them to the trap they'd set up. It was undisturbed.

'I should go back to the —'

'We do *not* separate,' Roh told him firmly.

Something nearby rustled and Roh pressed a single finger to her lips. He nodded slowly. They watched as the wild boar emerged from the foliage, sniffing determinedly. Roh's heart began to rise from the roiling pit in her stomach, hope filling her. The beast edged towards her trap, grunting and snorting into the ground, smelling its way to the apple bait. He was nearly there … Just a few more steps —

An arrow shot through the boar's eye with a bloody splat. Roh clapped a hand over her mouth hard to stop herself from crying out. Finn Haertel limped out from a hiding spot further down the path, gripping his crossbow, his right foot tied with bandages stained red. Seething, Roh watched the highborn approach the boar, his human close behind, holding his keeper's boot, pincushions to the shards of ivory sticking out. Together, cyren and man strung the beast up between them on a spear. Finn swore loudly as he staggered under its weight on his injured foot.

He found the bone splinters at least. There was small satisfaction in that.

But as Roh watched Finn and her prize disappear off into the labyrinth, panic set in. She and Odi had nothing, *nothing* to show for their efforts except the cut on her cheek. Their time was waning fast. She closed her eyes and took a moment.

Something buzzed by her ear and she froze. Her eyes flew open to see a nucrite, a tiny winged insect, fluttering near Odi's shoulder. He went to bat it away carelessly and she shot towards him, clamping one hand over his mouth and using the other to pin his arms at his sides. He was tense in her hold, his breath hot on her palm, but she didn't release him. She watched the nucrite, her mind racing with how she could create a flame to distract it, for where there was one, there was usually a swarm. Her heart hammered against Odi's back, but she refused to move, for fear of disturbing the dry leaf litter at her feet. All it would take was one small sound and a swarm would be upon them.

A moment passed. Then two … And the nucrite fluttered away.

A cry of relief nearly escaped Roh as she released her arms to her sides.

Odi turned to her, brow furrowed. 'It was just a moth,' he said.

Roh laughed darkly. 'Until it called all its friends to eat the flesh from your bones.'

Odi's face paled at that.

'Another gift from the council, no doubt,' she mused. 'It's gone now —'

A scurry amongst the undergrowth cut her off.

'Don't move,' she ordered Odi.

A bird, similar to the one that had darted past them earlier, appeared. It was smaller, perhaps the previous creature's offspring, but still sizeable enough.

Roh swallowed. This was their chance. It *had to be*. She watched intently as the bird scuttled towards her trap, spotting the apple sitting on the false floor beneath the wheel. It stalked towards it, suspicious, its movements skittish and unpredictable. Its long neck extended, reaching for the bait, pecking at the apple flesh but not quite on the false floor … It was so close …

One claw stepped forward and a screech sounded. The wheel came crashing down on the bird's head and Roh and Odi leaped towards it. Their prize was half stuck beneath the wheel, its legs and much of its torso hanging outside the trap as it flapped wildly and screeched loudly.

'It's going to escape,' Odi shouted, trying to push the rest of the bird's body into the trench.

'Hold the wheel down, just wait,' Roh told him, putting a foot on top of the wheel as the bird thrashed within. Its head came through the spokes and attacked her boots with furious pecking.

'What now?' Odi said, his hair damp with sweat.

'Wait.'

'But, Roh —'

'*Wait.*'

For once, Odi did as she told him and the only sound was the panicked flapping of the bird's wings and its desperate cries. Gradually, its movement slowed and its squawks became less frantic and then quiet. Finally, it slumped in the dirt, lying lifeless in the trap.

Slowly, Odi removed the wheel atop the trench, his mouth agape. 'What happened to it? How …?'

Roh picked up the apple. 'I spiked it with some of your wine from the gala. The poor beast has had a very heavy dose of coral larkspur.' She tossed the apple aside and pulled the limp animal from the trap. It was heavier than she expected, which was a good thing, given their goal. Odi took it from her and slung it over his shoulder. Roh adjusted the rucksack on her back as a flicker of movement above caught her eye.

The hourglass. Down to its final grains.

'Odi,' she croaked. '*Run!*' She didn't wait a second longer, staggering into a panicked sprint.

Odi raced beside her, the unconscious bird bouncing awkwardly on his shoulder.

They ran, weaving through the trees, darting across clearings and ducking through hubs of coral and kelp. Somewhere in the distance, something chimed. Panting raggedly, Roh looked up just in time to see the final grain of sand fall in the hourglass.

The forest flattened.

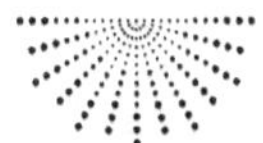

CHAPTER TEN

The entire forest had vanished, leaving Roh, Odi and the other competitors exposed and vulnerable in the open. Everything the forest had contained – coral, kelp, backahast, nucrites, and the rises and falls in terrain – was all gone. There was nothing but flat space. Roh found herself stepping closer to Odi, scanning the sudden change in scenery wildly. *What now?*

The hovering hourglass floated to the ground, landing with a soft thud. Was that a water-warlock enchantment, too? Her hand flew to her mouth, stifling a strangled gasp. For behind where the forest had stood was a filmy veil, a shifting, transparent wall, and turquoise waters shimmered against it as it held back the sea. A portal. She heard Odi's intake of breath beside her as he also saw it. She'd been right, the sea *had* been near, and upon seeing it, she could smell the salt all the more strongly and hear the rhythm of the current. It called to her in the way the music of the lair did, as it did to all cyrens. How long had it been since she had felt the kiss of the tide against her skin? As a nestling, she had heard ancient stories, going back thousands of years, of when all cyrens had had wings, when they had roamed the seas and lands above with little care. What had happened that tethered all cyrens to their lairs?

The hair on her arms prickled and Roh wrenched herself from the song of the current. She had forgotten where she was, but the increasing hum of the crowd forced her to turn back to where judgement awaited them. Her stomach churned as she surveyed the tiered seating of the stands, which seemed fuller, thousands of unfamiliar faces watching her and the others, a mix of lilac eyes full of anticipation. All around Roh, the competitors were gathering themselves, wrenched from the height of the hunt and the enclosed forest to this starkly open space. Applause broke out as Finn Haertel, his face contorted in pain, began to limp towards the podium, his boar on a spear held up by himself and his human. Roh eyed the bloodied bandages on Finn's foot. Her hand went to the dried blood itching her cheek. A shredded foot for a cut face … Perhaps it had been a fair exchange.

There was no sign of the human Odi had found impaled on the stakes, nor his master, the kitchen hand, Ferron. They spotted Darden Crezat following close behind Finn; though he was covered in blood, he was seemingly uninjured. But behind him, he dragged his unconscious human across the ground by his shirt. The crowd gasped in unison from the stands. The human's arm was missing, the joint at his shoulder no more than a bloody pulp.

Roh's throat went dry.

'Did *you* do that?' Odi whispered to her.

'*What?* Are you mad?' she hissed back, watching assistants come forward to take the maimed human, his sandals dragging behind him in the dirt. Roh couldn't look away, not until the poor man was out of sight.

She could feel Odi shaking beside her. 'The bracelet … The things we stole as bait, and the poison from my wine.'

Roh started towards the marshalling area, all too aware of the competitors doing the same around her and the crowd's eyes on her. 'Coral larkspur doesn't do that,' she said, teeth clenched.

'You said it can cause *death*.'

'*In large doses*. The few drops I rubbed on those possessions was *nothing*.'

'Well, what does it do, then?' Odi walked beside her, the limp bird still slung over his arm.

'Funny, you weren't asking questions in the forest, were you?'

'*What does it do?*' he pressed.

Roh looked around and pointed. 'That.'

Odi followed the line of her finger to the podium in the marshalling area, where the highborn Savalise Vinnet was waving her hands frantically as she argued heatedly with Elder Winslow Ward. She motioned flippantly to her human, who was slumped at her feet, disoriented, covered in a nasty rash.

'She's alive, is she not?' Savalise said loudly. 'Therefore I have done my duty. I have fulfilled the obligations of the tournament rules.' Savalise's catch, a sizeable fish, hung dead at her belt.

But Elder Ward's gaze was locked on the human, who gave a moan of pain.

'Your duty was to keep your human unharmed and whole. She is not fit for anything. You are eliminated from the tournament.'

'No. She is fine. She —'

Elder Ward was already walking away, completely disinterested in Savalise's pleas as commotion sounded and the bleat of a terrified animal echoed throughout the cavernous space. The army leader, Miriald Montalle, caught up with the rest, wrangling a live deer with a length of rope.

Another cheer sounded from the crowd as Yrsa reached the podium. Roh's brows shot up in surprise. A rope hung between Yrsa and her young human, sporting an array of smaller game: numerous klyree, fish and strange small birds.

So this is how it will be determined, Roh realised. *By weight, not size ...*

'Clever,' she murmured, glancing back at Yrsa and her game as the attendants transported it into a tent that had been erected by the stands. Feeling uneasy, Roh continued to size up her competitors and their prizes. Neith had a single klyree, Zokez's human carried a goat of sorts, while Estin and Arcelia both had small geese. Roh spotted the other lowborn competitor, Lillas. Both she and her human were dazed, their faces and arms covered in a savage rash that seemed to spread before her eyes. They would not be making it to the next trial.

Roh swallowed. While she had not permanently harmed anyone, she may as well have signed a death sentence for the humans. They would be turned out into the passageways of Saddoriel and left to face the lure of the lair. A slower, crueller death, perhaps. She knew of no tale where humankind survived Talon's Reach alone.

More attendants appeared at the competitors' sides to collect their prizes, bringing them to a giant set of scales inside the tent. A female cyren took the bird from Odi, its strange feathers ruffling against her shoulder as she walked away.

Neither the competitors nor the crowd could determine anything from this process, with the scales and prizes hidden from view, no doubt to protect the sensitive sensibilities of highborns who were perhaps not used to seeing their meals in this form. It took forever, or so it seemed to Roh, whose stomach was churning more uncomfortably with each passing moment. She needed to know, had they done enough to keep their place in the tournament? Her scattered mind took her through a series of unpleasant what-ifs: What if they hadn't made it? What if she had to return to the bone-cleaning workshop a failure? What if she had betrayed Harlyn and Orson for nothing? What if one of them had competed rather than her? Would they have been better? Would they have —

The crowd was buzzing with excitement once more and Roh turned, realising why. Bloodwyn Haertel had taken to the podium, a roll of parchment in her hand and her hard gaze surveying the competitors, then the cyrens in the stands.

'A valiant effort from our competitors,' Elder Haertel said, making a show of looking at each of the battle-worn cyrens below her. 'Your methods were, for the most part … inspired.'

With her talons extended, Elder Haertel unfurled the parchment and scanned its contents.

'The victor of this trial,' she said slowly, fuelling the hunger of the crowd with her deliberate pause, 'is Yrsa Ward. Ward's catch tallied to the most weight, and she has provided an extensive bounty for tonight's feast. Congratulations, Yrsa.'

The applause that followed was thunderous. Roh felt the ground beneath her boots tremble. She looked to the stands, where thousands of lilac eyes were filled with awe. Cyrens called Yrsa's name, and some threw flowers at her feet. To Roh's right, Yrsa Ward took to the podium and bowed gracefully, her gaze falling upon her uniformed partner at the forefront of the crowd.

The elder inclined her head to the highborn before returning to the parchment. 'Miriald Montalle's deer was next, followed by Finn Haertel's boar.'

More cheering erupted, echoing in Roh's ears long after it had faded.

'Alas, in order to have victors we must also have losers …'

Roh focused on her breathing. A steady inhale through her nose, then a quiet, slow exhale through her mouth.

'Eliminated from the tournament are: Ferron and Lillas from the Lower Sector, Darden Crezat from the Mid Sector and Savalise Vinnet from the —'

'Elder Haertel,' Savalise ventured, her voice honeyed. 'I'd like to challenge —'

Bloodwyn Haertel's gaze was steely and unblinking. 'You failed,' she said, her words cutting clean through the objection like a hot blade. 'Your human was to remain unharmed throughout the tournament.'

'But —'

A subtle arch of one brow was all it took to silence the highborn. There would be no more protests. Visibly swallowing her fear, Savalise bowed her head and backed away from the steps of the podium. The debate, if one could call it that, was over.

But that didn't matter to Roh. Nothing did other than one single fact.

'We made it,' she whispered. 'We … we made it.' She saw Odi's whole body sag with relief. She could sympathise with that; she too felt relief, but it meant so much more than that to her. Turning her eyes to the crowd, Roh searched for the two familiar faces she knew would ground her. Harlyn and Orson would be there, no doubt jumping up and down, hysterical with joy at her small victory. Roh had done what she had to, to get through the trial and it had paid off. She was one step closer to the coral crown and now she wanted to revel in that feeling, just for a moment, to celebrate the achievement with those who knew her best. But it was Ames' eyes that latched onto her and stared back. From the lower tier of the stands, her mentor's expression was unreadable.

Is he disappointed I didn't win outright? Is he proud I made it to the next round? Ames gave nothing away.

Elder Haertel had stepped down from the podium and was now addressing the remaining competitors. 'Tonight at the twentieth hour, the feast will be held for the victors in the Queen's Conservatory,' she was saying. 'Until then, you are encouraged to return to your chambers and use the time to see to any ... injuries.' She said the last word with a pointed look at Finn Haertel's bandaged foot. Was that disappointment in her eyes?

'Dismissed.'

When Roh looked up to find Ames again, he had disappeared as the spectators dissipated, breaking from the stands and into the marshalling area, spilling like a river through floodgates. Roh was jostled roughly and she grabbed hold of Odi. She wasn't going to let him out of her sight amongst all of this. She pulled him by the wrist through the throngs. Cyrens were clambering to get to the victor and runners-up; Roh was invisible to them, and for once she was grateful for that fact. She found a quiet spot on the edge of the stands, waiting for the excitement to die down.

Odi slumped against the stone column behind him,

letting his head fall back and rest there, eyes closed. Roh knew the feeling, yet she wouldn't let her guard down, not here amidst all these vipers. One last time, she craned her neck, trying to find Harlyn and Orson, but the stands had emptied. Only a few stragglers remained, none of whom Roh recognised, and without the presence of the highborn victors, the lingering spectators' curiosity turned to Roh and Odi.

She pulled at Odi's shirt. 'Time to go.'

Roh stared at the clothes that had been laid out for her on the bed. Loose-fitting linen pants and a lace-trimmed camisole, with a colourful silken robe to be layered on top. A new jewelled belt to cinch the whole outfit together lay next to the luxurious fabrics. Roh glanced back to her own clothes in a pile at the foot of her bed – her muddy boots, dirt-spattered pants and the droplets of blood on her once-white shirt. The highborn fashions taunted her. As did the scabbed cut on her cheek. It ran through her old scar, creating a zigzag of disfigurement across her face.

She got dressed while Odi was in the bathing chambers, willing herself to relax now they were in the safety of their rooms. But she couldn't shake the events of the day from her mind: the jagged coral swinging at her face, the human impaled on the sticks, the man whose arm had been maimed ... After all that, they were expected to dine opposite each other? It was some sort of sick joke. Not even the thought of Finn Haertel's cut-up foot could salvage her mood. She felt restless, an uneasy churning still roiling in her gut.

At last, Odi emerged from the bathing chamber, hair dripping, a towel slung across his hips. Roh averted her gaze. 'You didn't want to change in the bathing room?'

'I left my clothes out here.'

She didn't reply; instead, she busied herself cinching the jewelled belt around her waist. She willed herself not to blush. It seemed incredibly intimate, not to mention unnecessary, to have a shirtless human wandering around her sleeping quarters, piquing her curiosity. She couldn't remember the last time she'd seen one of the male cyrens without a shirt on; she had been in all-female quarters for years now. While Odi was a little on the scrawny side, his frame was corded with lean muscle. The job he did in the human world was clearly a physical one.

To Roh's relief, Odi scooped up his clean clothes from the bed and returned to the bathing chamber. While she waited, Roh wiped the mud from her boots and tugged them on, deciding that no matter what luxurious dresses or pants they put her in, she would stay grounded in her own shoes. And she was going to need some semblance of normality tonight. It was one thing to stand around at a gala with her fellow competitors, but to attend a formal sit-down dinner was another. She would be forced to make conversation with them ... and what could she possibly have to say? Would they even be speaking New Saddorien? Or would she have to endure an evening of private conversations held in front of her in the old language she didn't understand? The anxiety was already building up within her, making her chest tight and her mind race.

Odi emerged once more, in fresh, stiff clothes. She didn't say anything as he pulled on his fingerless gloves and boots. Perhaps he needed something to ground him, too.

At last, Odi straightened, amber eyes bright. 'Ready?' he asked.

Roh lifted her chin. 'Always.'

The Queen's Conservatory was nothing short of spectacular. The giant rectangular room had been transformed into an opulent formal dining hall. Two long tables ran parallel down the length of it, adorned with silver plates, cutlery and goblets, as well as jewelled candelabras and embroidered serviettes. Each high-backed chair was cushioned with rich, colourful velvet, and large, shiny cloches ran down the centre of each table, glinting in the flickering chandelier light. The windows and doors to the surrounding private gardens were open, and the sweet fragrance from the vibrant blooms wafted in, mixing with the mouth-watering aromas of the roast game.

'This is certainly different to the lair I stumbled into,' Odi said.

'And to the Lower Sector I was born in,' Roh murmured, tilting her head back as the music began.

At the front of the room, atop a small carpeted dais, was a human musician, seated on a small stool, with a large hourglass-shaped instrument placed between her legs. As the woman drew her bow across the strings, Roh let the melody wash over her. It played to a piece of her soul she kept locked away within her.

To her great annoyance, Odi nudged her gently and she opened her eyes. The room was filling with competitors and highborns.

Of course the nobility are here, Roh mused. She reluctantly moved towards the tables, spotting the place cards that had been positioned on the glittering dinnerware. It didn't escape her notice that Neith, the other lowborn, was seated at the other table.

As Roh reached for a drink on a passing tray, she noticed the tremor in her hand. She clutched the goblet to hide the shaking from Odi. When she pressed the cool metal to her lips, Odi leaned in closer to her.

'Be careful,' he whispered. 'Remember the poison last time?'

Roh only just refrained from flashing her talons at him. Who was he to lecture her? It had been she who had caught the poison before he ingested it. But she gave the goblet an exaggerated sniff before taking a large gulp. The flavour of smoked berries burst across her tongue, causing her mouth to water. She fought the urge to guzzle the whole goblet.

Arcelia Bellfast approached them, standing straight and tall, an untouched drink in her hand, her human so close to her side they nearly brushed shoulders. 'I've noted that my human wasn't missing any belongings,' she ventured cautiously.

Roh swallowed her mouthful of wine. 'That's because we took nothing from her.'

Arcelia's eyes bored into hers, and finally, the former teacher dipped her head. 'Understood, Rohesia.'

As Arcelia walked away, Odi looked from Roh to her, confused. 'Why didn't we set one of those traps for her?'

Roh strummed the stem of her goblet. 'I didn't set one for Neith's human, either.'

Odi's frown deepened. 'Why not?'

'Because we're playing the long game, Odi,' she told him. 'We may need allies later, and the more cyrens who owe us favours or underestimate us, the better.'

Roh's attention snagged on the cyren who had just entered the conservatory. A thrill rushed through her and the events of the trial momentarily faded as she fantasised about the conversations she and Estin Ruhne could have. Roh watched the renowned bone architect in awe as she crossed the room and addressed the nobility in a dignified manner that Roh could only dreamed of imitating. Estin Ruhne was probably the only cyren here she had anything in common with. Roh longed to talk with her, despite the fact that she knew she'd gush and make an absolute fool of herself.

A delicate bell chimed, cutting through the quiet melody floating from the dais. Elder Winslow Ward, Yrsa's aunt, took to the stage. Her robes trailed after her, and her jewelled belt winked in the candlelight.

'Welcome to tonight's feast,' she said, greeting them with more warmth than Roh had ever witnessed from a council elder. 'And congratulations to our victors. The queen has expressed her explicit satisfaction with your performances today. Her Majesty has bid me to pass on her congratulations, also. We have glimpsed the extraordinary qualities of true leaders today. Her Majesty has organised a reward for all eight of our remaining competitors. Tomorrow, you will be given an exclusive tour of Talon's Reach.'

A tour? Roh couldn't help scanning the faces of the other competitors. The Jaktaren and the highborns gave away nothing, but the rest looked as confused as she felt.

Elder Ward smiled again. 'Now, we invite you to take your places, for this great feast is about to begin.'

With Odi as her shadow, Roh found their place cards in the centre of the first table. She took her seat on the plush chair, and Odi sat beside her. He picked up his place card and showed it to Roh.

'What does this say?' he asked, pointing to the cursive Saddorien scrawl across the parchment.

'It says your name,' she told him. But Roh followed his gaze to the place card of the human two cyrens down from him. The writing was the same there.

Odi picked at his gloves, fingers flexing. 'What does it really say?'

Roh chewed her lip for a moment. 'It says *vinarah.*'

'Which means?'

'*Outsider.* It's what we call humans in our language.'

Odi's fingers continued to twitch, but he gave a stiff nod and placed his serviette on his lap with what looked like as much dignity as he could muster.

With a flourish, the cloches were removed from the

dishes and fragrant steam drifted up from the roasted game before them. If Roh had been impressed with the food last time, this banquet was something else entirely. She eyed the food greedily. Since her first unfortunate encounter with food from the Upper Sector, she'd been eating carefully, letting her body adjust to the richness of the meals. Now the thought of the gruel they served in the Lower Sector turned her stomach. She reached for the roast boar tentatively, serving herself a thin sliver of meat. She cut a small piece and put it in her mouth, chewing slowly, not wanting to make herself ill again.

The scrape of a chair sounded and Roh looked up from her plate in time to see Finn Haertel take his place a little further down her table. He offered no apologies for his tardiness as he sat; he simply reached for the crystal decanter of wine and poured himself a generous glass. He caught her staring and glared back at her, disgust etched on his face. Trying to ignore him, Roh served herself a spoonful of steamed root vegetables. Beside her, Odi was eating as though he hadn't touched a meal in days.

Good, she thought. *I need him strong and fit for whatever trial is next.*

As she reached for the roast potatoes, her hands brushed someone else's. Yrsa Ward's. The highborn beat her to the dish and served herself first. Roh waited. She felt oddly compelled to say something to her fellow competitor. She wanted to praise Yrsa for the outside-the-box thinking that had led to her victory. Roh wished she'd thought of that herself.

On both long tables, the conversation was flowing.

Except Roh hadn't said a word. She was reluctant to make substantial conversation with Odi in front of all the nobility, but no other cyrens had so much as looked in her direction. She needed to make a conscious effort, she decided. She reached for her goblet and searched the table. A cool gaze met hers and Roh's heart soared. Now was her chance …

'Estin.' Roh found her voice as she met that gaze with her own moss-green stare. 'I … I just wanted to tell you … We … I mean, *I'm* a big admirer of your work. Your design for the music theatre —'

Quiet settled on the table around her as Estin's nostrils flared and her talons scraped the table's surface. 'You,' she said, her voice low but audible to the whole table. 'You think you were clever? Implementing tactics formerly used against the very crown you compete for, *isruhe.*'

The word hit Roh like a blow to the face in the icy silence. She could no longer hear the subtle melody from the instrument on the dais. All she could hear was: *isruhe.* It was the second time that day someone had wielded that word against her. It was like a stain. There was no harsher insult, no fouler name.

Roh's rebuttal snagged in her throat. As Odi had been upon his arrival to Saddoriel, she was speechless. She couldn't breathe for the sudden pressure sitting heavy on her chest. *They think I took things too far? What of the body impaled on the spikes? Or the swinging coral meant to shred my face to pieces?*

'What do you mean?' she finally croaked.

'Don't play ignorant now,' Estin crowed. 'Using someone's personal treasures against them … The water warlocks used that tactic against us in the Scouring of Lochloria. Just as you used it to your advantage today.'

Roh's blood pounded in her ears.

Another voice filled the silence. 'It's little wonder,' said Taro Haertel, down the far end of the table. 'The offspring of such a beast in the dungeons is bound to share the same foul blood.'

The wine coating Roh's mouth turned sour. *He knows …?*

'Don't tell me,' Estin said, outraged. 'This *isruhe* is the offspring of Cerys the Slayer? She sits here dining with us? Competing for the crown?'

The scrape of cutlery on porcelain ceased and gasps sounded from all around the table.

Roh's cheeks burned. She didn't dare look at Odi, whose sideways glance she could feel boring into her temple. How could she have been so naive? To think that her heritage would remain a secret up here? To think that someone like her could partake in the Queen's Tournament without consequence? So this was what her kind truly thought of her.

'I hope to have misheard the conversation occurring at this table.' Queen Delja's voice cut through the air like a sharpened blade. She stood behind Estin Ruhne, sipping from a silver goblet of wine.

Estin paled, her chair scraping. 'Your Majesty —'

'Don't get up,' the queen said.

'We weren't expecting you, Your Majesty.'

'Can a queen not change her mind?'

'Of course, I only meant —'

'We do not use the language I heard only moments ago in Saddoriel,' Queen Delja said, her lilac eyes settling on Roh's flushed face. 'It is an insult to me to use such terms in my halls.'

Shock radiated across the group, and to Roh's great satisfaction, Estin grew paler still and fumbled for words. 'My deepest apologies, Your Majesty. I … I meant no disrespect to you.'

'And yet here I am, disrespected. Let's leave the matter to lie, shall we? I've already grown tired of it.' Roh could have sworn there was a glint of amusement in Queen Delja's gaze and a brief thrill shot through her. However, when she looked around the table, the stares were worse than before.

'Rohesia,' the queen said. 'I would have a moment with you in the gardens.'

Roh blinked – had she heard correctly? The sharp elbow to her side from Odi told her she had. She fumbled with the serviette on her lap and nearly knocked her chair over as she made to leave the table. With a glance around the vicious faces staring back at her, she motioned for Odi to follow her. There was no way she was going to leave him with them.

If Queen Delja was surprised by the human's presence, she didn't let it show as she guided Roh to the glass entrance of the gardens, the hems of her flowing trousers dragging behind her. Roh could feel the eyes of every guest on them as they disappeared down a narrow path bordered with tall Aching Fiirs, the single cobalt blooms atop shoulder-high stems wavering as they passed. There were all kinds of plants and flowers here, many of which Roh didn't recognise. She stared at a dark flower that seemed to have a thousand charcoal petals.

'Laceflower,' Queen Delja told her, gesturing to the bloom in question as they turned a corner. 'This place used to be called the King's Conservatory,' she mused. 'Did you know that?'

Roh shook her head, not quite trusting herself to speak. She glanced at Odi to her right, who looked just as baffled, if not terrified.

'Here should do.' The queen paused beneath the shadows of several giant ferns.

'Your Majesty?' Roh asked, clutching her hands behind her back to keep herself from fidgeting.

Delja smiled kindly and said in the common tongue, 'I thought you might need to escape all that for a moment.'

Roh's shoulders sagged. 'Thank you. Your Majesty is kind.'

'Estin should be punished for using such a term.'

Panic sparked in Roh. 'No, Your Majesty. Please —'

'I will not make matters worse for you by doing so, Rohesia,' Delja said. 'But she should be.'

'It's true, though, isn't it? I am what she says.'

'Are you?'

'I am Cerys' daughter. Cerys the Slayer.' She had never said those words aloud. The truth of it was that part of her had always believed Cerys had somehow been caught in the crossfire of someone else's battle. That perhaps she'd simply been in the wrong place at the wrong time. It wasn't hard to imagine that alternate reality, given her current state of mania. An entire Council of Elders had been killed, but there had to be something Roh didn't know, something that *everyone* didn't know about Cerys, that explained her actions all that time ago. But facing the poisonous words of the highborns, it was clear to Roh that her mother was exactly who they said she was.

Queen Delja studied her. 'You are Rohesia of the Bone Cleaners. Competitor in the Queen's Tournament. Is that not what matters most?'

Roh didn't understand this new relationship with the Queen of Cyrens. How well had Delja known her mother? What secrets did they share? And why now was she speaking to Roh, helping her? It was one thing to converse with her in invisible pockets of the prison, but to single her out in front of the Council of Elders and highborns of Saddoriel …

'They would never accept me … if I won,' Roh started, the black inky fear leaking from her. It was the question that kept her awake in the dark and early hours, the very thing she feared most. 'Would I even be allowed to take the crown? Is it against our laws? As an … As the offspring of a criminal?'

Queen Delja adjusted the coral crown atop her head and met Roh's gaze. 'A queen must know the Law of the Lair better than she knows herself.'

Roh thought the queen was going to say more, but she didn't. Instead she turned her attentions to the small white flowers encasing the fern trunks and plucked one from a vine.

'I came here often as a young nestling,' she ventured, seeming to marvel at the bloom in her grasp. 'It is one of the few places in Saddoriel that has not changed immensely over the centuries.' The queen's voice was melodic, even in speech. Not for the first time, Roh found herself wondering about her deathsong.

'What did you make of the water forest?' the queen asked.

'It … it was beautiful … in a dangerous sort of way …'

The queen smiled at this, motioning for Roh and Odi to follow her back up the path. 'I find that often the most beautiful things are the most dangerous. That forest was one of my favourites. One of the oldest lungs of Saddoriel.'

As Roh listened, she could have sworn the garden moved with the queen's words. She glanced at Odi, whose face told her he had noticed it, too.

'But it's gone now?'

'Yes, it's gone. I had best leave you and your human here and return to my guests,' Queen Delja said with an apologetic smile. 'Remember, Rohesia, know the Law of the Lair better than you know yourself.'

And with that, the Queen of Cyrens turned another corner and was gone.

Roh looked at Odi, incredulous. 'What was —'

But Odi was staring at the ground.

'What are you looking at?' Roh asked.

Odi pointed to a stream of white flowers along the

edge of the path, just like the one the queen had been holding. 'Were they there before?'

'What?' Roh said, frowning.

'I could have sworn …' Odi trailed off at the look on Roh's face. 'Never mind. What now? We're not going back there, are we?'

Roh shook her head. 'Not a chance. Now … now we find someone who knows the Law of the Lair.'

Roh and Odi found Andwana in an empty common room of the Lower Sector. The older cyren held a book in his lap and a pipe to his mouth, smoke spilling from his lips.

'If it isn't the bone queen to be,' he said, looking up as they approached. 'And a new pet, apparently,' he added, eyes fixed on Odi. 'What do you want?'

Roh couldn't tell if Andwana's tone was in jest or if something sinister lay beneath. She decided that it didn't matter.

'I want to borrow a book,' she told him, taking a seat in the chair opposite. Odi remained standing at her side, looking very much out of place.

'You? Borrow a book?' he scoffed. 'Do you even remember how to read? You've never shown any inclination before. All those mealtimes I've come round with the trolley …'

'I have an inclination now.'

'Well, my trolley's not here.'

'Could you —'

'If you're about to suggest that I go fetch it for you …
You're not queen yet.'

Roh sighed and slipped three bronze keys from her
pocket. 'Will this cover your troubles?'

Andwana removed the pipe from his mouth and
considered her. 'It might.'

'I want a book on the Law of the Lair,' Roh told him.

The older cyren coughed a laugh. 'One book that
contains the Law of the Lair? Are you daft, fledgling? The
Law of the Lair is a beast, a living, breathing, changing
thing. It does not fit in a single volume. You'll have to be
more specific.'

'Fine,' Roh ground out. 'A book on the Law of the Lair
regarding the Queen's Tournament.'

'Hmm. Lucky for you, I don't have to go far for that
one.' Andwana stood. 'Wait here.' He left them in a haze of
smoke.

'Can we trust him?' Odi asked, staring after the cyren.

'Trust?' Roh snorted. 'Have you learned nothing of
Saddorien cyrens so far?' She gauged his expression and
sighed. 'First lesson, then, Odi Arrowood: never trust a
cyren.'

'You're a cyren.'

Roh shrugged. 'I'm a cyren whose best interests align
with yours, for the moment.'

'And when they no longer align?'

'Well, we'll either be dead, or —'

The door swung inwards. 'Found it,' Andwana said,
pushing a heavy book into Roh's hands. 'I borrowed it

myself, in case I managed … Well, my skills at Thieves proved a hindrance there, but nevertheless, here it is.'

Roh looked down at the faded title: *Life, Law and the Lair, Volume XI: The Dawning Queen's Tournament.* 'How many volumes are there?'

'Don't know,' Andwana said, relighting his pipe. 'You'll need to return it in three days' time.'

'Three days? You expect me to compete in the tournament *and* read *this* in three days?'

'Rules are rules.'

'Fine.' Roh stood and offered a bronze key.

Andwana frowned. 'What about the rest?'

Roh shrugged, tucking the book under her arm. 'You didn't have to get your trolley, did you?'

'What?' Andwana blustered. 'You little —'

'Thanks for the book,' Roh quipped, leaving the room.

Odi was fast on her heels. 'I don't think you should have done that,' he said. 'You might need —'

'What was the first lesson, Odi?'

There was a flash of irritation across his face. 'Never trust a cyren,' he said begrudgingly.

'Let's hope that one sticks. Hurry up.' She walked the familiar passageway, intending to go straight up to her new quarters and read, but down in the dark, a melody echoed.

She paused, Odi nearly crashing into her.

'Is there a human playing?' Odi asked softly.

Roh frowned at him. 'It's Harlyn's lute.'

Confusion was written across his face. 'But I thought cyrens couldn't play instruments?'

'Of course we can,' Roh dismissed. 'We choose not to.'

It was long after workshop hours, but the music told Roh that her friends had not yet retired. She followed the vibrant notes all the way to the workshop, almost forgetting that Odi shadowed her. As she drew closer, she heard Orson's voice accompanying the quiet chords being strummed on the lute. Roh listened, realising that what she was hearing were the core notes of Orson's deathsong. Roh paused before she reached the workshop door, a lump thick in her throat. Orson had never sung her deathsong to them, she had always been too shy, but now … now the notes danced from her, clear and confident, and *dark*. There was a dangerous undercurrent to the striking music projecting from her friend, a beautifully twisted sound that didn't quite match her sweet and considerate nature.

Roh's insides prickled uncomfortably. *Is this the first time they've shared their songs? Do they hide these little singalongs from me?*

Odi was at her side, his palms upturned in question as to why they remained in the shadows. But Roh's feet wouldn't move. Even though she knew it was wrong to stand there eavesdropping, there was something ugly in her that wanted to know what went on in her absence.

Orson cut the song short. 'It's not complete,' she said quietly.

Roh imagined Harlyn shrugging her shoulders as she said, 'At least you know that much of it. The sound is completely your own, and you only need, what? One final verse?'

'Something like that,' Orson admitted.

'Exactly. Whereas mine keeps changing, or I keep changing it – I don't even know which.'

'You're younger than me. You'll get there. Some cyrens are as old as sixty before they —'

'I know, I know. I just wish I could be one of the ones who gets it early, you know?'

Roh was hurt. Why had they never spoken of this before? Hearing that Harlyn shared the same fears as her warmed her, but now her knowledge of it was a secret. She had put the wall between them by hiding outside, and if she was completely honest, by cheating in the game of Thieves. Her guilt was like a cold, constant embrace. Swallowing her pride, she pushed the door open with a creak and her friends' conversation ceased.

'Roh? What are you doing here?' Orson rushed forward and hugged her tightly. Roh inhaled her friend's familiar scent, the scent of home. Pulling back, she spotted Harlyn at their workbench, her lute clutched in her hands.

'You're alive,' Harlyn said by way of greeting.

'I am.'

'We're sorry we couldn't watch, we had work to catch up on down here.'

Roh heard the words she hadn't said: *your work.*

But Orson showed no signs of bitterness. 'How did it go?' she asked, her brow furrowing with concern as she reached for the cut on Roh's cheek. 'Well enough, I'm guessing. You smell like a feast.' She dropped her hand.

Roh felt instant regret. She shouldn't have come down

here smelling of an exotic banquet when she knew the others had only eaten slop. She should have thought to pack some food for them … The thoughts raced through her mind, each barely fully formed before the next one came crashing in.

'It was …' But she couldn't find the words. 'I'm still in,' she managed eventually.

'I see you managed to keep him in one piece.' Harlyn nodded at Odi.

'Nice to see you again, too, Harlyn,' Odi said darkly.

It was during this charged exchange that Roh noticed the flowers decorating the grimy workshop window. In all her seventeen years in the Lower Sector, she'd never seen flowers down here before.

'What's that about?' she asked.

'Oh, those,' Orson said. 'They're for Neith.'

'Neith? The water runner?'

There was an awkward pause and Orson glanced worriedly at Harlyn, who merely shrugged her shoulders.

'They're calling her the "Saviour of the Lower Sector",' Harlyn inserted bluntly.

'*They?*'

'The lowborns.'

Roh's stomach twisted. 'All of them?'

'Nearly all,' Harlyn said with another shrug. 'Cyrens from all over the Lower Sector have been leaving her gifts and such.'

Roh bit the inside of her cheek. She knew Harlyn well enough to recognise a jab when she heard one. The last unnecessary detail had been a barb designed to hurt Roh, and it had found its mark. Flushing and repositioning the book under her arm, Roh refused to take the bait. Harlyn, who had wanted to compete as much as she had, was jealous. Perhaps it wasn't as easy to be happy for the one who'd made it through as they'd thought. While Roh understood that pain, she couldn't help the sadness that coursed through her. She longed to debrief with her friends, to unpack the events of the trial and the banquet, to tell them about the queen, to see the whole thing through their eyes. But she would not be offered that comfort, not tonight. She glanced towards the back of the workshop, her eyes finding her secret project still hidden by the sheet of cloth, as she'd left it. The memory of the music from the Upper Sector filled her with a sudden inspiration to work on her model.

Harlyn followed her gaze, and Roh forced herself to dull the passion in her eyes. She knew that the inspiring music and architecture she'd seen in the last few days would only fuel her friend's envy.

Something clattered to the ground and all three cyrens whirled around. Odi was mid-crouch, picking up a bone scraper he'd dropped. Roh had forgotten he was there. Frustration rushed through her. He was *always* there, even in her most private moments with her friends. She opened her mouth to snap at him, but as she did, the scab on her cheek itched, a stark reminder. She swallowed her harsh words and checked her temper. Were it not for the human, she might not be here.

As Odi stood and carefully placed the tool back on the

bench, Harlyn fixed him with an icy glare. 'Watch what you're doing,' she hissed.

Gods, she's out for blood today.

But Odi didn't break Harlyn's stare, didn't flinch at the unveiled fury in her voice.

'Let's go, Odi,' Roh interjected, nearly swaying on her feet. Exhaustion had barrelled into her and the refuge she'd hoped for here was nowhere to be found.

Finally breaking Harlyn's stare, Odi followed her.

At the door, Orson's hand found hers and squeezed. 'Give her time,' Roh's gentler friend said, glancing worriedly back at Harlyn, who had already returned to her work. 'She's still accepting the fact that it's you out there. You understand, don't you?'

Roh steeled herself against the guilt that tried to lance through her at that moment. She'd done what she had to do and Harlyn had done the same. The only difference was, she had won and Harlyn had lost.

'I understand.' Roh gave Orson a grim smile before she and the human left her friends and the bones behind.

CHAPTER ELEVEN

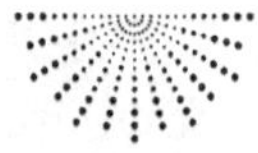

Any flutter of excitement Roh had felt about the impending tour of Saddoriel and what elusive parts of the territory she might see had been quelled by the events of the previous night's feast. Now, thick dread settled in her stomach at the thought of seeing her fellow competitors. As she and Odi reached the meeting point, her insides squirmed. Although the tunnels and turns had seemed familiar upon approach, she couldn't quite place when or why she'd been here before. But it didn't matter where they were; Roh wasn't ready to see the others. Her cheeks burned as the contenders arrived in pairs and stood waiting for a council elder to appear. There was no doubt that those who had not heard last night's conversation firsthand had heard it by now, distorted and exaggerated, as was the nature of hushed whispers. Estin Ruhne, Miriald Montalle and Arcelia Bellfast stood together a few feet away, and Roh averted her gaze immediately, feeling the familiar burn of shame spread across her cheeks. The architect's words still echoed in her mind, and with that element of her anonymity stripped away, she felt naked, exposed. She had thought of Arcelia as something of an ally, but after the poisonous murmurings of Estin Ruhne, Roh wasn't so sure.

The Jaktaren and their humans appeared from a passage Roh didn't recognise. The highborns who had been injured in the first trial had been tended to with great care; there was certainly no limp to Finn's gait as he strode around the hall, his chest puffed out arrogantly, laughing with Yrsa and Zokez.

A collective intake of breath sounded and Roh's stomach dropped, expecting another verbal confrontation. Her paranoia was erratic in her mind, but as she looked up, she realised that the wave of shock rolling over the group had nothing to do with her. Although Roh had never met the arms-bearing cyren standing before her, she knew *exactly* who she was. By name *and* by the thick rings of scars that wrapped around the length of both bare arms.

'Today's venture is courtesy of Her Majesty's generosity,' Toril Ainsley's silvery voice cut through the chatter. She wore a sleeveless leather vest and fitted leather pants, very unlike the traditional free-flowing garments of the Saddorien territory. Toril, once a trader from the Mid Sector, was the only former tournament competitor Ames had told Roh anything about. According to him, Queen Delja had been so impressed with her efforts and resilience that she'd allowed the trader to break custom and join the Jaktaren late in life. And sure enough, the cyren standing before them had the zigzag pattern of the guild shaved into the side of her head. It highlighted a thick, white burn that cut through the scales at her right temple. Roh couldn't help but stare at it and the scars that marred the cyren's otherwise flawless skin. They made the scar on Roh's own face look like a beauty mark. She wrung her hands. They were only one trial in, and she'd scarcely scraped through that. It certainly wasn't the first time she had felt out of her depth since entering the tournament, but it *was* the first time she'd seen the permanent consequences of the trials presented so starkly before her. She swallowed. Would she emerge from the Queen's Tournament whole, if at all?

Toril gave the group a cursory glance before continuing. 'Our queen wished me to impress upon you that should one of you take up the crown, the deepest understanding of Saddoriel and Talon's Reach must be fostered. Follow me.' The trail of Toril's cloak was already disappearing around a sharp corner.

Roh started after the others. Odi was keeping so close to Roh that he might as well have been holding her hand. But she said nothing as his shoulder brushed hers; this was safer. Soon after, they came to a halt before an archway of bones, the smaller twin to the one at the entrance of Saddoriel. Beyond it, the torches illuminated intricate mosaics in the stone walls.

'Welcome to the Passage of Kings,' Toril said.

'The what?' Odi murmured in Roh's ear.

'The Passage of Kings,' Roh hissed, frowning. *That's*

why these tunnels feel so familiar. She didn't bother to hide the blatant disappointment on her face. Every cyren in Saddoriel had been to the Passage of Kings. It was a mandatory part of their history lessons as nestlings. She cursed silently. She'd stupidly been hoping for unprecedented access to the more secret parts of the lair, perhaps even the Vault, where it was rumoured the *Tome of Kyeos* was kept, but instead … Instead, she had almost died in order to receive a tour she'd already had in her ninth year. She wasn't the only disgruntled cyren, judging by the snippets of conversation that broke out around her.

'She can't be serious.'

'Everyone's seen the passage.'

'What could she hope for us to learn *here?*'

'Are you finished?' Toril's voice sounded again, sharper than a blade, and the chatter fell silent at once.

Then again, Roh mused. *Perhaps it's all been worth it just to see Toril Ainsley in the flesh.*

They passed through the small archway of bones and Roh blinked at what she found inside. Her childhood memories did no justice to the passage before her now. As a nestling, she had been far too young to appreciate the artistry and the history that stretched across the high walls. Her mind had been filled with thoughts of mimicking Orson's straight-backed stance and evading Ames' scoldings. It was a different story now as Arcelia pressed a torch into her hand, its flickering flame revealing the deep lines of the ornate relief tiles.

In a flash, Roh was nine years old again …

'What did I say about touching the reliefs?' Ames' deep voice was terrifying as it echoed off the walls.

'Sorry, Master Ames,' Orson said quietly, glancing back at Roh and Harlyn, who had ducked to take cover behind her legs. They crouched lower, stifling a fit of giggles, knowing they rarely got into trouble if Orson was with them.

Roh shook the memory from her head and stepped into the passage.

'Take your time here.' Toril's words echoed. 'The Passage of Kings is one of the most sacred parts of Saddoriel, preserving the memory of our kind for millennia. The ruler of our kind must be intimately familiar with our history, our magic and our nature. Which is why we begin here.'

The competitors fanned out, taking their humans with them as they covered various tunnels, wandering into different periods of cyren history. Roh crossed her arms over her chest against the cool air pricking her skin and roamed with Odi until they found the starting point. She could feel Toril Ainsley's gaze on her. The former competitor had probably heard about last night and the nature of the circlet that lined Roh's head. Roh ignored the attention and tugged Odi in front of the first mosaic scene. It was the first cyrens of Lamaka's Basin and Lochloria, a not-so-distant territory, tunnelling beneath the East Sea, with the water warlocks at their backs enchanting the sea so that it remained in place and didn't flood the region that would later become Saddoriel. Their magic was depicted with deep spirals and swirls that resembled the great waves and currents above.

Roh had never been good at studying and retaining facts. Her mind was usually so crowded with an array of tangled thoughts that remembering moments in cyren history was often like trying to scoop the last remaining drops from an empty bucket. But with the scenes portrayed before her in such stunning detail, the stories she'd learned as a nestling came back to her ...

'Those are the birthstones of Saddoriel,' she told Odi quietly, pointing to the rectangular tile. 'The gems you've seen in the queen's coral crown.'

'They're not in a crown there,' Odi said, frowning at the artwork, where the three stones were depicted on an altar.

'Well, they didn't just come from nowhere, did they?' Roh mocked. 'They originally belonged to the water-warlock founding families. They enchanted them at the creation of the lair, in order to maintain balance between cyren and water-warlock magic.' The words were not Roh's own, but Ames', coming back to her a decade later.

'How?' Odi asked, keeping up with her as she moved along to the next exquisitely detailed tile.

'Each stone possesses its own power.' Without thinking, Roh ran her fingers over the outlines of the stones in the next mosaic: a close-up depiction that showed the banded rings of the first gem. 'The Gauntlet Ruby gives its bearer clarity and can detect poisons and broken vows.' Her fingers moved to the second stone, its brilliant honey colour undocumented here. 'Mercy's Topaz guides its bearer to sincerity and shows them the way when they're lost.'

'And the third?' Odi asked, pressing his half-gloved fingers to the tile.

'The Willow's Sapphire supposedly provides its bearer with endurance, and faith when all faith is lost. Do you see a theme?'

Odi frowned at her. 'Magic?'

Roh rolled her eyes. '*Truth*, Odi. The powers are themed by elements of truth. It was a choice made by the water warlocks in order to help them combat the cunning nature of cyrens.'

'I see.'

Roh doubted he did. The intricacies and secrets of cyren history were rarely understood by anyone, let alone a scrawny human.

'Who's this, then?' Odi pointed to a carving of a cloaked figure, holding a crown between his hands.

'That's Taaldin the Great. The first cyren king. He oversaw the expansion of Saddoriel into Talon's Reach and linked it to the other territories.'

'Roh!' came an enthusiastic voice. Roh had to suppress a sigh of frustration as Neith and her withered old human sidled up next to them. Her chest twinged as she recalled the flowers in the workshop and Harlyn's hurtful words: *Neith – Saviour of the Lower Sector*. Gods, Roh didn't know why it had stung so much. She had never cared about what the other cyrens thought of her, so long as she had Harlyn and Orson … Did she still have them? Would she, at the end of all this?

Roh cast a sideways glance at Neith and the feeble

human practically clinging to the hem of her shirt. *How in the realm did they make it through the hunt? The human's practically on his damn deathbed.* But when Neith smiled at her, the hardness within Roh softened and the sigh that escaped her was one of relief. It was *nice* to see a friendly face, it was *nice* to be met with something other than hostility and cunning. As a fellow Lower Sector competitor, Neith understood where Roh came from and there was much comfort to be found in that. So, Roh smiled back.

'How did you find yesterday?' Roh asked quietly as they moved onto the next historical scene.

'Terrifying.'

Roh nodded. 'Me too.' She glanced at Neith's human. 'Must be hard with an old one like that.'

'His name is Aillard,' Neith said, with a note of fondness.

Aillard turned at the sound of his name and gave Neith a somewhat toothless grin.

Neith laughed softly. 'We're a good team, aren't we, Aillard?'

Interesting, Roh mused. Neith hadn't struck Roh as a human-lover, and yet she conversed with the old man as though ... as though they were *friends.*

Roh didn't realise she was frowning until Odi frowned back at her. 'What?'

'Nothing,' she muttered.

Neith chatted away at her side as they continued through the Passage of Kings. 'Can you believe the sleeping quarters up here?' she was saying. 'I swear you could fit the water-runner common room in mine five times over!'

Roh's skin prickled as she became conscious of Neith's voice echoing. She could hear no other voices and she realised why. No one else was talking, not like Neith. This was a *sacred* site.

'And the food. Have you ever —'

'Neith,' Roh interjected in a whisper, peering after the other competitors who had trudged ahead.

'Hmm?'

'Perhaps we should explore the passage? Quietly?' Before Neith could answer, Roh peeled away from the water runner and her human and led Odi deeper into the passage, silently hoping that Neith wouldn't be offended.

They passed the mosaics of dozens and dozens of previous rulers, the coral crown resting atop their heads, flanked by their Councils of Seven Elders. The vastness of their history, millennia rich with detail Roh had never encountered, left her breathless. Who was she in the face of all this? For a moment, she allowed herself to imagine her name, her story being carved here. She pictured a time, millennia in the future, where young cyrens were told the great tale of Rohesia the ... What would they call her?

She paused at a new set of tiles, recognising the overly long talons of Asros the Conqueror. He was the second-most recent ruler before Queen Delja. Asros had been known for his brutality, and the scenes sprawling across the tunnel walls depicted as much. His long talons slashed through humans and cyrens alike as his greed gave birth to a campaign that would see cyrens attempt to conquer the shores of the human realms as well as their seas. The very one Roh and Odi had briefly mentioned during one of their first encounters.

'The Age of Chaos,' Roh said quietly, taking in the sight of the cyren army inflicting their death chorus upon not one, but three human warships. It was the bones of these crews that adorned much of the southern end of the Great Hall.

'Who's this?' Odi was pointing to a female cyren wearing a trailing cape standing beside King Asros.

Roh didn't have to dig deep for the memory of that figure. 'It's Freya, one of Asros' consorts. She saw how many cyren lives were being forfeited during his rule and she tried to stop his warmongering for over a century. She was well known amongst our kind – the people called her *Ramehra*.'

'What's that mean?'

'*Chosen Majesty*, or "chosen by the people". It's an ancient phrase in Old Saddorien. As far as I know, that term has never been bestowed on another ruler in our history, only Freya. It's a term of the utmost respect, and to be called it is the highest honour.'

'No one calls your queen a … *Ramra?*'

'*Ramehra*,' Roh corrected. 'And no. Not yet. Come on.' She tugged Odi's sleeve, aware that Neith and Aillard were closing in on them once again. Roh wasn't ready to leave their rich history for incessant chatter just yet.

'The Age of Chaos led to many cyren deaths,' she

whispered to Odi. 'It's one of the reasons we do not rule the seas above as we once did.'

'How did it end?'

Roh paused at another story she knew well. 'Uniir the Blessed defeated Asros at The Dawning, which is what they used to call this tournament.' The carving displayed Uniir's proud, imposing figure, standing between the goddesses Dresmis and Thera, their wings outstretched, as though sheltering the cyren king, protecting him. From what Ames had told Roh and the others over the years, Uniir had been a fanatic. His obsession with Lamaka's daughters was evident in Saddoriel's temples, and the statues of the deities scattered around all sectors of the lair.

'Peace didn't last long with him, then?' Odi asked, standing before another well-known scene.

The Scouring of Lochloria. Roh had read about it as a younger fledgling and had badgered Ames endlessly for more information. However, unlike her other quests for knowledge, Ames did not support this one. In fact, he refused to speak of that time, other than to call it 'one of the darkest periods in cyren history'.

Roh shook her head. 'It did not,' she answered Odi. 'Decades before his reign began, rumours spread that water warlocks were gaining too much power in Talon's Reach. Many of them left, thinking it safer to return to Lochloria. In one of his fanatical rages, Uniir claimed that water-warlock magic was unnatural, that warlocks were cyrens who had never fully matured. According to him, it was Dresmis and Thera's will that Uniir rid the realm of them, so the hunting of water warlocks began.'

'He killed them?'

Roh nodded. 'He sent the cyren army to wipe their kind from the world.'

'That's insane.'

'From what Ames told us, Uniir believed he was reclaiming Lochloria for Dresmis and Thera, ridding their sacred home of the unworthy.'

Odi swore.

Roh pressed on, the facts coming to her quickly now. 'In the past, Talon's Reach was far bigger and its passageways full of life. Thanks to Uniir, our kind split into distant clans.'

'He wiped out an entire race and split up his own people?' Odi was wide-eyed with disbelief.

'He did.'

'That's barbaric.'

'That's history,' Roh corrected him. 'Surely yours is just as bloody?'

'No, I don't think —'

'I'll wager it is *exactly* like this. History is just an ongoing violent exchange of power, whatever the cost.' Roh stopped once more at a new series of mosaics. A pair of great wings spread wide before Uniir, a taloned hand clutching a double blade. 'King Uniir opposed Delja's entry into the tournament,' she explained. 'But somehow, she got through. And when she won, her wings sprouted. Then and there, Uniir dubbed Delja the descendant of Dresmis and Thera, and claimed his work in Saddoriel was done. He flung himself onto her blade, talking nonsense about making sacrifices to the gods.'

'Really …?'

Roh nodded. 'Those who wish to pray to Dresmis and Thera are still free to do so. Cyrens still pay homage to them – they are our ancestors, after all. But those who wished to live by prayer rather than by the Law of the Lair left Saddoriel and joined the clan in Akoris. Apparently there, they still worship as Uniir the Blessed did.'

'So your queen saved your kind?'

'She became Delja the Triumphant for that.'

Odi nudged Roh and she tore her eyes away from the carvings to see the competitors gathering at the far end of the passage. Their time in the Passage of Kings was at an end, it seemed.

'The Triumphant?' Odi asked. 'Not *Ramehra?*'

Roh shook her head. 'When a cyren becomes ruler, the king or in this case, queen, drops their family name and adopts a title bestowed upon them by the Council of Elders.'

'I see.' Odi considered this before frowning at her. 'I don't know your family name.'

Roh rubbed the bridge of her nose. 'I don't have one. No lowborns do.' The bone cleaner, Rohesia … She was *nothing* in the face of the millennia of great cyrens and events that surrounded her. In the presence of the mighty rulers who had shaped their kind, she was a speck of dust merely to be wiped from the halls of history.

The group of competitors began to move on and Roh

craned her neck to see the back of Toril Ainsley's head, leaning in close to Finn Haertel.

What are they whispering about? She edged closer in time to see Yrsa elbow Zokez in the ribs, spurring him on.

'Toril,' he ventured. 'Might you tell us about your time in the tournament?'

Roh clapped a hand over her mouth, yanking on Odi's shirtsleeve to bring him closer to the group. *Of course* the highborns had dared to ask such a question, for what could happen to them as a consequence?

Toril's nostrils flared and a taloned hand lifted to the burn that ran through the scales at her temple. Her eyes narrowed and she looked as though she were about to bite Zokez's head off.

'Please,' Yrsa added. 'We'll likely not have the chance again to speak to a former competitor.'

What? But Toril is a Jaktaren. Surely she speaks to Yrsa and Finn all the time?

'Please, Toril,' Finn implored beside Yrsa.

Roh couldn't contain her shock. Finn Haertel using manners? *Did he hit his head somewhere?*

At this, Toril's furious expression softened and she gestured for the group to follow her with a long-suffering sigh. Roh gathered this wasn't the first time Toril had been badgered about her experiences. As they turned a corner, her voice carried down the tunnel.

'I competed in the most recent Queen's Tournament. Exactly fifty years ago. Some of you more mature cyrens may remember, I made it to the third trial.'

Roh saw Estin and Arcelia nod.

They turned another corner.

'I was the crowd favourite against three others in this last trial,' she continued. 'It took us to the most savage parts of the seas – a challenge of speed and agility. I had taken the lead early and was a hair's breadth away from the finish line, when one of my competitors gained on me suddenly.'

Notes of music became louder as they moved down the passageway, but Roh and everyone else was hanging on Toril's every word.

'I knew that should she catch up, I no longer had the stamina to race talon to talon to the finish line. I had swum those particular currents before, and knew of something that lived amidst the coral on the seabed, something that might hinder her progress, should I manage to stir it into action. It was a risk,' she admitted. 'A risk I was willing to take for a chance to hold the coral crown as my own.' Toril ran her talon down one of the ringed scars on her arm. 'I dived down fast and deep … and awoke a reef dweller.'

'*Dresmis and Thera*,' Neith muttered in disbelief somewhere nearby.

Roh resisted the urge to shush her.

'It had camouflaged itself against the coral and I miscalculated its exact position. It shot up as if out of nowhere, its giant tentacles thrashing in all directions. I remember hearing my fellow competitor's scream and feeling the briefest sensation of victory. That was until I realised my screams had merged with hers. The reef dweller had wrapped its tentacles around me as well, and its poison was eating through my skin.' Toril paused and rotated her arms before the group, Roh flinching at the depth and breadth of those scars once more.

'It even damaged my scales,' she said, gesturing to the gruesome burn on her temple. 'I can no longer communicate with other cyrens under water because of it … I nearly died. My fellow competitor did.'

The silence was deafening.

'Does that satisfy your curiosity?' Toril asked flatly.

No one spoke.

'Good,' she said. 'We're here.'

They turned a final corner and music, brighter and clearer than ever, flooded the tunnel, emptying all thought from Roh's crowded mind.

'The Passage of Kings,' Toril called, 'is one of many entries to the queen's music theatre.'

Roh's heart nearly froze mid-beat in her chest. She had dreamed of this place all her life, imagining what it would be like in the flesh.

'Some of its newer additions,' Toril said as they paused at a pair of elaborately embellished doors, 'were designed by one of your fellow competitors.' She dipped her head in acknowledgement to Estin Ruhne, who stood at the front of the group.

Roh chewed her lip. As a kindness, Ames had shown her those designs, a demonstration of what true architectural prowess looked like. But seeing lines on a piece of parchment was wholly different to —

The doors opened and Roh had no words. As she

stepped inside the queen's music theatre and the melody drifted up from the stage, she thought her chest would burst. The entrance opened out at the back of a small, exclusive tiered seating section that was nestled in the curved edge of the half-circle structure. It looked out onto an open, flat stage, where a harpist sat at the centre. But above … above was the true feat of genius. Rows and rows of curved balconies looked down onto the stage, the levels of seating climbing up until they disappeared into a beam of light. The banisters seemed to flow from one section to the next, horizontally and vertically, designed to mirror the crest and fall of the waves in the sea. Roh loosed a breath. The sheer magnitude of the structure made her little model back in the workshop seem like exactly that: a little model. Though she detested the renowned architect after her comments at the feast, Roh couldn't help the begrudging admiration she still held for Estin Ruhne's work. Could she separate the creator from the creation? The music theatre sang with an astounding sense of creativity that Roh knew in her heart she would never possess.

'Our whole lair was enchanted by the ancient water warlocks so that the music reaches all corners of Saddoriel from wherever it is played,' Toril explained from where she stood halfway down the aisle to the stage.

Odi leaned in to Roh. 'Again, their magic remains, but they do not?'

'Their magic remains in a lot of places.'

'So, cyrens took their magic and then annihilated their kind?'

'Keep your voice down,' she hissed. 'And yes. Have you learned nothing of Saddorien cyrens yet?'

Odi's expression became sullen, and to Roh's relief, he turned away from her to face Aillard.

Thank the gods for that, she thought, turning her own attention back to the music theatre. He was irritating her to no end. She wished that Harlyn and Orson could see this place, the place that housed the very life's blood of Saddoriel, the music that was pumped to every major part of Talon's Reach. The music that Queen Delja and her council enjoyed so freely, coming and going as they pleased. She closed her eyes for a moment, trying to absorb as much of the song as she could, feeling it touch somewhere deep in her chest.

'— were it not for my wife, back home.' The snippet of conversation pulled her from her reverie. *Wife?*

'Where is home?' Odi was asking Aillard.

The old man grinned. 'We call it the fire continent.'

Odi's brows shot up. 'You're from *Battalon?*'

Aillard tapped a finger to the side of his neck, where a lick of flame was inked. 'This not proof enough?'

Roh hadn't noticed the marking before, but the human lands meant little to her kind. Her geographical lessons had been focused on the cyren territories, the currents of the seas and the coastlines above.

Odi let out a low whistle. 'Is what they say about those tattoos true?'

'That depends, what do they say?'

'Well, I've heard —'

'That's enough,' Roh said. Didn't they know that any

personal information they made public could be used against them? Didn't they know that one of these days they might come face to face with each other in a trial? Being friendly with the other competitors wouldn't help their cause.

'Come on, Odi,' she said, finding her voice softening at the hurt in his eyes.

They left the music theatre all too soon, before Roh could sink back into the cascading notes of the harp. Toril took them through a different exit that led to yet another passage. Roh had to admire the vast network of tunnels. They were a true feat of her kind and it was no wonder cyrens were born with an inner compass to navigate such labyrinths. Toril led the group, turn after turn, the path twisting around numerous sharp corners.

One of the other humans crashed into Odi, sending him sprawling across the wet ground.

'What in Thera's —' Roh's words died on her tongue as she saw Finn clap his human heartily on the back.

'In the dirt where you belong,' Finn sneered, stepping over Odi dramatically, avoiding making contact as though the human had an infectious disease.

'You bloody *bastard.*' The words were out of Roh's mouth before she had even thought to say them and they tasted like poison. Panic gripped her as what she'd said settled between her and Finn, his narrowed lilac eyes fixed on her. She had just cursed at a highborn ... In defence of a *human* ... What sort of consequences came with such an action?

But it was the water runner, Neith, who broke the

tension, as she struggled to help the much larger Odi up from the ground. She staggered under his weight, but eventually, the human was once more upright, brushing the clumps of dirt from his clothes.

'What's going on?' Toril's voice cut across them.

'Nothing,' Finn said, before stalking off after Yrsa.

Roh caught Neith's eye. 'Thank you,' she said, tugging Odi closer to her and checking him for visible signs of injury.

Neith simply nodded and motioned for Aillard to follow her.

'You alright?' Roh asked Odi as they once more took up the rear of the group.

'Yes. Fine,' he said, gaze forward.

Roh waited for him to meet her eyes, but he didn't. After a moment, she straightened her shoulders and pressed on. 'Good.'

They said no more as they followed the others, with Roh silently willing the tour to be over. But as they pushed on and started to descend through the levels of Saddoriel, Roh realised that the tour was far from over. As they walked on, the delicate notes of music grew fainter and the passages became damper and darker. Roh knew this scent … The stale aroma of the Lower Sector and beyond.

Her stomach churned with dread and the motive behind the tour became clear.

She knew exactly where they were going next.

. . .

A portcullis of bones, reinforced with iron, cast long shadows across the wet ground beneath Roh's boots. Thick, rusted chains and heavy locks wrapped through its latticed grille, a solid wall of algae-covered stone standing either side. In contrast to the harsh, looming structures was a crawling plant of white oleander, its vines firmly wrapped around timber beams, its delicate flowers peppered across bone and iron alike. Roh's skin prickled. Until now, she had never seen the official entrance to Saddoriel's prison, the one that, for whatever reason, highborns and officials used. It was formidable; a warning to those who were condemned to its confinement that they would never pass through its gate again. Roh cast her gaze upwards, abstractly wondering how long those bones had guarded the most damned creatures of Saddoriel's underworld. A long time, by the look of them. Centuries of dirt and grime coated them, and the chains looked like they had rusted in place permanently. Two guards manned the gate, dressed in formal black uniforms, leather whips coiled at their belts, backs to the stonework.

Roh felt the eyes of her fellow competitors on her like a red-hot brand searing into her flesh and recalled Taro Haertel's cruel words:

'The offspring of such a beast in the dungeons is bound to share the same foul blood.'

Toril Ainsley cleared her throat as she stood before the gate. 'This here is the only cyren prison in all our territories,' she said. 'Once reserved for deserters of the Saddorien Army and prisoners of war from the Age of

Chaos, it is now exclusively reserved for those who have betrayed the coral crown and the Law of the Lair. Prisoners from other cyren clans are brought here to face the consequences of their crimes. Part of our queen's duty is to oversee and judge such atrocities.'

Toril pointed up, a black talon extended. 'There you will find the prison records. Exactly who is imprisoned beyond these walls, and for how long.'

Roh's mouth went dry and she was filled with a premonition of dread. A stone slate hung from a spike hammered into the stone, its dark surface etched with the details. The hair on Roh's arms and the back of her neck stood up. There it was, scratched into the slate in an old script, the name she didn't want to see: *CERYS. FIVE MILLENNIA.*

It was the longest sentence on the list, with no marking to indicate when it had begun. An icy shiver snaked down Roh's spine. Knowing that cyrens generally only lived for two centuries, she had always shuddered at the symbolism of such a long punishment. Cerys must have been a true monster to deserve it.

Though there was no family name to connect them, Estin Ruhne's remarks from the feast were repeated in hushed tones and Roh heard her mother's name on the lips of Toril Ainsley and the highborns.

'I've heard it said that she is ancient, perhaps as old as Queen Delja.'

Roh tried not to react as she reeled in shock at their whispers. Could it be true? She had no way of knowing. She realised too late that their lilac eyes were on her now, staring at the gold circlet around her head, the very thing that solidified her connection to this nightmarish place, the thing that marked her for what she was – the daughter of the longest-imprisoned traitor in cyren history.

'So, not only are you the nestling of the Elder Slayer,' sneered Zokez. 'But you were actually *conceived* amidst this filth?'

Roh had no retort, no answer but a furious flash of her talons. She let the shame wash over her in a burning wave. What could one say in response to such a truth?

Rohesia the isruhe. *Cerys the Elder Slayer.*

She had no defence for herself, nor for her mother's actions all those centuries ago. But in that moment, all she could think of was the cell she knew best, somewhere behind that portcullis of bones. What most of the cyrens around her would never see: her incensed mother, hacking at her own hair with her talons, and the etchings of strange masks on the stone walls. In fact, there was only one person who had seen what she'd seen. Jaw and fists clenched, Roh turned to Odi, desperate for understanding.

He wasn't there.

She whirled around, scanning the group and the tunnel wildly. Her throat closed up. There was no sign of him.

CHAPTER TWELVE

Panic seized Roh's chest as she ran, leaving the prison and her fellow competitors far behind.

How could I have been so stupid? He had tried to escape once before. Why wouldn't he try again? She had to find him, before something happened. *If it hasn't already …* How far back had she lost him? How could she have been so *senseless?* Why hadn't she noticed he was no longer stuck to her side? She swore loudly as her boots pummelled the wet grit on the ground, retracing their earlier steps in a frenzy and following the tug of her inner compass. *It won't fail me this time,* she thought desperately. *It can't.*

She ascended the levels of Saddoriel at a sprint, sweat beading at her brow, her shirt damp. 'Odi! Odi?' she shouted as she ran, her voice straining. Would he answer once he realised how foolish he'd been in trying to escape the lair? If she didn't find him … If he was … She couldn't let herself think of it, not now. Instead, the image of Finn's smug face formed in her mind, along with the memory of him clapping his human on the back after shoving Odi. She spurred herself into an even faster sprint, her thighs and calves burning with the exertion.

'That. Fucking. Bastard,' she ground out. The common-tongue profanity was foreign on her lips, but its viciousness matched her rage. What had Finn done to Odi? What had she *let him* do? This was her fault, Odi was *her* responsibility. Once again, she had slipped up, underestimating the cunning of the competition. And it might have cost her the tournament, and Odi … It might have cost him so much more.

There was no sign of him. *None.* Mid-tunnel, she came to a stop, her rasping breathing the only sound she could hear. 'Odi!' she yelled, terror threatening to take complete hold of her. This couldn't be happening. Any semblance of hope was waning fast as she forced herself to run another yard down the dark passage, limbs heavy. What if she couldn't find him in time? What if she *never* found him? What if he had somehow succumbed to the lure of the lair and wandered its winding passages for the rest of his days? The thoughts caused a thick lump to form in her throat and she slowed once again. Hunching over, she rested her hands on her knees, sweat running freely from her hairline across the scales at her temples and dripping to the ground. The ground …

In her utter turmoil, she hadn't realised it had changed from wet grit to something soft. She narrowed her eyes and unsheathed her talons. Thick moss grew across the terrain here and the music around her quietened, as though what she was about to stumble upon was too sacred for sound, even the music of the lair. She raced down the mossy path, her heart in her throat as it opened up into an enormous grotto. From the ceiling of the cave, thousands of stalactites hung like daggers over a vast icy-blue pool. The surface of the water reflected its surroundings like a pane of polished glass. Weeping willows grew from the banks, their hanging leaves veiling much of the pool, and jagged rocks framed the water's edge.

Every cyren in Saddoriel knew of this place: *the Pool of Weeping.*

It was where the single most important ritual of cyrenkind took place: the First Cry. Even a lowly *isruhe* like Roh would have been brought here after birth, by Ames perhaps – but that didn't matter now.

'Odi?' she whispered, knowing that nothing good would come of her shouting in this sacred place. Her eyes followed a path of emerald-green moss that led from the border of the grotto out to the centre of the pool and stretched beyond the veil of willow trees. It was wide enough for only a single person to walk its length.

Something glinted in the corner of her eye. She lunged towards it, scooping up the item in her taloned hands: a shell. *Odi's* shell token.

'Odi!' His name came out as a desperate hiss. *He has to be here somewhere.* Clutching the protective token to her chest, she scanned the rippling ice-blue water and the fluttering leaves of the willow trees. There he was, swaying at the water's very edge on the far side, mesmerised by the infinite ripples.

Forcing herself to take slow and steady breaths, Roh approached Odi cautiously, mindful of startling him. When she reached his side, she grasped his forearm slowly but firmly.

'Odi,' she said softly. 'I've got you.'

His amber eyes were glazed over and his body careened from side to side, as though he didn't even realise she was there. The lure of the lair had him.

Quickly remembering what she held, Roh fumbled with the leather strap of the shell token in her trembling hand. It had been sliced clean through, she realised. Needing both hands, she placed herself between Odi and the water's edge, and knotted the two ends of the leather with numb fingers.

Dresmis, Thera, let this work, Roh prayed, looping the necklace around Odi's neck. The shell, slightly chipped, she noticed, dropped down to rest against his sternum.

Roh bit her lip hard enough to draw blood, her arms still resting on Odi's shoulders, poised to catch him should he fall. With her heart in her throat, hardly daring to hope, she searched his face …

As though a veil had been lifted, Odi's clear eyes slowly met hers. 'Roh?'

Her knees buckled and her whole body sagged as she staggered, only to be caught by Odi's steady arms before she could sink to the wet bank of the pool.

'Gods,' she muttered, head in her hands. If Roh ever cried, this would be the moment for it. But mixed in with her relief was the overwhelming grip of responsibility. It was her job to keep Odi alive. She had been so caught up in the prison, in Cerys, in the taunts and the whispers that she'd nearly blown her chance in the tournament, and had nearly cost Odi his life.

'For a moment, I thought you had meant to escape,' she said quietly.

'I didn't, not that time. But I've thought about it,' Odi replied. 'I *think* about it, still.'

'Even though you know you'd die?'

Odi flinched. 'Even then.'

Roh swallowed the hard lump in her throat, shock barrelling through her at Odi's admission. He would risk death rather than stay where he was?

'Roh?'

A second shockwave cascaded over her. Wasn't that exactly what she was doing in partaking in the tournament? She too risked death to challenge her place in the lair. Perhaps … perhaps she and this human were more alike than she cared to —

'Roh!' The urgency in Odi's voice wrenched her from the spiral of thoughts.

'What —'

The wail of an infant pierced the quiet and Odi pointed.

Icy fear and a pulsing premonition of danger gripped Roh. They shouldn't be here. She scrambled, dragging Odi by his sleeve and hauling them behind the thick exposed roots of a nearby willow tree, to peer through the gaps. A hooded, robed figure appeared, carrying a crying bundle in their arms, walking the length of the path that led to the centre of the pool beyond the willow fronds. The water rippled and the figure reached the end of the path, crouching, the infant still squalling. Roh's skin crawled as she witnessed the First Cry. The figure held the infant out over the pool, letting the tears fall in fat droplets to the water. At the offering, it was as though the whole lair shivered.

The piercing sound of the nestling's cries called an old verse to Roh's mind …

Oh hush now, little nestling,
One day you will find your song.
But quiet now, little nestling,
For in dream is where you belong …

This was what every cyren had in common; even those damn highborns Finn and Yrsa shared this with her. Every one of them had offered up their tears to Dresmis and Thera, to Saddoriel. To become one with the water, to be linked to cyren territories all over the realms. Keeping to the shadows, Roh motioned for Odi to follow her from the grotto, shaking her head. The Pool of Weeping was the beginning and the end of anything she shared with the rest.

When Roh and Odi returned to the entrance of Saddoriel, the archway of bones seemed more imposing than ever. It towered above them, its ivory components gleaming in the generous torchlight as they passed beneath it. The entrance was busy. Cyrens of all ranks crossed the open space, shooting her and Odi curious looks but not interfering. Still rattled, Roh had never felt so grateful to have a human, *her* human, at her side. She glanced in Odi's direction frequently, finding his lean frame a comforting presence in her peripheral vision, his ridiculous half-gloves failing to bother her as they once had. He was *alive*. He hadn't succumbed fully to the lure of the lair, and they still had a chance in this gods-forsaken tournament.

'You found him!' exclaimed a familiar voice. 'When you ran off like that, I feared the worst.' Roh turned to find Arcelia Bellfast approaching them, her human close behind.

'So did I,' Roh admitted, smiling at the warmth in Arcelia's tone. That too was a comfort.

Arcelia rested a hand on Roh's shoulder. 'You missed the instructions for the second trial,' she said.

Roh's heart sank. 'What?' She couldn't have missed that vital information. She couldn't have triumphed in finding Odi only to have missed the —

'We have to build something.' Arcelia's words cut into her panicked thoughts.

This was all part of Finn's plan. Rage simmered just below the surface. She was going to —

'Roh?'

Her eyes snapped back to Arcelia.

'We have to build something. That is the trial. It will be judged by the Council of Seven Elders.'

'Why … why are you telling me this?' Roh stammered, realising what her former tutor was doing.

Arcelia gave a strained smile. 'You warned me of the poisoned drinks at the gala. You laid no trap for Fasiel in the hunt. It's only fair that I share this with you. I owe you.'

Roh studied Arcelia's lilac gaze. She could sense nothing but sincerity and a keen sense of honour, not common amongst their kind. With another glance at Odi, Roh nodded slowly.

'Can you tell me – *us*, in the common tongue?' she asked.

Arcelia released Roh's shoulder. 'Very well,' she agreed, changing languages without missing a beat. 'The criteria for the second trial are as follows, with each criterion offering a maximum of five points. First, the item must have significant meaning to the cyrens of Saddoriel. Second, the item must be created with sophistication and finesse. Third, the item must have a practical application. Fourth, we will be scored on the originality of our concepts. And finally, we must meet the deadline as stipulated by the council. The projects are to be presented within the next moonspan.'

Ignoring the look of disbelief Odi was aiming at her, Roh herself gaped at the cyren before her. 'What?'

Arcelia's mouth was set in a straight, grim line. 'I know,' she said. 'It's not much time.'

'*Much time?* It's not *any* time.'

Arcelia merely shrugged.

'And that's the whole trial? That's all the instructions?'

'You have my word, Rohesia. That is all we were told.'

Roh believed her. 'Thank you,' she said, knowing full

well that none of the other competitors would have shared this information with her.

'Yes, thank you,' Odi's voice sounded from her side.

Arcelia looked at him, brows raised in surprise before a hint of a smile tugged at the corners of her mouth. She turned back to Roh, dipping her head slightly. 'We are even now, you and I?'

'We're even.'

'Then, I wish you – both of you,' she added, 'the best of luck.'

'You too, Arcelia,' Roh said, and meant it.

Build something. It sounded so *simple*, yet between the two little words lay a churning sea of doubt. What would be worthy of the lair? What made something original? What sort of creation was practical for a sector of highborns who had everything they needed?

Down in the workshop, Roh tried to palm the exhaustion from her eyes. After the ordeal of the tour and Arcelia's news, she and Odi had wandered all over Saddoriel, searching for inspiration for the trial. But it was as though upon mention of the trial, a solid wall sprang up between Roh and any semblance of an idea, blocking her at every possible turn. It hadn't helped that all throughout the evening, the phantom echo of the nestling's cry from the Pool of Weeping filled her mind, rendering her listless. For a time she had tried to lose herself in the heavy tome she'd borrowed from Andwana: *Life, Law and the Lair,* but in truth, she had no idea where to start. The table of contents alone was twenty pages long. Which was why they had ended up in the workshop, yet again. Roh, Harlyn and Orson sat huddled around Ames' desk at the front of the workshop, while Odi paced between the workbenches, toying with the protective token he'd come so close to losing.

Harlyn monitored him suspiciously, not taking her eyes off the human as she talked. 'Why don't you use your music theatre?' she asked, waving a hand to the back of the room where Roh's model sat hidden beneath its cloth.

Roh shook her head. 'It has to be built specifically for this tournament.'

'So build another.'

Sighing, Roh went to the back of the room and brought the model back to the bench, removing the fabric. She'd never shown her friends what it looked like up close and in detail, but now seemed like the right time. 'This took me *months*,' she explained. 'The initial sketches alone took weeks.'

'But you have the sketches,' Harlyn argued, turning the model around to examine it from all angles. 'It won't take half as long if you start again now.'

Odi stopped his pacing, approaching curiously. Roh found herself wringing her hands as she watched him wordlessly take in the details of her design. Her stomach swooped uncomfortably and she curled her toes in her boots; she didn't like feeling like this – exposed. Besides the tournament and her friends, her miniature music theatre was everything she cared about. She'd poured her heart and her soul into its design and creation for so long and now … Odi was seeing it, judging it. She may as well have been naked.

'I don't think the Council of Elders will see this to mean much to Saddoriel,' Orson said quietly.

Although Roh had already been disagreeing with Harlyn, her heart sank.

'Not because it's not incredible,' Orson added quickly, with a worried glance at Roh's fallen face. 'But because it's for the Lower Sector. If it's not for *them* … Well, they won't see the meaning, will they? They want for nothing up there. They *need* nothing. Did you not just visit the queen's music theatre today?'

'Yes,' Roh admitted. 'And it was a thousandfold better than this thing.'

Orson sighed. 'What about —'

'No, it wasn't,' Odi said suddenly.

Roh struggled to swallow. 'What?'

'The one we saw today, it wasn't a thousandfold better than yours.' Odi's voice was clear and sturdy. 'It was just different, Roh.'

Roh and Orson fell quiet, looking at the human boy with a begrudging admiration. Harlyn eyed him dubiously, a sharp comment undoubtedly poised on her tongue.

'But Orson's right,' he continued, resting his palms flat on the workbench and meeting Harlyn's gaze as if in challenge. 'Even if Roh somehow managed to build another model in time, the Upper Sector already has its music theatre. And I get the sense that your Council of

Elders are not the sort to use valuable resources and currency on those lesser than themselves.'

It was the most Roh had ever heard him speak. His eyes were bright with amusement as he surveyed their surprise. 'You could always just make another big cage to trap us useless humans in?'

Roh braced herself for Harlyn's bloodletting. Her friend was barely tolerating Odi's presence as it was, and now, Odi had outright provoked her. Orson looked as panicked as Roh felt, and had not-so-subtly placed herself between Harlyn and the human. Harlyn, however, looked thrilled.

'Finally,' she said, drumming her talons against the bench. 'I was wondering when you'd come out of that sad little shell of yours.'

'As soon as you three stop talking in circles and come up with a decent plan,' Odi quipped, holding her stare. He drew a stool up to the bench and took a seat.

Roh froze, waiting for the others' outrage to hit, that a human dared to join them at their table. A human boy thinking he was part of their ranks? But Orson and Harlyn were quiet, watching him with renewed interest, as though he were now something other than an inconvenience. Harlyn gave Roh a sideways look, for once saying nothing.

Roh took this as her cue to continue. 'What about a suit of armour?' she asked. 'For the queen?'

'The queen already has armour,' Harlyn said flatly. 'And last time I checked, you weren't an armourer.'

'The queen's armour is made out of sea-serpent

scales,' Orson said. 'I'm sure one of our tutors mentioned it during our lessons.'

'Ah yes, our extensive education,' Harlyn said with mock fondness.

Orson gave a roguish grin before continuing. 'It used to be some sort of sport – hunting sea-serpent scales.'

'*What?*' Odi choked. 'Sea serpents are … *real?* I thought they were just myths, made up to scare little children.'

Orson ignored this. 'Glory seekers would attempt to acquire a scale for the ruler's armour. It went on for centuries, but the sport got outlawed after the Age of Chaos. So many cyrens had already perished that it was deemed senseless for more of our kind to die for a simple sport.'

Roh stilled her tapping foot beneath the workbench with a glance at Odi, who looked just as impatient. 'This is all very well and good,' she told her friends. 'But I think it's safe to say that both these options are out. What else?'

The trio reeled through numerous items Roh could build, each one struck off the list of possibilities faster than the previous. Their ideas were too impractical or unrealistic, or even worse, unoriginal. They debated the meaning of the criteria hotly, frustrated that their intended audience knew nothing of need.

Roh rubbed her temples, a headache starting to bloom behind her eyes. 'The practicality aspect of the criteria is basically redundant,' she sighed. 'I need to *build something.* What *can* I build?'

Odi rolled his shoulders. 'Maybe it's not a matter of what *you* can build, but what *we* —'

The door to the workshop creaked open, and young Jesmond poked her head in. 'Busy?' she asked.

'Yes,' Roh replied curtly.

But Jesmond, as she always did, ignored the social cue and strode in, a money purse bulging proudly at her belt.

'I wouldn't go wandering around with that on display,' Harlyn muttered as Jesmond joined them at the bench.

Jesmond grinned, patting the pouch fondly. 'Plenty more where that came from.'

'Profiting off the back of the tournament, are you?' Roh asked, eyeing the purse.

The bone-cleaner-turned-gambler gave a dark laugh. 'Isn't that what you're aiming to do, Roh?'

'Jes, what do you need?' Orson asked gently. 'We're in the middle of something here.'

'As a matter of fact ...' Jesmond produced a wrinkled sheet of folded parchment and a short quill from her pocket. 'I thought Roh here might have some insider tips for me.'

'Tips?'

'That's right. On the other competitors. On the inner workings, you know, to help me point my ... clients ... in the right direction. You and your human look pretty chummy. A good dynamic forming there, that works in your favour.'

Roh scoffed in disbelief. 'You're not serious.'

'When it comes to the exchange of our beautiful currency, I'm always serious.' Jesmond spoke with a straight face and now stood patiently waiting for Roh to divulge tournament gossip.

'Oh, get out of here, Jes.' Harlyn waved her off.

'What?' Jes looked genuinely perplexed. She shrugged off Harlyn's protests and pulled up a stool, turning her attention to Odi. 'You, human … How are you feeling about the pending trial? What do you think your odds are?'

Odi looked the younger fledgling up and down, and burst into laughter. The sound came from deep within, his shoulders shaking.

I've never heard him laugh, Roh realised. Like Orson's, his laughter had a contagious nature and Roh soon found amusement on her own lips.

'Well, I don't know about *odds*,' Odi was saying, eyes watering. 'But I do plan on living a lot longer than the next four weeks.'

Jesmond's expression was still utterly serious as she put quill to parchment and noted down his words, nodding to herself. 'Good to know,' she said.

This only incited more laughter from Roh and Odi, with Harlyn and Orson joining in as Harlyn got out of her seat to shoo the youngster towards the door.

Jesmond tried to evade Harlyn's arms. 'You'd stop me from making an honest living?'

'Your honest living is cleaning bones,' Roh called after her as Harlyn finally got Jesmond to the door —

Both cyrens had frozen on the spot.

'What is it —' Roh stopped when she saw. It wasn't a matter of *what* it was, but *who*.

Finn Haertel pushed past Harlyn and Jesmond, and with his burly human close behind, strode into the workshop as though he owned it. As though he owned everything anyone had ever touched.

'Where's Master Ames?' he demanded, his harsh lilac eyes going straight to Roh.

Roh gritted her teeth. 'What do you need Ames for?' she said quietly, remembering the last words she'd spat at the highborn, remembering what he'd done to Odi's token and all that had nearly happened because of him.

'That's none of your concern,' Finn retorted, scanning the room. 'Where is he?'

Roh's talons itched to be unsheathed.

'He's not here.' Orson stepped in, her voice soft and calm. 'You might find him in the mentor quarters, two levels up.'

Roh elbowed her. 'What are you doing?' she hissed angrily.

Finn eyed her with utter disgust, his gaze lingering on the fresh pink scar that now marred the old one on her cheek, before he turned on his heel and left, his human trailing behind him. Roh's fingers went to the cut that had now healed over, though she still remembered the sharp slice of the coral through her flesh.

'Roh,' Orson said, her eyes full of reproach. '*You* might be competing against him, but to us, he's still the son of a council elder.'

The frustration in Roh deflated and she gave Orson a grim smile. 'I know. Sorry.'

'What's that lech doing, showing up here, anyway?' Jesmond dropped into Harlyn's seat and made herself comfortable, despite Harlyn's protests.

Roh sighed heavily. 'I don't know, but I can't say I like it much.'

Three days went by in a blur and Roh was no closer to deciding what to build for the second trial. She spent much of her time pacing back and forth, in her chambers, at the workshop and at the Great Hall in the early hours of the morning, when she found it deserted. But no matter the amount of walking, no matter how many great feats of architecture she exposed herself to, her mind remained blank. She was at a complete loss, and her growing anxiety took her from one scattered thought to the next, always dismissing her ideas as reckless, stupid or unoriginal. She felt the walls of pressure closing in around her, leaving her with less and less room to breathe.

The bathwater had grown cold as Roh lay fuming in the tub, her arms draped over the sides. She had thought a long soak might force her to relax and consequently unlock some brilliant idea at the back of her mind. She'd been wrong. All the solitude had done was feed her obsessive worries, and though she hadn't acknowledged it aloud, Finn Haertel's appearance at the workshop had unnerved her more than she cared to admit. Alone in the bath, she could no longer deny it to herself. Seeing him there, pristine as ever and making demands, had made her skin crawl. His presence in the Lower Sector, standing before her friends, in *her* workshop ... Her worlds were colliding and it made her gut clench. He and his poisonous ways did not belong there. He brought an icy coldness to one of the few places in Talon's Reach that held any sort of warmth.

Roh let herself sink to the bottom of the tub, submerging herself completely in the cool water, pretending just for a moment that it was the salt-kissed sea. She watched the bubbles of air float leisurely from her mouth up to the surface, where they broke. It had been a long time since she'd used her cyren ability to breathe under water, but the skill was instinct. She closed her eyes and took a breath.

The warlocks, male and female, were preserved in the state they'd been in when they broke into the prison. They wore frayed travelling cloaks and heavy boots, coated with blood and dirt after whatever skirmish had taken place. Some of their fatal wounds could be seen – a slashed throat, a dagger embedded in the side of a neck and a gaping hole in a gut. Others were hidden beneath layers of blood-soaked clothing. Eerily, the warlocks had been propped up in standing positions, their eyes frozen open to stare dead ahead, some of their mouths twisted in agony or surprise. One warlock, a female, held a scythe at her side in a bloodied hand, while the one that stood directly across from Cerys' cell ... Roh found him the most disturbing. His frozen half-snarl, the smear of red on the quartz dagger clutched in his hand ...

Roh broke the surface of the water with a gasp. Her dreams had been addled with scenes like this of late and they always left her with a keen eagerness to visit her mother, drawing her to Saddoriel's prison like a sailor to a cyren's song. She got out of the tub and pulled on one of the soft bathrobes hanging on the back of the door, its fluffy material softer than anything she'd ever owned.

She opened the door a crack and called out to Odi: 'I want to visit Cerys. Get yourself ready.' She didn't wait for a reply before closing the door. As she towelled her hair dry, she thought of her last visit and wondered if she might see the queen down there again. For a moment, the queen hadn't been Queen Delja the Triumphant, she'd been a sad cyren who had once known Roh's mother, centuries ago. A cyren who knew things Roh had only ever dreamed of knowing. Sighing, she pulled on her undergarments and clothes over her damp hair and caught a glimpse of herself in the mirror. The days of endless anxiety had made themselves known in the deep purple smudges beneath her moss-green eyes, and despite the superior food of the Upper Sector, she had lost weight, her collarbone jutting out from beneath her loose shirt. She made a note to herself to eat a second portion of dinner that night. The last thing she needed was her strength wasting away.

She entered the main quarters, braiding her hair down one side to find Odi sitting at the window bench as usual, his expression far away with the delicate notes of the fiddles playing somewhere beyond.

'Are you ready?' she asked him, searching for her boots.

Odi continued to gaze out the window. 'About that …'

'About what?'

'I don't think we should go to the prison, Roh.'

Roh folded her arms over her chest. 'Since when?'

Odi turned his head, taking in her combative stance. 'Since ever, actually. No good comes of it.'

The tips of Roh's fingers tingled, her talons ready to spring free. 'How would *you* know?'

'I've been there with you. I know better than anyone. Why do you *want* to go?'

Roh had asked herself that question a thousand times, but it had never been posed aloud. What did she want? A mother. A father. Answers. The constant ache of loss she carried in her chest didn't make sense, because how could she miss what she'd never known? Before she could answer, a knock sounded at the door.

'Don't hate me,' Odi said, turning his gaze back to the window.

'What? Why —'

The door opened and Ames entered, his expression stern.

'What are you doing here?' Roh asked, forgetting herself.

Ames closed the door behind him with a click. 'I was informed that you wished to make one of your unofficial visits to the prison.'

Roh shot an incredulous look at Odi, who was pointedly ignoring her. 'Informed? You've got my own human spying on me?'

'Your own?' Odi laughed darkly. 'I am not yours to own. And I did it *out of concern*. Last time, we saw *the queen* down there.'

'You what?' Ames' lilac eyes flashed and he took a step towards Roh.

'It's nothing.' Roh waved her hand dismissively. 'She said she often goes down there.'

'If Queen Delja is visiting the prison cells of Saddoriel, it's certainly not *nothing*.'

'But, Ames —'

'*How many times must I tell you, Rohesia?* You should *not* be visiting Cerys. It's dangerous.' Ames had never raised his voice to her before; Roh had to fight the urge to cower beneath its deep rumble. She fell quiet, face burning.

'She has nothing to offer you,' he said, gentler this time. The older cyren went to her and squeezed her shoulder. 'I do not say this to be cruel.'

She sniffed. 'I know.'

'And you know that reality is long lost to her, don't you?'

Cerys' off-kilter smile and hacked, uneven hair came to Roh's mind. 'Yes.'

'Good.' Ames released her shoulder and went to the settee at the foot of her bed. 'Now tell me of this trial.'

Roh sighed, massaging the ache that had begun to pulse at her temples. 'I have to build something,' she said. She would rather be thrown into the fray of another hunt than turn up to the second trial empty-handed.

Ames clasped his hands in his lap and looked to Odi. 'I see.'

Roh frowned. 'See what?'

'Odi,' Ames said. 'What do you make of it?'

'I think the trial, and your whole damn way of life, is barbaric.' He said it with a venom Roh hadn't heard before, and she waited for Ames to snap, to preach the virtues of preserving the cyren culture.

'True,' Ames said, to Roh's utter disbelief. 'But nothing can be done about that. *Yet*. So tell me, what do you make of the second trial?'

Roh watched Odi eye her mentor with a steady gaze before he shrugged and turned back to the window. Roh could have sworn a glimmer of disappointment crossed Ames' face before he stood and met her eyes.

'Promise me you won't return to the prison?'

Her stomach churned uneasily as she grappled with herself. Finally, she ground out the words: 'I promise.'

'Good,' he said, before something caught his eye. The book on Roh's bedside table. He picked it up and turned it over in his hands, running a taloned finger down the thick spine. 'I'm glad to see you're taking some interest in the Law of the Lair.'

Roh frowned. 'Why do you say that?'

'For one, you've always had a difficult disregard for authority. Two, knowing what restricts you can also highlight that which liberates.'

Clicking her tongue in frustration, Roh snatched the tome from her mentor. 'Can you elaborate? This thing is one of a million volumes. I can barely get through the first. Even if I could, there's no way I could remember everything.'

'True,' Ames mocked. 'You do have a rather narrow mind.'

Roh glared at him.

Ames adjusted his collar, covering up the small patch

of discoloured skin that had started to show. 'Just keep reading. You never know when a piece of knowledge will serve you well.'

When he had left, Roh watched Odi carefully. He still hadn't moved from where he was perched on the window bench, his brow furrowed in concentration. Roh hadn't really taken a moment to consider what it had been like for him down here amongst the cyrens, forced to partake in something that he didn't believe in and that regularly jeopardised his life. And yet, he had committed to it. He had proposed as many ideas as Harlyn and Orson had. And he had saved her life during the first trial.

She approached the window bench and waited for him to move his legs aside so she could sit. He didn't budge.

'Why did you tell Ames I wanted to go see Cerys?' she asked, leaning against the wall instead.

'He told me to send for him if you were in trouble.'

'How?'

'There are water channels.'

'What do you mean?' Roh demanded.

'Channels that Ames uses to communicate, mainly with your kind —' Odi cut himself off. 'I can't tell you more than that.'

Roh's brows shot up. 'What? You and Ames have *secrets* now?'

'I gave my word, Roh. He cares about you. More than you know. Let it go.'

There was something about Odi's tone that made Roh acquiesce. 'I wasn't in trouble,' she muttered.

'It felt like … It felt like you might be on the brink.'

'Of what?'

'Making a bad decision. You had this look in your eyes, like no one could stop you. And seeing Cerys – seeing your mother – it's not done much good in the past, has it? You need to be focusing on this trial. Not running off chasing ghosts.'

Roh let herself slide to the floor, tilting her head back to rest against the cool surface of the wall. He was right. Deep in her bones, she knew he was right, and yet she still couldn't escape the harrowing temptation of those tunnels.

'Odi?' she asked quietly.

'Hmm?'

'Do I look like her?'

The human turned his amber gaze to her, taking his time to study her features. She watched his eyes scan her own, then her nose, her cheeks, her jawline … 'Sometimes,' he allowed.

'Only sometimes?'

Odi gave a nod. 'Most of the time, you just look like you.'

Later, they ate on the floor in their quarters, an array of hot dishes and bread spread out before them. But the rich stews and roasted vegetables may as well have been gruel as Roh chewed mechanically, tasting nothing, unable to shake the feeling of despair that had blanketed her. It had been days since Arcelia had given her the instructions and she still had nothing, not an inkling of an idea of what to build. Each hour that ticked by took her further and further away from her dream. Her dream of freedom, of power, of a better Saddoriel for her friends and herself. A place where cyrens were encouraged to explore without fear of retribution or judgement. A lair that was generous with its magic and music, no matter in which sector a cyren resided. A Saddoriel that offered its inhabitants choice, *real choice*. Choices that Roh and Harlyn and Orson had craved all these years. She sighed. She had taken to flipping through the law tome in silence, hoping that some random image or sentence would inspire a groundbreaking idea.

'What?' she snapped without looking up, feeling Odi's gaze linger on her.

'Why was Ames asking for my opinion of the trial?' he asked.

Roh gave an irritated shrug. 'I thought that was something you'd know, being his new best friend and all.'

Odi rolled his eyes. 'I'm serious.'

'So am I.'

'Has it ever occurred to you that the other cyrens might not utilise their humans' strengths and skills?'

Slowly, Roh lifted her gaze to his. 'You said you were a … shopkeeper in your realm. What sort of shop?'

Odi placed his wine carefully on the floor. 'A craftsman, really. It's my father's shop. We sell and fix instruments.'

Roh sighed with frustration, picking up her goblet and taking a long drink. 'Well, we have to build something from scratch. Not mend something that's broken.'

'I didn't just *mend* them,' Odi told her quietly.

'What else did you do, then?'

'I made them.'

Roh blinked. 'Made *what*, exactly?'

'Pianos.'

'And what is a piano?'

'*What?* How do you not know what a piano is? Your lives down here revolve around music.'

Roh refilled both their goblets with a generous pour of wine. 'Just tell me.'

'It's a musical instrument. It … Well, you sit down at it, you play it with your fingers on what we call keys.'

Roh tilted her head. 'Keys? Like money?'

'No, we call our money "coin", not "keys" like here. Keys on a piano are … Look, why does it matter? It creates music.'

'Beautiful music?'

'It can.'

'And you know how to make one of these … pianos?' Roh said it slowly.

Odi nodded, taking a sip from his goblet. 'I do.'

An ember of hope glowed in Roh's chest, though she didn't yet dare let it flare to life. 'This could work … If it does what you say it does … We could build one.'

'We would need the right materials,' Odi countered.

Roh forced herself to exhale slowly, containing the fire within. 'And if we found the right materials? Or similar materials at least?'

'Then it could maybe be done.'

Something dawned on Roh. 'We would have to be able to demonstrate what it can do. Could you do that? Could you show them?'

Odi had started shaking his head before she had even finished her sentence. 'I can only tune the instrument. Perform basic scales to test the inner workings of it.'

Roh felt as though her chest had caved in, the glowing ember within completely snuffed out. They had been *so close*. The idea was a good one, she was sure of it. But without proof of the instrument's abilities, it was useless. 'We can't do it, then,' she said, her voice hollow. 'We have no way to show the council what it can do.'

Odi was studying her tentatively. 'I can't show them,' he said slowly. 'But … the Eery Brothers can.'

CHAPTER THIRTEEN

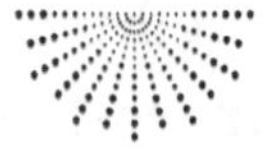

'How do you propose to *pay* for all of this?' Ames asked the next morning, scowling at the list of materials Roh handed him in his study. As his eyes scanned its contents in disbelief, she looked around. The place hadn't changed much. Ames' dimly lit study was in the mentor quarters two levels above the workshop. Nearly every surface was covered in piles of parchment and small vials of who-knew-what, which had always struck Roh as strange, even as a nestling, because everything she knew about Ames told her he was not a scholar. She had found herself here a number of times over the years, mainly when she and Harlyn had skipped lessons as nestlings. They had stood exactly where Roh and Odi stood now, and Ames had worn the exact same stern frown as he'd reprimanded them. If only Harlyn could see him in this moment, Roh knew the two of them wouldn't be able to contain their laughter at the absurdity of it.

'Maple wood, felt, nails …' Ames rattled off the list of items that she and Odi had spent all night creating. On the floor of their chamber, Roh had watched Odi put charcoal to parchment and sketch the curves of the piano. He had explained the main parts to her before starting a fresh design, detailing the inner workings of the instrument. To say it was a complex task was a vast understatement. But as Odi's half-gloved, charcoal-smudged fingers had worked their way across the parchment, his brow furrowing in deep concentration, Roh couldn't help the flutter of excitement in her chest at the thrill of creating something, and the possibility that this might *actually* work.

'Rohesia?' Ames was saying, the list still clutched in his weathered hands. 'How much do you have to your name? A handful of bronze keys, if that? Are you expecting your friends to pool their savings for you?'

The comment was like the flash of a hidden dagger, no warning but for a glimpse of silver before it drove straight into her heart. Ames knew the barb had hit home; Roh could tell from the flash of satisfaction in his eyes. Was he testing her? Or was this the messy aftermath of his decision to help her?

'Never,' she said coldly as she forced her gaze to his. *You made your choice,* she tried to convey with her eyes.

The lines of Ames' face softened and the single nod he gave told her he had understood, and that she was right.

'Then I'll ask again: how do you propose to pay for all these materials?'

'I'm going to be resourceful,' she said.

'Wonderful.' Impatience laced his tone. 'Then why are you here showing me this?'

'Because we need a workspace —'

'The workshop is *completely out of the question,* as you very well know.'

Roh cursed herself for not asking Orson to negotiate on her behalf. Her sweet-natured friend had a way with Ames, and the hardened old cyren definitely had a soft spot for that pretty round face and wide eyes.

'I'm not asking to use the workshop, Ames,' Roh countered.

'What, then? You seem to think I have endless hours to stand here playing guessing games with you.'

'Roh said you mentioned a place to her, months ago,' Odi ventured, taking a step towards Ames. 'An old tree-felling site?' Odi's eyes were alight, as though the project had awakened new life in him, too.

'Rohesia twists the truth. I told her of no such thing. I mentioned it to a fellow cyren in passing, and her overly large ears happened to hear,' Ames said sourly.

Roh felt the corners of her mouth tug upwards. They were close to convincing him – she could always tell when he started to use superficial insults. Sure enough, Ames was considering Odi thoughtfully.

'You know all the others will be getting help,' she added, as Ames patted his pockets in search of something.

'Who said anything about help?' Ames frowned,

snatching up a bundle of keys from amidst the documents on his desk and striding towards the door, his robes billowing behind him.

'Ames?' she asked slowly, frowning at his left hand by his side.

He gave a frustrated sigh. 'You really are in the gambling mood today, aren't you, Rohesia? Perhaps you should seek out Jesmond after this. Tell me, what now?'

'I just …' Her frown deepened. 'What's wrong with your hand?'

Ames looked down and saw what she was seeing: an uncontrollable tremor. 'Oh, that,' he allowed, turning his shaking hand over to examine it himself. 'The lasting effects of an illness I had as a child,' he told her. 'It flares up now and again, *particularly* when someone causes me stress,' he added pointedly, shoving his hand in his pocket.

Roh didn't dare say another word as she and Odi followed him down a slippery spiral staircase and into a dark tunnel. Ames held a torch high as they walked the length of the unknown passage, tripping over gnarled roots, droplets of water from the ceiling hitting their heads. They walked for an age, it seemed, but Roh stayed quiet, lest Ames change his mind. At long last, they came to a thick timber door, reinforced with iron embellishments.

Ames produced the bundle of keys from his robes and unlocked the door with his good hand, straining to push it open with his shoulder. Odi leaned in as well and the heavy door creaked inwards. A forest – or what had once been a forest – lay before them. The majority of the trees had been chopped down, leaving only stumps sticking up from the ground like round stakes, dried pollen cones wrapped in webs of spider silk littering their bases. Roh stared into the pattern of rings in each one of the felled trees' trunks, a circle within for every season of memory.

'They harvested these trees to make improvements on the Elder Council meeting room and residences,' Ames explained. 'No one comes down here now, and won't until the next crop is due to be planted.'

Roh stared in wonder at the tree graveyard. 'Where are we, exactly?'

'The eastern outskirts of Talon's Reach,' Ames replied.

'What about those trees over there?' Odi pointed to the few dozen remaining trees, their trunks thin and pale. 'What type are they?'

The corner of Ames' mouth twitched. 'Sea birch. And as far as Saddoriel is concerned, this crop has been harvested.'

A kernel of hope flickered in Roh's chest. 'So we can use those trees?'

Ames slid his gaze to hers and raised a brow. 'What trees?'

Roh bit back a triumphant grin. That would have to do. She gave Odi a gentle push. 'Go see if we can use them instead of your maple wood. And if there's enough of them.'

Odi nodded and left her with Ames.

'He's … an interesting fellow,' her mentor mused, watching the human weave through the rows of stumps towards the living trees on the far side. When he reached them, he ran his palms flat across the trunks and tested the suppleness of the lower, smaller branches, bending them between both hands.

'Do you want me to look at the design?' Ames said in a low voice, not taking his eyes from Odi.

Roh started. After all his protests, was Ames offering to *help*? She contemplated the charcoal drawings tucked safely away in the pack she'd brought. The numerous pages detailed the working layered parts of the instrument and how they fitted together, each line, each curve painstakingly drawn by Odi. He had sketched without hesitation, jotting down the various dimensions and calculations.

To her own surprise, Roh found herself shaking her head at Ames' offer. 'Thank you, but … the design is solid,' she told him.

He wiped the apprehension from his face. 'You can borrow tools from the workshop – we have saws, clamps and glue. You'll need to return everything once you've used it.'

'Of course.'

Ames fumbled with his bundle of keys, the metallic jangling echoing in the barren space. There was a soft thud in the dirt.

'I seem to have dropped my key,' he said vaguely. 'Let me know if you find it.'

Roh smiled, a speck of bronze glinting up at her from the ground.

Ames cleared his throat. 'I hope you know what you're doing, Rohesia.'

Roh sighed, watching Odi, who was still running his hands across the tree trunks. 'So do I.'

When Ames had left, Roh pocketed the key and approached the remaining trees. 'What do you think?' she asked Odi, gazing at the sea-birch leaves fanning out above. 'Will they do?'

Odi had snapped off several branches to examine the density and flexibility of the wood. He took up a stick and forced it to bend between his fingers. 'We usually use layers of maple to create the body of the instrument,' he told her. 'But this seems supple enough. See how it bows to the pressure but doesn't snap? That's what we want. What are these trees usually used for?'

'I'm not sure. Furniture … Building frames?' Roh took a guess.

Odi nodded. 'That sounds like the sort of timber we need.'

'Well, that's a start,' Roh allowed. She took in the small pocket of woods before them. 'We will have to cut these down ourselves.'

Odi shrugged. 'Then we'll cut them down.'

Roh huffed a laugh. She didn't know if she was relieved or overwhelmed by the fact that suddenly, things were that simple.

'Have you got some sort of lever or pulley system that could get it onto a trolley once it's built?' Odi asked, scanning the otherwise barren cavern. 'It's a heavy instrument.'

Roh nodded, thinking of the types of machinery and mechanisms she'd seen over the years. If there was one benefit to being from the Lower Sector, it was that she knew how things got done down here.

'Then that just leaves the strings.'

Roh ran her fingers across her circlet. 'The strings?'

'You have the designs?' Odi asked, palm upturned, waiting.

'In here,' Roh said, rummaging through her pack and passing him the handful of folded parchment.

Odi crouched, smoothing his crumpled drawing across the ground and running a finger across the charcoal lines. 'These. They create the notes, the music.'

Roh knelt in the dirt beside him, studying the detailed design and following the arrows he'd scribbled to show where the strings went. 'What sort of string do we need?'

'Specialty string.'

Whatever Roh had eaten that morning curdled slowly in her stomach. *Of course.* Why hadn't she foreseen this problem? There would be no special music string in Saddoriel. 'And where do we find that?' she ground out, furious with herself for not interrogating him more intensely the night before.

'Home,' Odi said simply. 'My home.'

Roh sucked in a deep breath, fuelling the fire within. '*Your* home? As in, the *human* realm?'

'We can make do with different wood and felt and keys from Saddoriel, but the strings … We need the true strings if this has any chance of working at all.'

Roh stood, drawing herself to her full height, letting

her talons slip from their sheaths. 'You tricked me.' Her voice was deadly quiet.

Odi got to his feet, now eye level with her. '*What?*'

Roh stared into those bright amber eyes, trying to grapple with the fury that was simmering just beneath the surface. 'You're trying to dupe me into letting you go home.'

'No, I'm not, Roh.'

She hated the way her name sounded on his lips: familiar, as though the time they had spent huddled over charcoal and parchment now somehow gave him the right to manipulate her. Did he really think he could match the cunning of a Saddorien cyren?

She closed the gap between them in a single step, eyes flashing. 'Do not lie to me.'

But Odi didn't back away as she'd expected. With his jaw and fists clenched, he took a step towards her. 'I'm no liar.'

Roh's eyes bored into his, waiting for him to crumble, to run. He *should* run. Didn't he know where he was? Didn't he know what her kind did to humans like him? But neither human nor cyren was willing to yield; the tension between them was palpable, almost a living, breathing entity in itself. Roh stared him down, but Odi, damn him, stared right back.

Roh exhaled hotly through her nose and swore. 'Fine,' she snapped, stepping back and sheathing her talons. This was the plan they had, the *only* plan. If she wanted to stay in the tournament, she would have to make it work. They could address the issue of strings later.

At least Odi had the good sense not to look smug. 'We'll cut down the trees,' he said, moving back to the drawings at their feet. 'And prepare the timber. We'll also need a supple metal to weld into a frame of sorts. To make the body.'

The rage that had coursed through Roh's body only moments before ebbed away, replaced by an urgent sense of purpose. She crossed her arms over her chest as Odi pointed to the sketches. 'We'll leave the metal to Orson,' she heard herself say. 'She's far more likely to get results from the welders than my circlet-wearing scar-face.'

Odi glanced up, a tentative smile tugging at his mouth. 'Come now, your face isn't *that* bad.'

A laugh burst from Roh and she shook her head. 'You're unbelievable,' she told him. 'Enough messing about. We've got to get our hands on a saw.'

They spent the rest of the morning gathering tools and materials around Saddoriel, stopping by the workshop briefly to ask Orson for her assistance in obtaining the metal Odi needed. With all the other materials they could manage, Roh and Odi returned to the abandoned forest, bringing a supply of food and drink with them as well. If Roh knew anything about working long hours, it was how important sustenance was. They heaved the tools towards the far corner of the crop, where the trees still stood. Saws, clamps, sanding papers, hammers, nails, cans of glue ... Roh was quietly impressed with what they'd achieved in such a short span of time, but now ... Now the true work began.

Odi picked up one end of the felling saw. 'Ready?'

Roh took up the other end. 'Ready.'

The physicality of cutting down the birches was liberating. Each time they put the serrated edge to a pale trunk and began to saw, a new wave of relief rushed through Roh at the singularity of her focus. She thought only of the motion of the felling saw and the tally of trees. The sea birches groaned beneath the blade, its teeth digging into the fine grain, sending a shower of shavings floating to the ground. Roh pushed and heaved, the rhythm of each pass across the timber taking over, completely numbing her mind as she focused on sliding the saw back and forth across the cut. Her arms ached and her hands blistered beneath the rough handle. The fabric of her shirt became damp against her back, and sweat lined her circlet and stung her eyes, but she pressed on, relishing the distraction. An ear-splitting *crack* sounded and the trunk they'd been sawing leaned dangerously to one side. Odi motioned for her to move as he put his boot to it and kicked. The birch fell, its leaves cushioning its fall.

Roh dabbed at the perspiration at her hairline. 'How many do you think we need?'

Dabbing at his own sweat with the sleeve of his shirt, Odi looked around, mouthing the numbers as he counted. 'We've done seven ... Let's do sixteen, maybe seventeen more?'

Roh nodded, digging deep into her rucksack for the

water skein she'd brought. She handed it to him wordlessly.

'Thanks,' he said gratefully, drinking deeply before handing it back.

'Can't have you passing out mid-build,' Roh said, taking a swig herself. She surveyed the materials and tools they'd piled nearby … There was much work yet to be done.

'Guess not,' Odi replied. He rummaged in their rucksack and took out a loaf of crusty bread. Tearing it in half, he handed the larger piece to Roh. With a murmur of thanks, she took it, aware of the newfound ease between them. The quiet they shared as they worked was comfortable. There was a rhythm to their movements that reminded Roh of working with Harlyn and Orson, where each party knew what needed to be done and performed their tasks without complaint.

When they had finished felling the trees, Odi showed her how to remove the bark from the tree's body. Her back ached as she hunched over the fallen trunks, hooking an iron rod beneath the bark and levering off the tree's skin. It was not too dissimilar from cleaning bones. Splinters bit into her palms as she tore the bark away, the ripping sound loud in her ears. She didn't know how long they'd been working, but the bone cleaner in her was used to pushing through exhaustion and hard labour. They shed the trunks of their scratchy husks, finally dusting their hands on their pants when they were done. Roh's skin itched as dirt settled into her sweat.

'Now what?' she asked, wiping her eyes with the hem of her shirt.

Odi lifted another saw and Roh sighed. With a grunt, she tore one of the sleeves from her shirt and tied it around the lower half of her face. She knew that inhaling shavings was no good and slowed her work immensely. She ripped off the second sleeve and handed it to Odi. 'Tie this across your nose and mouth,' she told him, another exchange of small kindnesses between them. She didn't want to think about what those meant, not as their work crept towards the uneasy matter of the strings. Odi did as she bid and took up his place at one of the naked logs, saw in hand.

The hour was late when the duo could work no longer. They collapsed on the dirt, grimy and exhausted, hands blistered, tugging down their makeshift masks.

'How much more?' Roh panted.

Odi pushed the sweaty hair from his eyes. 'I think that should do it for the sawing.'

'Are you sure?' Despite the tight soreness wrapping around her body, she wasn't sure she was ready to be finished with the brunt of the physical work. It meant that she was all the closer to having to make a decision on what to do about the damn strings they needed. Her mind was already pulling her in a hundred different directions.

'No. We'll cut more if we need it, but I don't think we can do any more tonight.'

Roh hated it when he was right, so she said nothing as she reached for the rucksack once again and made them eat, though neither of them wanted to. The flatcakes she'd packed were bland, but it was just as well. She couldn't have stomached anything more decadent if she'd wanted to. They passed a second water skein between them, resting with their backs against the discarded offcuts of timber.

'We'll rest here for a few hours,' Roh said.

'Here?'

'Do you fancy the trip back to the Upper Sector, only to come back down?'

Odi glanced at the door, clearly calculating the time it would take to get to their chambers, pulley systems and tunnels included. 'Fair point.'

With a terse nod, Roh got up and checked the locked door back to the passageway. She returned to their patch of dirt, dropped to the ground and shoved her rucksack into a makeshift pillow.

'Roh?' Odi said, voice filled with trepidation.

'What?'

'I'm not trying to trick you.'

Uneasiness roiling in her gut, Roh closed her eyes and didn't reply.

Roh awoke bleary-eyed and aching to a sudden hammering at the door. With a moan of pain, she staggered to her feet, her muscles protesting loudly as she stumbled towards the persistent pounding.

'We don't have all day,' Harlyn's voice called through the thick timber and iron.

With callused, blistered hands and no sense of the hour, Roh fumbled with the bolt.

'Finally,' Harlyn said as the door swung open, her lute strapped across her back as usual.

To Roh's great relief, her friends stood with a wad of light metal sheets between them. 'Odi,' she called. 'Come and help.'

Odi was as bleary-eyed as she was, but he stumbled over to them all the same and took up Orson's end of the metal sheets.

'Is this what you needed?' Orson asked worriedly, following them inside.

Harlyn let out a low whistle. 'What is this place?' she asked, taking in the sight of the tree graveyard.

'An old sea-birch forest,' Roh told her, watching as Odi flexed a single sheet and it warped to his touch. 'What do you think?' she asked him, ignoring the tightness in her chest.

He looked to Harlyn and Orson. 'This is perfect,' he said. 'Thank you.'

'Yes, thank you,' Roh added, knowing how little time her friends had to run around Saddoriel helping her. 'How did you manage to get it?'

As they carried the metal sheets to the far corner of the cavern, Harlyn gave Orson a conspiratorial wink. 'Our Orson here sweet-talked old Nusgaard the head welder —'

'Did not —'

'Did so. Why else would he give us all this stuff?'

'He —'

'He *fancies you*, that's why. Sweet little Orson,' Harlyn mocked, batting her eyelashes.

Roh laughed; the sound of their teasing soothed her. 'Everyone does.'

Orson gave an exasperated sigh as she often did. 'It's times like these when I truly feel the decade between us,' she said.

'Nonsense.' Harlyn slapped her on the back. 'We make you feel young again.'

Roh grinned as she spotted the familiar smile tug Orson's lips. So often she tried to remain stern and serious, but Harlyn always knew how to put a crack in her resolution.

Taking advantage of the light mood, Roh gestured to their workspace once they'd placed the sheets on the ground. 'Do you want to have a look?'

'Actually,' Odi interjected, 'we could use your help for this next bit.'

'More help?' Harlyn quipped with a brow raised, but turned to survey their work anyway, hands on her hips.

'You've done so much already,' Orson said, taking in the tree stumps and the pile of timber they'd prepared.

'There's still a lot to do,' Odi explained. 'We have to make the case, which is what this metal's for, then the soundboard and the keys.'

Harlyn removed her lute from her back, placing it carefully out of the way, and folded her arms over her chest. 'Well, quit your jabbering and tell us what to do.'

Roh could hardly believe her eyes as they set about following the human's instructions, clamping the metal sheets into place so they formed a large curved mould. It was an impressive structure, but Roh had no idea how they were going to get the timber they'd so painstakingly felled and cut into it. But Odi moved about the structure with complete calm and confidence, checking his measurements as the three cyrens held everything in place.

'Where's the glue?' she heard Odi ask.

Standing beside the others, she pointed, intrigued. Odi proceeded to slather thick layers of glue along the thin planks they'd cut and sanded, placing them together to form a thicker sheet. Then, he picked up each one, bent the wet timber to his will, to the metal mould, and fitted it within the curved shape they'd created. Roh watched on as he painted the timber with more glue and fitted the final pieces of wood to the template.

'This will be the case,' he told them, ignoring their stares.

'How *that* is supposed to make music is well beyond me,' Harlyn said.

To Roh's surprise, Odi laughed.

'Speaking of music,' Roh ventured, knowing Harlyn always felt a little more generous after she'd made someone smile, human or not. 'Do you think you could play us something?'

Roh could have sworn she saw Harlyn's cheeks flush, but she shook her head. 'Orson and I should be getting back. We have lots of work —'

'Oh, come on, Har. Please?'

There was definitely a pink tinge to Harlyn's face as she looked to Orson, who allowed a smile.

'I'm sure a song or two won't put us too far behind.'

Roh gave their friend a grateful smile. Had she been spending too much time in the Upper Sector that she now felt the absence of melody so keenly? She watched Harlyn gently take her lute from its case and sit cross-legged on the ground. The bulky instrument always looked awkward in her friend's long, elegant arms, but as soon as she balanced it on her thigh it became a part of her. Without looking up, Harlyn placed her fingers over the frets and began to play.

Something greater than relief, greater than gratitude filled Roh. A creation of Harlyn's own making danced between the skeletons of trees, the sound so rich, so vibrant that Roh could almost see it. The melody passed through Roh like a phantom breeze, and though the notes poured from but one person, the sound was that of a symphony. Roh had watched Harlyn play the lute countless times before, but here, with an audience of just three, her expression changed from her usual scowl. Here, she looked at ease, graceful even, and the music at her fingertips was a collage of colour.

The piece was over before Roh was ready. She stared, along with Orson and Odi, but it was Odi's gaze Harlyn's eyes met.

'What?' she snapped.

A smile played on Odi's lips. 'You're … you're good.'

'I know,' Harlyn quipped.

'If you adjusted the pegs at the top there …'

'Did I ask for your opinion, human?'

Odi raised his chin. 'You didn't mind so much when it was complimentary.'

But Harlyn was already packing away her lute and getting to her feet. She turned to Orson. 'We're due back at the workshop,' she said curtly.

'I was only going to say that if you adjusted the pegs slightly, the sound would be more expansive,' Odi pressed on.

'Orson,' Harlyn barked. 'Let's go.'

'Har, surely you're done with your shift?' Roh interjected. She wasn't ready for the music to end and for her friends to leave. She'd barely seen them.

'Actually, no. We've caught up on our usual work, but an order's come through that Ames says must be attended to, so we're due back at the workshop any minute.' Orson sounded unusually bitter.

Roh didn't miss the consoling pat Harlyn bestowed upon her arm as they made for the door.

'Thank you,' she heard herself say. She pointed to the metal frame she still didn't fully understand. 'We really needed that, so *thank you.*' She wondered if they could hear it in her voice: her gratitude amplified by guilt. Would they be helping her like this if they knew what she had done to secure her place in the tournament? Roh had desperately tried not to think about that question, but on the receiving end of her friends' kindness and generosity, it penetrated her mind with a vengeance. Roh walked them to the door, thoughts churning so loudly that she didn't realise Harlyn was speaking.

'… you know?'

Roh blinked, slowly returning to the present. 'Sorry?'

Harlyn lowered her voice and gave Orson a sideways glance. 'I'm just saying … you're putting a lot of faith in *him*.' She jerked her chin in Odi's direction; he was hunched over the metal frame once more, lathering glue across the timber.

'I know,' Roh said hoarsely.

Orson gave a sad smile and Harlyn shrugged. 'So long as you know …'

The door clicked shut behind them and Roh bolted it. When she turned back to their project, Odi was already sanding another plank of timber. According to his drawings, which she glanced at over his shoulder, he was now working on the soundboard, whatever that was.

'Harlyn doesn't like to be told what to do,' Roh explained.

Odi quirked a brow. 'I don't think that trait is specific just to Harlyn.'

Roh ignored this; instead, she watched him work for a moment, studying his half-gloved hands as they guided the rough paper across the wood, patiently smoothing out its imperfections.

Harlyn's words still fresh in her mind, Roh paused by their tools. 'Odi?'

'Hmm?'

'About these strings.'

'What about them?'

'What could we use as a substitute?'

Odi frowned as he smoothed over a particularly

rough part of the timber. 'I don't know. I don't think anything else would work. They have to make the right notes. Otherwise, the Eery Brothers won't be able to play it.'

'Well, what are the strings like? I'll ask Ames if we have anything similar – like the wood. We didn't have maple and we managed.'

'The case of the instrument is different. But if you really mean to find a replacement for the strings … Well, to start, they're more like wire than string, I suppose. We just call them strings.'

'You humans are always calling things by the wrong name.'

Odi raised his brows. 'Do you want my help or not?'

'Fine.'

'They're more like wires. They're struck by hammers, which create the unique sound.'

Roh's heart was already sinking. She couldn't think of a place in the Lower Sector where she might get her hands on *wire* of all things. Rope, perhaps, but not wire. 'How many do we need? Of these wires?'

'Two hundred or so.'

'Two hundred?'

Odi's hands stilled and he looked up at her, his dark hair falling into his eyes; he pushed it back. 'I told you, they're not just any strings. We need three for the tenor and treble notes. For bass notes the number of wires per note decreases from three to two. When you approach the lowest bass notes, it decreases to one. The strings are different lengths, too, shorter for going from low to high notes, and the thickness changes as well, depending on how high in pitch the note is.'

'What ...?' Roh said. 'There's ... there's *nothing* like that here.'

Odi shrugged and turned back to the timber he was sanding. 'I said from the beginning we'd have to get them elsewhere.'

And he had. He'd been honest with her from the start. She just hadn't wanted to listen. Despite what her kind had done to him, despite being trapped down here, he had done a great many things for her, not the least of which was saving her life. She began to pace. There was no *rule* about leaving Saddoriel or Talon's Reach stated in the tournament orientation ... She shook her head. *I can't possibly be considering this.*

The question left her lips all the same: 'How long do you think it took you to get to Saddoriel from where you entered the tunnels?'

Odi frowned. 'It's hard to say when there's no natural light down here, but I wouldn't have guessed more than two days?'

What he didn't know was that time moved differently in the outskirts of Talon's Reach. There was a magic to those tunnels that warped one's sense of the days, hours and minutes. But it was a start. 'How far from the entrance of the tunnels is your home, and these supposed wires?' she asked.

'Under three hours at a walk, less at a run.'

Two days there, six hours of Odi being out in the human realms. Two days back ... If he came back ... But with Roh at his side, the journey would be quicker, if all went as she wished. With her inner compass, she could navigate the passages easily, and she *did* have a general sense of where Odi had been found. Roh surveyed the skeleton of the instrument before them. 'Does it leave us with enough time? To build the rest of the ... piano?'

Odi looked from the framework and elements assembled on the ground to his drawing and calculations on the crumpled piece of parchment.

'We have three weeks left until the end of the moonspan?' he asked.

'Two weeks, six days now.'

'Then that should be enough time. It won't be my best work, won't have the same finishes a true piano made in our shop would, but it will work. It will sound as it should.'

Roh took a deep breath. 'And tell me, why should I trust you?'

Odi stood and wiped his hands on his already dust-covered trousers. He met her gaze. 'If this is what you want to build, you'll just have to.'

Roh studied him carefully, her green eyes boring into his amber gaze. 'It's not in my nature to trust anyone. Least of all a human.'

Odi didn't look away. 'And yet, here we are,' he said, his voice calm and steady. Then he did something that Roh did not expect. He offered her his hand, palm upturned.

They had come this far ... Nerves roiled in Roh's gut

as she grasped his hand with her own and shook it. 'Here we are.'

They returned to their chambers in the Upper Sector to bathe and pack for the journey. They made quick work of their tasks, Roh snatching food from the dining hall that she thought would last the trip: flatbreads, hard cheese, cured meat and oatcakes. Her main concern was water, and so while Odi used the bathing chamber, she loaded their packs with water skeins, praying to Dresmis and Thera that it would be enough.

From what Odi had told her, Roh knew the place where he'd been found by Taro and Bloodwyn Haertel and which passage to take. The real test would be what came after, once they started out into the real outskirts of Talon's Reach.

When they were ready a few hours later, cyren and human shouldered their packs and slipped out of the Upper Sector residential quarters, determined to remain unseen. Though their plans weren't against the rules, Roh very much preferred that her fellow competitors and the Elder Council judges remained in the dark when it came to their journey. They managed to get through the residences, the foyer and the Great Hall without being seen, but at the entrance to the lair Roh stopped in her tracks.

'Where are you skulking off to?' Finn Haertel's voice matched his lazy stance, leaned up against the side of the archway of bones. His human was nowhere in sight.

'We're not skulking,' Roh snapped. 'And it's none of your business.'

Finn's eyes narrowed with dislike, his menacing gaze shifting between her and Odi. What was his problem? Before the tournament, Roh had never clapped eyes on the highborn, had never even set foot in his sector, and yet he was intent on sabotaging her, on infiltrating the only space she had known as home, on speaking to her friends as though they were dirt. Roh had had enough of the bastard. He'd taken every opportunity to hurt her and Odi, and had used his position, or rather, his parents' position, as a shield. He was nothing but a coward.

'Stealing Odi's token was a low move, even for you, Haertel,' Roh said, venom coating her words.

'Well,' he sneered, eyes brightening at the challenge. 'You'd know all about *low moves*, wouldn't you. Being what you are. Your despicable mother being what she is.'

It seemed an unnatural moment to bring Cerys into things, but he did it often, Roh realised. All of his snide remarks and insults led back to her mother, and suddenly, it was clear to Roh: this was *personal*. How had she not recognised that? It was not just Finn flexing his superiority over her, it was not just some sport he enjoyed. There was something deeper here that *mattered* to him, in a way he hadn't let slip, until now. That knowledge fuelled the fire within her even more. 'What is it that you have against me? Why do I get under your skin so badly?' she taunted.

'*You?*' Finn laughed darkly. 'You are nothing to me. A speck of mud on my shoe, perhaps. But your mother …

That murdering piece of filth rotting away down in her cell … The Haertels owe her a death debt.'

Roh's skin went cold. Although she knew what her mother stood accused of, what she carried her sentence out for, she had never stopped to question *whose* lives Cerys had impacted. If it was true, it was too ugly. If the Haertels owed her mother a death debt, then her mother had … killed a member of the Haertel family.

'You're just getting desperate now,' Roh heard herself say, her voice icy.

'Am I?' Finn smirked. 'You know *nothing, isruhe*. And you *are* nothing. That fear you have, that you'll never understand it all? It'll consume you. And I'll be here, waiting and watching with joy when it does.'

All her life, Roh had been the source of disdain and dislike for the cyrens around her. Her very presence offended some. However, not until she had come face to face with Finn Haertel had she known such raw loathing. To be the subject of uncontained hatred made her feel dirty, as though something tainted her very skin. Roh kept her face neutral as, with a final sly smile, Finn turned on his heel and strode back into Saddoriel, his words clinging to her like a poison.

She looked down to find her hands shaking. Swallowing the lump in her throat, she asked Odi, 'What do you call the Finn Haertels of your realm?'

Odi wrinkled his nose as he watched Finn cross the entrance and disappear into the Great Hall. 'We call them "highborn pricks",' he said.

Roh felt the tension dissipate from her shoulders and

she released an unexpected bubble of laughter. Odi grinned back.

Adjusting the pack on her shoulders, Roh motioned for Odi to walk ahead, and together, they passed beneath the archway of bones.

CHAPTER FOURTEEN

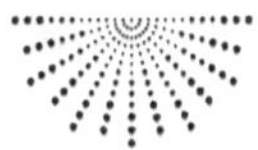

Along the path before Roh and Odi, gnarled roots crept through the surface of the earth. They grew up the walls and even across the top of the tunnel, thick, dark and knotted. She heard Odi stumble beside her, an imaginative curse echoing down the tunnel as he caught himself before he landed face-first. Roh put her hand to the wall, running tentative fingers across the rough surface, feeling the ridges and patterns. The wet ground beneath their boots became puddles, wider and deeper the further they walked. A few moments later, it made sense.

The passageway opened up into a prolific water forest. All manner of enchanted trees, shrubs and kelp sprouted from the water-covered ground, filling the space with rich greens and blues. It stretched on as far as Roh could see. She inhaled deeply, savouring the cool, soothing sensation inside her chest. It was the freshest air she'd ever breathed.

'I don't remember seeing this on my way in,' Odi murmured in awe.

Roh frowned. She hadn't gone the wrong way – it was impossible. Her inner compass pointed her south, and she knew in her very bones that they were in the right place. Her attention went to the shell token poking out from Odi's shirt laces.

'Take that off for a moment,' she said.

Odi grasped the token protectively. 'Not a chance.'

Roh rolled her eyes. 'I'm here, what do you think I'm going to let happen to you? I need you, remember?'

'You said to never take it off.'

'And you shouldn't, unless I say.'

'That's awfully convenient.'

'For Dresmis and Thera's sakes, just do it.'

To her surprise, Odi obliged, pulling the leather cord over his head and pressing the token into her palm.

He gasped. 'What in the …?'

'You can't see it?' Roh guessed.

Odi shook his head, mouth agape in astonishment. 'I … I don't …'

'What *do* you see?'

'Darkness,' he told her. 'It's dark and eerie. And … and I hear my stepbrothers again.' Odi took a step back in the direction of Saddoriel, and another. His eyes glazed over, as though he were in a trance.

Roh flung the shell token over his head and he stopped abruptly.

'What …?' Odi blinked.

'The lure of the lair,' Roh said, waving her hand casually towards Saddoriel.

'That's …'

'Impressive?'

'I was going to say horrifying.'

Grimacing at the water soaking through her boots, Roh led them into the water forest, careful to keep her torch away from the foliage. A quiet yearning thrummed amongst the silent trees. There was something sacred about being surrounded by so many, especially here in the outskirts of Talon's Reach. Each tree was its own, with unique veins and scars in its skin and bark, rich verdant leaves fanning out in the branches above. Long fronds of grass swayed in the rippling waters around the bases of the trunks: a silent guard. This forest was ancient, created by ancient magic. Roh felt it in her bones as a phantom wind rustled the foliage around them and the water swirled at her ankles. It seemed to know her, to beckon her into its embrace. She and Odi marvelled at the beauty of it, at the wide boles wrapped in vibrant emerald vines and carpeted in pale moss that resembled tiny icicles. Roh didn't know how she knew – she just did: this was one of the original lungs of Saddoriel, an enchanted forest that provided the passageways and the lair with clean air to breathe —

A near-deafening rumble shook Talon's Reach, rattling the entire forest and creating small waves in the water around them. Roh clutched the nearest tree for support, the rough tremor causing her knees to buckle.

Somewhere far away, a muted screech filled the air, creating another spasm, the vibration so turbulent Roh bit her tongue. The quake stopped as abruptly as it had begun, though the water still surged, cresting at the mercy of an unnatural tide.

'What was that?' Odi asked, eyes wide as he surveyed the forest.

Tasting blood, Roh released her grip on the tree, her skin crawling and her stomach churning with unease. 'I can't be sure,' she told Odi. But she remembered the violent tremor that had occurred during the first trial. They had been close to the sea then, too … The image of the veil of water, the sea portal, was clear in her mind; she had no doubt they were near something similar now. Which meant that all manner of creatures lurked just beyond. Elongated reef dwellers with poisonous tentacles, giant piranha with razor fangs … But there was only one creature large enough, only one monster connected so strongly to the sea's magic that it could make such an impact on the lair. Yet it couldn't be …

Roh's fear must have been etched plainly on her face.

'Roh?' Odi's voice sounded from beside her, echoing down the passageway. 'Are you alright?'

It was ludicrous to her that this human, whom she had only known for a matter of weeks, was suddenly in tune with whatever storm of emotion stirred beneath her skin. She had always thought she masked it well.

'Because if you're, you know, not fine, that's okay,' Odi continued, his voice carrying through the tunnel.

Roh sighed, turning the torch towards him, the

earnestness shining in his eyes. She chewed her lower lip. When was the last time she'd confided in someone? Truly? Not even Harlyn and Orson knew all her secrets, not now. And Ames? There was no way he understood her the way she wanted, the way she *needed*. But here, in the dark outskirts of Talon's Reach, perhaps her secrets could be safe? Something caused her to falter, however, to keep her secrets hidden.

I'm not ready, she told herself.

After a time, the water level receded and the forest thinned out, narrowing into a dark passageway once more. Roh led them through the tunnels, each one whispering unique magic, offering a singular presence, which made navigating their twists and turns as easy as breathing. Odi looked perplexed but followed her dutifully, never questioning. The music of the lair had long since ceased, and although Roh felt its absence keenly, she was used to operating without it; she had done so all her life.

The silence between her and Odi was comfortable, and yet Roh couldn't bear it, for it left her alone with her thoughts, fed by the darkness around them. Roh's mind flitted from death debts and sea serpents to Cerys and the etchings on her cell walls, each thought spiralling down into the next until they became obsessive, leaving her to imagine what the *Tome of Kyeos* might look like, locked away in the Vault.

'Where are you from?' she heard herself say, her voice hoarse. She had to get out of her own head, to focus on something other than every tiny detail of hurt in her mind. She had asked this once before and hadn't cared much for the answer. Things were different now.

If Odi was surprised by her question, he didn't show it. 'A place called the Isle of Dusan.'

Unsurprisingly, Roh had never heard of it. 'What's it like there?'

As though sensing she needed a distraction, Odi told her. 'It's a group of small islands just off the south-east coast of the mainland. Three islands, actually, best known for their chalk-white cliffs and verdant grasslands. It's small, with very few people, but beautiful. My father and I have lived there our whole lives.'

'And what of your mother?'

'She died of the plague when I was young. My father remarried a few years later, but his wife doesn't like me much.'

'And she has sons?'

Odi nodded. 'Yes. My stepbrothers. I can't say they like me much, either.'

'Why not?'

'They didn't need another brother.' Odi shrugged.

Roh found herself scowling. 'They're unkind to you?'

'Not exactly.' He kept his gaze forward.

So, he has his secrets, too.

Roh could take a hint. 'This … Isle of Dusan? That's where we're going now?'

'Yes, that's where my father's shop is. People come from all over the realms to see him.'

Following the tug of her inner compass, Roh took the

next left turn. Some sort of yelp sounded in the distance. She stopped in her tracks. 'What was *that?*'

Odi frowned. 'Sounded like a dog barking, to me.'

'A *what?*'

'A dog.'

Roh stared at him blankly.

'It's … an animal. Humans have them as pets sometimes.'

Roh shook her head. 'There's nothing like that down here. Must be another trick of the lair.'

'If you say so.' Odi shrugged, toying with his shell token.

When Roh's legs became too heavy to lift, she granted them a rest stop. It felt incredibly exposed to break bread in the middle of a passageway, but there was no other option. They sat on the tails of their cloaks on the wet ground and ate.

'What do you think the next trial will be?' Odi asked, picking at the cured meat.

'You mean if we make it through this one?'

Odi smiled. 'I mean if we make it through this one.'

Roh sighed heavily. 'I have no idea.'

'None?'

She shook her head. 'This is the first tournament that's occurred in my lifetime. I only know what Ames has told us of the previous ones, and from what I understand, they never repeat a trial. For every tournament, they come up with new tasks.'

'So it could be *anything?*'

'Anything.'

Odi tore at a piece of flatbread but didn't eat it. 'Are you scared?' he asked.

Roh hesitated before she said her next words. 'I think part of me is always scared.'

'Of what?'

She had never admitted that to anyone, not even Harlyn and Orson. 'That … I'll never be more than what I am. And I want … so badly to be so much more.'

Odi didn't say anything, as though he knew there was no comfort to be found in words of reassurance. Roh only ever found comfort in action, in taking a tangible step closer to her goals. Those steps had led her here, to the outskirts of Talon's Reach with a human whom she was about to set loose from captivity. Slowly, her old doubts crept back in and once more caused her stomach to churn with nerves.

'You speak of the third trial as if you'll be here for it,' she said as casually as she could. 'How do I know you'll come back?'

'I thought we went over this.'

'Let's go over it again.'

Odi shook his head and bit into the piece of flatbread he'd been nursing.

What if once they were in the human realms, he ran off? What if she lost him? She needed some sort of reassurance, some guarantee that he'd stay with her. So Roh stared pointedly at his protective token. 'That'll wear off, you know.'

'What?'

'Once you're outside Talon's Reach, it'll wear off. And

you'll still wind up right back where you started. You've heard the lure of the lair now. It will always call to you.'

'What are you talking about?' he asked.

Roh shrugged. 'Once your token's enchantment wears thin, it'll draw you back in, only the next time, if I'm not there to protect you, you'll be at the mercy of the cyrens for real.'

Odi lowered his gaze to the shell grasped between his fingers, as though if he stared hard enough, the token would reveal its secrets.

Roh stood, shouldered her pack and started down the passageway once more.

The tunnels in the outskirts of Talon's Reach were the worst places Roh had ever slept. It was cold and wet, and the constant *drip, drip, dripping* of the walls drove her to near insanity. Her dreams were plagued by mask drawings and Estin Ruhne and Finn Haertel's words, and the screeches of deadly sea creatures.

You know nothing, isruhe. *And you* are *nothing.* She tossed and turned as the voice washed over her again and again. Each time she awoke, Roh berated herself for letting the highborn bastard get inside her head and then steeled herself with determination to prove him wrong. To discover the truth. To beat him in the tournament. More than that, she wanted to rule over him. See how he'd like it once *she* was queen. Once *she* had unthinkable power. Once people were cheering her name. Though, her darker dreams spun a different reality. One where Finn won the tournament, cementing his place at the top, where he would lord it above the rest. Where Roh the bone cleaner, the murderess' daughter, would slink back to the workshop in shame, where she'd spend her eternity.

In their waking hours, Roh made a point of glancing at Odi's token whenever she could. As they drew closer to the human realms, she wanted him as nervous as possible about his fate with the cyrens. In the human realms, Roh herself would be at a disadvantage, and she couldn't have Odi using that to escape. She needed him to return with her and she would say anything, do anything, to ensure that he did so.

The lair was vaster than she'd ever imagined. They passed more water forests, glowing coral trails, glistening blue pools and marshlands. Roh kept to her inner compass, knowing that the various offshoots and prettier passageways were designed first and foremost to ensnare prey. There was no knowing what they might encounter in these parts of Talon's Reach, be it beast or enchantment. Although she was used to a lack of privacy with Odi by now, having to find an empty alcove and announce when she needed to relieve herself was mortifying.

Not long after their second night in the tunnels, the terrain began to incline, subtly at first, but then Roh's thighs and calves began to burn. Before long, she was sweating and swearing as her muscles strained beneath the arduous ascent. It felt as though this part of the trek would go on forever, but just as she was considering packing in her pride and taking a break, the air changed. It was crisper, fresher. And then, she saw a beam of sunlight. She nearly stopped in her tracks.

Sunlight. *Real* sunlight. Not the cavernous ceilings of the lair enchanted to mimic the outside realms. The pale-gold shaft of light was real. But Roh kept her awe to herself as they made their way to the top of the incline. There, the tunnel opened up to a vibrant woodland area. A strange sensation filled her as the air from the outside realms swept into the passage. Fear entwined with a yearning to explore the beyond. A place that didn't involve the workshop and its barrels of bones. A world that had real sunlight and moonlight. A realm that didn't deprive its inhabitants of music. A whole other realm of possibilities just out of her reach from the very tunnel in which she stood. Her inner compass spun uncontrollably, unable to point steadily as the glade just outside Talon's Reach beckoned to her.

She made to step into the light and froze. Her foot wouldn't budge from where it was suspended over the ground. She tried again.

Nothing happened. She couldn't leave the passage. Something ancient whispered in her veins, telling her she was bound to Saddoriel by the tournament, or was it more than that? She turned to Odi, terror forming a thick lump in her throat. This was the biggest risk she'd ever taken in her life, perhaps the stupidest thing she'd ever do: setting a captured human loose and expecting him to return.

'You'll be gone the better part of the day?' she heard herself say, her voice steadier than she felt.

Odi gaped openly. 'You're not coming?'

Roh wanted to tell him that she couldn't. That there was some sort of force physically stopping her from leaving that damn cave. Instead, she just shook her head.

Odi's fingers still toyed with his token. 'I know where everything is. I'll be as fast as I can.'

With difficulty, Roh swallowed. She opened her mouth to call out to him as he stepped out into the woodland, her instinct to threaten him again, but she didn't. She watched him go, and prayed with everything she had that he would come back.

CHAPTER FIFTEEN

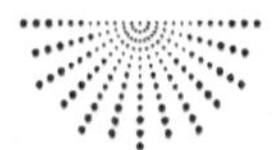

On the threshold between her realm and Odi's, Roh settled against the cool, damp wall of the tunnel and began the long wait. Nerves pricked holes at her insides as she wondered whether or not he'd return. Had she instilled enough fear in him? Or did he have some strange sense of loyalty to her after all they'd been through thus far? There was no way of knowing; only time, stretching, unending time, would tell.

Roh sighed and stared outwards in quiet fascination, watching the colourful woodland from afar. Tiny birds with vibrant yellow beneath their wings flitted about in the shrubbery, performing an erratic dance with one another. Larger birds called from above, swooping with the utmost grace to the forest floor to snatch insects from the leaf litter. When they had had their fill and ceased their dives, rabbits poked their heads from burrows beneath sage-green bushes, standing up on their hind legs, ears pricked, listening for predators.

Roh had only ever seen wildlife like this in books before. She breathed in every detail. It was a different kind of magic out here. She stretched out her legs, trying to rub the ache from her stiffening muscles. There, as the hours passed, the sunlight streamed into the entrance of the passageway, hitting her skin, soaking it in warmth. Although the absence of music had left a hole in her chest, the woodland offered a natural rhythm of its own, and the sun's rays seeping into her skin left her feeling content and sleepy, despite her worries. But as the sun moved across the glade and the hours started to pass quickly, Roh's fears crept back in, stronger and darker than ever. She wondered where Odi was now, and if he'd yet made the decision to betray her. How long would she wait? How long would she wait before she turned back to the network of tunnels and Saddoriel, defeated? Chilled, she rubbed her arms, watching the pattern of light become dappled across the woodland ground, the warmth receding from the mouth of the cave. Without the shafts of golden sunlight and nature's creatures to distract her, the wait turned torturous, and as was her habit, Roh's treacherous mind began to spiral.

Night fell and beyond the treetops Roh saw her first sliver of moonlight: a yellow smile against the inky-blue sky, and a smattering of stars. She longed to leave the confines of the cave, to find an open clearing and see the whole thing for herself. But her willpower and ambition had held fast all day, and would do so all night if need be.

When she was crowned victor of the tournament, Queen of the Cyrens ... Then she could see the sky whenever she wished, she promised herself as another hour passed without Odi's return.

Roh's breath turned to cloud before her face as night well and truly set in. She sniffed the air – the wind carried the promise of rain, though she wasn't sure how she knew that. It was instinct, as though she could hear its song in the distance. Shivering, Roh wrapped her cloak around herself tightly, not that it did much good. The woodland offered a new array of sounds in the darkness. Something hooted in the near distance and she could hear scurrying amongst the leaves. Lighting her torch, Roh cupped her hands around the small flame and thought of her friends in the workshop back home, feeling the sudden sting of senseless envy. And it *was* senseless. It had been *her choice* to separate from them. They were doing nothing wrong, nothing malicious. They were simply carrying on, as they had to. Deep in her bones, Roh knew no blame lay with them, but it didn't shake the pain of knowing they were together *without her*. Despite what she'd done to secure her place in the tournament, she envied the closeness that was so clearly developing between Harlyn and Orson in her absence. She recalled hearing the notes of Orson's deathsong for the first time, not by being at her side, but from where she had been hidden away in the shadows. The memory revived yet another ache in Roh's chest – the lack of her own deathsong.

Finn and Zokez's taunts haunted her. *'I heard a tale ...*

*about a little cyren who doesn't know a note of her deathsong
...'*

It had been many moons, perhaps even longer, since she'd last tried to find that sense of self within, the one that transformed into a storm of cyren magic, the chaos of song. Ames had continually told her to be patient, that he'd known cyrens to remain songless until they reached their first century, but patience had never been one of Roh's stronger virtues. She had always dismissed those tales, like Harlyn, refusing to be one of those cyrens. She didn't understand why she couldn't find her deathsong before her eighteenth name day.

Roh cleared her throat and straightened her posture. *Who am I?* It was one of the first things they were taught in lessons, that the knowledge of who they were, and their own magical potential, was vital to discovering their deathsong. Roh settled against the cave wall. She tried to find a meditative state, inhaling steadily through her nose and exhaling through her mouth, blocking the sounds of the night-time woodland. The way she imagined it, the note would bloom in her chest, where she felt the melodies of the lair hit home. Music was a part of a cyren's soul, so it made sense that the note would originate from her heart. She concentrated deeply. *I am Rohesia of the Bone Cleaners. I am Rohesia of the Bone Cleaners.* The words were a chorus in her mind and still, she felt nothing. Not a stirring, not a whisper of a note from within. *I am Rohesia of the Bone Cleaners.* She opened her mouth, calling upon her cyren instincts. A strangled noise escaped her. Her face burned deeply, despite the lack of audience. She had been to many a deathsong lesson, she knew everything her friends knew about the subject, she understood it just as well as they did, so why couldn't she manage a note?

She tried again.

The same wretched sound followed. Exasperated, Roh threw her hands up. She had always thought she'd known who she was, and exactly what she wanted. It was simple enough, wasn't it? At least it seemed so for everyone else. But her lack of deathsong told a different story. Perhaps … perhaps she didn't know herself at all.

Muttering one of Odi's curses, she got to her feet and turned back to the immediate task at hand. She had no way of knowing how many hours had passed. She had no timepiece like the highborns kept in their pockets, had never been taught the movement of sun and moon, or enchanted sun and moon in her case. Her stomach grumbled and she reluctantly fished through the rucksack Odi had left behind, finding some wrapped cured meat and a water skein. Seething silently, she watched the night sky, cursing its crisp air and glittering stars. Midway through a resentful bite of meat, she saw a flash. A bright streak across the inky canvas, leaving a trail of light in its wake.

Roh was still gaping at the stripe of gold when something rustled. Something was *moving* out there. Something bigger than a woodland rodent or bird. Her talons flashed and she pressed herself to the wall of the cave, staring out into the darkness, waiting.

CHAPTER SIXTEEN

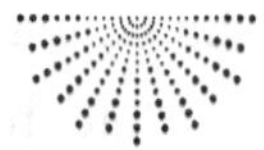

'Odi.' His name tasted like relief on Roh's tongue. She sheathed her talons and took a step towards him. She didn't know how long he'd been gone, and it didn't matter now.

He was *here*.

At last, the giant weight sitting atop her chest dissipated and her shoulders sagged as she released a long exhale of tension. Odi approached her through the velvety darkness, a huge sack slung across his back and another pack strapped across his chest.

'You're here.' The words came out as a croak and Roh wasn't sure he'd heard her.

In the torchlight, Odi's cheeks were pink and his brow was damp with perspiration. 'Sorry I'm late,' he puffed. 'They'd moved the wires and I spent ages trying to find the hammers and felt.'

'Hammers? Felt?' Those items had not been agreed

upon, had not been on the list of things to retrieve from the human realms. All the same, she offered him the water skein.

'Well, I was there, so I thought I'd get whatever else would make the piano as authentic as possible.'

Roh blinked away her shock. *Maybe I have instilled some sort of loyalty in him?* Fighting the instinct to rush them towards Saddoriel, she cleared her throat. 'Right … You … you should sit down and rest a while, before we head back.'

'I can manage,' Odi said.

Roh shook her head. 'You'll need all your wits for the lair.' She took the sack from his shoulder, placing it carefully on the tunnel floor, and did the same with the other bag. 'Sit,' she told him.

Noting her steely gaze, Odi gave in, sinking to the ground with a groan and stretching out his long legs. He pointed to the bag he'd brought. 'In that side pocket there,' he said, 'there's a flask.'

Frowning, Roh crouched and opened the buttoned compartment, rummaging until she took out a flask. 'What's this?'

Odi gave a rare grin. 'Rum.'

Roh tossed the flask to him, and he caught it, still grinning. Removing the cork with his teeth, he took a long swig and smacked his lips. 'Gotta celebrate those little victories, too, right?'

Roh slid down the wall beside him, crossing her legs beneath her, and accepted the flask from his outstretched hand, the liquid sloshing within. The sharp smell filled her nostrils as she put the mouthpiece to her lips and drank. The syrupy liquid that hit her tongue was complex, harsh at first, but with a sweet finish reminiscent of toffee. She took another sip.

Odi laughed. 'Good, huh?'

Roh took another swig, savouring the rich flavour, and handed the flask back to Odi. 'You should get some rest,' she said.

Odi shrugged. 'Don't think I'll be able to sleep just yet. My heart's still pounding from racing through the woods.'

'You ran?'

'Where I could. I didn't want you to think that I'd left for good … Did you?'

Roh couldn't stop the hint of a smile that tugged at the corner of her mouth. 'Not for a second.'

'Liar.'

Roh laughed, the sound rising along with the weight from her chest. 'Maybe.'

Accepting another swig from the flask, Roh met Odi's gaze with a serious expression. 'Did you see your father?' she asked quietly.

'I did.'

'And?'

'All is fine.'

Roh clicked her tongue in frustration. 'You've been gone for some time. What did you tell him?'

Odi removed his fingerless gloves and began to knead the lines of his palm with his thumb, flexing his fingers as he did, as though working out a familiar ache. He looked up at Roh through his dark fringe. 'I told him I was helping a friend.'

Roh held his gaze, not sure if it was the rum or the sentiment filling her chest with warmth. 'Thank you,' she managed, not quite knowing what to say next. Her mind scrambled. 'Is … is your father well?'

Odi smiled, continuing to massage his hands. 'He's well enough. Lonely, perhaps.'

'What of your stepbrothers? And stepmother?'

'My stepbrothers aren't around so much. They travel a lot. And my stepmother … She busies herself with running the business side of my father's shop. She enjoys counting gold more than she enjoys my father's company these days.'

Roh produced the leftover cured meat from her pack and passed it to him. 'You should eat something.'

'You're probably right,' Odi allowed, replacing the cork in the flask and accepting the parcel from her. 'Do you have any siblings?'

Roh laughed darkly. 'None that I'm aware of. But who knows? As you've probably gathered, my parentage is something of a mystery.' She waited for Odi to press her like Harlyn so often did, but he just gave a nod, flexing his fingers with a grimace before picking at the food.

'Are you injured?' Roh asked, frowning at his hands.

'No, no,' he told her, pulling his half-gloves back on. 'The muscles and joints in my hands, sometimes they ache. My father thinks it's because of the work I do. These gloves you hate' – he wriggled his fingers at her pointedly – 'the warmth from them helps the stiffness.'

'Have you seen a healer?'

'Once or twice. But a healer can't do much for you if you insist on doing the thing that inflicts the damage repeatedly, can they?'

Roh shrugged. 'S'pose not. Are you any good, then? At this work you do?'

Odi snorted. 'Bit late to be asking that, isn't it?' Smiling, he continued. 'We're *very* good. People travel to the Isle of Dusan from all over the realms to have us mend and create their instruments.'

'Is that so?'

'We've had royal commissions before. Made pianos for princesses and such.'

'I had no idea I had such an esteemed human in my company,' Roh said dryly.

'At your service, my lady.' Odi flashed another grin and gave a flourish with his hand, before turning serious once again. 'What about you? Have you always wanted to enter this ... tournament?'

Roh nodded vigorously. 'Always. Ever since I first found out about it.'

'For what? Glory? Fame? To be part of history?'

'*To be queen,*' Roh corrected him, frowning. With the words said aloud, her ambition hung naked between them, bare and vulnerable. Never before had she stated it so bluntly, never before had she offered up that secret piece of herself she had cradled and fed carefully for over a decade. And Roh hadn't realised how isolating that sort of ambition was, not really. She hadn't noticed the impenetrable walls that had built up around her, not only locking others out, but also caging her in.

'The ruler of cyrens is granted access to the *Tome of Kyeos*, an enchanted book that knows all. It can tell me … *everything*. *Exactly* what happened the night my mother became Saddoriel's prisoner. Who my father was. Who my family is. Who *I* am. And I *need* to know who I am, Odi, my deathsong demands it. And to know all that, I have to be queen.'

She half expected him to laugh; many others would if they ever heard a bone cleaner of Saddoriel say such a thing. She knew what it sounded like: the faraway dream of a child, and it had certainly started off that way. But along with her, it had grown into something far more, something that mattered so fiercely to her that she would do anything to protect it. She already had.

Odi didn't laugh. His amber gaze told Roh that he knew what it was like to want something that much. 'If you're crowned queen …' he said slowly.

'Yes?'

His eyes met hers. 'If you're crowned queen, will you let me go?'

'Let you go?'

Odi nodded. 'Will you set me free from Talon's Reach?'

Roh spotted the sack of wires in the corner of her eye and recalled Odi's flushed face from running back to her. She pictured the body of the piano they had already built and remembered how Odi always gave her the bigger chunk of bread. With a quiet sigh, she touched a finger to the fresh scar on her cheek.

'When I'm crowned queen,' she said, 'I will grant you your freedom.'

Odi exhaled shakily. 'I have your word?'

'You have my word.' Roh offered her hand, as Odi had done.

He took it in his half-gloved grip and shook it.

Roh nodded once. 'Now get some rest.'

At last, the human leaned his head against the cave wall and closed his eyes.

Descending the steep incline of the passageway was just as hard as climbing it. Roh found her thighs burning and her toes hitting the front of her boots painfully as she tilted backwards, trying not to lose her balance and go tumbling down into the darkness. She carried the giant sack of wires across her shoulder blades and the bag of hammers over her chest, having insisted that Odi had carried them all day. But she hadn't realised how heavy they were; one wrong step and she would plummet down the steep gradient. They were moving faster, however, so she didn't complain.

The lair's tunnels swallowed them as though they had never seen the outside realm, as though the feeling of the sun warming Roh's skin with its golden kiss was a distant dream. The passageways seemed darker than before, and the torch Odi held behind her only illuminated a few steps ahead of them. Frustrated, Roh lit another, despite it being difficult to hold with the additional cargo. Her inner compass pointed true. Now they had what they needed, Roh's sole focus was to get back to Saddoriel, to build the piano with Odi and *win*. The pace she set for them was gruelling, but she was determined to make good time. She needed to buy them as many hours as possible to complete their task. Odi kept up with her. With her promise echoing between them, he was just as invested in the outcome of the trial.

The tunnels of Talon's Reach lured them in and Roh recognised the numerous landmarks as they passed: the glowing coral trails, the pockets of willow trees, the caves filled with valo beetles amongst the stalactites. But on the previous journey, in her desperation to get to the human realms, she hadn't noticed the veil. In a cavern just off the main passage, it glimmered between the dark walls: a veil of magic between Roh and the sea. Unlike the one she'd seen after the first trial, this veil was familiar to her. She didn't notice the steps she took towards it, its magic and the power of the sea beyond calling to her. The smell was what triggered her memory. It wafted through the water and the portal to fill her nostrils: a subtle, bittersweet tang. She'd know it anywhere, especially after finding it in Odi's wine goblet. This was where she, Harlyn and Orson had come as youngsters, when they had drawn the short straw to harvest the lethal coral larkspur. Peering down past the wavering sheet of water, Roh could see the field of the poisonous flowers across the seabed. Despite Ames' insistent warnings, the trio had come here with excitement in their hearts, finally able to pass the threshold into the pulsing currents they'd so often dreamed of. She remembered what it had been like to dive through the veil, to feel the rush of cool water against her skin, against the glimmering scales at her temples —

'Roh!'

Odi's voice broke the spell and Roh found herself standing inches away from the veil, her hand outstretched.

'What are you doing?' Odi asked, catching up and pulling her back. 'Is this the lure of the lair? I thought you were immune to it?'

Roh shook her head slowly, shocked she'd been so enraptured, and took a step away. 'It's not the lair … It's … the call of the current. It whispers to us cyrens. The sea offers a different rhythm, a different music to that in Saddoriel. It … I can feel it in my bones. Anyway, I … I have a connection to this spot. I've been here before, with the others.' In that moment, she missed Harlyn and Orson deeply, as though a part of herself had been wrenched from her, leaving a hole that could not be filled. She gasped at its presence, the void yawning wider and wider.

Odi tugged on her sleeve. 'We have to get back, remember?'

Numbly, Roh allowed him to lead her away from the cavern, away from the veil and the current that called her name. She walked after him in a daze, letting the cool darkness of the passageway settle over her.

· · ·

Once again, Roh lost herself in the monotony of the trek, taking the lead from Odi and guiding them through the winding tunnels of Talon's Reach. It wasn't long before she was drenched in sweat and her breathing turned ragged. Wordlessly, Odi took the sack of wires from her and slung them across his own back. The return journey went on forever, despite the breakneck pace Roh set. Every now and then, though, she could hear faint notes of music, which told her they were getting close. She yearned to hear the rich, full movements of the fiddles and the delicate notes of the harp.

Not long now. She forced herself to put one heavy foot in front of the other.

When they eventually stopped for a rest, Roh was too exhausted to eat. She passed the rations to Odi, who dug in with great enthusiasm. She'd never seen someone eat like that before. When he was done, he sighed, tipping his head back and resting it against the wet stone wall. Despite being more than anxious to return to Saddoriel, she knew they had to listen to their bodies. If she pushed them any harder they might not be in any condition to build the instrument that would save them; they might not make it back at all. Roh couldn't help glancing at the token resting against Odi's sternum. The simple shell curling at the end of the leather cord. He followed her gaze and lifted it between his fingers, turning it over, following its lines with his fingertips. 'It was never going to wear off, was it?' he asked.

She lifted her moss-green eyes to his amber stare and swallowed thickly. 'No.'

'I didn't think so.'

'And you came back anyway?'

'And I came back anyway.'

Roh didn't know what to say to that, didn't know how to express the immeasurable gratitude she felt, or the relief. So a few moments later, she hauled herself up, dusted the seat of her pants and said, 'Let's go.'

Odi sighed heavily. 'But, Roh —'

A high-pitched shriek pierced the air, echoing down the passageway. Roh clapped her hands over her ears. 'What in the name of —'

It sounded again, wild and desperate. '*Help!*' the voice cried. 'Someone, *anyone*! Help!'

Without thinking, Roh started towards it, but Odi grabbed her by the wrist. 'It could be a trap,' he warned.

He was right. And knowing her competitors, it probably *was* a trap. But her inner compass was pointing her right to it, and that she couldn't ignore. Roh broke into a staggering run. Heart hammering, she raced towards the cries for help as another scream sounded, even more high-pitched than the last. Sheer terror. A left turn, another left turn, right and then left again. She left Odi behind and sprinted through the passageways. What if it was Orson or Harlyn? What if they'd been used as bait? She couldn't let them suffer, couldn't let anything bad happen —

She skidded to a stop just in time. The tunnel gave way to marshland. Swampy, boggy marshland punctuated with gnarled, stick-thin trees. *Stop*, her inner compass commanded, revealing what she hadn't seen straightaway.

Quicksand. She scanned it wildly, looking for the source of the noise.

'Help me, please!' The voice didn't belong to either of her friends, Roh realised, her eyes sweeping across the muck before her. A flash of a pale hand caught her attention. A human. And not just any human. *Yrsa Ward's* human. The girl was up to her chest in quicksand, flailing in panic. The swampy mud was sucking her down into its murky depths, moving faster the more she squirmed.

Roh felt heat on her neck and turned to find Odi panting behind her, laden with the supplies she'd left.

'What are you doing?' he said. 'We have to help her.'

The girl shrieked again as the quicksand glugged, pulling her in up to her throat.

'Roh!' Odi elbowed her roughly.

Roh watched, as always, calculating the risks and the consequences. 'If we leave her, Yrsa's out of the tournament. It's one less competitor to beat. One less highborn.'

'*You can't be serious!*' Odi lunged towards the girl, but Roh grabbed his arm, hard enough to bruise.

'Look closer, you fool.'

She waited for Odi to spot what she had moments before: not just a patch of danger – the whole marshland was quicksand, camouflaged as mossy, muddy grass.

'Gods,' he murmured, taking in the deathtrap before them. 'There has to be another way, Roh. We have to save her.'

There was another way. Roh had seen it only moments after she'd spotted the quicksand. There were slightly raised stepping stones across the marshland, leading to the little islands dotted around and the offshoots of the passageways.

'Roh! Is this the queen you'll be? A queen who lets someone suffer, lets them die, for the sake of a shortcut?'

The quicksand was past the girl's throat and her eyes were wide with panic, her strangled sobs of terror echoing across the swampland.

Fury surged through Roh. 'Damn you,' she hissed at Odi, shoving her cloak into his chest. She leaped out onto the first stone, catching her balance with a gasp as she slid across perilous algae. She didn't look back at Odi as she jumped from stone to stone towards the sinking human. Roh made for the small island of firm ground closest to the girl and dived onto her stomach. She couldn't believe she was here, doing this. The stench of the swamp hit her full in the face as she edged towards the quicksand.

The human girl struggled towards her, managing to free one of her swallowed hands from the sucking mud. Roh swore, inching her body further out across the marshland and stretching out painfully with her arm.

A wet, slippery hand found hers.

Roh cursed as the girl's grip slipped. '*Come on,*' she ground out through clenched teeth.

The hand reached for her again, covered in muck, and a rasping gurgle sounded as the human's mouth and nose went under. All Roh could see were the girl's terrified eyes.

With her talons retracted, Roh made a final lunge with her hand, lacing her fingers through the human's with a vice-like grip, and heaved the girl through the quicksand.

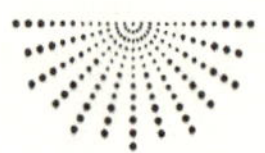

CHAPTER SEVENTEEN

The human was as unsteady on her feet as a newborn calf. A slight girl, no older than fifteen, with mousy-brown hair and a timid demeanour. Her cold, trembling grip clamped down on Roh's hand hard as she stood upright, dripping with slime, and Roh tried not to gag at the putrid smell.

How has she lasted this long? Roh wondered in bewilderment as she helped the sopping-wet human across the stepping stones back to Odi, who was waiting with his cloak open for her. The girl dropped Roh's hand as she stepped into the cloak gratefully and tugged it tightly around herself before turning to them both, still shivering.

'Th-thank y-you,' she said, making herself smaller beneath the cloak.

'What's your name?' Odi asked.

'T-t-t-Tess.'

Odi offered a kind smile. 'I'm Odi,' he told her. 'And that's Roh.'

Roh wiped her muck-covered hands on her pants. 'We need to get moving,' she said, scrunching up her nose at the smell coming from Tess. 'You'd best be able to keep up.'

'I-I … I c-can.'

'Good.' She made to continue down the passageway.

'Roh?' Odi's voice echoed down the tunnel.

'What now?' Her newfound truce with Odi wasn't going to last long at this rate. Thanks to him, they were now navigating Talon's Reach with a massive liability in tow.

'Tess' token,' he said.

'What about it?'

'Well, she doesn't have one.'

'And what do you want me to do about it?'

'Well …'

'Tess.' Roh turned to the cowering girl. 'Where do you last remember having your token?'

'I … I t-th-think it was b-b-back in the l-l-lair.'

Roh clenched her jaw as she faced Odi once more. 'Chances are, that's where she lost it, or where Finn Haertel and his underhanded human cut it from her neck as they did yours. We don't have time to go searching for another competitor's token. She's lucky we got her out of the quicksand. We owe her and Yrsa *nothing*.'

Odi opened his mouth to argue, but Roh raised a palm.

'That's enough,' she said. 'I won't hear another word

about it. Every moment we stand here is a moment less we have to work on our project, a moment taken away from something that might grant *you* freedom. Let's move.'

Thankfully, Odi didn't attempt any more protests as Roh turned on her heel and started down the passageway. She tried to walk far enough ahead that the stench of the swamp muck on Tess didn't cling to her nostrils, but the humans were slow and she couldn't leave them completely unchaperoned, not even with Odi's shell token still intact. She'd left the packs with Odi, figuring he deserved to carry them after his merciful stunt with Tess, but he was also keeping Tess on the right path, as she was continually wandering off, hearing phantom music and cries from people she once knew, down different tunnels.

'Mama? Mama, is that you?' she'd call quietly into the darkness.

'For Lamaka's sake,' Roh muttered, taking the packs off Odi. 'She's your responsibility,' Roh told him, nodding to the dazed girl.

'Fine,' he said.

Unbelievable. Fury rolled through Roh as she kept up her pace. She couldn't believe she'd allowed Odi to rope her into this fiasco. She had much bigger things to worry about than the safety of another competitor's human. Yet here she was, playing pack mule so her own human could play saviour.

Suddenly, Roh staggered with a gasp as the ground beneath her shook violently. Stumbling to stay upright, she looked back wildly, spotting Odi and Tess pressing themselves to the trembling cave walls. The uncontrollable vibrations dislodged several stalactites from the ceiling.

'Watch out!' Roh yelled, raising one of the packs to protect her head as a stalactite came shooting down towards her, its sharp point puncturing the delicate skin of her forearm as it fell, before it shattered on the ground. But Roh barely felt it as she watched in terror while Odi covered Tess' body with his own, pressing her flat against the cave wall. The dagger-like formations rained down on them, stabbing into the damp earth of the tunnel floor or crumbling upon impact. Roh saw Odi flinch as one skimmed his shoulder, but she was too far away to see how bad the damage was.

'Odi!' she shouted over the rumbling, but he didn't turn to her. Roh swore as another stalactite pierced her arm, and this time she felt the wet, warm trickle of blood. A heart-stopping screech sounded in the distance before the tremor stopped, returning the passageway to its former quiet stillness.

'Dresmis and Thera,' she panted, before dropping the pack and darting towards the others. 'Odi? Odi, are you alright?' She pulled him away from Tess, her hands going straight to the shoulder she'd seen hit. He winced as she pulled his shirt down from his neck.

'It's just a graze.' Relief surged at the sight of the raised pink welt. 'It didn't actually break the skin.'

Odi gripped her hand, turning it over, inspecting her arm. 'You're injured.'

'It's nothing,' Roh said. And when the concern in Odi's gaze didn't ease, she shrugged him off. 'Truly. I've had worse just from being in the workshop.' Though her arm pulsed with pain, she scanned the cavern, searching for any clue as to what might be going on. 'That's three times now,' she murmured, more to herself than to the others. 'Three times the lair has trembled like this.'

'You still don't know what it is?' Odi asked her as he checked Tess over for injuries.

Roh shook her head. 'All we can know for sure is that something is stirring in the currents beyond the walls of Talon's Reach. Something big.'

Odi nodded, as though he expected no less. 'Tess is fine,' he added, patting the girl reassuringly on the shoulder.

Roh eyed her warily. 'That's twice now we've saved you.' Pushing the damp hair from her eyes and sighing heavily, she started off again, her legs aching and sweat pricking at her scalp. Exhaustion had its claws in her and she tried to ignore the whispers of the humans behind her; she had no energy to take interest in whatever trivial matters the two saps were immersed in. Roh had places to be, a piano to build.

The monotony of the journey ate away at Roh, fuelling her impatience to get back to the task at hand. The cut on her arm pulsed with pain, but she navigated the passageways without a second thought and tapped her foot impatiently whenever Odi and Tess fell behind.

Every now and then, Tess' voice sounded the same question: 'Mama? Mama, is that you?'

Something about it made Roh's skin prickle. Had she ever asked after her own mother like that?

To her relief, they passed the original water forest they'd ventured through, and soon, she could hear the faint notes of the harp music playing from the heart of the lair. They were close.

When at last they entered Saddoriel, Roh realised it was night-time. The enchanted light above mirrored the image of the moonlight she'd glimpsed. But it wasn't the same. It didn't have the same depth and the stars didn't glimmer in the same way. There were certainly no falling stars to be seen. Roh allowed herself a deep breath with closed eyes, picturing what she'd witnessed from the entrance of their territory. She would see it again, just as she'd promised herself. After a moment, she motioned for Odi and Tess to follow her. She didn't want the three of them to be caught out here by any of the other competitors, knowing that it would be assumed she'd sabotaged Yrsa. That was the way the cyrens thought. It was the way *she* thought, most of the time. Roh led the humans across the foyer and into the residences at a jog. The sooner this was over with, the better. They encountered no one.

Thank the gods, Roh thought as she found Yrsa Ward's door and rapped her knuckles against it. The solid timber creaked on its hinges as it opened a crack.

'What are you doing here?' said a gravelly voice from within. There was a vicious hiss.

Roh looked down to see a horned serpent rising up from the ground. With a shudder, she ignored it and pulled Tess to her side, gently pushing the door further ajar. 'Returning something that belongs to you.'

The door opened fully and Yrsa stared at Roh open-mouthed. 'What ...?'

Roh decided then and there that she liked the look of surprise on highborns. 'Finn's been stealing human tokens,' she told Yrsa. 'You might want to retrace her steps.' She said no more. She didn't have the energy to explain it all – she was too focused on fighting down the feeling that this very moment would come back to haunt her. They left the sodden Tess with Yrsa, who stared after them from the door, her serpent coiled quietly at her ankles.

Though Roh wanted nothing more than to head straight to the abandoned water forest to begin work, she knew it was foolish at this hour, that they were both nigh on delirious from the journey and all it had entailed. She felt off balance, and the stench of the marshlands was still trapped in her nose, so she led Odi back to their chambers. Once they were inside, Roh dropped the packs with a moan and headed straight for the washroom. Frankly, she was sick of the sight of Odi and she needed to decompress in privacy. Did that make her selfish? That her gratitude had been so short-lived? She was too exhausted to delve further into the subject. The question of her own moral compass had been murky for some time now, anyway.

Miraculously, hot water had been left for them, and

she poured bucket after bucket into the wooden tub. She peeled away her clothes, leaving them in a heap on the tiled floor, and tested the water with her fingertips. It was hot, but that was exactly how she wanted it. She stepped into the tub and slowly lowered herself, inch by inch, into the near-scalding water. She tipped her head back to rest against the tub's edge and let the water flow across her chest. The heat soothed her aching muscles and the tension she carried in her body. *This is what I need.* She lay there motionless for a time, the silence washing over her. She hadn't realised how exhausted she was until this moment of stillness. Ever since her entry into the tournament, it had been one shock after another, one hurdle after the last and her mind … Her mind was so full of questions and worries that it felt tight in her skull, as though it might burst.

Roh sank down to the bottom of the tub, submerging herself. The water muted the world around her, drowned out the fears, the fury and the clawing desperation for truth. Beneath the surface of the water, she felt at peace. A similar sort of contentedness to when the notes of a melody settled in her chest. She watched her hair float up around her face, revelling in her ability to breathe under water. When she and the others had been nesters they had been given brief sea training. Small groups of them had been taken out into the currents and taught how to manipulate the tides, how to breathe water as though it were air, how to use their scales to communicate with each other soundlessly. But it had been a long time since then. Roh hadn't felt the salt water of the sea on her skin in years, not since she, Harlyn and Orson had gone beyond the veil to collect the coral larkspur. Saddorien cyrens belonged to the lair. The memory she had of her sea training was faint; the cool kiss of the current and the unending blue vastness seemed far away. She could pretend all she wanted, but it wasn't the same here. Her breathing abilities were second nature. She didn't have to think, didn't have to practise, but ... she missed the salt water.

Roh broke the surface, her troubles returning to her. Filled once more with a sense of urgency, she scrubbed at her skin with the lavish soaps provided, and watched as the bath turned from clear to cloudy. Her limbs felt heavy as she finished washing and heaved herself, dripping wet, from the tub. She would need to rest before starting work – there was no getting around that fact. She'd be useless otherwise. Roh towelled herself dry and pulled on a robe that hung on the back of the door. Tying it tightly around her waist, she entered their main chambers, hair still damp.

Spotting Odi sitting by the window, she said, 'Take tonight to bathe and rest. We rise before daybreak.'

Odi nodded and headed for the washroom. He paused in the doorway. 'You did the right thing,' he told her.

'We'll find out soon enough, won't we?'

The door closed behind Odi and Roh went to her bed, pulling back the covers and sinking into the soft mattress. She thought about picking up the heavy tome of laws that sat on her bedside table, long overdue for return to Andwana, and her fingers itched to pick up her sketchbook and stick of charcoal … There was so much to do, so much to think about. But tonight, she would give herself permission to sleep. And almost as soon as her head hit the pillow, slumber dragged her under.

Roh and Odi were in the abandoned forest long before the rest of the lair awoke. Everything was as they'd left it, with the exception of a few additions. Ames, Harlyn and Orson had seen to some of the items on the list in her absence. Beside the piano's case was a small stockpile of necessities: fresh parchment and charcoal, more glue and metal clamps, a hammer and nails, several planks of freshly sanded sea-birch timber, and … bones. The last item had been Roh's request, a tiny addition she'd scrawled onto the list at the last second without Odi seeing. He might have known pianos inside and out, but she knew Saddoriel and its cyrens. And she knew that no matter how good their creation was, it would have to fit in here, somehow. She tucked the parcel away from Odi's sight, deciding that she'd have to wait until the right moment to propose one final change to his design.

Scanning the rest of the items, she sighed with relief. 'Thank the gods for them,' she murmured as she placed her pack of wires beside the supplies and turned to Odi. 'We have everything we need, then?'

Odi dropped his own pack to the ground and glanced from the piece of parchment to the supplies before them. 'I think so,' he said, nodding.

'Good,' Roh replied, crossing her arms over her chest. 'Now what?'

Odi glanced across at her and smiled. It was a genuine smile, one that brightened his expression, making him look younger. He continued to smile as he went to the supplies and took up the parchment and charcoal. Then, sitting cross-legged in the dirt, he spread out the blank parchment before him. Roh stood beside him as he began to sketch the remaining aspects of the design. She watched on with a mix of awe and envy as his long fingers brushed the stalk of charcoal effortlessly across the parchment, outlining the hidden intricacies of the instrument.

'This is the soundboard,' Odi murmured, still sketching. 'The heart of the piano.'

'It creates the music?' Roh asked, noting the dark lines on the paper linking from one to another. The ease with which Odi drew the design told her that he'd done this hundreds of times before. That he drew each line with care, knowing what part it would play in the creation of a sound, singular and unified with others.

'Mmm,' he agreed, the charcoal stilling in his fingers as he studied the design. 'Each piano is unique, has its own character.' Still holding the parchment, he stood, taking stock of their tools and supplies once more. 'Every piece of material we use, every turn of a screw or beat of a hammer contributes to the predominant qualities of the instrument. Mellowness, warmness, the roundness of tone.' He was speaking more to himself than to her, Roh realised. But it didn't matter. Odi knew about music in a way that she could never articulate. She felt music in her chest, in her soul when it sounded, but Odi … Odi understood it. The words he used to describe it felt right to Roh, and more than that, they left her wanting more. To understand the notes, the *tone* in the same way he did. And so she followed his instructions, starting with the soundboard, the heart.

It was not one large piece of wood, as Roh had guessed by looking at the plans; rather, it was created by gluing smaller planks together. They placed the smaller planks side by side, at a diagonal angle.

'It acts as an amplifier,' Odi told her as they placed the clamps in place so the glue could dry. 'Its whole purpose is to radiate a large volume of sound over a wide range of frequency. We'll cut it to size when it's dry, so it fits perfectly over the rim of the case.'

Roh found herself nodding in fascination at this new language.

'That will take some time to dry, so we can work on the bridges now.'

'Bridges?' Roh didn't see how bridges had anything to do with musical instruments.

Odi smiled again. 'Different type of bridge,' he said. He showed her his charcoal sketch. 'On a piano like this, there are two bridges inside. They connect the strings to the soundboard.' He went to the pack he'd brought back from his home. 'They're a little trickier to create, so I thought it would be easier to bring them.'

He handed Roh a long, thin piece of timber and she saw what he meant. While the timber itself was simple enough, there was a piece of felt along it, with hundreds of small pins in a sort of zigzag shape.

'The strings thread through here?' she asked, running her fingers along the bridge carefully.

Odi nodded. 'Exactly.'

Roh held the bridges as Odi measured and marked their positions on the soundboard with his stick of charcoal.

'Pass me the long one?' he asked, hand outstretched.

She held out the longer of the two pieces and he took it, lining it up with the markings he'd just made.

'The treble and tenor strings pass over this one,' he told her. 'And the bass strings pass over the shorter one. These two bridges allow the strings to be cross-strung.'

Roh watched in silence as he applied glue to the bottom of the long bridge and pressed it onto its place on the soundboard. Odi chewed his lower lip as he took the short bridge from her and repeated the action.

'We'll leave the soundboard overnight now,' he said, knees cracking as he stood.

'Alright.' Roh looked around, unsure of what came next.

But Odi was already at the packs they'd brought. 'We'll sort through the strings. We can put them in order so when the soundboard is dry, we know what's going where.'

Roh went to him. 'I ... Uh ... How?' She could have kicked herself. She sounded like that stuttering human, Tess.

Odi threw her one end of a large white sheet and

motioned for her to open it and spread it flat across the ground.

'I'll show you,' he told her.

Over the course of the day, they worked to untangle and sort through the strings – wires – that Odi had taken from his father's shop. Slowly, they ordered them across the white sheet from shortest to longest. Roh's fingertips were tender from handling them. She surveyed their work so far, and still couldn't comprehend how a bunch of wires housed in a curved wooden box would make music befitting Saddoriel. But for the first time in a long time, Roh had faith. She had heard Odi talk about music; he knew what he was doing – he knew things that even the most gifted cyrens of the lair didn't know.

The task was a tedious and frustrating one. The journey through the human realms and the tunnels of Talon's Reach had tangled the wires into a messy ball, where the solution to one knot became the cause of another. Roh ignored the blisters swelling at her fingertips as best she could, but when they were on the verge of splitting open and weeping, she sat back with a bitter sigh.

Odi glanced up at the sound, placed another wire in the row and wiped his brow on his shirt. 'We're just about done with these,' he said. 'A couple more. I'll do them.'

Roh didn't know where he found the patience, and although she'd never say it, she admired the quality greatly. He reminded her of Orson in that regard. A pang of sadness hit her in the chest at the thought of her friend. It felt like it had been an age since she'd clapped eyes on Orson and Harlyn. She missed them, more than she could say. She missed the ease of conversation and silence alike. She missed *laughing*. How long had it been since she'd laughed? *Really* laughed? She couldn't recall. Everything since she'd entered the tournament had been so dark, so serious.

'There!' Odi's voice pulled her from her spiralling thoughts and her gaze came to rest upon the rows of wires they'd sifted through.

'Thank the gods for that,' she muttered.

Odi huffed a laugh. 'I know. I can hardly see straight.'

'Can we afford to take a break?' Roh asked, massaging her sore fingers.

'It would be unwise not to. I don't think anyone ever does their best work when they're exhausted. Do you?'

Roh shook her head. 'No. Let's go get something to eat, then we can start fresh on the next steps, whatever they may be.'

On their way back to the Upper Sector, they passed the workshop and that familiar pang of sadness hit Roh anew as she peered through the window. Both Orson and Harlyn were inside, their heads down. They looked thinner, more haggard than usual. Something about the workshop was different, though Roh couldn't quite place it. She noted the deep, dark circles beneath her friends' eyes. She knew that they had to cover her work while she was competing in the tournament, but that wasn't all.

'An order's come through that Ames says must be attended

to …' Orson's words came back to her as she willed her friends to look up and see her in the window. They didn't. They were working too intently, on something Roh didn't recognise.

It wasn't their usual work – Roh would know that from a mile away. It was then that she realised what was different about the workshop. Half of it had been sectioned off. The workers were crammed together, seated elbow to elbow, their brows creased with discomfort.

'What in the name of …?' Roh breathed. In all her seventeen years, she'd never seen the workshop transformed in such a way. Her hands clamped over the windowsill, her talons threatening to break through with the injustice of it all.

Neither Orson nor Harlyn looked up. Roh made to leave, but her eyes caught on something else … Her project, tucked away at the back of the room, covered up and untouched. A heaviness settled on her chest then. One day … *One day* she would make it a reality. And Harlyn and Orson would have front-row seats to music that could be heard throughout all of Talon's Reach.

Roh and Odi saw no other competitors in the Upper Sector except for Neith. As they were filling their plates in the dining hall, the water runner waved at them with a broad smile from across the room. Roh returned both wave and smile, though she felt anything but cheery. For a brief moment, she wondered what her fellow lowborn was building for the trial, only she didn't have the energy to ponder it for long.

'We haven't seen Tess since …' Odi trailed off as they passed the door to Yrsa Ward's quarters on the way back to theirs.

Roh shrugged. 'Why would we?' She didn't want to linger on what saving that human's life had cost her. To think there could have been one less Elder Council representative to contend with … Odi didn't seem to understand the risk she'd taken there.

'I don't know. But it'd be nice to know if she's alright? If she found her token.'

Sighing, Roh shook her head and said no more as they reached their chamber and Odi ducked away to bathe. Perhaps all the concern was a trait more common to humans. She certainly hadn't seen any cyrens worrying about fellow competitors like Odi did.

After she'd finished eating, Roh dropped onto her bed and pulled her sketchbook onto her lap, taking the stick of charcoal from the bedside table. Settling herself, she started her sketching exercises. She drew perfect straight lines freehand, developing the basic principles of construction: horizon, viewpoint and vanishing point. The exercises soothed her, and she revelled in how they showed off her technical talent. Roh lost herself in the points, lines and planes, creating basic geometric shapes, then defining the distances and clarifying the depths.

'What are you drawing?'

The charcoal snapped between Roh's startled fingers.

She hadn't noticed Odi emerge from the bathing chamber and come to stand beside her.

With a muttered curse, she set aside her sketchbook. 'Nothing.'

'You won't tell me?' Odi sounded hurt.

'There's nothing to tell. I'm just practising.'

But Odi didn't move; he stared down at the discarded sketchbook.

Roh sighed, sitting back so Odi could see her work. 'Ames says my technical ability is good, but I haven't yet developed the artistry, the imagination for truly inspired designs. That's why I find it easier to fix other people's work rather than create my own. I keep thinking if I just keep practising, something will come to me.'

Odi shrugged. 'Good things take time, Roh.'

Roh suppressed another sigh and headed to the bathing chamber. Time was one thing she didn't have much of.

Sleep didn't come that night. In its place, Roh recalled the dozens of banners she'd passed on the way up to the Upper Sector.

Neith, Spirit of the Water Runners.

Neith for Queen.

On Neith's swift wings ...

Roh had pretended she hadn't seen them after they'd left the workshop window, but she had. She'd seen every single one, each one essentially a vote against her. Word was out about her parentage and she hadn't realised that the resentment for her origins would come so hard from her own sector as well. There had not been one sign in support of her, Saddoriel's *isruhe*. In the brightly lit foyer and dining room, she had brushed the sting of it away, but now, as she lay in the darkness of her chamber, she recalled the script of every single banner. Each one like a low punch to her gut.

With a frustrated sigh, she rolled onto her other side, but she was only greeted with other worries she'd swept to the back of her mind. They filled the absence of sleep like a great wave rushing into a sea cave.

The days merged into a week, and then two. Roh and Odi worked tirelessly down in the abandoned water forest, both sporting bloodied bandages around their fingers from spending hour after hour stringing the wires through the correct bridge pins. Roh couldn't remember the last time she'd felt this tired, the kind of exhaustion that sank down to her bones, making her whole body heavy. It wasn't until one afternoon, when she was 'borrowing' a jar of glue and a pair of wire cutters from the workshop, that the full extent of her weariness hit. She had decided to leave Odi in the forest, deeming it more than safe if she locked him in. Alone at long last, she stood in the doorway in an utter daze, finally able to sink a little under the weight of the burden she carried. She found herself staring into the empty room, at the exact spot she imagined Harlyn and Orson had sat when they had been discussing their deathsongs. The memory stung Roh, sharper than before, heightened by her fragile state.

'You'll get there, you and Roh both.' Orson's sweet voice

filled her head, along with the notes she'd heard of her friend's deathsong. Despite the reassurances Roh had overheard, they gave her no comfort as she recalled her fruitless, strangled efforts in the mouth to the human realms. She was a failure. What sort of queen would she be without a deathsong? She would be the laughing stock of Saddoriel. If she even made it that far. Her thoughts echoed Finn and Zokez's taunts from the first trial. And why wouldn't those worries return to her? She couldn't understand why she was having such trouble. It was *instinct* to a cyren, like breathing under water, like listening to the melodic notes of the fiddles —

'What are you doing, Rohesia?' Ames' voice sounded from behind her and she jumped, jolted from her reverie.

'I …'

But Ames frowned at whatever he saw on her face. 'What's wrong?'

'Sorry?' Roh asked. She had known the old cyren all her life and *not once* had he ever asked her something so personal. She must have misheard him. The Ames she knew wanted no part in the emotional turmoil of his students.

'What's wrong?' he said again, peering into her face.

'Nothing,' she replied automatically.

Ames gave a frustrated sigh and strode past her, into the workshop. He sat at his desk, clasping his hands before him and waiting expectantly. *He truly wants to know*, Roh realised. Although Ames had never been a parental figure as such, he had known her longer than anyone else in the lair. He had taken her in when she had been cast out from her mother's prison cell. Roh took a step inside, glancing once more at the spot where Harlyn and Orson usually sat.

'It's my deathsong,' she told him reluctantly.

'Ah.'

'Everyone else is finding theirs and I ... I've got nothing. I'm useless. I —'

Ames shook his head. 'You are still young, Rohesia. *It will come.*'

'But what if it *doesn't*? Queen Delja sang her first note at *eight years old*! And she has *the most powerful* song in history.'

'Does she?' Ames tugged on his collar, as he usually did when he posed such questions.

'What do you mean?' Roh asked, brows furrowed.

'Does Queen Delja have the most powerful deathsong in history?'

Roh chewed her lower lip as she worked backwards in her mind, trying to find the precise source of that information. 'That's what everyone says,' she replied weakly.

'Ah, therefore it must be true,' he said dryly.

'Well, I —'

'Queen Delja *did* sing her first note at eight years old, but she didn't sing her full song until her later fledgling years. *However*, even then, it was not she who had the most powerful song in known history. That claim belonged to one of King Asros' battalion leaders, many hundreds of years ago, and if my sources are correct, she did not find her deathsong until long after her fifth decade. She was in the minority, that's sure enough. But when she did eventually find her song, Rohesia, it was something else entirely.'

Roh gaped at her mentor. She had *never* been told that story before. 'You heard it?'

Ames nodded. 'Once. And I'll never forget it.'

'Who was she?'

'Sedna Irons. She led King Asros' cyren armies across the seas in the Age of Chaos. A bitter end for such a talent.'

Roh didn't know what to say. All her life she had believed she was behind the others, that she was lesser, that she may always be lesser, but now … The most powerful deathsong in cyren history had belonged to someone who hadn't found it until her fiftieth year. There was hope yet.

Ames cleared his throat. 'Now, if you're done stealing supplies from my workshop, you might want to absent yourself before my class returns from break.'

All of a sudden, it seemed, the eve of the second trial was upon them. Roh hovered over Odi's shoulder as they at last prepared to test the piano's sound. He sat before the instrument on a makeshift stool he'd crafted from timber offcuts, his half-gloved fingers poised above the incomplete keys.

'I cannot believe I let you talk me into this,' he muttered, staring at the gleaming ivory at his fingertips. Bone.

'I had to link it to Saddoriel in a way that the highborns understand,' Roh argued, resisting the urge to press down on the keys herself.

Odi shook his head. 'You tainted it with cyren barbarism.'

'Cyren barbarism might be the thing that gets us into the final trial.'

Odi sighed in defeat. They'd had this argument several times already and Roh knew how it ended. 'Just test it, will you?'

With a curse, Odi hit the first key to test the hold of the wire and Roh gaped in utter, unabandoned awe. A note, a note of music. There was no mistaking it.

Odi nodded to himself and pressed another. 'This is promising.'

'Promising?' Roh crossed her arms over her chest.

'That's what I said.' Even Odi's quiet demeanour had a limit. They had spent days and weeks on end together and Roh's last-minute addition to the piano had caused a ripple in their otherwise calm companionship. Now in silent tension, they strung the last of the wires by hand, threading them through their rightful place on the long and short bridges between the pins, checking the pressure so that the hammers struck the string at their vital, accurate points.

Roh glued the bone keys in place, only noticing that her fingers had bled through the bandages when she had to wipe the red smudges from the piano. She was too caught up in what they'd made, what had taken shape before them. It looked completely foreign to her, but there was something about it …

Odi finally returned to the stool and glanced up at Roh, looking uncertain for the first time since they had started the build. 'I believe this is what they call "the moment of truth".'

Roh nearly baulked. Was something wrong? Why was he nervous now? Did it not look how it was supposed to? She crossed her arms, mainly to calm her thumping heart. 'So test it,' she said, sounding steadier than she felt.

He pressed down on one key after another, the notes climbing with his fingers.

'And?' she asked, scarcely daring to breathe.

Odi plunged his elegant fingers across the length of their creation. The strings vibrated, producing their own individual, specific, musical notes. Just as he'd said they would.

'These are just scales,' he explained. 'They help musicians warm up, but also help makers check the instrument for tonal perfection.'

Roh swallowed hard and sat down on the stool beside Odi. She knew nothing about tonal perfection, but if the notes humming beneath Odi's fingers could be turned into a melody, then … 'You're sure they'll be able to play?' she heard herself ask. 'The fiddlers? What if they only play the fiddle?'

'The Eery Brothers are two of the most famous musicians in my realm. Musicians of that calibre start on the piano. They learn these scales. They use the piano to tune their other instruments. They'll be able to play.'

A fist of anxiety clenched around Roh's heart. 'How can you be sure?'

Odi considered her, his fingers hovering above the unfinished keys. 'I just am. Trust me.'

Trust had never come easily to Roh, and the trust between her and Odi in particular seemed even more fickle. It came in unpredictable waves; one moment he was saving her life, the next he was urging her into quicksand. It was like there was a set of weights between them, each adding and taking away enough that neither side touched the ground, yet neither side was ever even. But as Odi's fingers picked up their pace again, gracefully dancing along the bone keys, climbing the so-called scales, Roh made a decision.

'Alright,' she said. 'I trust you.'

CHAPTER EIGHTEEN

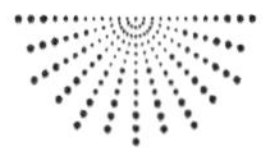

Roh stood at the entrance of the hall, between the statues of Dresmis and Thera, their wings outstretched as though ready to embrace her as she peered into the vast cavern beyond. Lanterns, candles and jars of valo beetles cast golden light across the immense platform that had been built over the narrow bridges of the Great Hall. She kept her clammy hands in her pockets as she entered with Odi and three porters behind her, carefully pulling a canvas-covered trolley in tow. Roh's eyes went to the great expanses of art stretched across the ceilings: goddesses and past rulers, all revelling in triumph after triumph. The sense of history bore down on her, the vast chronicles of her kind making her feel small, forcing the question of whether or not any of her own actions would ever be deemed worthy of art, of remembering.

As she walked, her knees felt weak, buckling slightly

when she came to a stop near the centre of the hall. The image of Tess trying to walk after the quicksand filled her mind; was that what she looked like now? Like some terrified newborn animal? She hoped she could mask her feelings better than the human had as she spotted the Council of Seven Elders, standing in a huddle beside Queen Delja. The queen sat in an impressive coral throne to match her coral crown, nodding along as her council murmured in her ears, but her attention was elsewhere. Her scales shone as she angled her head, focusing on the centre of the hall.

With her heart in her throat, Roh turned back to Odi and the porters, who were still inching the trolley down the makeshift ramp and into the main section of the hall. One of the bandages around Odi's fingers had come loose, leaving a ribbon of bloodied white hanging at his side. Roh glanced down at her own hands – she too sported red-spotted bandages around her fingers. Some points were still raw and pulsing beneath the linen strips. She recalled the scales Odi had played over and over into the early hours of the morning. They were as ready as they would ever be. She flinched as the trolley jolted loudly over a stone.

'*Be careful,*' she hissed. All that work, all those risks … It couldn't have all been for nothing.

Finally, the porters settled the trolley next to Zokez and his human. They stood beside something the size of a wine barrel, covered in a grey tarp, and didn't spare her a glance. Odi's shoulder brushed against Roh's as he came to stand at her side and she heard him exhale a shaky breath.

'Alright?' she asked softly.

He nodded stiffly, back rigid.

This is just as important for him now, a small voice said inside her head. She knew what the stakes were for him, too, that he was clinging to the promise she had made him in the tunnels. That he also now felt the cloud of pressure hanging over them, dark and rumbling, ready to burst. Odi had come back to help her, and had created the beautiful instrument that lay beneath the canvas on the trolley. And what if it wasn't enough? What if they didn't make it past this trial? What if she had to return to cleaning bones after everything they had done? What would become of *him*? What could she do to save him? From the corner of her eye, she could see the other competitors filing in, glancing nervously at the great queen before them, their creations hidden away by canvases and tarps, but she was already sucked into the whirlpool of anticipation that unlocked the darker level of her fears at a dizzying pace. Roh's fingers twitched at her side as she made to grip Odi's hand —

A cyren touching a human in the Great Hall of Saddoriel? Never. Her fingers stilled.

Odi nudged her, nodding to a figure across the hall. Tess. The human stood beside Yrsa Ward, her eyes bright and colour high on her cheeks.

So, they found her protective token.

'She looks …' Roh started.

'Safe?' Odi finished for her. It was a strange term for a

human to speak in the heart of the lair, but the word died on Odi's lips as a commotion from the entrance sounded. It was Finn Haertel. Behind him and his human, an entourage wheeled a massive contraption inside. It was larger than Roh and Odi's, only just managing to fit through the giant double doors. Roh couldn't even guess at what might lie beneath the numerous sheets covering it. Did she even *want* to know? She swallowed the rising panic in her chest and the lump in her throat. There was no way of knowing what any of the competitors had built, no way of knowing who would still be standing here at the end.

A bell chimed; the clear, singular note echoed throughout the chamber and Elder Colter stepped to the forefront of the council. 'Competitors, welcome to the second trial of the Queen's Tournament,' he said, his voice effortlessly projecting across the space. 'Our queen, my fellow council elders and I are eager to see what you have built for us. You will be called by name. You will tell the council what you have created, and where applicable, provide a demonstration. Our judgement will be reserved until the end of the presentations.'

Roh cursed silently. That meant she would be last, as always. As if her nerves weren't already in tatters.

'Finn Haertel,' Elder Colter called. 'If you please ...'

Everyone, Roh included, turned to face the highborn. His expression betrayed nothing, as though he were just as comfortable here as he would be in his own quarters.

And why wouldn't he be? Roh mused, hands clenched at her sides as she glanced towards the Council of Elders, where, despite their neutral composure, Bloodwyn and Taro Haertel stood proudly.

'My warmest greetings to Her Majesty, Queen Delja, and the Council of Seven Elders,' Finn said, his voice strong and clear. 'It is my privilege to present to you today.'

If Roh hadn't been so nervous, she might have scoffed. *As if he needs to bootlick.* The sideways glance she received from Odi told her he thought the same.

Finn reached for the corner of one of the sheets covering his creation. Roh thought her heart might stop as the highborn cleared his throat and pulled.

A unified gasp sounded all around, and Roh swore softly. It was … She didn't know what it was. A storage vessel of sorts … made of bones.

'This is a musician transporter,' Finn started. 'A completely new contraption specifically designed for the Jaktaren guild.'

'*What?*' Roh muttered to Odi. 'What does that even mean?' From the confused expressions of her fellow competitors, she wasn't the only one who had no idea where Finn was going with this. But as always, his expression was calm and smug.

'Allow me to demonstrate,' he continued, seeming to savour the suspense as he pulled a lever. A gate opened. 'This design has numerous special features: the ability to have separate compartments, so captured musicians can be held individually.' He pulled another lever and a row of bars came swinging down, splitting the cage into various chambers. 'It also has several smaller gaps where food and water can be delivered or retrieved from each section, without opening the larger doors.' He pointed to a small section and slid it open. 'But the best part …'

Odi ducked his head close to Roh's. 'There's a "best part" to this monstrosity?' he whispered with disgust. 'Just how many musicians do the Jaktaren steal from the human realms?'

Roh folded her arms over her chest; she was inclined to agree with him.

'It's completely collapsible, transportable, and reassembles within moments.' He unlatched a bone at the cage's side. The whole thing folded neatly to the ground. After several quick and effortless motions, it was no bigger than a crate. 'The Jaktaren can take this with them on assignments, with minimal strain on existing resources. It then assembles like so …' Finn pulled something else and the contraption sprang back to its full form. 'And can be used however the Jaktaren leaders see fit. Alternatively, it could be used as a bone transporter.'

Dazed, Roh fixed her gaze on the *bone transporter*, recalling the sectioned-off part of the workshop. *That bastard*, she realised. Haertel had had *her friends* working overtime to create this horrific contraption. This piece of junk had been there in her workshop when she'd peered through the window the other day. Her friends had cleaned and sorted the bones for him. The *highborn prick* hadn't lifted a finger, that much was clear. How could he do that? How could *they*?

'A *bone transporter*,' she muttered. 'What sort of garbage is that?'

'The same garbage as a *musician* transporter.' Odi looked equally horrified. 'From the looks of it, your council doesn't seem to think it's garbage at all.' Roh followed his gaze to the Council of Seven Elders, who were now walking around the contraption, some taking notes. Queen Delja, however, remained seated in her throne.

'Is this something your guild or army would actually use?' Odi asked.

Roh watched the elders make their final observations then return to their positions before the competitors. 'It seems completely unnecessary, but … I don't know.' As the words left her lips, she knew them for the lie they were. She *did* know. The answer was *yes*. Saddorien cyrens would indeed use such a device.

'Yrsa Ward.' Elder Colter's voice cut through Roh's turmoil and she grew rigid as the highborn cyren and Tess stepped forward. It was the 'moment of truth', as Odi had called it. Would this be when Roh's choices came back to bite her? She shifted from foot to foot as Yrsa clasped her hands together before her. She made no show of greeting the queen or the council. She simply launched straight into her presentation.

'What I have here today is just a sample of the larger project I have created,' she said, motioning to the covered structure before her, no bigger than the side table in Roh's chamber. Without further fanfare, Yrsa nodded to Tess, who removed the sheet.

Roh took a step forward, and another, and another, as did the other competitors around her. She still couldn't quite see what lay within the box besides straw and several jars of valo beetles, glowing brightly. Yrsa lifted the box, tilting it on an angle to reveal its contents to them. Eggs. Crimson, scaled eggs. And around them was Yrsa's horned serpent.

'It's a breeding program,' she explained. 'To increase the numbers of these rare and endangered creatures. Creatures who have been a part of our history for so long.'

Roh could hear murmurs of approval from the council, and she had to hand it to Yrsa. It was nothing if not original. Slowly, the ugly beast of envy within Roh writhed uncomfortably.

Zokez was called next. Roh shuffled away from him, feeling uncomfortable with the spotlight so close to her. Zokez presented a vault for currency, not even hiding his link to the Council of Elders as the son of Koras Rasaat, the authority on the treasury. Another name was called. *Arcelia Bellfast.* Roh looked to her former teacher eagerly, but before Arcelia could open her mouth, Elder Colter spoke again.

'Where is your human?'

Arcelia bowed her head. 'Dead, Elder Colter. She died earlier this week. She misplaced her token and was taken by the lure of the lair.'

Shock rolled through Roh and the other competitors. Arcelia's human was dead? She had warned Arcelia before the trials had even begun to watch out for sabotage. Had she not heeded Roh's warning? But then ... Roh, too, despite her every effort to keep Odi safe, had found herself in a similar position not long ago. She took a small step closer to him now.

'Very well, Arcelia Bellfast. You are hereby eliminated from the tournament,' Elder Colter said.

Stony-faced, Arcelia bowed deeply to Queen Delja, who inclined her head ever so slightly. In her crown, the birthstones of Saddoriel seemed to pulse with power.

Still bent at the waist, Arcelia cleared her throat. 'I thank you for the opportunity to compete before you, Majesty.'

Queen Delja said nothing. She merely watched blankly as Arcelia was escorted out. Roh stared after her in disbelief, then glanced across at Finn Haertel. As if he needed to resort to stealing humans' tokens. It was such an underhanded move. Arcelia deserved to be here, more than most, and yet … her time here was done. Roh averted her gaze. She had to focus on what was happening *now*. It would be her turn soon, and she had to do their creation justice. She had to ensure it wasn't *her* being escorted away.

Next was Estin Ruhne. Roh schooled her face into neutrality, despite the anger that simmered in her gut at the sight of the renowned architect. Estin revealed a miniature model of a library designed specifically for the queen's private quarters. Roh couldn't help the pang that hit her in the chest. It was a dazzling design. Swirling spiral staircases that ran the length of the room, bookcases that rotated, revealing additional chambers beyond for the queen's most prized tomes. There was no denying: it was a work of art. Estin bowed at the applause that broke out around her. Teeth gritted, Roh clapped as well. She didn't do so for the architect, who had lost her respect weeks ago, but for the creation itself. Although Roh had never really been one for books, she respected the intricacies and level of detail in the design, the deep thought that had gone into every shelf, every hinge.

The queen's talons rapped against the arm of the throne and Elder Colter cleared his throat, drawing their attention back to him. 'Miriald Montalle,' he announced.

The army leader wheeled something forward, sweeping the cover off quickly to reveal a freestanding crossbow. It was an imposing structure, and for a moment Roh pictured it on a battle shore, firing into an oncoming enemy. It had a daunting presence about it, that was for sure. But Miriald's hands were shaking as she fitted a bolt to its chamber and drew the lever back. She released the catch and —

Nothing happened.

Miriald muttered something to herself and tried again. But the crossbow failed to fire.

'I'm afraid your project isn't in working condition, Commander Montalle.' It looked as though Elder Colter's words visibly sank into Miriald. She nodded, head hung in defeat. Offering no final words, no thanks to the queen upon her departure, the army leader left before the guards could escort her, tugging her human behind her. She didn't look back.

Roh swallowed. The competitors were falling away faster than she had expected, severed from the tournament ruthlessly, with no ceremony. Would she and

Odi be next? The waves of shock were still washing over the rest of them, but before she could fully comprehend what had just happened, Neith was called.

Roh turned to face the water runner, ready to offer a smile of encouragement. But Neith's face was dark with anger as she and Aillard removed the cover of her project. What they revealed … Well, *incomplete* was the *kind* way to describe it; unrecognisable was more accurate. Roh's skin crawled. *Has it been destroyed? Sabotaged?* Splinters of timber jutted out at odd angles and water leaked from somewhere within, creating a puddle at Neith's sandalled feet.

'What is this?' Elder Colter asked, his tone still neutral despite the mess before them.

'It …' Neith wrung her hands. 'It was meant to be a … water fountain.'

'Meant to?' The question itself mocked Neith.

'It's not finished,' was all she said.

'Very well. Neith, you are hereby eliminated from the tournament.'

'But —'

'There are no exceptions here. You may leave.' Elder Colter nodded to a pair of nearby guards, who took Neith and Aillard by the arms and led them away.

'Where are they taking them?' Odi's voice sounded in Roh's ear, and she knew his concern wasn't for Neith.

'The others were escorted out, too,' Roh whispered back. 'We can't worry about them now, Odi,' she told him. 'It's our turn.'

Roh struggled to breathe deeply enough, fighting for

air in short, shallow gasps. It felt as though one of the marble statues from above was pressing all its weight on her chest. The fear was all-consuming. This was the moment they had been working towards. What if —

Odi elbowed her. 'Focus,' he commanded, and just in time.

'Rohesia,' Elder Colter called. 'Of the Bone Cleaners.'

A cold calm washed over Roh as she stepped forward, forcing herself to stand up straight, keeping her hands still rather than wringing them in front of herself. She glanced at Queen Delja, as straight-backed and regal as ever, and Roh could have sworn the queen winked.

She sent a silent prayer to Dresmis and Thera that her voice would remain steady, and then, she spoke.

'What you're about to see is something we have never had in Saddoriel before …' She nodded to Odi, who, with a showman's flourish, removed the white sheet from their creation. Here amidst the glowing lights of the Great Hall, the piano looked impressive. It stood proudly atop the trolley, as though on a grand stage of its own. Odi had told her that they were usually painted and varnished, but this one was all the more glorious in its natural finish. Checking that the porters had placed bricks behind the trolley's wheels, Roh clambered up onto it and lifted the lid, revealing the row of gleaming white keys, the bones she'd insisted upon, to honour cyren history. The ivory of the bones contrasted starkly with the black shorter keys – the sharps and flats, as Odi called them.

Silence blanketed the hall and Roh cleared her throat.

'This is a musical instrument,' she told the council. 'It's called a piano.'

Elder Colter frowned. 'A piano?'

'Yes,' Roh pushed on. 'It plays melodies and songs.' She didn't miss the strange look the council elder exchanged with the queen.

'Very well,' he said. 'Prove it with a demonstration, then.'

'I require the human musicians,' she said, her voice almost quavering. 'The two who play the fiddles. I need them to play it.'

'That can't be allowed,' Finn Haertel barked, standing before Elder Colter, his cheeks tinged pink.

'What?' Roh heard Odi say.

Without so much as glancing in their direction, Finn stepped forward to continue his protest. 'It's not in the tournament rules that we could use outside resources during the presentation of our projects.'

Fury coursed through Roh's veins. Her talons threatened to spring free and embed themselves in Finn's throat. *Steady,* she told herself. She approached Elder Colter slowly, very conscious of the fact that this was the closest she'd ever been to a member of the Elder Council.

'It's not in the tournament rules that we *couldn't* use outside resources during the presentation of our projects,' she said, her voice quiet but lethal. She turned to Finn. 'And I'm not sure *you,* of all cyrens, want to draw attention to what resources we can and cannot use.'

Elder Colter looked from Finn to her. 'I will consult the queen and council.'

He left them standing side by side, wrath pouring out of Roh in waves. She couldn't stand the highborn beside her. The bastard who had tried to sabotage her at every turn over some rumour he'd heard. This couldn't end here, not like this. She'd worked too hard to have it all derailed now, and by *him*.

As the council and queen deliberated, Roh paced, watching Odi from the corner of her eye as he stood guard by the piano. The competitors broke out into hushed whispers, and though she didn't dare look at Finn, lest she lose her temper, she knew he was staring daggers at her. *Let him*, she thought, inviting the challenge. Every fibre of her being wanted to rip him apart.

Odi came to her side, as though sensing she was on the verge of imploding. 'What if they don't allow the Eery Brothers to play?' he asked, his voice low.

Roh crossed and uncrossed her arms. 'You will have to just play the scales. And hope it's enough.'

'Do you think it will be?'

'No.'

'What then —'

Elder Colter returned to the forefront with an elegant sweep of his robes. 'We have consulted with the queen,' he said, facing Roh and the competitors. 'The bone cleaner is right,' he announced. 'We have sent for the musicians.'

A rush of relief pummelled into Roh so hard that she struggled to stay upright. She couldn't believe it. The queen, the council had *sided with her*? She was adamant in her disbelief until she saw Finn's reaction.

'*What!*' The highborn threw his hands up in the air and he looked at the council beseechingly. 'That can't be —'

But to Roh's shock, the elders ignored his spluttering. Slowly, a smile spread across her face. The Eery Brothers would play her piano, and the Elder Council would see what they had built. She savoured the moment, a little victory amidst the chaos. She knocked her elbow against Odi's, unable to stop smiling. *It's going to work.* She could feel it in her bones.

Several moments later, the Eery Brothers appeared at the entrance of the hall, flanked by two guards. The once-handsome men looked thin and dishevelled, their clothes much larger on them than they had previously been. Bewildered, they were escorted inside, and brought right up to Roh and Odi. When their eyes came to rest upon Odi, their expressions changed. From bewilderment to … regret? Anger? Roh couldn't quite read them.

'What are you playing at?' one of them hissed at Odi as they were shoved onto the stool before the piano. 'What have you done?'

Anger, then, Roh decided, watching them closely, suspicion stirring within her.

'Bought you more time,' Odi murmured back.

Roh frowned, saying nothing as the fiddlers arranged themselves side by side on the stool. Both took turns to glance up at Odi, frustration mingling with their fear. Fame wasn't the whole story, it seemed. Odi *knew* the musicians, knew them *personally* – that much was abundantly clear to Roh as she watched their nervous exchanges.

'What are you waiting for?' Elder Colter snapped impatiently.

The Eery Brothers' backs straightened and they adjusted their positions to sit on the edge of the seat. Then, their hands came to rest over the keys, their wrists relaxed, as Odi's had been.

'The Wolves of Wildenhaven?' one asked the other quietly. A human-realm song title.

The second brother gave a single nod. 'On my count, then … Five, six, seven, eight —'

Vibrant notes burst from the instrument, filling the Great Hall with a simple, warm melody beneath the deft fingers of one brother. It was like … like golden syrup, rich and sweet and welcoming. A song that warmed the soul and soothed the mind, until … until the second brother began to play as well, his long fingers weaving a complex theme amidst the layers of notes, dark and full in sound. It was nothing like their fiddle playing, nothing like it at all. Roh felt herself sway at the music's power, and let it settle in her chest and wash over her whole being. She watched the brothers in awe, their fingers trailing up and down the row of bone keys, their bodies rocking with the movement of the song. Gradually, the notes built and built, reaching a brilliant crest before spiralling downwards, Roh's heart hammering along with them. At last the song slowed and the final, poignant chords sounded. Silence fell but for the faint echo of those last notes.

The Great Hall was blanketed in shock.

Roh herself had clapped a hand over her mouth as the brothers had worked the melody into a frenzy. The others were staring at her, then at Odi and the fiddlers at the piano. Astonishment was etched on every face, and every mouth was slightly open in bewilderment. Even Queen Delja looked stunned. After a long pause, Elder Colter stepped forward once more.

'Very well. Take the musicians away. The Council of Seven Elders will now deliberate.'

The Eery Brothers looked panicked as they were escorted back out. Odi didn't take his eyes off them, his expression somehow trying to reassure them. When the council members and queen had disappeared into a side chamber, Roh turned to Odi.

'You knew them,' she said.

'I told you —'

'No, you *knew them*, you *know* them, beyond them being famous.'

'I … I've come across them before. Does it matter?'

Roh considered him carefully. 'I don't know yet.'

Odi's fingers drifted absentmindedly across the keys, before he yanked his hand away, remembering what they were made of. He caught Roh's gaze. 'I told you that you could trust me,' he said, with the hint of a triumphant grin.

Something crawled beneath Roh's skin that threatened to sour this victory. They had done it, the piano had worked brilliantly, but … there was a secret. Odi was keeping something from her. And Roh's experience with secrets told her this was no trivial detail.

But Odi's eyes were bright and she couldn't help the tug of a smile at her own mouth. 'I … I couldn't believe the sound,' she managed. 'It's *beautiful*. Better than anything I imagined it would be.'

'I know.'

There was nothing worse than the waiting, than the slow tick of the minutes passing, oblivious to the anticipation thrumming across the Great Hall. Sometimes it felt like Roh had always been waiting. Waiting for her mother to say something to her, waiting to be old enough, waiting to find her deathsong, waiting for this gods-damned tournament … The inaction didn't suit her. She found the helplessness of it suffocating, hating that it tested the power of her limited patience. She remained quiet in her thoughts, her gut writhing with nerves. Her skin prickled beneath the stares of the other competitors, as though they were only seeing her for the first time now.

That's right, she wanted to say. *I'm not just some lowly bone cleaner. I am someone to be reckoned with.*

The bell chimed once more, its singular note sounding strange in contrast to the richness of the melody they'd just heard. But it served its purpose, drawing the competitors' attention to the front, where Elder Colter appeared once more.

'The winner of today's trial …' Each word was slow and deliberate, a purposeful torment as he looked around, taking in their anxious faces. 'Is Rohesia of the Bone Cleaners.'

Roh didn't move. Didn't breathe. There was no applause. Only silence. Was it possible? Roh's gaze slid to Odi's and his wide eyes confirmed what she'd prayed in her heart was true. They had *won*. They had won the trial. Against all the odds and nepotism, the craftsmanship and originality of their work could not be denied, not even by the Saddorien Council of Seven Elders. She wanted to scream, to jump up and down with the joy of it. She wanted nothing more than to race down to the workshop to tell Ames, Harlyn and Orson.

But Elder Colter was still speaking. 'Estin Ruhne has received second place. Yrsa Ward has come in third place. Finn Haertel and Zokez Rasaat, while you did not place, you will continue on to the third and final trial. All of you are to leave your projects here.'

That was it. They were dismissed. Making for the exit amongst the other competitors, Roh's grin was wide. It didn't matter that there had been no more than a few words regarding their victory. The absence of deafening applause didn't matter. What mattered was what they had achieved. And together, she and Odi had achieved a great deal. The pair stayed close as they made for the exit, heads ducked together and eyes bright with unified camaraderie. When they reached the double doors of the hall, someone grabbed Roh's arm. She looked up, finding Neith at her side. *Good! I'm glad we've got a chance to see her.*

Roh paused beneath the statues of Dresmis and Thera,

holding a hand to her chest, the other squeezing the water-runner's shoulder. 'Neith! Are you alright? I'm so sorry that you were —'

'You don't belong here,' Neith cut her off, her voice icy.

The very air around Roh stirred with something unpleasant and she baulked. 'What?' She must have misheard her, picturing Neith's broad smile only days earlier.

'You. Don't. Belong. Here.' Each word was like a stab to the gut. 'What were you even thinking? An *isruhe* as our future queen? No one would bow to you.'

Roh stood frozen in the shadows of the great goddesses, shock rooting her to the spot. 'But ... we're the same, Neith. We were the lowborns in it together.'

Roh heard a snicker from behind her, but she didn't turn to look. She watched as pure loathing filled Neith's lilac eyes.

'There is nothing "together" about us. We *are not* on the same side. Why do you think I took your pathetic human's token?'

'What?'

'You were so quick to accuse Haertel, and I let you.'

Neith? Roh stared at her in horror, the realisation dawning. 'You ... you helped Odi up ...'

'Is that what I did?' Neith sneered as she turned to leave. 'I hope this tournament ruins you.' She stormed off.

'I tried to tell you,' said a warm voice from nearby. Neith's human, Aillard, appeared by the steps. He approached Odi. 'I told her she need not resort to such tactics, but … she wouldn't listen. Her actions were born out of fear.'

'She did it to Tess, too?' Odi asked with a meaningful glance at Roh.

Aillard nodded. 'And the one that belonged to the teacher. Poor Fasiel. She lost her life because of it. I'm sorry I couldn't tell you sooner, old friend.'

'You have nothing to be sorry for,' Odi told him. 'Do you know what happens to you now?'

Aillard gave a grim smile. 'Only the gods can know for certain.'

Roh tore her gaze away from the humans, trying to find Neith as the group dispersed outside the hall, but the bitter water runner had vanished. Completely dazed, Roh looked around, catching Finn Haertel's victorious gaze on her. He'd heard every word. He gave her a final satisfied look before slipping back into the hall.

It took Roh several moments after Neith had left to be able to move her feet. The shock had settled into her limbs like lead. How could Neith have done this? How could she feel that way about a fellow lowborn? Roh was reeling. The tournament brought out the worst in her kind and put it on irrefutable display. The nepotism, the cunning, the cruelty, the selfishness, it was all there, stark before them. It was bleeding from the creations the competitors had crafted, laced in the sacrifices they'd made to get there, seeping from those who had suffered in the name of it.

'Odalis Arrowood,' a firm, official voice called from behind them.

Roh's stomach dropped into her boots and her mouth went dry. *What? Odalis? Why are they calling him that?* Still at the entrance to the Great Hall, both she and Odi were forced to turn back. Inside, the Council of Seven Elders were crowded around the piano, where Finn Haertel stood beside Elder Arcus Mercer.

'What is this about, Elders?' Roh asked, her voice trembling. She didn't know how to formally address them.

Arcus Mercer ran a hand along the side of the piano in wonder. 'We need to speak with Odalis Arrowood. Come here, human.'

'Odalis?' Roh hissed in Odi's direction.

His eyes were full of apology as the pair of them were forced forward. The muscular chest of a guard suddenly pressed into Roh's back and she shot Odi a worried glance. *What have you done?*

Roh wet her lips. 'What do you want with him?' She was still being corralled towards the piano and the elders, and worse, the long shadows newly cast across the ground told her that the competitors who had left were now crowding at the entrance of the hall to watch whatever was about to unfold. Dread lurched within her, cloaked in a deep sense of foreboding.

'He is a musician,' Finn said, his voice cold. 'He plays the piano.'

'What?' Roh sneered. 'That's a *lie*. Odi can play no more than the rudimentary scales – the notes required to test and tune the instrument. *That's all.*' Her words were venomous. Finn Haertel was going to pay dearly for this.

But Finn turned calmly to the Council of Elders now. 'He can play. I've heard him before. He's known in the human realms as the Prince of Melodies.'

'That's absurd.' Roh planted her feet firmly on the ground, refusing to budge forward an inch more. Odi stood beside her, silent.

'The Jaktaren have sought him out for years. Saddoriel wanted him even as a child – his name is in the ledger. And yet he has evaded us, since before I was inducted into the guild,' Finn explained. 'His father owns a famous shop on the Isle of Dusan. He is the stepbrother to the renowned Eery Brothers, the musicians who performed just now.'

A chill ran down Roh's spine. *I was in the woods near my village foraging for truffles ... That's when I heard my stepbrothers ... I heard them so clearly. I just walked in.'*

'You have no proof,' Roh said.

Finn's gaze was icy. 'I have had my suspicions long enough to make enquiries in the realms above. The council is satisfied with my findings.'

Roh opened her mouth to demand he share his proof, but dread had begun to rise up in her and she pictured Odi standing before the cage of bones, the jewelled hairpin poised in the lock. *Gods, Odi. What have you done?* She didn't dare look at him. Couldn't bring herself to imagine what was next for him. For *her.* She looked wildly around the hall, desperate for help, in what form or from whom she didn't know. She only knew that this was bad. Incredibly bad, and she could do nothing to stop what was coming.

A gale of cold wind swept across the hall, and Queen Delja landed before them, flying back in from the galleries above.

Roh's chest soared with hope, but the queen didn't meet her pleading gaze.

'He will play,' Queen Delja said simply.

At the shove of a guard, Odi staggered forward. Roh opened her mouth to object, but she couldn't. There was no arguing with the queen. She tried to give him a reassuring look, but he didn't meet her eye as he was pushed up to the piano stool.

Roh's insides were screaming. They couldn't do this to him, they *couldn't* – Odi was shaking his head. There was some kind of mistake. There had to be. He couldn't, *wouldn't*. A blade pressed against the side of his neck and he stilled. Roh exhaled a trembling breath and blood trickled into her palms at her talons digging into her skin as she watched him forced onto the stool at the piano. She couldn't look away from the silver blade resting against his skin, couldn't stop herself envisioning his head tumbling from his shoulders.

'Play,' Queen Delja commanded softly.

Without acknowledging the queen, Odi straightened his posture and lifted his hands to the keys. Still wearing his half-gloves, he positioned his fingers, resting them just above the gleaming bones. Then, he closed his eyes, and began.

Odi's long fingers danced across the keys of bone as though they had been created for the very task. The melody that drifted from the piano was unlike anything

Roh had ever heard, had ever imagined possible. Each chord, each accent was richer, more powerful than the last, full of heart and heartache, like Odi was cracking himself open and baring his soul. The music flowed like a powerful river flooding through parched lands. Its tone was dark and tense, telling a tragic, mesmerising tale. Roh could see past the case of the piano and into its core, where beneath the lid and against the soundboard, the press of a key beneath Odi's masterful touch caused a hammer to strike, creating a unique note that vibrated against *her* soul. She had never seen or heard a musician like Odi. His fingers waltzed across the keys, exposing every pulse of feeling in the music. The song was full of colour, of life, and it flooded the Great Hall with thunderous chords and its volatile build.

Roh's eyes were burning. Unshed tears blurred her vision. She couldn't remember the last time she'd cried, but this? She blinked them back, and swallowed the lump in her throat as Odi played the final, heartrending note. Roh tore her eyes away from him, to find everyone around him transfixed.

A singular applause broke the silence. The sound was sharp and cold.

Queen Delja. Her wings flared behind her as she turned to her guards. 'Take the Prince of Melodies to the musician holdings,' she ordered.

'*What?*' Roh's talons shot out and she clawed her way towards Odi, knocking down an unprepared guard and shoving another. 'You can't!' she cried. 'He belongs with me for the duration —'

'Roh?' Odi called, his voice cracking as he was dragged away like an animal.

'He is in the Jaktaren's ledger,' the queen said. 'He belongs to the guild, and therefore Saddoriel.' But the queen's voice sounded far away as Roh fought against the swipes at her. She wouldn't allow this, she was going to —

Someone blocked her. Elder Winslow Ward dug her own talons into Roh's arm, the sharp pain wrenching her from her siege of madness. *The queen gave an order.*

And suddenly, Roh felt the eyes on her, the eyes of every single cyren in the Great Hall, realising what they'd seen … A Saddorien cyren, fighting for a *human.*

The grip on her loosened and Roh fell to her knees with a gasp. But he was gone. Out of sight. Hauled away like some beast. Around her, she heard the sound of the competitors and elders leaving. She was alone in the Great Hall, the lights not nearly as bright and golden as they had been before. She collapsed further into herself, not caring that the platforms had vanished, and now the gaping chasms either side of the bridges were back. *Where are the musician holdings? Will he be protected there? Does he still have his token? … What happens to me? To our place in the tournament? Why didn't he tell me? That he was – is – the Prince of Melodies?* Roh wanted to cry, wanted tears to spill thick and heavy, wanted to sob her heart out. For Odi, for her, for everything they had been through and everything they had done. Everything that hadn't been enough. But the tears did not come. They never did. Roh tipped her head back, and closed her eyes against the ghost gaze of the marble statues above.

She didn't know how long she stayed there, but all at once, music filled the Great Hall and all of Saddoriel. From somewhere in the lair, the song and its deep, sombre notes came from two familiar fiddles; the new melody more haunting than ever before.

Roh wandered the Lower Sector of Saddoriel listlessly, the empty place at her side like an open wound. Banners scrawled with Neith's name were still strung up across windows and archways, mocking Roh. *You don't belong here. No one would bow to you ...* The water runner's words tore open old hurts, most of which Roh had inflicted herself. In a flash of rage, Roh let out a cry and her talons tore through a *Neith for Queen* sign, the loud rip echoing down the passageway. She shredded the fabric, leaving it in ribbons on the damp ground. She whirled around, looking for another to destroy. She would find them all. She would tear them down one by one – she would show the lair what sort of cyren Neith of the Water Runners was. A traitor. An underhanded wretch. It wasn't until loose thread webbed her talons that Roh's fiery fury ebbed, fading into a lukewarm shame as she picked them out. The lowborns didn't know or care what the water runner had done. Roh herself was no better. She'd cheated her friends to enter the tournament. She'd set traps for humans to get here. And she'd allowed the guards to take Odi away to gods knew where ...

'Rohesia, of the Bone Cleaners?' a timid voice sounded, startling her.

Roh flushed, finding a messenger standing behind her. How much had the fledgling seen of her little outburst? Did Roh still look the part of the savage, raging beast? She must have, if the fledgling's cautious step towards her was anything to go by.

Roh tried and failed to muster her last shred of dignity. 'Yes?'

'This is for you.' The messenger handed her an envelope. Smooth wax brushed against her fingertips, a pair of outstretched wings stamped within. The *queen's* signet.

Roh took it, the parchment feeling heavy in her trembling hands as she turned it over. Scrawled across the face of it in black ink were two words: *Trial Three.* She looked to the messenger in disbelief, but the cyren had already gone, eager to escape the clawing talons of the feral animal she'd likely seen moments earlier.

Trial Three. Roh stared at the words, the wax seal on the back warming in her palm, Odi's absence at her side pulsing. Was this a trick? Was she not immediately eliminated without Odi? Was that why it was coming from the queen? Was this her way of helping Roh? This at least meant Odi was safe, and whole. But she wasn't ready to open the envelope. How could she be? There in the dim passageway, Roh slid down the wall, crumpling into a heap on the damp ground. Quiet hummed around her. She couldn't remember getting from the Great Hall to here. The last thing she could recall was Odi calling her name and talons piercing her arm. Sure enough, when she looked down, there were punctures in her skin and tracks of dry blood. Elder Winslow Ward had done that.

'The queen gave an order,' had been the words in Roh's ear. The queen had indeed commanded Odi to play, had ordered him away. The same queen whose sadness had been so poignant down in the cells of the prison. The same queen who had defended Roh at the victor's feast. The same queen who had winked at her only hours ago and now had offered a tether to the tournament, whatever that meant. Roh stared at the envelope in her hands, knowing that whatever it held would offer her no salvation. Standing, she shoved it in her pocket unopened.

It wasn't long before Roh found herself in the empty workshop, sitting at her old workbench, head in hands. Her fingers rested against her circlet and she wondered if this was where she belonged, after all. This whole time, had she been mad to want more? Her skin crawled as the image of Cerys filled her mind: jagged talons and chopped hair. Perhaps madness did run in her blood. Perhaps there truly was no escaping who had made her, or what she was. Roh surveyed the workshop. She had no idea of the hour, but it must have been late for the place to be abandoned like this. The space that had been sectioned off for Finn's hideous contraption had been converted back to its usual state. Benches and barrels of bones lined the room. She turned her attention to her secret project, which remained hidden beneath its sheet at the back of the workshop. Ignoring the nagging sensation of the unopened envelope burning a hole in her pocket, she went to it, pulling the fabric away. It looked smaller somehow, and simpler than she remembered. Even at first glance, she noticed the elements that she would change, after having seen much more complex architecture in the Upper Sector. She would have to change a lot if she wanted to be happy with it now.

'I heard what happened ...' Ames' voice drifted into the workshop. He was *always* the first to know everything and he had a strange habit of showing up without being summoned, Roh noted, not for the first time.

It was only upon hearing his smooth tone that she realised it was exactly why she had come here. For comfort, for advice, for familiarity. She had hoped he would find her. But she didn't look up, didn't let on what she was feeling. She never did with him. Their bond had always been a complex web of roles – mentor and student, guardian and nestling, ancient cyren and reckless fledgling. A thread of shared otherness linked them in mostly silent solidarity. They were not close, nor were they distant; they simply *were* with one another. Ames was the closest thing besides Cerys that Roh had to family, and yet there had always been a barrier between them, a wall of formality that Roh longed to break down.

'What are they saying?' she asked.

'That you fought for him. The human.'

Roh did look up then, her throat going dry. She met her mentor's gaze. 'I think … I think he might be my friend, Ames.'

'I see.'

Was it disapproval in his tone? Surely not, when Ames himself seemed so at ease with Odi that he'd secretly opened up a dialogue with the human.

'Do you know where the holdings for musicians are?' she asked cautiously.

Ames lifted a single brow. 'No.'

Was he lying? Ames was the master of knowing things that others didn't, and was even better at keeping that knowledge to himself. Roh studied his weathered face, but couldn't pick up on any of his usual tells. Perhaps she'd lost her touch. She sighed and turned back to her project, scanning the tiny pieces of bone she had so painstakingly glued into place so long ago. Back when the tournament had seemed like a distant goal. Ames came to stand beside her, peering over her shoulder at the model. Roh realised with a start that he'd never seen it before, not up close, not like this. All at once, she became too aware of its flaws. But the self-consciousness she expected to flood her remained at bay, her mind still tangled in thoughts of Odi.

'Is it …' She hesitated.

'Is it what?'

She mulled over the words before she finally spoke them. 'Is it wrong? For him to be my friend?'

Ames tugged at his collar and turned his gaze to her. 'Only you can answer that, Rohesia.'

'I need him to …'

'Complete the tournament?'

'To be safe. I owe him that much at least.'

Ames nodded slowly, his expression still unreadable. 'Well,' he said. 'What would you do if it were any other friend?'

'What?'

'What would you do?'

'I'd … I'd try to get them out.'

'Try? You wouldn't just *try*. If Harlyn or Orson had been taken from you, you'd get them back. It's as simple as that.'

'Simple? How can I, Ames? He's being held on the queen's orders.'

Ames gave an infuriating shrug. 'That's not for me to say. You know I can offer you no *official* assistance.' His stress on the word 'official' told her that he believed he'd already given her enough unofficial assistance.

'So, I'm on my own for this one,' she muttered, pulling the unopened envelope from her pocket and sliding it across the bench towards him.

Ames stared at it, as though he could see its contents through the parchment and seal. 'You haven't opened it.'

Though it wasn't exactly a question, Roh shook her head. 'I can't bring myself to. And what's the point, without Odi?'

'You're talking like you won't see him again.'

'I might not.'

Ames gripped her arm hard, startling her once more. Roh couldn't remember a time in the last decade when Ames had actually touched her. 'You were made for this tournament, Rohesia,' he said with intensity, his lilac eyes latched onto hers. 'Your human friend will be safe where he is for the time being. Take the night with Orson and Harlyn. You have a choice, Rohesia. You can give up, or you can do what you think you were born to do.' He slid the envelope back across to her. 'You have a choice,' he repeated, before he stood and left her staring after him.

Roh pushed open the door to her old sleeping quarters with a creak and stepped inside. It was smaller than she remembered. Less than half the size of her quarters in the Upper Sector and shared between six cyrens, or five, without her. It was dark, the fire at the centre down to its last glowing embers, and the room was filled with the soft rhythm of steady breathing. Roh could just make out the outline of her empty bed. Not knowing what else to do, she went to it, pulled the covers back and slipped beneath. It was surreal, being here. The bed was narrow and the mattress thin enough to feel each slat beneath it, the rough fabric itching against her skin. Had it always done that? She closed her eyes, embracing the velvety dark behind her lids, and sighed.

'Roh?' Orson whispered from beside her. 'Roh, what are you doing here?'

Roh opened her eyes to see Orson's outline sitting up in the dark, reaching over to nudge Harlyn.

'What?' Harlyn grumbled, tugging her covers tighter around her.

'Roh's here.'

'What?'

'Roh's here, Harlyn. Wake up.'

Harlyn muttered a curse before throwing off her sheets. 'What is it?'

'Not here,' Roh told them.

Harlyn scoffed. 'Oh, we'll just step into my private council room, shall we?'

'Harlyn!' Orson scolded. 'Roh, she's just tired.'

'It's alright. How about the bathing chamber?'

Quietly, they took their quilts and ducked into the adjoining washroom.

'Damn, it's freezing in here,' Harlyn murmured, wrapping herself in her covers before seating herself on the cool tiles. 'Can't you start one of your little fires for us, Orson?' Then, she looked around wildly. 'Where's the human?'

Once the three of them were huddled on the ground in a circle, Roh met their gazes. 'They took him.'

Harlyn gaped at her. 'Who took him? The Haertel worm?'

'The queen.'

'*What?* How? *Why?*'

Each question was a sharp blow to Roh's gut. She explained about Odi being a musician and being in the Jaktaren's ledger.

Harlyn let out a low whistle. 'So they can do whatever they want?'

'Apparently. And … that's not all,' Roh said.

'Gods, Roh, don't draw it out. What's happened?' Harlyn nudged her gently.

'It can't be worse than them taking Odi,' Orson blurted.

Roh produced the still-unopened envelope from her pocket and handed it to Orson. 'I can't bring myself to …'

'*Trial Three*,' Orson read aloud, glancing from Harlyn back to Roh. 'Do you want us to help you?' she asked.

Unable to find the words, Roh nodded, watching as Orson slid a talon beneath the wax seal and broke it.

'What does it say?' Harlyn said impatiently.

Orson unfolded the envelope, her eyes scanning the instructions within, until the piece of parchment she held began to shake in her hands.

'What is it?' Roh's voice came out raw, the pit of her stomach filled with dread.

'You …' Orson hesitated before she passed the parchment to Harlyn, whose eyes widened with utter horror as she too read the details.

Harlyn placed the instructions facedown on the cold floor and met Roh's gaze. 'You have to retrieve the scale of a sea serpent.'

Roh heard her own breath whistle. 'Say that again …'

'You heard me the first time,' Harlyn said, giving her a pointed look.

Roh nearly jumped as Orson balled her quilt up in her fists, burying her face in it. A muffled scream sounded, full of rage and disbelief. She screamed again, her body heaving. When she pulled her face away from the fabric, her eyes were rimmed with red and saliva stretched from her chin to the blanket. 'How …?' she panted. 'How could they do this? That tradition was *banned,* years and years ago. How can they …?'

Harlyn reached out and wiped Orson's mouth with the quilt with surprising tenderness before turning back to Roh. 'It's suicide,' she said.

Tears streamed freely down Orson's face. 'It was outlawed *for a reason.* So many cyrens died. Roh … you can't do this.'

The bathing room spun before Roh. 'Forfeit?'

'Yes. *Please.* You have to.'

The despair etched on her friends' faces made the final trial all the more real to Roh, unmasking it for the insanity it truly was. *Retrieve the scale of a sea serpent …* A deathtrap designed by the Council of Seven Elders to eliminate any threat to their current power. Roh recalled the tremors and the distant screech in the outer tunnels of Talon's Reach. She also remembered the texture of Toril Ainsley's scars and how she'd wondered if she'd leave this tournament whole.

Skin tingling, Roh traced her own scar. 'Odi … Without him I'm eliminated anyway.'

'*Good,*' Orson said firmly, palming away her tears. 'If it means you stay alive, then *good.*'

'Orson, it's not that simple.'

Orson's eyes were fierce and her tone unusually sharp as she said, 'No? How is not wanting you to die not simple?'

'It's just …' Roh didn't understand it herself, couldn't

process the warring emotions roiling inside her. 'This can't be it.'

'What do you mean?' Harlyn asked.

'It … it can't end here. Not after everything. What would you do?' As the question left her lips, she realised how much she needed to ask it, how much their opinions truly mattered to her. They had always been a trio, until, without their knowledge, she had severed that tie. At that moment, she wanted to tell them, to confess to them all she had done, how she had wronged them, her guilt nearly bubbling from her like the white foam of a wave. She bit her lip, holding back the flow of words. If she told them now, it would only be to relieve herself of her own pain. It would be selfish, she told herself. Her decision was something she had to live with; there was no point in destroying things for them, too.

'I don't know what I'd do.' Harlyn shrugged. 'And we'll never know. It doesn't matter, does it? It's about what *you'll* do.'

Roh's friends continued to talk, but their voices were distant. Roh's head was filled with a panicked fluttering sound, or perhaps it was coming from her chest, she didn't know. Harlyn and Orson blurred as blood rushed to Roh's head and sweat chilled her skin. Fear wrapped around her like thick, heavy chains. She imagined herself restrained from neck to toe, released into the current and sinking to the bottom of the seabed like a stone. Although she could breathe beneath the infinity of water, it was knowing she'd be trapped down there forever that cast an immovable shadow across her heart.

'I'm *afraid*,' Roh croaked aloud. Her chest was tight, as though those chains had indeed imprisoned her. Those two words revealed it all. The stark truth of the matter. The utter terror drowning her at the thought of what lay ahead.

A warm hand squeezed her shoulder. Harlyn. 'If anyone can do it, Roh,' she said, all traces of her past envy gone, 'it's you.'

Roh stayed in her old bed that night, listening to the comforting rhythm of her friends' quiet snores. Only emptiness awaited her in the Upper Sector quarters. She had to get Odi back. He was her responsibility. More than that, he was her friend. He'd risked it all to come back. And now, she would do the same. The only question was, *how?* Roh lay in the narrow bed, the sheets still scratching against her skin as her mind spun with an array of absurd options. None of them were right, none of them would see Odi returned to her side and the two of them still in the tournament.

There is one person who might know ... Harlyn's words from all those months ago lingered in Roh's mind like the after-effects of a poison. *Cerys ...* Cerys might know something, anything that could help her. She had been in Saddoriel for centuries. She knew the queen. If there was a possibility, even the slightest chance that Cerys knew something that could turn the tide in Roh's favour ... Silently, she swung her feet from the bed, feeling the cold floor beneath her soles, but a new voice filled her head.

'It felt like ... It felt like you might be on the brink.'

'Of what?'

'Making a bad decision. You had this look in your eyes, like no one could stop you ... You need to be focusing on this trial. Not running off chasing ghosts.'

Roh swallowed the lump in her throat. Was that what she did? Ran off chasing ghosts while the world around her fell apart? She waited a moment, and then swung her legs back into bed, yanking the covers up to her chin. As silence settled around her once more, she swore she could hear the faint notes of a melody. She knew it was Odi, wherever he was. It could be no one else. He had told her that each piano was unique, had its own character. Well, so did each musician, Roh realised as the song washed over her, loud and clear now, despite her being in the Lower Sector. The way Odi played was different to his stepbrothers. There was more soul, more feeling to the sounds that poured out of the instrument at his hands. At long last, Roh fell asleep, with the melody in her heart and a promise to help Odi on her lips.

Roh made her way to the Upper Sector in the quiet hours of the morning. Odi's music was long gone, replaced with the clear notes of a duo of fiddles. She passed through the Great Hall, weakly hoping to find Odi there, but it was empty save for the enchanted music that filled the domes above. As she entered the foyer to the residences, the song still wrapped around her, Roh realised that she'd never felt so conflicted about her yearning for music before. The sounds she now heard were encased by rage and guilt. How could there be so much pain and suffering at the root of something so beautiful?

'There you are!' a husky voice exclaimed. Yrsa Ward was charging straight for Roh. 'I've been looking everywhere for you,' she said, irritated.

Roh frowned, spotting Tess at Yrsa's heels. 'Clearly not everywhere.'

'Request an audience,' Yrsa demanded.

'What?'

'Request an audience,' Yrsa repeated impatiently. 'With the queen. She can't change the rules mid-course.'

'I think she's proven that she can.'

'There's a difference between re-introducing an old tradition and breaking the rules of her own tournament.'

'I don't —'

'Do you know nothing of Saddorien cyrens? We choose our words carefully. Choose yours carefully, and you'll get your human back.' Yrsa was already walking away.

Roh started after her. 'Why are you —'

But Yrsa and Tess had slipped into the Great Hall, the door swinging closed behind them.

In her chambers, Roh sat at the bay window, looking out onto the empty foyer below. A dozen voices filled her head. She couldn't stop the onslaught of their words. Harlyn, Orson, Ames, Odi, Finn, Yrsa, Tess, Cerys, Queen Delja, Toril, Elder Ward and several of her own. A wild debate raged within, questioning her abilities, her motivations, her moral compass and everything in between. Each word echoed, ricocheting off the walls of her mind. Shaking her head, as though she could rid herself of the doubts, Roh made a decision. She went to the side table and took up a piece of parchment. There, cringing at her poor handwriting, she scribbled upon the page with her talon:

I, Rohesia of the Bone Cleaners, request an audience with Queen Delja the Triumphant.

CHAPTER TWENTY

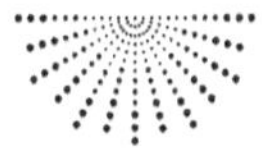

The next morning dawned with enchanted hues of violet and rose gold spilling through the chamber window. When the knock sounded at her door, Roh was ready. Washed and dressed in simple clothing, with her boots polished and laced tight, she gave herself one final glance in the washroom mirror. Her eyes went straight to the line of gold around her head. Her dark curls escaped beneath it, hanging past her shoulders. The circles beneath her eyes were darker than ever.

An audience with the queen ... She hadn't thought of anything but this very moment since she'd scrawled the words on the parchment. Now, her chest felt like a hollowed-out cage, dozens of insects flitting about inside, rattling her thoroughly as she followed the messenger from the competitors' quarters. She did so in silence, listening to the music that skittered across her skin. Somewhere in Talon's Reach, Odi was playing the piano again. There was no one else whose melody could be so sorrowful and astounding; Roh imagined his half-gloved fingers dancing across the bone keys.

They did not, however, take the pulley system to the ground floor as she expected. They went up, the music growing louder as they passed level after level, until they finally came to a stop at the very top.

'Where are we going?' Roh asked quietly.

The messenger looked startled, as though she didn't know whether or not she should speak to Roh. 'To the queen's private quarters,' she whispered back, in a tone that told Roh she ought to know. The pulley system opened, revealing a brightly lit foyer and two formal guards standing either side of a pair of silver doors.

'Her Majesty is expecting the bone cleaner,' the messenger told them, nodding to Roh.

Without a word, the guards opened the doors and the messenger led Roh into a grand hall. *So, these are the queen's quarters ...* Roh stared in wonder at the pristine white walls, the shining blue marble beneath her boots and the chandeliers of bones above. However, it was something that glimmered at the end of the hallway that caught her eye. She squinted as she and the messenger drew closer.

Is it ...? Roh had to stop herself from clamping a hand over her mouth in shock. It *was*. A veil of water, much like the one she'd seen in the first trial and then in the outskirts of Talon's Reach. An enchanted portal to the seas surrounding Talon's Reach and Saddoriel. The queen had one of her very own ...

'This way,' the messenger said, turning left.

Roh wanted to protest, the veil and the current beyond calling to her with its shimmering turquoise blue, but she had no choice other than to follow the messenger, each step bringing her closer to Odi and his music.

You can do this, she told herself, clenching her fists to stop her hands from trembling. The messenger pushed another door open, and pine-green walls greeted them, lined with silver architraves, but Roh's eyes went straight to the source of the music, where the ornate furnishings had been pushed to one side to make room for a piano. Odi sat at the stool, straight-backed, his wrists poised over the keys, music pouring from his fingertips.

Roh started. It was not the piano of their making. This one was black and shining, the polished twin to their creation.

How ...?

'It's why the Prince of Melodies has been hunted so ferociously by the Jaktaren,' Queen Delja's voice sounded.

Roh whirled around. On a chaise longue in the corner, surrounded by plush velvet cushions, sat the queen. Her wings were hidden, a sketchpad and a stick of charcoal in her hands. Her crown rested on a small dark table to her right. Roh met the bright lilac gaze that latched onto her and didn't look away.

'The instrument was brought to Saddoriel over a century ago,' Queen Delja continued. 'Only the Jaktaren and I know of its existence. For decades it has sat here, untouched, because something so beautiful should not be played by anyone but a master. For an age we waited for a musician worthy of it. Your Prince of Melodies has been on the ledger since he was six years old. A *child prodigy*, they called him. But I instructed the Jaktaren to wait, wait until he was of age, until he reached his full potential.'

Roh was reeling. The queen had had a piano all along? Why had she not stepped in and told the council she possessed a flawless, finished version of what Roh and Odi had created for the trial? It could have meant one less competitor challenging her reign. Not to mention it was thanks to her that Roh had received the details of the final trial. Apparently, Queen Delja was a riddle of secrets and contradictions ...

Somewhere behind Roh, the messenger left, the door clicking closed behind her and momentarily snatching Roh's attention away from the queen. Her gaze trailed to the ceiling and she blinked slowly, not quite able to believe her eyes. The entire ceiling was *glass*, transparent glass, revealing the sea above. The current pushed against it as a school of flame angelfish swam above it, the deep blue beyond utterly mesmerising.

'Your Odalis evaded us for a long time ...' Queen Delja's melodic voice made Roh's skin prickle, but she faced her again.

'We captured his brothers easily enough,' the queen was saying. 'Both talented in their own right. We should have known the lair would use them to call to him. All those years of effort.' The queen lowered her sketchbook and placed the charcoal on the table by her crown, her fingertips smudged with black. She had drawn two young cyrens, both with wings outstretched behind them,

herself so they were eye to eye. The guards lifted the pointed double blades instantly.

'The bone cleaner is right,' the queen allowed, her voice sharp. 'For the duration of the tournament, the human is hers.'

Roh didn't dare move, even as the music ceased abruptly behind her and Elder Colter and his guards gaped openly at the queen. Roh couldn't remember the last time a song had ceased playing in Saddoriel, incomplete. Without looking in her retinue's direction, Queen Delja waved a hand of dismissal and the council member and guards left them.

Roh bowed deeply once more. 'Thank you, Your Majesty.'

The queen ignored this. 'You understand why I had to do it, don't you, Rohesia? That it was expected of me? *Sacred is the ledger.*'

Roh blinked, feeling slowly coming back into her limbs. Did she understand? *What in the name of Dresmis and Thera is she talking about? Why is she explaining herself?* But now was not the time to disagree. Roh nodded quickly. 'Yes, Your Majesty.'

The stool scraped against the marble floor and Odi came to stand beside Roh, filling the void that had pulsed in his absence. Roh didn't dare to look at him yet. She focused on trying to find the words, the excuse to leave. As she opened her mouth, her eyes fell upon a leather-bound tome that peeked out from the cushions on the chaise and she stilled.

The *Tome of Kyeos*. Or at least, one of its many

volumes. It was calling to her, in rhythmic whispers. The rest of the world around her was gone. She took a step forward. A song filled her mind and the turquoise waters above shimmered against the glass, as if in time to the melody. She knew those words …

'Hush, hush, little cyren, so strong yet so small,
For down in deep Saddoriel, we let no tears fall.
Oh hush now, little nestling,
One day you will find your song …'

But who was singing? The tome itself? Why would it sing a nestling nursery rhyme to her? She was just about to reach for the book when —

'Your mother always had a fascination with it, too,' Queen Delja said quietly.

The blood rushing through Roh's veins froze and she snapped from her trance, all notes of the children's song vanishing, leaving her cold. *My mother? What does Cerys know of the* Tome of Kyeos?

Queen Delja's expression gave nothing away. 'Just like the lair, the tome and all its volumes are a living, breathing thing. It has its own will. She never saw it. Not in the end.'

'How …?' Roh's voice was small, as though in the presence of new information about her mother, she had returned to the bewildered state of a young nestling. 'How?'

But Odi was tugging on her sleeve, bringing her back to reality.

'It seems your human is eager to leave my chambers, Rohesia,' Queen Delja said, retrieving the volume from the chaise and placing it carefully on the table beside her crown.

Roh stared. The two things she wanted most in all the realms were but an arm's length away, practically within her grasp. She could have sworn she heard the book whisper her name and saw the gems in the coral crown wink at her. They called to her, they wanted her to have them – but Odi was pulling her away. She barely registered her legs moving beneath her, and yet she found herself outside the queen's chambers, the tome, the crown and the veils to the sea all ripped away.

'Keep walking, keep walking,' Odi muttered, pulling Roh towards the pulley system by her elbow. Odi kept checking over his shoulder, as though he could hear footsteps behind them. As though someone was bound to stop them and order him back to the queen. The fear that spiked in his eyes brought reality crashing back to Roh. Had she really just got away with taking Odi from the queen?

'Odi, slow down. I'm going to trip!'

But he didn't pause until they were in the pulley system, the cage closed, feeling the strange sensation of being dragged down. His face was pale when he turned to her, and suddenly Roh needed a moment to gather herself, before she told her friend that she had freed him from one nightmare only to drop him in the middle of another.

When they arrived at the level for competitors' residences, Odi had still barely said anything. It wasn't until they were safe in their own quarters that Roh could no longer stand the silence between them. 'Odi,' she began, unsure of what to say, but knowing she needed to say something, *anything*. 'Odi —'

'I'm sorry,' he blurted out as soon as the door clicked closed behind them. 'I wasn't honest. The Eery Brothers, the fiddlers, they're my stepbrothers, you see.'

'I'd gathered as much,' Roh allowed. 'When you said you heard them in the tunnels, you meant their music.'

Odi nodded. 'Mason and Brooks Eery.'

'You helped with the piano because … You came back for them, didn't you?'

Odi stopped in his tracks. 'I knew if they had a piano, it would mean a lot more songs would become available to them. That they would have more time. That I would have more time to figure out a way to save them. I always knew cyrens hunted musicians, but I didn't know about that ledger. That I was on it.'

'You still risked yourself for them. I thought they treated you poorly?'

Odi's brow furrowed at that. 'They're family, Roh.'

'You had a chance to escape this place.'

'It doesn't matter, does it? I'm here now. They've got more time, and we still have a shot in this tournament, if you're not too angry with me?'

The onslaught of fury Roh expected did not come, and she was filled with something foreign to her … Understanding. She found herself waving away his apology. 'What right do I have to be angry?' she said, surprising herself. 'You didn't choose to enter this tournament. You were lured into our lair and trapped. All three of you were. And it's not like I'm known for my stellar decision-making.'

Odi gave a small smile at that. 'You got me back.'

'I shouldn't have let them take you in the first place. I … I was in shock. I froze. Are you … Are you harmed?'

'I'm fine,' Odi told her, settling into his usual spot by the window.

'Where did they take you? What happened?' Roh asked, sitting on the floor nearby, stretching out, eager to keep the reality of the third trial at bay for just a little longer.

'I was taken to the musician holdings. Mason and Brooks were there. Despite appearances, they're alright. I talked to them. I told them about our piano, to use it and their full repertoire of songs.'

'I hope they were grateful.'

Odi smiled. 'Mostly, they were angry at me for putting myself at risk.'

Roh must have looked confused.

'Our relationship … Things are complicated with them, Roh. We may not get along, but at the end of it all, we are still brothers. In any case, I wasn't there long. The queen sent for me less than an hour after I'd been taken from the hall.'

'What did she want?' Roh asked.

'You saw the piano. It's one my ancestors made. She said they'd been waiting for me, and she made me play for her.'

Roh waited.

'So I played for most of the night. One or two of those

council members visited, but they spoke your language, so I couldn't understand what they were saying. The whole time, that damn viper of hers watched me. It's disgusting, Roh, shedding its skin everywhere. Honestly, that creeped me out more than the queen of Saddorien cyrens.'

'The queen isn't creepy.'

'What?' Odi blurted.

'She's not. She's beautiful.'

'You can be both,' Odi argued.

Roh ignored this. 'What else? What else happened?'

'I looked through the book.'

'What!'

Odi gave her a sheepish look. 'Well … she left for a while. Said I should have a break and it was … Well, it was just lying there on the table. And you'd told me how important it was in the Passage of Kings.'

Roh realised that she was gripping fistfuls of carpet, her whole body tense.

'I couldn't read it,' Odi told her, his tone apologetic. 'But …'

'But?'

'It showed me something. It was so strange, Roh. There I was, frantically turning its pages, trying to understand why you're so obsessed —'

'I'm not obsessed.'

Odi rolled his eyes. 'Even though I couldn't read it, I still looked. I don't know what I was expecting, but … It showed me Orson, Roh. She was standing all alone, in some dark, empty space.'

'What do you mean?' Roh said, turning to face him.

'That's it. I don't understand it, either.'

Roh didn't know what to make of these visions. The *Tome of Kyeos* had been trying to tell Odi something, but what, she had no idea. And what did Orson have to do with anything?

'Did you get caught?' she asked.

Odi shook his head. 'No. No one came back for a while after that. And besides, I think the queen assumed I couldn't read it or didn't know what it was, so … she was never suspicious of me in the first place.'

'Alright.'

'Alright?'

Roh ran her fingers along her circlet, preparing herself for the blow she had to deal him now. 'I think it's time I told you of the third trial.'

Odi started. 'You know what it is?'

'I do. You're not going to like it.'

'I expected as much.'

'No, you're *really* not going to like it.'

'Tell me,' Odi said simply.

'We have to retrieve the scale of a sea serpent.'

Thick silence filled the space between them, the tension growing with each passing moment. Roh could hear her own heart thumping in her chest until —

Until Odi tipped his head back against the wall and laughed. The sound burst from him, loud and rumbling.

And though there was absolutely nothing funny about the impending trial, Roh felt her own face split into a grin, a huff of laughter escaping her as well.

Disbelief, defeat, terror … Their laughter encompassed it all. When the pair finally stopped, Odi wiped his eyes and seriousness settled around them once more.

Odi got to his feet. 'We need to prepare.'

'*Prepare?*' The word was laced with incredulity. 'We can do nothing to prepare for this.' Roh had already made as much peace with that fact as she could, but Odi was still processing the news. He began to pace their quarters at a dizzying speed, looking around wildly, as though some bolt of inspiration would come to him through the gold lattice headboards.

'I'm sorry,' Roh heard herself say, her voice small.

Odi looked up from his panic. 'What?'

'I'm sorry that you got dragged into this. I asked to be a part of this tournament. You didn't,' she told him.

'True,' Odi said, stopping to push the loose hair back from his face.

Roh smiled grimly. 'I don't think there's anything we can do.' If they had more time, more knowledge of the creature, she might have tried to design a trap, but her parchment and charcoal lay discarded at her bedside, no use to her now.

Odi went to the rucksack crumpled in the corner of the room and rummaged through the outer pockets until he produced the flask he'd brought back from his father's shop. 'You know, I think you might be right, Roh.' He tossed her the flask. 'We'll have to leave it up to fate.'

Roh removed the cork and breathed in the toffee-sweet scent. 'I don't believe in fate.'

'No?'

She took a long swig. 'No.'

'What *do* you believe in?'

'Doing whatever it takes to get what you want.'

Odi took the flask from her and drank. 'When's the trial?' he asked, his voice hoarse.

'Tomorrow,' she told him.

CHAPTER TWENTY-ONE

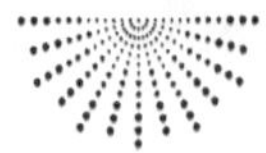

On the morning of the third and final trial, Roh and Odi broke their fast in the competitors' dining room. What had once been a bustling hub filled with cyrens and humans was now near empty, and a sombre atmosphere lingered heavily at its heart. The pair sat together on the end of a long table, pushing their food around on their plates, quietly watching the tension of the morning unfold.

Roh's stomach was in knots, twisting so intensely she thought she might be sick. Odi looked equally terrified, his face colourless and his fingers rapping against the table uncontrollably. Roh felt as unprepared as she had at the first trial, not knowing what was to come, or who, if anyone, would survive. Ames had always said the trials got more and more difficult, dangerous, deadly. Somehow she hadn't believed him. She wished she had now. Though, would it have changed anything? She had been so determined to be here. In her bones, she knew that no words from Ames would have stopped her. That thought calmed her. It had been her choice, all of it. At every twist and turn of this tournament, she'd made a decision that had brought her here. From the game of Thieves at the very beginning, to leaving Saddoriel with Odi and saving Tess. Every single moment had been a choice belonging to her and only her. She had to face that, but also acknowledge that it wasn't the same for everyone. She stilled Odi's tapping fingers on the tabletop beside her, covering his hand with hers, hoping that the warmth of her palm would offer some sense of comfort. Odi hadn't chosen this path for himself. He hadn't had the free will that she had, up to a certain point. But he too had started to make decisions for himself. He had chosen to build the piano. He had chosen to return to Saddoriel, when he'd had the chance not to.

These thoughts roiled wildly in Roh's mind as she watched the dining room, spotting Yrsa and Tess entering from the far corner. As though sensing Roh's attention, Yrsa's gaze slid to hers, before shifting to Odi at her side. Stony-faced, Yrsa gave a single nod of acknowledgement before nudging Tess in the direction of the serving trays.

'Well, that was new,' Odi said.

'Hmm,' was all Roh could manage. She didn't feel like talking. It was a form of self-preservation. She knew she would need all her energy, all her wits before the day was out, and so she continued to survey the others. Finn Haertel had just entered, his face a mask of livid rage. But for once, he didn't spit venomous, hateful words at her. In fact, he didn't so much as glance in her direction. A flurry of movement caught Roh's eye. Estin Ruhne was talking to Zokez Rasaat, her hands moving erratically before her, her eyes frantic.

Zokez was shaking his head, gesturing in a way that told Roh he wanted nothing to do with the renowned architect. Fascinated, Roh watched as Estin approached Yrsa next. She was too far away to hear their words, but Yrsa's frown and subtly wrinkled nose told Roh that Yrsa didn't like whatever Estin was saying.

Odi leaned in close. 'What's going on?' he whispered.

'By the looks of things, Estin's asking for something that no one wants to give.'

Indeed, Estin approached Finn next. Roh had to admire her for that, given Finn's furious expression and rigid stance.

'Please,' she heard Estin say. 'We have to be in this together.'

'Leave me be, Estin,' Finn brushed her off, his words harsh, unfaltering.

'But, Finn, what they've asked of us … It's madness. We'll all die.'

'So don't enter.'

'You truly believe you can achieve what has been —'

Finn drew himself up. 'I truly believe that you should leave me be, or —'

'Or what?' Estin snapped. 'You'll do something worse than feed me to a sea serpent? For Thera's sake, Haertel, open your gods-damned eyes.'

'No, Estin. You open *yours*. And do it somewhere else. I'm tired of looking at you.'

Roh saw Estin's body sag with defeat. Finn's razor words had found their mark at last. But what Roh did not expect was Estin's eyes to fall to her and Odi, and this time, her gaze was not filled with the disgust and loathing Roh had experienced at their mercy before. As Estin approached their table, she seemed almost … timid.

She cleared her throat. 'Rohesia …'

Roh kept her face neutral as she looked up at the architect she had admired so greatly once. 'What is it, Estin?'

'I know that we haven't always … seen eye to eye.'

Roh couldn't help the scoff that escaped her. 'That's an understatement.'

Estin didn't bite back. This Estin lowered her head in something akin to regret before she continued. 'What are you planning to do about this trial?'

'What do you mean?'

'Well, surely you don't mean to compete? A sea serpent? You'd have to be —'

'Mad?' Roh asked with her brows raised.

Colour bloomed on Estin's cheeks. 'I'm sorry,' she said. 'I'm sorry for my part in all that. But, we have bigger problems facing us now, don't you think?'

Part? The part you played? Roh wanted to say, anger heating beneath the surface. *You humiliated me in front of everyone who matters in Saddoriel …*

'Rohesia? Surely you're going to do the sensible thing and forfeit?' Estin added desperately.

Seeing the utter terror in Estin's lilac eyes, Roh bit back all the rage she had for the cyren.

With a glance at Odi, she faced Estin. 'I wasn't planning on forfeiting,' Roh told her. 'But if that's what you want to do, there's no dishonour in that.'

'But … but we should *all* forfeit. We should stage a protest together.'

'You know as well as I do, that will never happen.'

'Well, then,' Estin stammered. 'You and I can forfeit, together. I … I heard that you're something of an architect yourself. Perhaps … perhaps when this is all over, I could be your tutor.'

Roh stared at her, nausea subsiding. To be the disciple of Estin Ruhne … There once had been a time when Roh would have done anything to hold claim to such a title. To learn under such a renowned bone architect would hone her skills in unparalleled ways. Her music-theatre model flashed in her mind and she imagined how much it would improve at Estin's instruction.

But slowly, Roh shook her head. 'I'm sorry, Estin,' she said. 'I'm not ready to forfeit.'

Estin swore loudly, throwing her hands up in a rage. 'The madness lives on in you then, *isruhe*,' she spat at Roh.

Roh waited for the insult to pierce her; however, it didn't land as it previously would have. It bounced harmlessly from Roh, as the architect gave her one last filthy look and stalked away.

'I didn't think there was anyone I could respect less than you, bone cleaner,' said a smooth voice.

Roh spun to find Finn Haertel now at her side.

'Imagine my surprise when I discover that person is Estin Ruhne,' he said.

Roh opened her mouth to hiss a retort, but the dining-room doors opened, revealing Elder Colter.

'You are due at Saddoriel's entrance in one hour,' he told them. 'Gather what you need.'

When Roh turned back to Finn, he was gone.

Roh and Odi were solemn as they stared at the rucksack on the floor of their quarters.

'*Gather what you need,*' Roh remarked quietly. 'Like there is a prescriptive list of items for handling a sea serpent.'

Odi shrugged unhelpfully. 'It seems stupid to bring a pack like that.'

Roh agreed. 'It'll just slow us down.'

'Us? That sounds like you think I'm expected to breathe under water alongside you.'

Roh rubbed her temples, an ache blooming there. 'I don't know what's expected …' The thought of Odi attempting to swim and breathe beneath the seas with her was terrifying, but she pushed it aside. 'You're right about the rucksack, though.' She opened it up and took the coil of rope, shoved it into a much smaller satchel, and tucked a simple dagger into her boot.

'That's it?' Odi asked, brows raised.

'That's it.'

The music of Mason and Brooks Eery filled the passageways as Roh led Odi from the competitors' quarters into a network of tunnels. Roh's inner compass pointed the way, taking her down paths she'd never encountered before, as though it somehow knew she needed this extra time away from everything and everyone to gather her strength. Ignoring the queasy feeling in her gut, Roh led them towards the entrance of Saddoriel. She could already hear them, the hungry crowds lusting after her blood. Resentment clamped a cold fist around her heart as the towering archway of bones came into view, the sound of the crowd deafening now. Cyren and human peered outwards, taking in the formidable entry to the lair, and the masses that congregated there.

Odi glanced at her, like he wanted to say something, as though yet another of his questions was on the tip of his tongue. Instead, he pointed, and Roh's mouth went dry. Surrounding the base of Queen Delja's stone-column throne were five tall glass tanks.

'What in the realm?' Odi murmured.

Dread sank to the pit of Roh's stomach like a stone. She should have known there would be an unforetold element to this already horrific task. High up, the galleries were brimming with cyrens. As in the first trial, Roh could tell they were from all over the realms above. The different fashions, the snippets of conversation in various dialects … Roh couldn't see the queen, who was sitting up high in her throne, but her great, open wings cast long shadows across them all.

A fist of panic clenched hard around Roh's throat, and

suddenly the words she'd sworn she'd never utter aloud came bubbling out. 'I cheated,' she said.

Odi's amber gaze met hers and he waited.

'To get my place in the tournament,' Roh explained. The cord that had been wrapped so tight around her heart loosened ever so slightly as the confession peeled away from her. 'I rigged the deck. I used a sleight of hand in the card game we played. I lied to Harlyn and Orson. If I hadn't, it might have been one of them standing here with you. I'm … I'm a fraud.'

Applause burst from the crowd beyond the passage, but Odi didn't look away. 'Do you regret it?' he asked.

Roh chewed her lip. Did she? She regretted how it made her feel. She regretted that it had driven an invisible wedge between her and her family, one that they were not even aware of. But would she take it back? Would she relinquish her place in the tournament?

'I …'

Odi's long fingers gripped the curve of her shoulder. 'It doesn't matter how you got your place,' he told her. 'Not now. You got to this point by surviving each trial. We can never know who might have stood with me had you not cheated. But *you* are standing here and I'm glad it's you.'

The sound of a pebble skittering across the ground echoed off the walls.

'Someone's coming,' Roh whispered, wishing the moment hadn't been broken. She turned back to Odi. 'Thank you,' she said.

He frowned. 'For what?'

'Just … thank you.' She knew that confessing to Odi didn't absolve her of her crimes against her friends, against the whole Lower Sector, but it helped. It helped to tell someone who understood her, who delivered no judgement. Before facing a sea serpent, it helped to know that perhaps she wasn't a complete monster herself. Roh pushed her hair from her face and stepped out of the shadows, into the light.

The same messenger who'd brought Roh to the queen's quarters approached them and took them to where the rest of the competitors were waiting. They passed through the archway of bones, its ivory tones brilliant against the darkness of the cavern, loose fragments of bone rattling underfoot. Roh found herself trying to catch Yrsa's eye, but the highborn was staring straight ahead. At something Roh hadn't yet noticed … Something had been curtained off beyond the glass tanks. Beside Yrsa, Finn Haertel sported the usual crossbow strapped across his back and seemed to be ignoring the numerous groups of female cyrens in the crowd who called out to him, waving canvas banners with his name scrawled across them. Next to him, Zokez bore no visible weapon. Roh's gaze went to Zokez's foot, which tapped the ground erratically. Behind him, his human was as pale as bone. Estin Ruhne's head was bowed into her hands, hiding her expression and whatever decision she had made for herself.

A single note of music filled the air and hummed upwards through the galleries. The insatiable crowd fell silent as Elder Colter stepped out into the open.

'Welcome once more to Saddoriel, cyrens of the realms. Welcome to the third and final trial of our great Queen's Tournament,' he said, his voice magically projecting to the top reaches of the galleries.

Roh wriggled her toes in her boots, suppressing the urge to run.

'Our competitors have been given a valiant task,' Elder Colter continued. 'One that honours an ancient tradition, one that will test their endurance, their perseverance, their strengths and their dedication to the crown. Our competitors have been asked to retrieve the scale of a sea serpent.'

Shocked gasps echoed throughout the galleries and the crowd broke out in excited murmurs. Roh's skin crawled. These were her people, this was her kind.

'The scale, if retrieved, will be used for the royal armour that has yet to be completed over the course of our history. At the commencement of this final trial, each competitor's human, whom they were tasked with keeping alive, will be placed in one of these glass tanks you see here.'

Ice shot down Roh's spine.

'For the duration of the trial, the tanks will fill with water, until each respective competitor returns.'

'Gods.' Odi glanced at Roh, his eyes filled with horror.

'Each human will be measured and placed on a block within the tank, so they are of equal height and the competitors get equal time to retrieve the scale.'

'Roh ...'

She could feel Odi trembling beside her. But Roh

could do nothing to soothe the panic in her friend, nor within herself.

'The first cyren to return with a sea-serpent scale, within the allotted timeframe, will be our victor and future ruler. Those who return after, or not at all, lose.' Elder Colter surveyed the competitors. 'Given the nature of this trial, every competitor has the opportunity to forfeit.'

Forfeit. The word reverberated in Roh's mind, more of an option now than it had been at Estin Ruhne's request. *I could get out of this unscathed. I could return to bone architecture having lived through a Queen's Tournament ...* The thoughts flitted from one to the next, Roh's head spinning.

From the corner of her eye, she saw Estin Ruhne step towards Elder Colter. 'I wish to forfeit,' the architect said shakily.

Elder Colter considered her and bowed his head. 'Very well, Estin Ruhne.' He gestured for her to leave the competitor area. She did so, without looking back, leaving her human to be taken away.

'Elder Colter?' Another voice laced with tremors sounded. 'I also wish to forfeit.'

It was Zokez Rasaat, his hands trembling at his sides.

The council elder nodded. 'Very well, Zokez. You may join Estin in the viewing gallery.'

Zokez shoved his human towards the messengers and avoided eye contact with the other competitors, even Finn, as he hurried out of the staging area.

What is happening? Roh watched Zokez until he was

out of sight. Somehow, she hadn't been expecting the highborns to forfeit. *Surely, they all have something up their sleeves for this trial? Some insider knowledge?* But their tightly drawn faces and silence said otherwise.

'Roh?' Odi's voice whispered in her ear. 'What are you going to do?'

Roh was searching for familiar faces in the crowd, and unlike during the first trial, she found them – Harlyn and Orson, sitting with Ames and Jesmond in the second tier of the stone galleries. *How did they manage to get those seats?* These mundane observations seemed to occur at the oddest times and Roh forgot herself for a moment. Orson was waving at her, Harlyn standing stoically beside her, her cool expression still full of pride. They were here. *If anyone can do it, Roh ... it's you.* Her heart hammered as she came to her final decision. But it wasn't just her. She and Odi were in this together.

'Finn Haertel, Yrsa Ward and Rohesia of the Bone Cleaners, do you enter into this trial freely?' Elder Colter's voice sounded.

Odi elbowed her. 'Roh, what's happening? What are we doing?'

Roh eyed the glass tanks. 'It's your choice, Odi. I will not force you into one of those.'

Finn and Yrsa gave a nod, and their humans were hurried away by messengers, led towards the great glass tanks for measurement.

'The alternative?' Odi whispered.

'If the queen doesn't keep you as her musical slave,

you'll be relieved of your protective token and released into the passages of the lair,' Roh told him.

'If I'm released, would I stand a chance of surviving?' His words were hushed, desperate, and Roh wondered if, like her, he was picturing Tess being swallowed by thick quicksand.

'No,' Roh said.

'So, my choices are between two forms of certain death?'

'Essentially.'

'Rohesia of the Bone Cleaners, what say you?' Elder Colter called.

Roh waited. The eyes of the crowd, of Odi standing beside her, and the burning gazes of the Council of Seven Elders and Toril Ainsley bored into her.

From the corner of her eye, she saw Odi give her a subtle nod. Slowly, Roh dipped her own head, swallowing the hard lump in her throat. 'We will compete.'

A roar erupted from the crowd, though in her numb state, Roh couldn't tell if it was in support or outrage. Perhaps one extra body in the water simply made things more interesting.

Messengers appeared at Odi's side and Roh gave his hand a firm squeeze before they led him away. She hoped he knew, knew how hard she was going to fight for them, to shake the certainty from at least one of the paths of certain death.

Before Roh and the other competitors, Elder Colter removed the fabric covering the passageway. It was a veil of shimmering water, a portal to the sea. Like those she'd seen before, contained by an invisible force. Water-warlock magic. Without realising it, she'd been walking towards it, following the others.

Without warning, Elder Colter was directly in front of her, holding something out to her. He pressed it into her palm. Odi's protective shell token. 'Your humans will be safe from the lure of the lair in the tanks.' He directed his speech to all three of them. 'While you search for the serpent, you will wear this. As time passes, it will change from hot to ice cold. When you can no longer bear it against your skin, it means your human is submerged under water, and that you have run out of time.'

Roh's hands were trembling as she looped the leather string around her neck. Sure enough, the shell was hot against her breastbone. Roh's whole body trembled as she approached the veil, the shimmering entrance to the sea. She felt unmoored from herself, as though she wasn't contained to her physical form, and she was looking down on what was occurring, detached, separate ...

A single note sounded once more. Finn and Yrsa launched themselves through the veil and into the abyss beyond. The crowd exploded.

Hunting a gods-damned sea serpent ... Roh shook her head. Numb, she pushed her boots off at the heel, and, without giving herself a chance to second-guess, she threw herself into the sea.

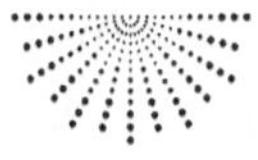

The sound of the crowd vanished and Roh was greeted by the muted, soothing tones of the sea. The current sang its own song, the water cool, not cold, humming against her skin. Her breathing changed immediately, her magic effortlessly pulling the air from the water around her and filling her lungs. The sea embraced her, becoming one with her, wrapping around not only her body and mind, but her soul, recognising her for what she was: a child of the current. She felt the connection slide into place, and once it did, with a single kick she shot through the water, and with a single flick of her wrist, the waters parted for her, the currents taking her where she bid. It was a thing of beauty, as vast and dark as she remembered it. She felt *alive*, untethered from the lair, becoming one with the water and the hypnotic lull of the sea —

The image of Odi trapped in the glass tank flashed

before her eyes and terror seized her. She couldn't succumb to the sea's song, couldn't fall prey to the power of the ancient deep, couldn't forget *why* she was here. Shaking herself from her daze, Roh spotted the trail of bubbles Finn and Yrsa had left in their wake and started after them. It looked like the highborns were working together, which was completely against the rules, but … how else could a handful of cyrens, even Jaktaren, take on a fully grown sea serpent? Roh kicked her legs, willing herself through the water, manipulating the currents, allowing her to swim faster. She swam hard, determined to follow the others. There was no doubt that they had obtained some knowledge about the creature; they had likely been hand-fed the information from their Elder Council relatives. Her best bet was to shadow them. It would be suicide for her and Odi if she simply darted off into the dark waters, hoping to randomly encounter the serpent and tackle it head on with nothing but a coil of rope and a dagger. She needed to be smarter than that, to use her cunning. Both she and Odi had risked so much to get here, and Odi's life was yet again hanging in the balance, so she couldn't afford to act brashly. Kicking her legs and parting the water with her will, she relished the feeling of power that rushed through her as she moved within the sea. For a moment, she wondered if Orson and Harlyn remembered what it was like to swim, to feel the currents skim across their skin and draw air from the water.

The expanse of sea was like a slumbering giant before Roh. As she swam, her panic became a constant but quieter, duller sensation in the pit of her stomach. Shoals of violet trout, silver carp and pink-spotted bass darted past, giving her a wide berth. She gazed in wonder as a bloom of jellyfish floated past, their underbellies glowing in a lavender hue.

Down here, sounds were subtler, but Roh could still hear the flurry of fins and tails skimming through the current, and the quiet sigh of the seaweed waving in the tides. She could taste the salt on her lips and feel the prickle of the ancient water on her skin. *What if I swam and swam, and didn't go back?* The seabed was alive with coral of all colours and textures, tall and spiky bushels of velvety fronds. Here, the sea had its own ballad, accented with creatures and beautiful plant life. *Why would anyone want to leave?*

The pulse and pull of the water had a powerful energy and rhythm that sang to the ancient part of Roh, the part that longed for the magic of music. While a cyren's call could lure humans to their deaths, that ancient magic was crafted from the very essence of the sea's song, a song that cyrens themselves found hard to resist. Roh allowed just a touch of sea water to fill her lungs. The burst of cold and salt brought her back to herself, and realising the trail was fading, she kicked violently, determined not to lose it.

It was hard to keep track of time down here. Roh had a feeling that it hadn't been too long since she'd left Saddoriel, but her senses were muddled. It felt as though she'd been in the sea her whole life. Her only tether back to the lair was the shell token resting against her breastbone, its temperature slowly changing from hot to warm, making Roh all too aware that although it may not feel like it, time was indeed ticking. Every minute that passed signified an increase in the danger Odi faced back in Saddoriel. She gritted her teeth. Odi would hold strong. He *had to*.

Something tickled at her nose. A scent, through the water and the salt. She'd recognise it anywhere – blood. It lingered in Yrsa and Finn's wake.

Is one of them hurt? Have they attacked each other? The possibilities spun before Roh in a blur as she pushed on through the water, closing the gap between them while trying to remain unseen. Around her, the waters changed. They became warmer and more light penetrated the deep blues. She realised they were drawing into a bay, where serpents usually made their kills, where, according to legend, they destroyed warships with a single swing of their powerful bodies. Shuddering, Roh continued to swim, at last spotting the others ahead. She squinted, not quite able to see if they were injured as they ducked into the darker currents. Quickening her pace, Roh followed them, finally close enough to see them disappear into the mouth of a cave.

What are they up to? She pushed through the tides, approaching the cave with trepidation. Peering inside, she could see a flicker of light from within —

How? What are they doing in here? She could wait no longer, for fear of losing them in the darkness. Roh's feet touched down on the gravelly floor of the cave and she palmed her dagger as she stepped inside. The light ahead illuminated the walls. She stepped forward, once, twice … Something wasn't right. Did the cave lead somewhere? Had the Jaktaren stored the serpent scales here for this very purpose? It wouldn't surprise her. Finn and Yrsa were working together, why not the whole guild? Wouldn't it be their dream to see a Jaktaren upon the throne? She moved further inside, soft currents still swirling around her. The cave felt small and constricted compared to the open waters outside, but Finn and Yrsa were somewhere in here … and they would lead her to the very sea-serpent scale she needed to win.

The light ahead went out.

A rush of water surged around Roh in the darkness, and for a second she froze, before looking to the mouth of the cave, where to her horror, a gate swung down, trapping her inside.

'*No!*' she screamed from her mind, the scales at her temples warming as she found her water voice, the one meant for her cyren deathsong. '*Please – you can't leave me here! Yrsa, Finn, don't!*' Roh yelled telepathically, as loud as she could through the water, rattling the gate with her hands, talons extended.

The Jaktaren paused on the other side.

'*Yrsa,*' Roh implored.

But the highborn shook her head. '*We are even,*' she said. '*I owe you nothing.*'

Roh blanched. '*You can't —*'

'*I told you we should have killed her. Or at least gagged her,*' Finn interjected coldly.

'*It might work in our favour,*' Yrsa said, her eyes scanning the bay.

'*What are you going to do?*' Roh rattled the gate again. '*Please!*'

The Jaktaren were already swimming away.

Roh cursed the highborns and then herself. How could she have been so stupid? What was she always telling Odi? *Never trust a cyren ...* She quelled the panic rising within her and examined the contraption she'd fallen for. She had to focus on getting out of here, and she knew design better than any highborn fool. As she ran her hands across the iron, she knew the trap had been forged in the Lower Sector by the metal workers. Its design had likely passed across Ames' desk, perhaps even her own workbench. She just needed to stay calm, to think ...

From where she was trapped, the scent of blood filled Roh's nostrils once more and she at last spotted its source from between the bars of her cage. Finn and Yrsa were corralling a wounded southern whale into the bay. Ribbons of blood stained the water like spilt ink, pouring from several crossbow bolts jutting from the beast's body. The smell of impending death was crisp in Roh's nostrils.

They're baiting it, she realised. Yrsa and Finn were baiting the sea serpent. Roh scanned the turquoise waters around her, her eyes drawn to the shadowed parts. Didn't they know that spilling blood like that would attract all manner of predators? She pictured a mighty reef dweller, wrapping its poison-laced tentacles around one of the highborns, leaving rings of thick, white scars like those on Toril's arms.

Squinting, Roh spotted two packs on the seabed, and ropes – no, some kind of net. *They're going to trap it? Are they mad?* Roh couldn't believe what she was seeing. But how —

A ripple shuddered through the sea. The temperature dropped abruptly and a rush of pressure swayed Roh. Gods, she needed to get out of this trap. She *would not* sit here while they took the scale and the crown from her.

A flash of pale gold tore through the currents and the turquoise waters went dark.

The sea serpent had come.

Roh watched in sheer terror as the gigantic beast carved through the water, racing towards the poor wounded whale. Its thick, muscular body covered in pale-gold scales hummed with unyielding power. Worst of all, its forked tongue flickered from its mouth with a hiss Roh could hear through the current as it approached the whale.

Ignoring the hammering in her chest, Roh forced herself to focus on the trap. It was a weight-loaded contraption – she had seen its like many times before. It was difficult to find its hinges in the dim light, but she followed the bars with her hands and explored by touch until she felt the juncture with her fingertips. As she suspected, a pin and barrel —

A vicious hiss vibrated through the waters as the sea serpent gnashed its fangs at its prey. Through the bars of her cage, another flutter of movement caught Roh's eye and she clapped a hand to her mouth. Finn and Yrsa split up from where they were hiding below, making a mad dash for the serpent, the net opening like a giant mouth between them. They were lightning fast, and as the serpent's jaws closed around the weakened whale, the net closed over the serpent.

An enraged shriek pierced the muted sounds of the undercurrent as the cyrens brought the net to a close with unnatural speed, as though they had been hunting serpents their whole lives. Roh stared, unable to tell who was more impressive, the highborns or the water beast. The legendary creature lashed and writhed in the restraints, bubbles and foam forming in the water around it. But Yrsa and Finn held strong.

The net's enchanted, Roh realised. *It has to be …*

Amidst the screeches and the vortex the captured creature was creating in the net with all its thrashing, Roh could hear the pair arguing.

'*It won't hold*,' Finn yelled telepathically.

'*It will*,' Yrsa countered, her voice straining. '*Long enough for us to grab a scale —*'

'*It* won't. *I can barely hold —*'

The serpent pummelled the water more wildly still, and for the first time, Roh seriously debated whether she was safer locked away in the trap. But no – she needed a scale. She would not remain a bone cleaner. She would not let Odi drown in that tank. Using her talons and dagger, she set to work on the pins of the hinges.

Finn nearly lost his grip on his end of the net; he fumbled, managing to only just maintain his grasp. The beast's barbed tail struck through the net, aimed right at Finn's exposed middle —

'*That's it,*' Finn coaxed, reaching for the crossbow strapped to his back.

Yrsa screamed, '*Finn, don't —*'

But in one swift motion, Finn had released his part of the net and loaded his crossbow. He shot. A bone-rattling roar filled the water and Roh looked up to see waves on the surface rise and crash into foaming masses. Her blood froze in her veins. *What has he done?*

A flash of gold blinded her, followed by a guttural shriek of terror. Roh regained her sight just in time to see the net shred apart and the barbed tail whip through the water with unnerving speed, lashing into Finn's unprotected body. His eyes went wide as the barb pierced his middle, detaching itself from the serpent's tail. A cry of pain died on Finn's lips and his limp hand released the crossbow, the weapon sinking, as if in half-speed, to the sea floor. Finn followed after it, unconscious or dead, his body hitting the sand in a heap.

The trap door came loose beneath Roh's expert talons, and before she could think, she was darting towards Finn. When she reached him, his lips were blue and his whole body was trembling. The barb of the serpent's tail was embedded in his stomach, his shirt stained red. It was only as Roh looped her arms under Finn's that she questioned whether or not she should help him. After all, he'd done everything he could to sabotage her from the moment the tournament began. Her grip loosened. He'd tried to disfigure her with flying coral, he'd tried to have

Odi taken away from her, and now this? Just moments ago, she'd been trapped in a prison of his making.

Before Roh could move, the roar rattled her bones again. With a crossbow bolt sticking out from between its golden scales, the serpent turned its vicious gaze to Yrsa, who was looking down at Finn and Roh, still clutching the net in shock.

Gods, Roh cursed, making a final decision and pulling Finn's limp body through the current towards the shelter of the cave.

She glanced back up, panic spiking. *'Yrsa! Watch out!'*

The serpent struck. Blade-like fangs gnashed and Yrsa screamed. Fresh blood seeped into the water as fangs sliced through her arm. Writhing in pain, Yrsa became tangled in the net, sinking to the seabed, leaving a trail of blood in her wake.

Roh shoved Finn into the cave and made a dive for Yrsa. Above, the sea serpent whipped its body through the water and lunged a second time for the Jaktaren. But Roh already had her. She half dragged Yrsa, still tangled in the net, through the currents, shaping the water to her will, and propelling them towards safety. They burst across the threshold, just as yellowed fangs gleamed at the mouth of the cave. Roh gasped for air, thanking the gods that the entrance was too small for the giant creature to penetrate. Leaning against the wall, Yrsa was panting, her face twisted with pain. Outside, the serpent screeched and thrashed, as though trying to shake the bolt free from its scales. Unsuccessful, it gave a final roar, snatched the dead whale in its jaws and glided through the currents, disappearing into the dark tides beyond.

Yrsa's eyes were scrunched shut as she clutched her arm. Untangling her from the net, Roh surveyed the injury. It wasn't life-threatening. She'd seen worse in the workshop.

'*You'll be alright,*' Roh told her.

Yrsa waved her away and pointed to Finn. '*Help him. The barb is poisonous.*' The voice that spoke into Roh's mind was weak and Roh hesitated, but Yrsa gave her a frail push. Roh went to Finn, not quite able to believe what she was doing. He was in much worse shape than before, alive but fading, his lips now near black and his arms stiff and cold. Roh pulled the barb from his flesh, hoping that the salt water around them would clean the wound, or would at least keep the poison at bay until help no doubt arrived for the highborns. She retrieved their packs and rummaged through them. Finding a cloak, she wrapped it around Finn without thinking, tucking it at his sides as though he were a young nestling. Her damn human had rubbed off on her, that's what had happened here …

Yrsa reached, not for her, but for the crossbow and Finn's bolts.

Roh palmed her dagger, ready to fight, but Yrsa simply loaded the weapon and handed it to her. '*You'll have one shot,*' she said into Roh's mind, then nodded to Finn. '*I'll get him back to Saddoriel. Go.*'

There was no time to ask why or how, and Roh didn't really care. All she cared about was the delicate cooling sensation of Odi's shell token around her neck. With a final glance at the two injured highborns, she left the cave. And, strapping the crossbow over her back, the *isruhe* of Saddoriel kicked her feet through the current and began hunting the sea serpent.

Roh followed the fresh scent of death from the whale carcass. It clung to the sea serpent's trail and left ribbons of blood in its wake. On she swam, careful not to get too close, careful not to let her own scent drift too far ahead. As she manipulated the currents around her, willing them to pull her through the waters faster, she couldn't help but revel in the power at her fingertips. The sea became deeper and darker as she pressed on, the waters swirling around her, dancing to their own rhythm, playing in their own orchestra. *Orchestra.* Odi had taught her that word. *An ensemble of instrumentalists.* It seemed to suit the sea as well. With Odi's lessons on her lips, Roh realised she was running out of time. The shell token against her skin wasn't even lukewarm anymore, and little by little, the coolness grew stronger. *How high is the water in Odi's tank now? Up to his hips? His waist?* Her thoughts began to spiral. Even if she did somehow manage to follow the creature and retrieve a scale, she still had to find her way *back* to Saddoriel, back to Odi. Would there be enough time? Roh forced herself to swallow the rising panic. It would do her no good here.

As she swam, powering her way through the dragging tides, the efforts of Finn and Yrsa were fresh and despairing in her mind. If she approached the beast in the same way, she would fare no better, likely worse. Now that the serpent was angered and suspicious, if it caught her, she would die. She had to do things differently, but how? She pictured the beast carving through the water, the much larger ancestor to the serpent pets back in the lair, leisurely wrapped around the arms of council elders, or coiled about Yrsa's ankles, or hissing at Roh in Queen Delja's private chambers, sizing her up with molten-gold eyes.

'The whole time, that damn viper of hers watched me ...' Odi's voice filled her head. *'It's disgusting, Roh, shedding its skin everywhere.'*

As the sea caressed Roh's skin, the seed of an idea formed.

Further and further out to sea she swam, trailing the scent of blood and death through the ever-changing tides. She clutched Odi's token to her chest. It had definitely grown cooler. How much longer did they have? If she turned back now, could she save him? But how? Once again, Roh allowed herself to taste salt to steel herself. *She* was their best chance. She had to push on, to achieve what she'd set out to do. To find the serpent. To not let Odi, or herself, down. Both their lives were in her hands.

The scent was getting stronger, the whale and serpent blood entwined with a path of tiny air pockets in the water. Around her, the temperature was suddenly colder. She slowed as she caught sight of the seabed, where the dead whale had been discarded. But there was no sign of the serpent ... Roh's bare feet touched the sandy floor and it shifted beneath her soles, sending sparkling granules of sand floating up before her face, getting caught in the current and drifting away. Cautiously, she put one foot in front of the other and passed the whale carcass, scanning her surroundings, heart in her throat. Spotting the line of tiny bubbles, Roh followed it to an opening in a massive rockface, where light glowed within.

A nest ... She couldn't stop the tremors that racked her body. She didn't know what she'd been expecting, but this ... There was no way she could enter a sea serpent's nest undetected. And any moment, it might come back for its meal. It was absolutely impossible. The creature also now knew the scent of her kind and no doubt associated it with danger and pain. Roh looked around frantically, her fear latching onto the ever-cooling token at her chest. Again, visions of Odi flashed before her – this time in her mind he struggled to keep his head above the water inching up his chin, but he was weighed down with stones tied to his ankles.

Roh's eyes fell to a particularly muddy part of the sand bank. No, it wasn't mud ... It was clay, a thick and heavy deposit of it amidst the sand. Dropping the crossbow from her shoulder, Roh knelt on the sea floor, and scooped up great handfuls of the substance. She covered herself from head to toe in it, smoothing it over her skin and running it through her hair. It masked any scent that clung to her, any foreign odour that the creature could detect in its nest. It was better than any shield. She had made herself invisible. Palming her dagger and leaving the crossbow behind, Roh entered the serpent's territory.

Something deeper inside illuminated the mouth of the cavern. At first, it looked like a simple cave, a burrow within the jagged seabed rocks. But as Roh moved further inside, she gasped. Reefs upon reefs of coral glowed against the boulders and stone in an array of colours. Bronze staghorn, its antler-like arms brushing against the branches of rose-pink tree coral, blue algae blooming between them. Tiny star-shaped leaves radiated a soft green hue, while sunburst florals pulsed orange. It was astounding, a botanical garden, flourishing at the seat of the sea's true ruler.

Roh continued to creep further inside the nest, her chest tight and breathing shallow. Trapped in a confined space at the mercy of a sea serpent was no place she wanted to be. If she was detected now, she was dead. She stepped carefully, tiptoeing around the various shoots of coral and algae. Until something glimmering snagged her attention. She paused, her gaze drawn to her feet, where flecks of pale gold were scattered sparsely across the ground as she approached the heart of the nest. *Scales.*

Mouth agape in disbelief, Roh crouched, tracing the face of one with her fingertips. It was smooth. Her magic still snatching the air from the water, she picked it up, turning it over in her hands.

It's heavy, was her first thought. Then, she marvelled at its colour. The purest of pale gold, similar to the gold of her circlet. Curious, that the same colour could mark both a feared, powerful creature and a *vermin of the deep.*

Roh stared at her prize. *I'm holding the scale of a sea serpent ...* Disbelief coursed through her. Never in her darkest, wildest dreams had she imagined herself here. Everything she had done to get here flashed before her eyes, from planting her deck of cards in the game of Thieves and setting bone-splinter traps, to travelling to the edge of Talon's Reach and now this ... She gaped in wonder at the scale glimmering between her talons a moment longer, before she at last slipped it into her satchel. It was as though a weight had been lifted from her shoulders, but she did not allow premature relief to rush through her just yet. She turned on her heels, looking to the exit. Now she had to get away from here as fast as possible. She had to channel the seas with everything she had to return to Saddoriel, to claim the crown, to save her human.

But as Roh made to leave, the contents of a small side passage caught her eye. She stopped short, nearly losing her balance. *It can't be ...*

Roh blinked, her thoughts slowly bringing the pieces together, picturing the barb protruding from Finn's abdomen that marked the serpent they'd seen as a male ... But what she saw now ... This was not the nest of a male sea serpent ...

For beyond the threshold, was an alcove and inside it ... was something else entirely.

With the loaded crossbow strapped to her once more, Roh swam from the nest with lightning speed, not even glancing over her shoulder as she powered through the water, racing towards Saddoriel. The shell token pressing against her sternum was far cooler than before and she couldn't help the surge of panic that rushed through her. She could not have come this far, only to fail now. She kicked through the currents with all her might, willing the rhythm of the sea to help her back to the cyren lair. She imagined hearing notes of music, calling out to her like a torch in the night as she manipulated the dark waters and the ever-lapping tides. She was running out of time. Odi was running out of time —

An ear-piercing screech curdled Roh's insides and forced her to falter. Her hands shot to her ears to block out the agonising sound as a powerful swell surged through the current around her. Thick dread filled Roh. She knew what she had done, what she had set in motion. Heart pounding, she dared to look back. The sea serpent was in pursuit, only —

It felt as though she'd left her insides behind as she raced through the water, the horrific realisation finally dawning on her. Giant shadows cast either side of her across the sea floor, darkening the turquoise hues once more to almost complete black, blocking out any glimmer of drifting sand.

Wings.

It was not a sea serpent, but its female counterpart. Stronger, more powerful and even deadlier, with its legs tucked under and its great wings outstretched.

A *sea drake*. The true queen of the sea.

A soft cry of terror escaped Roh then, salt water finding its way into her lungs in her panic, blood pounding in her ears as she swam and swam, darting left and right and up and down. But these small manoeuvres meant nothing to the giant creature who covered great distances with a single beat of its wings. Roh churned the waters behind her, attempting to distract and slow the formidable beast.

It knows what I've taken ... What have I done? The question was a hot brand on her mind as she shot through the water. She had been in the drake's nest, had seen what it prized above all else. It knew her now. The clay had peeled away from her and she was like a beacon in the darkness, calling out to the creature with her terror-drenched scent. The dagger in her boot would do nothing to penetrate those fierce golden scales, nor would a single bolt from the crossbow strapped to her back. *This* was how she would die. The sea that had bent to her will before was barely manageable in the presence of such an ancient, powerful creature, but still Roh tried. She flicked her wrist behind her, a whirlpool of water and sand whipping into action, blocking her from sight, but the drake shot straight through it with a roar.

Faster, Roh urged herself, *faster*. She dropped the coil of rope she'd kept strapped around her chest, not stopping to watch it float to the seafloor or be gnashed between the drake's fangs. Roh kicked, gripped by a terror unlike anything she'd known before. She cut through the sea like a hot blade, using anything and everything she could to slow the beast: masses of tangled seaweed, a volley of coral shards from the seabed ... Between the roars of the drake charging after her, she heard the first faint notes of music. She dived down, weaving through the narrow gaps between coral and kelp, but the drake simply crashed through them, tearing the beauty of the seabed apart in its raging pursuit.

Roh gasped for air. She knew she was almost there, if she could just shake the beast from her trail —

A searing sensation pulsed at her breastbone. Roh would have cried out in despair were it not for every ounce of her energy being used to evade the fangs of the crazed creature behind her. A flurry of movement below caught her eye and Toril Ainsley's voice filled her mind:

'It had camouflaged itself against the coral ...'

Roh's limbs were burning with the effort, her breathing ragged, and more and more salt water was finding its way into her lungs. She was overexerting herself, and her magic wasn't working at full capacity.

The drake's noise had already disturbed what lay amidst the seabed. It just needed a little more encouragement ... As she manipulated a path of water before her, she wrenched the crossbow from her back and pointed it at the moving coral below.

She released the bolt.

A low, guttural roar sent a wave barrelling upwards and Roh saw a flash of garnet tentacles shoot up through the current. The sea drake screeched as the reef dweller launched itself into its path. For a second, Roh faltered, watching legendary beast against legendary beast —

But the icy exterior of the shell token was nearly unbearable on her skin, and another screech sounded behind her as the shimmering light of Saddoriel came into view.

Just a little further ...

With a strangled sob, Roh burst through the veil and into Saddoriel, skidding across the bone fragments on the ground, gulping for air. A flash of gold and garnet passed outside the shimmering shield, and then it was gone. Coughing uncontrollably, Roh scrambled to her feet, looking around wildly for Odi – *there!* Inside the glass tank, the water skimming his mouth, he stood on the very tips of his toes, his head tilted back and his eyes wide, full of panic. Roh staggered towards him, wrenching an unattended stool from its feet and slamming it into the face of the tank. The glass cracked, veins splitting across its polished surface. With a cry of rage, Roh lifted the stool and hit the tank again, and again. Finally, glass shattered into thousands of pieces and the water poured from the tank in one giant wave, spilling across the ground, sending fragments of glass sailing past Roh. Odi collapsed into her.

The world around them slowed at last. Nearby, Finn was being tended to by a handful of healers, while Yrsa's partner was fussing, heaping blankets on her. The Elder Council was huddled together at the base of the stone-column throne, whispering amongst themselves. Roh scanned the second tier in the audience for Orson, Harlyn and Ames, but they weren't where they'd been before. There was no sign of Tess, Yrsa's human, or Finn's – their tanks were whole but empty. *What happened to them?*

Odi panted in Roh's arms. 'Did you ...?'

Roh met his gaze and gave a single nod, just as the

crowd fell silent. She saw why. Queen Delja had flown down from her throne. Her slippered feet hit the ground silently, just in front of Roh and Odi, avoiding the water and shards of glass. Unreadable lilac eyes met Roh's moss-green stare. Willing herself not to tremble, Roh carefully retrieved the serpent scale from her bulging satchel. She bowed deeply, her legs shaking uncontrollably as she held the scale out to the queen.

Queen Delja took it. Her eyes narrowed as she examined it, turning it over in her hands just as Roh had done in the serpent's nest. The pale gold glinted in the torchlight. A muscle flickered in the queen's jaw, just for a moment.

A sudden invisible pressure pushed against Roh's forehead and she staggered back. A sharp *crack* pierced the silence, followed by the sound of metal clattering to the ground. Roh blinked, staring at her bare feet, where in a puddle of water and glass fragments, her gold circlet lay broken in two.

CHAPTER TWENTY-THREE

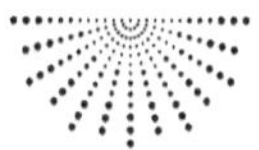

A queen ... *The queen of all cyrens ...* Roh didn't say the words aloud; she let them sink into her chest, into her very being. *Queen. Queen. Queen.* No one could take that from her now. There would be no more workshop, no more picking flesh from bones down in the dark depths of the lair ... Perhaps no more bones at all. Saddoriel and all the cyren territories – Lochloria, Csilla and Akoris – were hers. She stilled her fidgeting hands and took a moment, narrowing her focus. Was she imagining it, or was that a whisper of song stirring beneath her skin?

The violent roar of the crowd was still ringing in her ears as Roh found herself back in her chambers, preparing for the official presentation.

'I won,' she murmured to herself in shock. Against all the odds, she had beaten and outsmarted eleven others, including those who'd had inside advantages from the start. She'd bested a *sea drake*, for gods' sake … A sense of victory swelled in her chest, but she dared not believe it. Not yet.

While Odi was in the washroom, Roh fumbled with her satchel, still wet from the sea, and pushed it under the bed carefully, shuddering at the memory of the sea drake careening after her. Amidst the coral and scales of the nest, she had made an impulsive decision … and now what she'd stolen was burning a hole in that bag. No one aside from the sea drake and Roh knew its contents, and that was how it had to stay.

When it was her turn to use the bathing chamber, Roh's fingers wouldn't work as she tried to unbuckle her belt. She needed to get out of her damp clothes and wash off the patches of clay before she could change into something … more befitting of a sovereign. But what? She tried to recall what sort of attire Delja wore, without success; her mind was blank. She almost laughed. After all she had faced, attire was now her gravest concern? As she entered the main chambers, staring at the wardrobe, trying to find inspiration, the sound of teeth chattering made her turn. Odi, wrapped in the quilt from his bed, was shivering at his place by the window.

'Still not warm?' she asked, frowning.

'N-n-no,' he replied.

'Here.' She took the quilt from her own bed and piled it on top of him as well.

'Th-th-thanks.'

'I think you're in shock,' she told him.

Odi raised his brows, his long fingers toying with the

protective shell token she had returned to him. 'Aren't you?'

I am going to be queen ... The words filled her mind, prickling her skin with a rush of goosebumps. 'Yes,' she told him. 'I'm definitely in shock.'

Turning back to the wardrobe, Roh caught a glimpse of herself in the mirror and froze. She had been wearing her circlet since she was born. Now, without it ...

'You look like a different person,' Odi said weakly.

Roh traced her naked forehead with her fingers, following the faint line the circlet had left. 'I suppose I am different.' The prison flashed before her with its black passageways and dead water warlocks. And Cerys ... Had the news filtered down to Roh's mother yet? Roh inhaled sharply, realising that the *Tome of Kyeos* was now hers. The truth about Cerys was at last within reach.

She selected a pair of flowing pants and a loose shirt from the hanging space, and a simple but lush wide-sleeved robe to be belted over the top. She returned to the washroom to change, forcing her trembling fingers to work the laces and buckles. Thankfully, her boots were still dry and she tugged them onto her feet, the flowing fabric of the pants covering them completely. She wasn't quite ready to wear the traditional slippered shoes or sandals yet.

A sharp knock sounded and she poked her head out to the main rooms. The door swung inwards, revealing Orson and Harlyn, their mouths agape. Roh ran to them, dragging them inside by their arms and throwing herself at them, bringing them into a hard embrace. She breathed in their familiar scents, their bodies warm and solid against hers.

'*This* is where you've been staying?' Harlyn managed, stepping back and spinning around to take in every detail of the luxurious chambers.

As victor, Roh had been informed she was to invite family and friends to the official coronation. And here they were. She beamed at them.

'Congratulations,' Orson cried, tears streaking her face already. She reached out and traced the faint line of pale skin where Roh's circlet had been.

Harlyn squeezed Roh again. 'Yes, congratulations.' Gone was any trace of jealousy or fear. This was what they had all worked so hard for. This was what they had dreamed of since they were but small nestlings.

Roh reached out and cupped Orson's wet face. 'Don't cry,' she said. 'We did it. We actually did it.'

Orson laughed, sniffing loudly. 'We did … These are tears of joy.'

Harlyn slung her arms back around both Orson and Roh. 'Of course they're tears of joy. Now, more importantly. When are you going to tell us how *in the names of Dresmis and Thera* you retrieved that scale?'

Unable to contain the aching grin stretching across her face, Roh eyed the hour. 'That's a tale for another time, Har. We have to be at the Great Hall in just —'

Orson clapped her hands gleefully. 'What does one wear to a coronation?'

Roh flung open the wardrobe doors and gestured to

the highborn clothes draped within. 'Choose what you like, but be quick. I can't be late for my own —'

Harlyn burst out laughing, the sound from deep within her belly. 'You're going to be queen. You can do whatever you like!'

Grinning, Roh watched her friends rifle through the contents of the wardrobe, paying the shivering Odi in the corner no heed. Roh eyed him worriedly. There hadn't been time to speak of it yet, but Roh's promise hung between them. *'When I'm crowned queen,'* she had said, *'I will grant you your freedom.'* She knew Odi was waiting for her to broach the subject; her stomach squirmed uncomfortably as she considered what it would mean. Freeing him … would mean losing him. Sensing her attention, Odi's amber eyes lifted to hers. Roh had every intention of keeping her word.

'What shall we call you?' Harlyn was asking, tugging a gown over her head. 'Rohesia the Serpent Slayer? Rohesia the Untouchable? Rohesia the Risen?'

Odi quickly averted his gaze as the others changed, some colour at last returning to his cheeks.

Roh snorted. 'I don't know.' Still, her chest was swelling with pride. She was going to have a full title. No longer would she simply be Roh the bone cleaner. If Delja was *Delja the Triumphant*, what name would Roh be given? She would find out soon enough.

When her friends turned to her, a wave of goosebumps rushed across her arms. They looked different, too. Like highborns. Roh had never seen them wear anything other than lowborn workshop attire.

'You both look …'

'We know,' Harlyn quipped with a wink.

Roh led Harlyn, Orson and Odi through the residences and the foyer, towards the Great Hall. The paths were so familiar to her now that she didn't have to think about it. She watched her friends' expressions of awe and smiled to herself. They too would grow used to the Upper Sector. She was sure of it.

The Great Hall's galleries were packed. Roh had never seen a crowd of this size, not even for the trials. The stone balconies seemed to swell with bodies and the noise from the crowd rattled the very bridges they stood upon.

The Haertel elders approached Roh, heads bowed. 'Rohesia, this way.' They ushered her away from her friends, but seeing the panic in Odi's eyes, she gripped his arm. 'He comes with me,' she said, taking no chances.

They led her to the centre of the hall, where she was completely visible. All eyes were on her, gawking as though she were a savage beast trapped inside a cage. But she was caged no longer. She was free. Roh lifted her chin, letting them stare at the faint line of skin where her circlet had been. She was no longer a bone cleaner … She was about to be their queen. Beside her, she felt Odi shivering as a cold rush of wind surged through the hall.

Queen Delja, wings flared, landed deftly before them. *Is she just 'Delja' now?* Roh wondered abstractly. Delja was no longer wearing her crown and she looked strange, in the same way Roh did without her circlet.

'Welcome, cyrens from near and far,' Delja called, her

silken voice projecting to the far reaches of the galleries. 'Welcome to this monumental occasion.'

Roh fought the urge to rub her arms. Her skin was prickling, unable to shake the nagging sensation that something wasn't as it should be. She told herself she was being paranoid, urging herself to leave her tendency for spiralling thoughts behind her as she came into her throne.

'It has been five decades since our last tournament, and this one, like the ones before it, was a demonstration of our kind's courage, tenacity and cunning. The challenges faced by our competitors were designed to push their limits, to test their endurance and the very fibre of their being. They did just that. The efforts of all were nothing short of valiant.'

Odi was fidgeting and Roh realised that he couldn't understand the Saddorien language Delja was speaking. Roh leaned in to translate for him, but Delja's gaze suddenly turned to her.

'However,' she said. 'If there is to be a champion, there can only be one. Which is why we are gathered here now.'

Roh was as still as death.

'Rohesia of the Bone Cleaners has won the third trial of the Queen's Tournament. Come forward, Rohesia.'

Elder Mercer appeared next to the queen, presenting a cushion covered with a piece of silk.

Delja removed the silk with one smooth sweep, revealing a crown sitting atop the velvet.

'A new crown, for a new queen,' Delja said quietly.

It was certainly a new crown, striking, majestic even,

with delicate detailing carved into its ivory peaks. Roh gazed at it in wonder, finding her fingers aching to reach out and touch it. And why shouldn't she? It was *hers*. She had *earned* it. But as she stared at its beautiful craftsmanship, she realised that it was not at all like Delja's former coral crown. This one was a crown of bones.

The crowds realised it, too. Murmurs burst across the galleries, and whispers washed over the Great Hall in a tidal wave. All the while Roh stood before Delja, gaping at the former queen as she lifted the crown from the velvet cushion.

You're about to be made queen, Roh told herself. There would be a time to address the insult and her unending questions later. But as she bowed her head for the moment of her coronation, the bareness of the crown struck her. The birthstones of Saddoriel were missing. The crown was placed on her head, the weight of it settling atop her hair. Roh stood up straight, meeting Delja's eyes.

The former queen's gaze was triumphant. 'The Council of Seven Elders has made an additional decision,' Delja continued. 'Due to Rohesia's questionable heritage, a further task has been added to prove her dedication to Talon's Reach and the cyren race.'

What? Roh nearly choked. The queen's words were poison-coated thorns emerging from the garden of Roh's dreams.

'Rohesia can choose to forfeit her victory and return

to her work with the bone cleaners, or … she can prove herself worthy of our kind and our clans once and for all.'

Bile hit the back of Roh's throat, her knees buckling beneath her. Her eyes watered as she fought to keep herself upright. *This is … No one else would have had to do this.*

Odi sensed her panic, his eyes imploring her to explain.

Delja wasn't done. 'The birthstones of Saddoriel have been placed in the care of the cyren territories of Akoris, Csilla and Lochloria. Should you choose to accept this final task, you must find and win the stones. Once you have returned all three birthstones to their place in the crown, Talon's Reach will accept you as its rightful queen. Saddoriel and the *Tome of Kyeos* will be yours.'

Roh felt faint. She swayed against Odi.

'You have one hour to decide.'

In a chamber tucked away from the Great Hall, the soft, mournful notes of the Eery Brothers' fiddles sounded. Gentle chords rose and fell around Roh, Orson, Harlyn, Odi and Ames as they sat at a round table in the centre of the room. Roh's hands were shaking as she removed the crown of bones from her head and placed it before her, the gaps where the missing birthstones were meant to sit staring back at her.

How could I have been so naive? How could I have thought that the rules would be the same for an isruhe?

Everyone at the table was looking at her, waiting for

her reaction, waiting for her plan, but … An ache in her chest silenced her. She didn't know what to do.

Harlyn exploded on her behalf. 'This *has* to be against the rules,' her friend spat, slamming her palm on the table.

Roh said nothing, continuing to stare at her crown, studying the network of small bone fragments that had been carved and shaped to form elegant peaks.

'It's not against the rules.' Ames' voice was soft, followed by the rustling of parchment. Roh looked up to see him producing a thick bundle of papers from his robes. He placed them before her on the table, pointing to twelve signatures scrawled in a single column. Roh spotted her own messy hand. It was the contract she had signed.

Ames turned through the pages, to the very last one, and pointed to the final clause.

'*Clause fifty-two*,' Roh read aloud, her voice quavering. '*If the victor is of questionable birth or morals, an additional task may be deemed necessary by the Council of Seven Elders.*'

'This is *utter shit*,' Harlyn hissed. 'And they've given her *three* additional tasks, not one. What in the name of the gods did Roh ever do to Saddoriel?'

'She was born the daughter of our kind's most infamous murderer,' Ames said quietly.

All Roh wanted to do was hide. After everything she'd done, after everything she'd been through to get here, her dreams had been at her fingertips, only to be snatched away. She couldn't bear it.

Orson sat down beside her and gripped her arm gently. 'Did you know about this clause, Roh?'

Numbly, Roh shook her head. 'We … we didn't have the opportunity to read it. Or at least, I didn't think we did. No one else read it.'

'I'm guessing they were given copies to peruse at their leisure prior to signing,' Harlyn said bitterly. 'This is so —'

'Unfair?' Roh gave a dark laugh. 'We should have known.' She massaged her temples, shocked to find that her fingers didn't brush her circlet, before she remembered that it wasn't there anymore.

Would she be forced back into one, if she didn't become queen now? She traced her naked forehead once more. Could she go back to that?

'What can I do?' Her voice was small. Just how she felt.

'You can forfeit,' Orson said. 'You've risked your life enough, Roh. Forfeit and live.'

'*Or*,' Harlyn interjected, her eyes fierce. 'You can *fight*. Do the tasks, find the gems, become queen and *punish them all*, Roh.'

The room fell silent as Harlyn's brutal words lingered between them. Roh felt a flicker of gratitude for her friend, as she herself certainly couldn't muster up the strength to rage the way she knew she should. All the energy she had felt in her chambers with Orson and Harlyn while they dressed had evaporated, replaced by utter exhaustion. Her limbs felt heavy from the effort of racing through the currents, but more than that, her heart felt raw and swollen, as though there was no way she'd be able to repair it or return it to its previous state where it fit snugly inside her chest.

Ames pushed a card towards Roh. 'These are the official rules of the next stage of the tournament, should you choose to continue.'

Roh stared at the list before her. They had been prepared for this from the very beginning. She cleared her throat, forcing herself to sit up.

'*The competitor will have seven moons to obtain the three birthstones of Saddoriel. The competitor may choose up to four travelling companions to assist their quest. The competitor may be challenged thrice throughout their journey. Once for cunning, once for strength and once for magic, the very virtues cyrenkind reveres ...*' Roh trailed off and scanned the tight-lipped faces around her. She knew nothing of the other cyren territories. Nothing of travel, save for the brief venture to the edge of Talon's Reach with Odi. She ran her fingers over the crown of bones, tracing the settings where the jewels would sit. *Seven moons ...* Seven more moons fighting for something she had already rightfully won. Her warring thoughts must have been etched across her face.

Harlyn placed a firm hand on her forearm. 'You wouldn't be alone this time,' she pointed out. 'You can take companions with you. To help.'

'But she can be challenged at any time, Har,' Orson argued. 'And in foreign territories. It sounds like a deathtrap.'

'We said the same of the trials just past, did we not?' Ames offered, straightening his collar.

Together, they debated the options, as though picking apart each aspect of the trial would somehow lead them to a solid conclusion. The conversation seemed to go around and around in circles, and Roh felt more trapped here than she had her whole life in the Lower Sector. She sighed heavily. 'I have survived three trials. Surely, I'm due to run out of luck any day now?'

'Who says it's got anything to do with luck?' Harlyn quipped.

'Doesn't it?'

'Only you know that for sure.'

Roh glanced at Odi, who had remained quiet throughout their debates. She nudged him with her elbow. 'You're not going to say anything?' she asked. 'You're usually all about the questions.'

Odi gave her a blank stare. 'You're not officially queen.'

'Is that a question?'

Odi just continued to stare.

'No,' Roh said sharply. 'I'm not officially queen.'

'So, you can't grant me my freedom.'

Guilt, hot and harsh, hit Roh in the chest. 'No … I don't think so,' she said, quietly this time. 'I'm sorry.'

Odi shrugged defeatedly. 'Then I have nothing to ask you.'

'Ignore him,' Harlyn snapped, dismissing Odi with a wave. 'There is hope here, Roh. Look how far you've already come.'

Roh glanced between Harlyn, Orson and Ames, unable to look Odi in the eye. She was increasingly aware of the minutes ticking away, just as she had been out in the currents of the sea. With each passing moment, the pressure and panic rose within her, as the water had in Odi's tank. She felt as though she were about to be submerged, without the ability to breathe under water.

She massaged her aching temples again and looked to her friends in despair. 'I just wish I knew what was right …'

She didn't hear the click of the door opening. 'Perhaps a game of Thieves would help you decide.' Neith stood in the doorway, her eyes bright.

'What?' Harlyn said, the crease in her brow deepening.

Roh's stomach dropped to her feet and she was wrenched back to the moment when she had placed her final cards upon the bench.

'Well, Roh had some luck with that last time, didn't she?' Neith leaned against the doorframe, her arms folded over her chest. Long gone was the timid water runner. Here stood a cunning, vengeful cyren, who had waited until the very last moment to play her own final hand.

Roh's face heated. 'Neith …'

'What's she talking about?' Orson asked quietly.

'Neith.' Ames' voice was low in warning. 'Take your petty squabbles elsewhere.'

But Ames was not Neith's mentor. She did not answer the master of the bone cleaners.

'You don't know?' she continued, looking at Harlyn and Orson and resting a taloned hand against her breast in mock surprise. 'Here I was thinking she shared *everything* with you two.'

Roh felt it, the moment the web of lies she'd spun began to unravel. She knew she should say something, *do something* to shut Neith up, but any words she offered now would be inadequate. It was too late.

'Rohesia cheated,' Neith said, her cold, triumphant gaze meeting Roh's, her words a final knife to the heart. 'I heard the confession from the *isruhe* herself.'

A pebble skittering across the ground, echoing off the walls. Someone hadn't been coming, someone had *been there*, listening to her spill her guilty guts to Odi in the passageway before the final trial. *Neith.*

'Roh?' Orson's eyes were lined with silver. 'Tell us it's not true?'

A palpable silence weighed over the room as Roh looked at her hands, unable to swallow the hard lump in her throat. She could feel their eyes on her, and Odi's and Ames', too. The beast of panic raging within clawed at her throat. She opened and closed her mouth, trying to find the words, an explanation, anything that would stop her from losing them.

A loud shredding noise filled the air and Roh flinched. Pieces of parchment fluttered around her, tickling her face, raining down upon her shoulders and her hands resting on the table.

'Of course it's true,' Harlyn snarled, pieces of the ripped contract still in her talons. 'Look at her face.'

'I —'

In a flash of movement, Roh found herself shoved up against the wall, pinned there as Harlyn clenched a fistful of her shirt. 'No,' Harlyn cut her off. 'I will not listen to another lie from you.' Her words were venomous blades, cutting long and deep. 'How could you? Has a lifetime of friendship and acceptance meant nothing to you?'

Harlyn's face was mere inches from her own. From the corner of her eye, Roh saw Neith give a satisfied smirk before she slipped away.

'Harlyn,' Ames' voice sounded. 'That's enough. Leave her.'

Harlyn's grip loosened. She gave Roh a rough shove against the wall as she tore her talons from Roh's shirt and crossed the room in two short strides. She turned back at the doorway only to look at Orson, waiting.

Hurt shone in her friend's glassy eyes. 'You … you cheated *us*.' Orson's hands withdrew from the table as she stood, shaking her head.

'Wait —' Roh croaked.

But they were gone.

With a ragged gasp, Roh collapsed over the table, burying her head in her arms, fighting the onslaught of panic, struggling to take in enough air.

'Roh …' Odi's voice sounded, his half-gloved hand gently gripping her arm. 'Roh, you have to calm down. It will be —'

'Your hour is up.' Ames' soft voice cut through Odi's attempts at reassurance. 'What are you going to do?'

CHAPTER TWENTY-FOUR

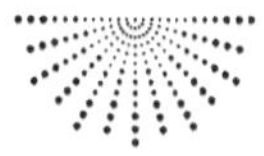

A pair of fierce, green-speckled lilac eyes stared out at Roh from behind bars of bone. Dark hair, chopped at odd lengths and angles, framed an intense expression, a gaze that flicked from the jagged scar on Roh's face to the crown of bones atop her head. Knowing she had succumbed to her weakness once more, Roh felt utterly depleted. It was against the wishes of Ames and Odi, the only two friends she had left, but she couldn't *not* see Cerys, not on the cusp of this pivotal decision and not in the wake of losing her friendship with Harlyn and Orson. At the thought of them, a dull ache pulsed right at the centre of her chest, a beat of pain that dragged inside her, trying to pull her to the floor. Now, more than anything, she wanted to cry. She wanted to feel that release cleave through her. But as always, the tears did not come. Roh sighed, the noise rasping and weary, sounding as heavy as she felt. She hadn't spoken to Cerys yet and she wasn't sure if she was going to. Every time she did, she felt like a fool, trying the same thing over and over again and expecting a different outcome. Roh had heard cyrens say that was the very definition of madness. She blinked at Cerys, whose head was tilted to one side, hands grasped around the bars of her cell.

Madness ... I certainly have some experience with that.

Cerys was watching her intently, an unhinged smile tugging at the corner of her mouth as her eyes lingered on the hollows in the crown of bones. Roh's fingers went to them automatically, tracing the vacant spaces, picturing the birthstones of Saddoriel as they had appeared in Delja's coral crown. Cerys followed the movement, still smiling crookedly.

Roh matched her mother's stare. 'Surprised?'

Cerys smiled wider, her cracked lips parting, revealing surprisingly white teeth. 'No.'

Roh froze. An icy hand had reached inside her and clutched her heart. Her heart pounded within its grip, threatening to burst as she gaped at Cerys.

'You ...' But the words wouldn't come. After all this waiting, after all this time, the words *wouldn't come*. The ice within had frozen her tongue, her mind, her ability to process what had just happened. It had sounded ... like her mother had answered her question, *completely lucid.*

'What did you ...?' Roh rasped, taking a step closer to the bars, reaching out with a shaking hand. She didn't break eye contact, terrified that if she did, reality would come crashing in around them.

'I am not surprised,' Cerys said clearly, releasing her

grip on the bones and taking a step back into the shadows of her cell, as though she couldn't bear to have Roh close to her. 'I am not surprised to see a crown upon your head. Nor am I surprised to see that it is not complete.'

'You …' Roh stammered again. 'You can talk …'

'She hid the stones. The keys to the tome.'

'How do you …?'

'He has already come.'

Roh threw herself against the bars, clutching the lengths of bone in her hands as Cerys had done so many times before. 'What? What do you know of the stones? Of the *Tome of Kyeos*?' she pleaded. '*Who* has already come?'

'Marlow,' Cerys said simply.

Roh's heart sank instantly. *Marlow*. Her supposed long-dead uncle.

'You'll find another like him,' Cerys prattled eagerly. 'Another like him amidst the gilded plains.'

'What do you mean, "like him"? What are the gilded plains?'

A bark of manic laughter burst from Cerys' lips as she leaped back, her body convulsing in an erratic dance as she dragged her ruined talons across the stone, creating an ear-piercing screech. 'It's begun. It's begun!' she sang.

Roh shook the bars of the cell desperately. 'Come back,' she yelled, her voice trembling as she rattled the bones in her grip. 'Answer me!' But the ember of sanity was gone, Roh realised. Her mother flung her arms open grandly at the carvings on her walls, something innately childlike about her in this state, a proud nestling showing off her drawings to her education master. The etchings were more of the same: the same design over and over, layered one on top of the other, so at first they seemed like senseless scribbles, but upon closer inspection showed hundreds of mask sketches peppering the stone. Roh squinted through the bars, so that her nose nearly pressed against bone.

All she felt was emptiness throbbing within. She released her grip on the bars and stepped back, feeling as though some part of her had been ripped away. She had to get back. Odi was waiting for her in their chambers. But as she turned away from Cerys, she found herself face to face with the dead water warlock at the centre. Roh's blood ran cold, a small detail catching her eye. She studied the man she had seen so many times before: the blue tinge of his preserved skin, the curl of his thin lips in a half-snarl suspended in time, the specks of blood on his worn cloak – the smear of red jogged Roh's memory and her eyes went to his hand. It was frozen in the same grip it had always been, but … What he usually held, the quartz dagger … It was gone.

'He has already come ...' Roh's skin prickled. An ancient cyren, risen to rob a water warlock's corpse? Did Cerys see the spirits of the dead now? Whatever she saw, there was no denying that the dagger was missing. If not a ghost, then who? Who had been here before her and taken it? And *why*? She whirled around to Cerys, but her mother was humming an off-key tune, swaying back and forth in some strange dance. Cerys had retreated back into her madness. Would she ever return? Would they ever converse like that again? Roh shook her head,

dusting off her dirty palms on her pants. She couldn't stay down in the prison forever to find out.

Roh stood at the opening of a dimly lit cavern, waiting for the former queen. Stark against the dripping walls was a thick, circular iron door, a large wheel at its centre, embellished with an array of intricate locks, gears and mechanisms, like the inside of a clock. The Vault. The very place Roh had wished to go during the now infamous tour. One of the most elusive parts of Talon's Reach, so elusive that many doubted its very existence. And yet here she was, the peaks of her crown of bones casting shadows across the door to the *Tome of Kyeos*. For a moment, she imagined the coloured reflections of the gems there, too ...

'You came,' said Delja's silken voice as she entered the antechamber alone, her gaze snagging on the crown of bones atop Roh's head. Her wings were nowhere to be seen, but even without her crown, the cyren looked regal. 'I assume that means you've made a decision?'

Roh's eyes went straight to the pale-gold breastplate Delja wore, honed from the very scale Roh had retrieved, had nearly died for, that *Odi* had nearly died for. At the sight of its pale sheen, Harlyn's voice rang in her ears: *'Become queen and punish them all ...'*

Roh met Delja's gaze. 'I mean to seek the gems,' she told her, voice steely. 'I mean to take what I have earned, what is mine.'

Roh could have sworn she saw a flicker of pride cross

Delja's face before the ancient cyren bowed her head. 'So be it, Rohesia.'

The weight of her decision spoken aloud settled around her, but somehow it was a comfort. It felt right, like armour sliding into place.

Delja cleared her throat. 'It is customary for the new queen to be introduced to the *Tome of Kyeos*.'

Roh raised her brows. 'New queen?'

'Well, perhaps that's not the correct title for you … yet.' She said the last word as though it were an apology, and Roh, for the life of her, couldn't understand the ancient cyren's place in all this, or what she wanted.

Delja grasped the wheel at the door's centre with a firm grip, turning it once, twice, thrice, before stepping back. The giant door groaned loudly beneath its own enormous weight and slowly began to spin, round and round. Its detailing blurred as it spiralled, making a whirring sound that continued to amplify to the point that Roh thought it might shoot off its invisible hinges. Just as she was about to look away to stop the dizziness, it snapped to a stop and swung outwards.

Roh's gaze went straight to it as they stepped inside, towards the beam of light in the heart of the chamber, illuminating the very thing she wanted most in the world. The thick tome hovered in the light, as though weightless. It held all the answers she'd ever wanted. All of them, about her mother, her father and who they had been. About what her mother had really done all those centuries ago … But without the birthstones of Saddoriel in her crown, she couldn't so much as touch the *Tome of Kyeos*.

'What do you know of the book and its volumes?' Delja asked.

Roh gazed longingly at the enchanted tome that seemed to bask in the light. 'It contains our histories,' she said cautiously.

'We both know that's an understatement.'

'It's all-knowing, all-seeing. It writes itself.'

'That's better.'

'How much does it record?'

'As much as necessary.'

'What about the card game?' Roh swallowed. 'How I cheated in Thieves?'

Delja nodded.

'That's a small detail for a book that contains such epic moments in our history,' Roh said slowly.

'Is it? Was it not that small detail that led you to stand where you do now?'

Roh didn't respond. Would this be how she was remembered? The *isruhe* queen whose reign began with a falsehood? What else had the book recorded? How much of it had Delja read? Did she know … Did she know what lay hidden in Roh's satchel under her bed? Delja could no longer access the tome's pages, but …

As though reading her thoughts, Delja faced her. 'Curiously, your movements stopped being recorded the moment you entered that sea serpent's territory.'

The moment she'd picked up the … Roh schooled her face into an expression of neutrality.

'You wouldn't know why that is, would you, Rohesia?'

'No idea,' she said blankly. But something in her chest soared. So it was true, what Orson had told them about the sea-serpent scales. No wonder Delja now wore hers over her chest. Protection. Magical protection. It was the most confirmation Roh was going to get. Delja suspected something, but couldn't know what Roh had taken.

Delja's smile was strange. 'We are not so very different, I think you'll find, Rohesia.'

I don't understand, Roh wanted to say. She didn't understand how the queen could flit between seeming to care about her and then being so cold, so unfair. Between talking of Cerys like she knew her and then taking Odi away.

'Who rules while I'm gone?' Roh asked.

'The Council of Seven Elders will preside over Saddoriel in the interim.'

Roh tasted blood as she bit the inside of her cheek. 'And your role?'

Delja tilted her head again. 'To offer guidance where requested.'

'That sounds a lot like ruling to me.'

'Rohesia,' Delja implored. 'I will do my best to help you, from the inside.'

Something squirmed in Roh's gut. 'Why?'

'Because six centuries is a long time to rule. Because …'

'Because?'

'Your mother … She was important to me once, more than I could say. Perhaps I couldn't help you when you were born, I couldn't change where the Law of the Lair forced you to go, but perhaps … Perhaps now I can change where you're going.'

Roh let Delja's words wash over her as she gazed at the mighty tome and its endless volumes. Delja, the most powerful ruler in cyren history, wanted to help her. Could she be trusted?

Roh made to leave.

'The human,' Delja said quietly. 'The Jaktaren want him, now the tournament is over.'

A chill rushed over Roh's clammy skin.

'They will go to great lengths to preserve the integrity of their guild, Rohesia. You know this. Mighty is the Law …'

'Sacred is the ledger.' Roh murmured the response. In the iron-framed doorway, she turned fully to face the former queen, rage simmering in her veins. 'According to them, he is property of the crown, and you no longer wear one. *I do*, whatever it's made of. And the tournament is not over,' she replied, her voice as strong as steel. 'They made damn sure of that. Odalis Arrowood stays with me.'

Whatever emotion flashed in Delja's eyes, Roh didn't recognise it. She left the former queen and the tome behind. She was out of patience and out of time.

With her decision made, in the privacy of her Upper Sector quarters, Roh packed her bag. Maps, her sketchbook, spare clothes and various items were spread out across the bed.

'I went to see Cerys,' she admitted to Odi and Ames.

'Rohesia.' Ames glowered from where he was perched at Odi's usual place by the window. 'What did I tell —'

'I know,' she snapped. Roh had debated confiding in them at all, but … She couldn't bear the thought of being entirely alone in this, of another secret coming between her and those she cared for. 'I couldn't help it,' she said more softly. 'Who knows if I'll ever return here, Ames. She's my mother. It was right to say goodbye.'

'And did you?'

'Well … not exactly.'

'What do you mean?' Ames ground out. Wisely, Odi was staying quiet.

'She told me something,' Roh said. 'Something that might help.'

From his bed, Odi sat up straight. Ames didn't move from the window bench.

'What did she say?' Odi asked.

'That I … would find someone. In a place called the gilded plains.'

'Someone? Who?' Ames barked, his arms folding across his chest.

Roh flinched. 'Someone who … who could help.'

'She said those exact words, did she?' Ames pressed heatedly. 'Your perfectly sane mother told you where you could find someone to assist you with winning the crown?'

'I've already won *the crown*,' Roh ground out. 'This … this is about the gems, the keys to the *Tome of Kyeos*.'

Ames shook his head in disbelief and long-suffering frustration. 'Pray tell, what *else* did she say?'

Roh shifted uncomfortably, fiddling with the straps of the pack, her mother's words filling her mind. She chewed her lip. To mention Cerys' hallucination of a dead brother would discredit the rest. Roh glanced across at Odi. 'That's about it.'

Odi threw his hands up in frustration. 'That's nothing, Roh!'

'I think she was trying to tell me something *real*, something that could lead us to the birthstones.' She turned to her mentor. 'Do you know anything about the gilded plains? Anything that might help?'

Ames pinched the bridge of his nose, his patience wearing thin. 'I thought you understood your mother's condition. She is of no use to us. She is dangerous.'

'Ames, she was trying to *help me*. I know it. Please, do you know anything? Anything at all?'

Sighing heavily, Ames stood and retrieved his goblet of wine from the table. He took a long drink and came to stand at her side, looking over the map she had laid flat on the quilt.

'Gilded plains,' he murmured to himself, his dark talons tracing over the different cyren territories. 'You know I am no scholar. Certainly no geographer. I've not heard of any gilded plains … I don't —' Ames stopped, a single talon tapping a marker Roh couldn't see.

'What is it?'

Frowning, Ames turned to her. 'Well, I know not of any official location, but … On the route to Akoris, where many of the Uniir worshippers still dwell, there are tussock networks …'

'What's tussock?'

'Like small patches of thicker grass,' Odi answered.

'These tussock networks,' Ames continued. 'I suppose they could be described as golden? Gilded, even.'

Roh loosed her held breath. 'And they're on the road to Akoris?'

'There is no "road to Akoris", Rohesia, but yes, I suppose one could pass through them.'

Roh turned to Odi, triumphant. 'Akoris is one of the cyren territories guarding a birthstone.'

Odi's jaw was clenched. 'I don't think we should base our decisions on some crazed comment your mother made.'

'She wasn't *crazed* when she said it,' Roh argued. 'And, it's *on the way*.'

Odi shook his head in despair, throwing Ames a look that told Roh they'd spoken of her stubborn streak before.

'Rohesia, you've barely seen Saddoriel, let alone anything of the realms above. You have to be strategic about this,' Ames said. 'You cannot make rash decisions.'

'I know.'

'This only gets more complicated, more dangerous from here on.'

'*I know.*'

Ames gave a resigned sigh. 'You're determined to visit these so-called gilded plains, aren't you?'

Roh nodded. She had to trust her gut and her instinct

was telling her that Cerys was trying to help, that Cerys knew *something*.

'Fine,' Ames said. 'But remember, you need to have obtained all three gemstones within seven moons. Do you understand?'

'I understand.' Again, Roh nodded. 'Ames?'

'What is it?'

She had been pondering the next question since the day before, only now working up the courage to voice it. 'Can you … Am I able to select you as one of my companions for this part of the tournament?'

For the first time, Ames' gaze softened. 'No. I am a mentor of the bone cleaners. I am bound to my duties here.'

Roh had guessed as much, but it felt like a blow nevertheless.

'I'll meet you in Akoris,' Ames said quietly.

'What?'

'I cannot go with you on your quest to the gilded plains, but I'll find a way to meet you in Akoris.'

It was more than she could ask, more than she could hope for. Quiet fell between them and Roh looked to the map once more. Akoris, Csilla and Lochloria … The three cyren territories that now held the birthstones of Saddoriel. Roh ran her talons across the seas and vast lands she would soon travel, the complete and utter unknown.

'You know who *has* crossed those shores and entered those lands?' Ames asked.

Roh met his gaze and nodded. She did indeed.

'Good.' Ames folded up the map and slotted it into the side pocket of the pack. 'Are you still coming to the workshop?'

'Yes.'

'Then we must hurry. You're due at the entrance soon.'

It wasn't long before Roh found herself rooted to the spot in the doorway of the bone-cleaning workshop. Inside, it was full, and every single face within was staring back at her. Roh willed her face not to flush. She hadn't seen Orson and Harlyn since they had found out about the card game. Now, they sat in their usual seats, glaring at her and her crown of bones, their eyes full of loathing.

With Ames sitting at his desk at the front of the room, Roh straightened her stance. 'I need to speak with Orson and Harlyn,' she announced, the words coming out louder than she'd intended.

'Whatever you need to say, you can say it in front of everyone,' Harlyn said, her gaze lingering on Roh's crown. 'The circlet suited you better,' she added. 'Marked you for what you truly are.'

Beside her, Orson flinched slightly, but for once didn't defend Roh, didn't dilute Harlyn's cruel words. The blood rushed to Roh's head and she had to stop herself from swaying.

'We were the only ones who treated you like that circlet didn't matter. Well, it turns out it did. Only an *isruhe* could have been so cold to the creatures who'd been the kindest to her.'

Roh had never heard Harlyn use that term before. It sounded the sharpest on her lips, a blade poised to make Roh bleed. Roh felt as though she *was* bleeding, right from her chest. And then, she spotted it at the back of the workshop … Her music-theatre model. Shattered into a thousand pieces. Left discarded on the floor with the rest of the bone fragments. She wasn't ready for the pain that tore through her, or the shock that left her near breathless. But they couldn't see her like that.

She raised her chin, steeling herself. 'Harlyn,' she said, her voice hard. 'You will meet me at the entrance hall in half an hour.'

'Not a chance, traitor.'

'It wasn't a question.' The words came to her hard and fast. Words she never thought she'd be directing at her friend, in a tone she never thought she'd use. Nevertheless, she continued to speak. If they weren't going to like her, they could certainly fear her.

'There will be a pack waiting for you. Bring your lute.'

Silence fell, but the hatred pouring from Harlyn was deafening. And beside her, Orson's eyes were lined with tears. To be betrayed was one thing, but to now be left behind, alone in the depths of Saddoriel … Roh knew it was unforgivable.

'Are you sure that was a good idea?' Odi asked Roh later, as the pair made their way towards the archway of bones at the entrance of Saddoriel. 'They … they hate you now.'

'They're not the only ones,' Roh said, pausing midway

down the quiet passage to check her pack. She was increasingly aware of what exactly she carried, to the point where she was desperate to leave the confines of the lair, for risk of being discovered. As she rifled through the top layer of supplies, her hand brushed against what she hid: something warm, tucked away securely. She sagged with relief. Safe – it was still safe, her secret, hidden from the world.

'You've got everything?' Odi's brow furrowed with concern.

'Yes, I've got everything,' she replied, shouldering her pack and starting off down the path again.

'Roh,' Odi pushed. 'To have Harlyn with us … when she feels like that …'

Roh gave a hollow laugh. 'You're not going to like my other choices, either.'

At last, they reached the entrance of Saddoriel and beneath the archway of bones stood three figures: a stony-faced Harlyn, Yrsa Ward and Finn Haertel.

'Are you *mad?*' Odi hissed in Roh's ear.

'Perhaps,' she murmured. 'But the Jaktaren know the realms above. They know how to travel, how to reach the cyren territories. We need resources and knowledge, Odi. Not friends.'

Delja and the Council of Seven Elders were waiting as well.

'You have seven moons,' Taro Haertel said, stepping forward and offering his hand, his grip as icy as his smile. 'Happy hunting, Queen of Bones …'

· · ·

Upon their departure, the sound of two fiddles had filled the air. The song of yearning and sorrow now followed Roh and her cohort through the passageways and the water forests, past many filmy portals to the sea. She let the notes and the elder's words wash over her as they travelled through the outskirts of Talon's Reach for hours on end, towards the human realms beyond. As she put more distance between herself and the lair, worry churned in Roh's gut. The last time she had tried to leave the cyren territory, something had stopped her from following Odi into the woodlands. Now, as she walked, she tried to sense the invisible cord that had bound her to Saddoriel. Just how strong was it? Exactly what was the connection? Silently, she searched deep, keeping her fears to herself and not faltering a single step.

Time passed in surreal waves, the silence between the companions making the tunnels all the more stifling, although it was better than the bickering. Roh pressed on, keeping her head high. *Queen* ... She would hold that title one day, if it was the last thing she ever did.

After what seemed like days of arduous trekking and burning calves, something caught Roh's eye. A beam of pale light up ahead. Something stirred within her as cool, fresh air kissed her clammy skin. Gritting her teeth, Roh adjusted the heavy pack on her shoulders, her secret buried deep within it, and took the lead, quickening her pace, heart in her throat.

When she reached the mouth of the cave, she nearly cried out at what lay beyond. She didn't need to look at the map she carried to know where they were. They had made it. They were exactly where they ought to be: at the very beginning.

She lifted a foot and made to step forward, rigid, waiting for the tether to snap in place, waiting for her freedom to be leashed —

Smooth, black pebbles crunched beneath her boot.

The threshold between her realm and Odi's was behind her. A stony shore greeted her with a breeze that tasted of salt and whipped through her hair.

Rohesia the bone cleaner breathed it in deeply. With her band of unlikely companions at her back, she stepped into the new world that beckoned.

ACKNOWLEDGEMENTS

Back in 2018, I took myself on holiday to New Zealand, where I planned to rest, wander, eat, drink and ride horses through the rolling valleys. It had been a long time since I'd had any time off and I needed to hit refresh, to refill the creative well. New Zealand is perfect for just that. Only a few nights in, I found myself scribbling down the initial idea for this very book at a bar. In fact, it was at this bar that I wrote the opening line, practically verbatim. At some point, I looked up from my notepad and a blue-eyed stranger asked, 'What are you writing?'

Gary, you were there from the exact moment this book came into being and for all the moments after. Thank you for spending countless hours listening and talking with me about this project, and for offering up your own ideas and creativity. You were such a vital part of this novel's creation – it certainly wouldn't be what it is without you and everything you do for me.

Not long after this trip, I moved to New Zealand permanently and the entirety of this book was written in that first year I lived abroad. It was not without its challenges, and were it not for the thought-provoking Messenger conversations and book recommendations of Hannah Jermyn and Aleesha Paz, I might have actually gone mad. I can't thank you enough for keeping me connected to our trio, to the book community and to my roots as a publishing grad.

Imagine my surprise and delight when the beta readers from my previous books agreed to continue reading for me on this new venture. Claire, Aleesha and Kelly, I don't know how you're not sick of me and my inane questions at this point, but I'm forever grateful for your patience, your sensitive feedback, your unwavering support and for making me a better author.

My gratitude also goes to Lisy and Eva, as I'm sure it will in all the books yet to come. The laughs, the conversations and the enduring friendship we all share brings me so much joy. As you know, this book holds a bit of all of us, and nothing makes me happier.

To my OG publishing bestie and fellow author, Benjamin Stevenson. Thank you for all your advice regarding blurbs and publishing options, and for inspiring me with your own incredible drive and success.

Tara Bennett, your Hikari candles have got me through every draft so far. I can't write a book without you, it seems. Thank you for your support and friendship, as well as your beautiful products that make me feel at peace, no matter where I am in the world.

To Mum, Dad and Yas back in Sydney, you've been so supportive since I decided to go indie back in 2017 and it's meant the world to me. But especially since I moved to New Zealand, you've held the author fort by posting out books around Australia on my behalf … Thank you for everything you do.

I also can't leave without saying a special thank you to the following people: Margot Butler, the O'shea family, the Mulhollands, the Zapperts and Delzoppos, Auty Lawler, Natalia Hunter, Fay Wood, Erin Mealey, Snez Georgieva, Brad Davis, Kyra Thomsen, Liam Casey, Mel Clarke, Emily-May Norman, Jenny Ryan, Gilly Haines, Sofia Casanova, Jodie Sloan, Fay Robson, Mira Bagtas, Jordan Meek (and Jordan's mum!), Anne Sengstock, Phoebe Woodward and the 'Supertrampers' (Zane, Liz and Podge).

Last, but never least, I want to thank YOU. My readers. Whether you've been with me since *The Oremere Chronicles*, or you're a new friend, thank you. Thank you for taking a chance on this strange, dark, ambitious book and its cunning characters. I hope we meet again when the adventure continues.

ABOUT THE AUTHOR

Helen Scheuerer is the YA fantasy author of the bestselling trilogy, *The Oremere Chronicles* and the *Curse of the Cyren Queen* quartet. Often likened to the popular series *Throne of Glass* and *Game of Thrones*, her work has been highly praised for its strong, flawed female characters and its action-packed plots.

Helen's love of writing and books led her to pursue a Bachelor of Creative Writing at the University of Wollongong and a Masters of Publishing at the University of Sydney. Now a full-time author, Helen lives amidst the mountains in Central Otago, New Zealand and is constantly dreaming up new stories. You can find out more via her website: www.helenscheuerer.com

The Oremere Chronicles:

Heart of Mist

Reign of Mist

War of Mist

Dawn of Mist

Cyren Queen Origins (novellas):

A Song in the Deep

The Law of the Lair

The Tides of War

Curse of the Cyren Queen:

A Lair of Bones

The *Cyren Queen Origins* are a series of prequel novellas available for free via Helen Scheuerer's newsletter.

Follow Delja and Cerys throughout their younger years as their friendship develops and they face dangerous challenges of their own. Discover their secrets and learn vital clues to who they become in the *Curse of the Cyren Queen* series.

Visit www.helenscheuerer.com to sign up and receive your free copies of the novellas, *A Song in the Deep*, *The Law of the Lair* and *The Tides of War*.